Bodies
in the
Bayou

Cheryl Campbell

sonarpress.com

Published by Sonar Press,
Hopedale, Massachusetts 01747
sonarpress.com

First Edition
Printed in the United States of America
ISBN: 979-8-9906251-3-6 (pbk)
ISBN: 979-8-9906251-2-9 (e-bk)
Library of Congress Control Number: 2024918543

ALSO BY CHERYL CAMPBELL

SCIENCE FICTION
Echoes Trilogy
Echoes of War
Echoes of Darkness
Echoes of Fate

FANTASY
The Burnt Mountain Series
The Monster Within
One in the Chamber
Do and Die
Rhyllia
When Heroes Fall

Dedication

From 1979 to 1981, there were at least twenty-nine murders called the Atlanta child murders. All the victims—twenty-one boys and adolescents, two girls, and six adult men—were Black. The children's ages ranged from seven to seventeen. The adult victims' ages ranged from twenty to twenty-eight years old. Twenty-nine bodies were recovered, and one missing boy's body has yet to be found. One person, a Black man, was convicted in 1982 of two of the adult male murders. Despite questionable evidence, he was linked to several of the other deaths, and all the cases were closed. The cases of the Atlanta child murders were reopened in 2019.

On June 27, 2023, Atlanta dedicated the *Eternal Flame* memorial, created by artist Gordon Huether, to the thirty victims. Remember their names.

Aaron Jackson, 9
Aaron Wyche, 10
Alfred Evans, 13
Angel Lenair, 12
Anthony Carter, 9
Charles Stephens, 12
Christopher Richardson, 12
Clifford Jones, 13
Curtis Walker, 13

Darron Glass, 10

Earl Terrell, 10

Eddie Duncan, 21

Edward Hope Smith, 14

Eric Middlebrooks, 15

Jeffery Mathis, 10

Jimmy Ray Payne, 21

John Porter, 28

Joseph Bell, 15

Larry Rogers, 20

LaTonya Wilson, 7

Lubie Geter, 14

Michael McIntosh, 23

Milton Harvey, 14

Nathaniel Cater, 27

Patrick Baltazar, 12

Patrick Rogers, 16

Terry Pue, 15

Timothy Hill, 13

William Barrett, 17

Yusuf Bell, 9

Chapter One

The girl stirred in her drug-induced slumber and rolled onto her stomach. The man pulled his gloves tighter, then returned her to lying on her side. He tucked her arms and hands where he wanted them for the photograph. He needed her displayed and appearing peaceful in her last moments, not flopped over and drooling.

The other children, even one on chemotherapy, had responded to his mixtures and dosing regimen, allowing them a final restful sleep.

He left her to check the camera, returned to adjust the headband holding her curly black hair away from her face, then stepped back to the camera and checked the viewer.

She lay tucked under a flowered, ruffled comforter and matching pillow. The pastel purple and green colors created a beautiful backdrop and contrast to her dark skin and hair. She wore pajamas she'd picked out from the stash he kept for the children. She was adorable in the ones with cartoon kittens and puppies. A brown teddy bear sat atop the small white table next to her bed.

The man shifted the tripod to the right and refocused. He had the correct angle now, and the girl appeared to be sleeping.

That was the goal.

He'd spare her the trouble of growing up with an illness plaguing her life. Her family would not have the burden of medical bills that her parents could not afford. Medical treatments would prolong her death. Killing her was his gift to her. She would pass in her sleep soon. It was a simple and kind gesture.

The man pressed the button on the camera, then examined the captured image.

Perfect.

This new photo would join the others of children he'd helped over the years.

The girl snuffled in her sleep, rubbed her cheek and then her mouth. Her palm became slick with saliva. She rolled onto her belly and sighed.

The man lifted vials from his black case and used droppers to create another mixture in a separate vial. He capped the new vial, shook it a few times, then drew the contents into a new dropper.

He moved without a sound when he lifted a white chair from the corner of the room and placed it next to the girl's bed.

He turned her to lie on her back and then sat in the chair. The man placed his palm on her forehead. Her eyes cracked open.

"Is it time for me to go home now?" she asked, her words sluggish and a little slurred.

"It sure is," he said, his voice soft and soothing.

She nodded and closed her eyes.

"Open your mouth. One more bit of medicine and you'll be all better and on your way home."

She opened her mouth, and he emptied the dropper into the inside of her cheek.

"Swallow that," he said.

She obeyed, wrinkling her nose. "Tastes icky."

"I know. I'm sorry. Here's your new bear."

The girl took the soft brown bear from him, yawned, then curled into a ball with the bear against her chest.

He remained at her side while her breathing slowed. There was no struggling and no pain. The man touched the pads of his first two fingers against the artery at the bend in her elbow. Her heart slowed too.

Her mouth sagged open, and it was the last movement she made before drawing her final breath.

The man kept his fingers on her arterial pulse a moment longer, though it had stopped.

When he withdrew his hand, he said, "Goodbye, Letitia."

Chapter Two

Denial. My favorite coping skill. It didn't matter that it wasn't effective; I already knew this. Self-medicating layered on top of denial was even better. My second-best coping skill was avoidance. Combining the three created a trifecta of dysfunctional perfection.

I drained the wine from my glass, then refilled it.

New Orleans.

Hot. Humid. Gross as hell.

Also damn fine music and food.

I should have taken the time to eat something, but from my small table in the rear of the bar, I enjoyed the wine and music too much to bother.

People danced, some made out while they danced, and I took another swig of wine.

I had numerous things to do before tomorrow, but I was content with my current state—buzzed from the alcohol and not doing any tasks on my ever-growing list of things requiring my attention.

The button-down collar of my shirt brushed against the side of my neck. I adjusted the collar to straighten it, then smoothed the front of my blouse. I realized that the burgundy-red wine in my glass matched the color of my shirt.

Air travel always created wrinkles in my clothes, but my earlier flight from Boston hadn't wreaked too much havoc. My black trousers remained crisp and free of unwanted creases. I admit I could be reckless when drinking, but when it came to my clothes, I didn't fuck around.

My thoughts drifted to the funeral tomorrow. The last adult from my childhood I gave a damn about had been murdered. I didn't want to be in New Orleans at all. And a funeral was the *last* thing I wanted to attend.

Hopping on a plane back to Boston and pretending I'd never arrived in Louisiana a few hours ago seemed like a viable plan. I could pop back over to the hotel, grab my things since I hadn't bothered to unpack after checking in, return the rental car, and get on the last flight back to New England. Except I was already somewhat drunk and needed time before I should drive … unless I drove anyway and hoped for the best. I'd been guilty of that before.

I checked my watch. Tomorrow's funeral was now today. Shit.

I'd missed the last flight out while wandering the French Quarter and then taking up residence in this bar.

The remnants of the bottle of wine on my table required consumption, and I was no quitter. I chuckled, then drained the glass in a way that would make a wine connoisseur shudder. I was a total quitter.

My fancy hotel room with a balcony overlooking the Quarter waited for me. But tonight, I preferred the bar and lots of intoxication.

My head swam after that last glass, so I slid one of the empty chairs at the table next to my chair. I draped one arm over the back of it and squirmed my ass in the seat until I felt comfortable and not at risk of tipping over onto the floor.

I moved my glass and bottle a little closer to me, then refilled the glass from my new position.

Uncle Jack wouldn't approve of me getting shit-faced while traveling alone, but he couldn't complain about my behavior. It was his funeral I had to attend, and the wine prevented any grief from surfacing.

A woman weaved through the dancers and approached my corner. The fitted black shirt that clung to her body left tattoos covering her arms exposed. She had a thick but athletic build like she either spent a lot of time in the gym or worked where she did a lot of lifting. Her brown skin accentuated her black lipstick and heavily lined eyes. Her black hair was close-cropped on the sides and back and longer on the top. Not everyone pulled off that hairstyle, but this woman owned it *and* the Gothic vibe.

I didn't want any company, but shit, this Goth woman was hot.

The woman sat in the empty chair I had my arm draped across, and I kept my arm in place.

"You drink that wine like it has wronged you in some way," Goth said. "Do you even taste it when you plow through half a glass in one gulp?"

"Watching me from the shadows?"

"A little."

"Stalk much?"

The woman's laughter was genuine and joyful. I liked the sound.

"I'm not drinking it for the taste," I said.

Goth watched me for a few seconds. "Do you prefer another type of drink instead?"

"The one that fucks me up the fastest is what I prefer."

Goth reached into her pocket. She removed a small, clear plastic baggie containing a dozen or so yellow, triangular pills.

She removed two from the bag and placed them in her palm. "These will get you there. Interested?"

I *did* have a funeral to attend about ten hours from now. "What are they?"

"Does it matter?"

I observed the little pills with a smiley face stamped into them. "No."

Goth popped one pill into her mouth. She took my glass and drank my wine to wash it down. She placed the second pill on her tongue, keeping her mouth open.

Without hesitation, I leaned in and kissed her, sweeping the pill off Goth's tongue and into my mouth. I dumped the remaining wine from my glass into my mouth and swallowed the pill. Goth slipped her hand around the back of my neck, pulling me close. I fumbled to return the glass to the table without toppling it while we kissed.

My evening had improved. I was drunk *and* getting laid tonight.

A warm flush from more than the wine flowed through my veins while we made out in the dark corner of the bar. I would have been fine dragging Goth off to the restroom and having her right there, but I stopped to take a breath instead. This woman had me turned on in all sorts of ways.

Goth nodded. "Not bad." She removed two more smiley pills. "Put this one under your tongue. Bite it first to break it into a few pieces so it'll dissolve and kick in faster."

I selected my tablet and put it in my mouth. I didn't like the *crunch* sound it made when I bit it. I slid the pieces under my tongue and frowned. "It's bitter."

"It'll be worth suffering through the taste," Goth said, and then she snapped the remaining pill with her teeth. She slid it under her tongue. "How long are you in town?" she asked, returning the little bag to her pocket.

"What makes you think I'm not a local?"

"You don't have even a hint of a Southern accent."

"Fair. I'm not sure how long I'll be here."

"I like your shirt," she said.

"Thanks."

"I'll like it better when I take it off you." Goth poured the last of the wine from the bottle into my glass. She drank half of it, then passed the glass to me.

I drank the rest. "Shall I get another bottle or should we leave?"

"How about we leave and get another bottle on the way?"

What death in the family? "That works."

Chapter Three

The man never liked seeing the dead children on the cold stainless steel table, but cleansing their bodies was part of the process. For him to continue his work, he couldn't get caught. He'd already finished spraying the girl's body with water, and while the final drops fell from the table, he used a push broom to force the excess water toward the drain in the center of the floor. He'd wash this room several more times over the next few days, but the first pass was complete.

He adjusted the long-sleeve, splash-proof apron on his body and checked to be sure the edges of his rubber gloves were tucked under the apron's elastic cuffs. Water dripped from her saturated pajamas, but his rubber boots kept his feet dry.

He retrieved a pair of scissors and cut the pajamas away from her skin. He covered her exposed body with a towel, working around her to remove the pajamas and dry her off. Then he eased the girl's body into his arms.

A second table nearby, covered in black plastic and lined with a layer of clear plastic, waited for her. The man placed her on the clear layer, removed the towel, then folded the plastic to cocoon her within it. He then wrapped a black layer over her corpse, positioning the final flap over her face last. He lifted her body again and carried her out the basement door to his car, where the trunk lid was already raised.

The orange glow of sunrise peeked through the leaves on the trees around his house. He'd taken too long, and he'd have to wait for another day, perhaps tomorrow, to remove her from his home.

He carried her back inside and placed her on the table. The man gripped the edge of the table, pulling it behind him. He opened the heavy, shiny door to his walk-in freezer. He kept the temperature high enough to act as a refrigerator so that when he needed to hold a body for a day or two it wouldn't freeze.

The man left the table in the center of the chilled holding area. He glanced at the adult-sized body in plastic on another table nearby. The girl was young and pure. She did not deserve to be lying in death next to the filth he'd killed and had to hold in the cooler too.

The adult male had screamed and thrashed during his punishment for being a liar and degenerate. The killer didn't care and had even enjoyed witnessing the man's dying twitches.

The killer placed his hand on the girl's head once more. The plastic crinkled beneath his gloved palm.

This was all part of his ritual, caring for the dead children with the same respect as he'd cared for them when they were alive. It was a kindness he felt he owed them. He even took time in advance to plan where he'd release the bodies. Once nature and the elements had them, what happened to them was out of his control. But until then, he would never be sloppy or a brute and toss a child's body into his trunk or fling it off a bridge into a swamp.

Never.

The adult corpse next to her would not receive respect. That man was not fit to be dropped into a hole or mourned. The killer would dismember him and discard the parts over time.

He strode out of the cooler, and the heavy door thudded closed behind him.

Chapter Four

I had been in this situation before. Hungover, naked, tangled in sheets with a woman whose name I didn't know, and in need of at least twelve more hours of sleep. The alcohol, drugs, and sex-fueled evening had already caught up to me. I rolled to sit on the side of the bed and dropped my head into my hands.

My head throbbed even more, so I straightened. Goth's fingernails scraped down my back to my ass. It aroused me, and I wanted another romp with the stranger in my hotel bed. But I had too much to do.

"Where do you think you're going?" Goth asked.

"I have to leave." I left the bed. "So do you," I said, then staggered my way to the desk in the room and the envelope sitting on top of it.

The person at the front desk had given me a note when I'd returned to the hotel last night with Goth, but I hadn't bothered reading it. *J. Martil* had been written on the outside of the envelope. I broke the seal and removed the plain, cream-colored card.

I hope your stay in the city is pleasant. I look forward to seeing you, Janette. ~Wilson Landry

I hated my name, and Mr. Landry was the only person allowed to call me Janette. He was too old and too sweet to correct. Everyone else called me Janie. The note wasn't in his handwriting, so I assumed he had called in this message to me. It didn't matter. I tossed the card and envelope into the trash bin by the desk, then headed to the bathroom.

I turned the shower on, and while the water heated, went to the sink and splashed water on my face. The brown of my Creole skin somewhat hid the shadows under my eyes but did nothing to hide the puffiness around them. I rummaged in my toiletries bag to find the drops to take the redness out of my eyes. After applying a few to each eye, I reassessed my looks.

The verdict was unpleasant.

I ran my fingers through my hair and frowned. A bun could at least keep the wavy black but acceptable mess off my shoulders and get through the day. I touched the swollen areas around my eyes. I'd wear sunglasses. The funeral service was inside a church. I could pass for a mourner. Shit, I *was* a mourner ... Well, I *should* have been mourning. Instead, I'd been busy getting trashed and having sex with a nameless woman.

I stepped into the shower space with floor-to-ceiling tile and a wide glass door. I increased the water's temperature and steamed up the bathroom.

I closed my eyes, allowing the water to flow from the top of my head and over the rest of my body. I lowered my face into my palms, but my head snapped up when the glass door opened. Goth entered and closed the door behind her.

Goth reached for me, and I stepped back. "I don't have time for this, Goth." I winced.

Goth tilted her head, her brow creased.

"That's ... I ... shit. I don't know your name. It's what I was calling you in my head."

The woman nodded. "Goth. I like it." She neared and passed her hands over my hips.

My gaze followed her fingers, and I liked the contrast of Goth's darker brown hands against my own lighter brown body.

Surely I had enough time for another round. But I'd be late for the service.

"In my head I've been calling you Bougie," Goth said.

"I'm not bourgeois."

Goth laughed. "You have expensive taste in hotels."

I shrugged. "It's a nice place, and I like staying here when I'm in town."

"Uh-huh. The button-down shirt you wore last night that I had the pleasure of removing, did you iron it yourself?"

"They do it at the dry cleaners, but I can iron in a pinch."

"Dry-cleaned shirts as your daily wear. Bourgeois as hell. I don't mean it as an insult though. I like it."

My gaze left her hands and met her light-brown eyes.

Goth moved in closer.

I shook my head. "I really don't have time."

"No?" One of Goth's hands traveled down the outside of my thigh before moving to my inner thigh, then traveled up.

All sorts of pleasurable chills flooded me when her fingers neared my groin. I shuddered.

Goth pressed her breasts against mine, and her breath against my neck was electrifying.

"Are you sure?" Goth asked, her fingers gliding through my wetness.

What funeral? I kissed her.

Chapter Five

My late entry earned me several turned heads and frowns when the church door clicked shut behind me. The place was packed. I knew it would be, but the volume of people inside the building made my insides quiver. It looked like the whole population of Jardin, the rural community an hour west of New Orleans, had opted to attend the service. I slid into one of the few open spots in a pew in the back of the church. Once seated, I slipped my sunglasses off and kept my head down.

The elderly Black woman next to me glanced over, but I kept my eyes averted. I needed this to be over. A young Black boy seated in front of me twisted in his seat, smiled, then waved at me.

"Hi," he whispered.

I managed a small smile and flicked my hand in a tiny wave.

A young woman, I assumed the boy's mother, said something into his ear and he sat facing forward again.

The minister continued his message to those gathered for Uncle Jack's service. "Jacques Montpelier was a devoted son, brother, uncle, and friend to many," he said, his voice booming into the microphone and coming down from above.

I risked glancing up. Of course, I'd picked a spot directly

under one of the speakers embedded in the ceiling.

My gaze drifted over the crowd. The woman next to me smiled upon making eye contact, and I reciprocated before returning to my head-down-and-eyes-on-my-lap pose.

I didn't want to think about anything with this funeral and why my presence was required. I'd left this town a long time ago. I figured I'd return at some point since my parents had left me their estate, but I had secretly hoped to die before having to come back.

Yet, here I was.

I tuned out the minister. Goth had given me her number before we parted ways this morning. Another evening with Goth would make me forget a lot of things.

I flinched when the minister barked his words to make his point about whatever he was saying. The moment of being startled jerked me back to the present. God. Salvation. Everlasting love. The minister droned on, and I mentally gagged. They could keep their God to themselves.

I shouldn't be here, because Uncle Jack should be alive.

Per the police, he'd been stabbed in New Orleans East by a mugger. Another dead Black man. Another unsolved murder in the greater New Orleans area. I wondered how much investigating the police had actually done. Injustice was rampant, and I'd abandoned belief in the system a long time ago. I'd given up on believing in most people in this shit-hole world—Uncle Jack being one of the *very* few exceptions.

My parents' dying in a small plane piloted by my father when it went down in Manchac Swamp had sparked some suspicion, but with me as the sole heir and only six years old at the time, I was not a suspect. The matter was deemed a piloting error, and I was shuffled off to New England to live with my mother's sister. The shitty child care system and my psychopathic aunt had created twelve years of abuse and neglect for me.

Fuck the system. Fuck everyone.

Upon leaving my aunt, I had spent the next decade doing whatever I wanted while avoiding Jardin.

The people sang a hymn, and I refused to sing. The rage inside never stopped simmering.

With no closure for my parents twenty-two years ago, the odds of getting any justice for Uncle Jack were zero.

I wanted the service over so I could scamper back to the city. Instead, I remained stuck inside a church in Jardin. The small town west of Vacherie got its name from the French word for garden, and the *J* was pronounced softly, like the *J* in Jacques. It was known for its plantations, sugarcane fields, and food. I had no plans to take a tour, eat here, or do anything else. I had to drive back to the Quarter and my hotel. I would get wasted with Goth again, then fly out.

Maybe a couple of nights with Goth, then fly home.

The minister babbled on, and my thoughts wandered.

Home was an illusion. My Boston apartment was someplace I slept. I had no home, and Uncle Jack was gone.

I brushed away the tear that had the audacity to spill from my eye. I forced my self-pity into the corner with the rest of the emotions I refused to release. I'd numb the hell out of every emotion later with bottle after bottle of wine.

Another fucking hymn.

I stood with the masses but kept my eyes down, arms crossed, and mouth shut. Someone got up and went to the podium next for a long-winded prayer. I almost screamed when they called for the attendees to turn to a different page in the hymnals.

I had had enough. I glanced around to plan my escape. I had a clear path to the back door, except there were two sheriff's deputies next to it. The male deputy, a tall man with muscles that barely fit inside his uniform, was occupied with something on his phone. The female deputy, an attractive woman around my age with a lean build, stood against the wall with her arms crossed.

I caught her eye, then looked away. Shit.

If I moved too quickly during my escape, I might wobble. Goth's little yellow pills remained in my system. The fluttering in my chest from an ongoing, elevated heart rate informed me that the smiley-faced pills hadn't worn off yet. I was thirsty as hell, too.

The mourners sat again, and I fantasized about stabbing myself in the eye with a fork. That had to be less painful than this bullshit.

The minister said, "Before we conclude …"

I almost leapt from my pew, but I managed to remain seated a bit longer. Another round of standing and singing happened before the group was dismissed to proceed to the cemetery. This was my moment to slip away, but the elderly woman touched my arm.

"Will you be staying for the fellowship after, *chère*?" the woman asked.

I hadn't been called *chère* since I was a little girl living in Jardin. That one little word brought me back to living in a giant house with towering oak trees dripping with gray and brown moss. I blinked, realizing that I hadn't responded to her question. "Oh, no, ma'am. I have a flight to catch."

"Pity. How did you know Jacques?"

I glanced at my watch and feigned an apology. "I'm so sorry, ma'am. I need to go."

I weaved through people, whispered a sarcastic "hallelujah" to not see the deputies anywhere, and hurried out the door. I winced when the heat and suffocating humidity of the day slapped me in the face. I could never live here without spontaneously combusting.

I spotted my car, parked way the hell down the street because of my late arrival, and headed in its direction.

"Janette! Janette, wait up."

I recognized Mr. Landry's voice, stopped, and turned. It took me a moment to recognize him. I'd only ever spoken to him on the phone over the last decade, and it had been equally as long since I'd seen him in person.

"Hi, Mr. Landry," I said.

He smiled, and his million wrinkles seemed to fold his face in on itself. "It's so good to see you. I can't believe it's been so long. I called the hotel last night, but you were out. Did you get my note?"

"I did. Thank you."

"You look like you did when you turned eighteen. Beautiful as ever."

"Thank you."

"I can't believe it's been ten years since the last time I saw you."

Mr. Landry had been my parents' lawyer and executor of their estate until my eighteenth birthday. Everything had passed to me on that date, but I'd kept him on for all the legal crap while Uncle Jack had continued to manage the maintenance of the main house, grounds-keeping sheds, gardens, and land. I'd tried to give everything to Uncle Jack, but he'd refused.

There were millions of dollars in the property to be had, but he wouldn't take it, and I didn't want anything to do with it. So Uncle Jack managed the estate all while I, its legal owner, hid in Boston.

I wiped at the sweat beading on my face. "It's good to see you, Mr. Landry, but I need to head back to the city. I'm flying out."

"You'll have to postpone your flight, Janette. We have

paperwork to manage here first."

"Can't we do it online like before?"

"Jacques was very specific in his request."

"I don't understand."

"He managed your property, but he had his own home."

This wasn't news to me. "Yeah."

"He left it to you, including instructions."

Oh, fuck me. I closed my eyes and rubbed my right temple, the site of the growing headache I had now on top of the hangover headache. I lowered my hand. "Why me? He has *loads* of family here."

"It was his choice."

"How long will this take?"

"A few days, at least."

"Can we deal with it tomorrow?"

"Oh, sure. Sure. You must be devastated."

I nodded, devastated that I couldn't run away.

"Come to my office at, say, eleven, tomorrow morning? And we'll ride out to his home."

Home. There was that word again. "Okay."

He left and my retreat to the car had to wait. The female deputy was waiting for me.

Chapter Six

People poured out of the church, some going to their vehicles, but most headed in the opposite direction, on their way to the cemetery. I had nowhere to hide, and there weren't enough people around me to get lost within them. The deputy came straight for me. I did my best to look calm and even faked a smile while my pulse spiked, causing an unwelcome whooshing sound in my ears.

"Hello," I said when the deputy arrived.

"Leaving already?" the woman asked, her Southern drawl thick but genteel.

Lying about a flight could result in an easy cross-reference to find out I was indeed lying. Could a deputy even check that without probable cause? I wondered if I'd done anything to raise suspicion. Had I wobbled when I walked into the church, indicating my compromised state? I couldn't remember.

"Are you okay?" she asked.

I brushed sweat off my forehead. "Sorry. I'm not used to this heat."

The deputy smiled. "I'd expect not since you've been away for so long."

Her smile seemed familiar. "Do I know you?" I asked.

"Yes and no. It's been a while since we've seen each other, but you look exactly like the pictures Uncle Jacques had of you."

My mind worked at a furious pace to come up with a name, but my ability to keep my rising panic under control wavered while I feared melting in this abhorrent heat. Uncle Jack had three brothers and two sisters but no children of his own. I had no idea how many nieces and nephews he might have running around these parts.

The deputy smiled again. "I'm Lina."

I dragged up a vague memory of a Black girl I always played with at school. A more vivid memory emerged of me and this same—I thought it was the same—school friend clinging to each other and sobbing before hands pulled me away to put me in a car for the airport to deposit me in Boston. I refocused on the woman, and I recognized the striking, light hazel-green eyes that were the same as my childhood friend's.

"Holy shit!"

Lina laughed, and I recognized that sound, too.

"Wow," I said.

"I wish we were reuniting under better circumstances."

"I agree." My vision blurred. I must have swayed, because Lina caught my arm.

"You're quite the wilting flower in this heat," she said.

I somewhat nodded. The heat wasn't the only thing kicking my ass. "It's like being trapped in a giant's sweaty armpit."

Lina snorted. "After all these years, you're still so funny. C'mon. Let's get you some water, and I'll go with you to the cemetery."

I wanted to leave, but everything was catching up with me. Dying and going to hell had to mean dying and going to Louisiana. It was so fucking hot. How did people live here?

I walked beside Lina and willed myself to not pass out, but

subsequent events turned fuzzy until I got some cold water into my mouth. I wasn't sure where or when Lina had procured the water bottle.

My hand trembled when I took another sip from the bottle. Lina had at least found me a bit of shade and a tree to lean on during the graveside service. I tried to block out the sounds of weeping family members seated under the canopy near the casket. Part of me wanted to weep with them. Part of me wanted to run away from this pain like I always had.

The minister got going again on his message to the masses, and I gave up. I sat on the ground. Lina knelt next to me.

"I'm fine," I whispered.

Lina nodded, then stood. Now it was like being a guarded prisoner. I'd need a few more bottles of water to rehydrate before I attempted the drive back to the city. I really was a prisoner—of my stupidity of getting fucked up with Goth, then trying to make it to a funeral. I promised myself I'd never do it again and took another long drink from the bottle.

Being seated on the ground and eye-level with so many headstones made my insides twitch. I glimpsed a little redheaded girl darting between the headstones. I shifted for a better angle, but there was no girl in sight.

Heat and drugs. Those had to be the reason I'd seen something that wasn't there.

My gaze wandered over the crowd, and I spotted the boy from the church pew. He watched me and waved at me again. I smiled at him, then shifted my gaze to the browned grass around my feet. I kept this pose, allowing my mind to wander nowhere in particular. I heard Lina sniffle a few times, but I refused to look at her.

My personal mission was to keep my shit together until the service wrapped up sometime this century.

When the service concluded, I was rather proud of my

accomplishment of not passing out, except I wobbled again when I stood.

Damn drugs.

"C'mon," Lina said. "Let's get you inside."

I spotted a tall, lanky man in a nice suit among the crowd. He smiled and shook hands with several people around him. Others who had worn suits to the service had their jackets draped over one arm, but this man remained in his jacket.

"Who is that?" I asked. "The one in the jacket."

Lina raised an eyebrow. "That's your uncle. Franklin Martil."

"Huh. Haven't seen him since I was little."

"Do you want to go speak to him?"

I'd forgotten all about Uncle Frank until now. Vague memories bubbled up from the depths of my past. I couldn't remember much about him, but images of my parents and the estate house surfaced with a vengeance.

"You okay?" Lina asked.

I was *so* not okay. "Yep."

"You sure?"

Frank spotted me, and I couldn't sort the mix of emotions attacking me. I hadn't spent much time with him when I'd been little, but where had he been during my stint in Boston with my shitty aunt? Uncle Jack had told me that my aunt wouldn't allow him to visit me in New England. But I was never sure if I'd believed his story. Maybe Frank hadn't been allowed to visit me either.

None of it mattered. Everyone had abandoned me after my parents were dead.

I fumbled with the bottle cap wishing the water could be turned into wine—*a lot* of fucking wine. I dumped the rest of the water into my mouth and swallowed. I wiped my mouth with the back of my hand. I wasn't bougie when I was losing my shit.

"Janie?" Frank said.

The polite thing to do was to respond to him, but the gears in my mind ground to a halt.

Lina intervened. "Frank, let's talk inside. Janie's not doing well in this heat."

"Of course!" he said.

Frank moved to stand beside me, and I cringed. I didn't want to be touched or forced to rely on someone else to help me, but I didn't have a choice.

"I'm fine," I said. "I got drunk last night, and I'm a little dehydrated. That's all," I said, knowing that if I tried to walk on my own, I'd fall.

Frank placed a gentle hand on my lower back. "I had one too many beers last night, so I understand. I've been drinking water all day to stay ahead of the heat."

"We'll get you inside where it's much cooler," Lina said.

My shoulders slumped, resigning myself to their assistance. At least they walked in silence and didn't badger me with questions or talk about stupid shit like how nice the service was or what the weather would be like the rest of the week.

Chapter Seven

The air-conditioned fellowship hall attached to the church felt magnificent, and I didn't mind sitting at a table not sweating my ass off while guzzling another bottle of water.

Frank brought me a new bottle. "You're looking much better," he said.

"Thanks for helping me."

"Anytime."

Lina slid a plate stacked with food in front of me and placed a second plate on the table. She pulled out the chair closest to the additional plate.

"Frank, are you staying to eat?" Lina asked.

"No. I have work today."

"Where do you work?" I asked.

"Real estate," he said.

"Should I bring Janie by the hospital?" Lina asked.

"No!" I barked. I quieted my voice, but my annoyance remained. "No. Why are you asking *him* if I should go?"

Frank chuckled. "I was a paramedic in a former life, Janie. You don't need to see a doctor, but drink plenty of water today."

I nodded, and the prickly heat of embarrassment crept up my neck.

Lina and Frank hugged, but when Frank leaned toward me, I stiffened. I couldn't help it. He was a family member, but he was a stranger. Thankfully, he backed off.

"I'm really glad I got to see you," he said to me. "I'd like to visit with you more while you're in town. It's unfortunate that funerals sometimes turn into family reunions."

He left, and I stared at the plate before me. I hadn't felt hungry until now and couldn't remember when I'd last eaten a piece of fried chicken, green beans with bits of bacon, mashed potatoes with brown gravy, and baked mac and cheese. My mouth watered. Cornbread too? Maybe Louisiana wasn't a total hell.

Lina sat next to me and picked up her fork. "Wasn't sure what you would like, so I grabbed a bit of everything."

"Thank you. This is great. I'm not sure I'll eat it all."

The male deputy arrived with his plate and lowered himself into the other chair next to me.

If he hadn't been a lineman on Louisiana State University's football team, he should have been. He was a hulk of a man with a kind smile and eyes similar to Lina's, except his were darker with more brown. His uniform was different, and I noticed the patch on his shoulder. He worked in a different parish than Lina.

I didn't like being flanked by them, but I was too hungry to be nervous. The fork next to my plate was crooked, so I straightened it and then placed the napkin in my lap. I wasn't sure where to start with all the food Lina had brought me, so I went for the cornbread perched on top of the mound like a crown.

"I could eat a horse today. You?" the male deputy asked me.

"Anthony, manners," Lina said.

"Nah," he said, waving her off. "We're all family here in one way or another, even if I don't know her name."

Lina rolled her eyes at him, then turned to me. "Do you remember my cousin Anthony?"

I had too much cornbread in my mouth to speak, so I shook my head.

"He was older than us, so he didn't spend much time with us as kids," Lina said. "Anthony, this is Janie."

His mac-and-cheese-laden fork stopped halfway to his mouth, and he stared at me. "Janie Martil? Martil Plantation?"

I inwardly groaned. The plantation wasn't a real plantation. My mother's fascination with the Deep South, grand homes, and expansive properties had allowed my wealthy father to gift his wife a swath of land—and some swamp—to build up exactly how she wanted. My mother had named it Martil Plantation, though it lacked the history of the Laura, Oak Alley, and Whitney plantations.

Anonymity was the gift of the North. In Jardin, as a Martil there was no hiding since I was one of the two Martils left in Jardin and possibly in St. James Parish. At least they knew how to pronounce it here—Mar-*teel*. New Englanders tended to botch it and call me Martin or Mar-till. Over time, I'd stopped correcting them.

"Yes," Lina said. "Let the woman eat."

I sent Lina a mental "thanks" for the intervention on my behalf.

"You're staying out there while you're in town?" Lina asked me.

I retracted my gratitude since the conversation remained centered on me. I picked up my fork, surveying what to eat next, and stabbed it into the green beans. "I'm in the Quarter tonight, then flying out." I remembered Mr. Landry's appointment tomorrow. "Well, I'm there until I'm done with the lawyer."

Another thought struck me. I wasn't related to Uncle Jack,

and here I sat with his niece and nephew.

I hoped nothing came up about the will. If someone contested me for Uncle Jack's property, I'd let them take it and have Mr. Landry throw the paperwork together for me so I could get the hell out of this state.

"Do you have someone else lined up to be the estate caretaker with Uncle Jacques gone?" Anthony asked.

I bristled. Sure, Uncle Jack was indeed "gone," but Anthony's tone irked the shit out of me. I shouldn't have to replace Uncle Jack at the estate at all. He was supposed to be alive! "Do you have any leads on his killer?"

Both Anthony and Lina stopped eating.

That was probably too much, and I lowered my fork. "I'm sorry. I'm not feeling well and emotions are running high." My chest tightened, and I coughed into my elbow.

Panic. Panic was running *really* fucking high for me now.

I hated the plantation, hated my family's history, and hated that Uncle Jack was dead. My heart rate was on the verge of out of control. I risked standing and was pleased to find my legs in working order.

"Lina, it was good to see you again, and thank you for looking out for me when the heat got to me. Anthony, good day." I left the table and snagged two bottles of water on the way out. In my attempt to escape, I collided with a little boy whose head barely reached my waist.

"I'm so sorry," I said. "Are you okay?"

It was the boy from the pew.

He flashed the cutest smile. "I like you."

"Uh, thanks," I said.

"What's your name?"

"Janie."

"I'm Samuel."

"Wonderful to meet you, Samuel."

He beamed. The young woman who had sat with him at the church arrived and put her hand on his shoulder.

"I'm sorry. Is my son bothering you?" she asked.

Lina was headed my way. "Not at all, but I do need to go."

"Bye!" Samuel said, giving me an enthusiastic wave.

My rotten mood brightened with his cheerfulness. "Bye," I said to him and the young woman, then rushed to my car.

I hopped in and then yelped when the heat from the inside of the car and the scorching seat and steering wheel welcomed me. "Fucking hell! Like really, this is fucking hell!" I screamed inside the vehicle.

I touched things with my fingertips when starting the car and turning the air-conditioning all the way up. I put my sunglasses on and drank more water while the car's interior cooled. Upon spotting Lina rounding the corner of the church building, I put the car in gear and left, kicking up loose gravel with the tires when I hit the gas pedal.

The initial part of the drive was a blur until I neared the interstate. Only a couple more turns and I'd be on I-10 and well on my way back to New Orleans. While stopped at a red light, I noticed the signs in the grassy areas at the intersection. One with a Black girl's smiling face was larger than all the others. It contained one word in large font: *MISSING*.

My gut knotted like I'd been punched in it. My light turned green, so I drove through the intersection, then slowed the car to ease off the road and into the empty parking lot of an abandoned gas station. I wondered if it was a cramp from all the water or the cornbread I'd practically inhaled. Maybe it was a side effect from the mystery drugs I'd consumed last night.

There was another sign for the missing girl near the parking area. It had a number listed to call with any information. Now my chest ached, a little at first, then worsening into a sensation like a belt was wrapped around me, preventing me from taking a deep breath.

Here we go. Panic attack.

I closed my eyes and tried to focus on slowing my breaths. I struggled before finding the right rhythm I needed to relax my mind and body.

The redheaded girl I thought I'd seen in the cemetery.

The sign.

The smiling girl's face.

MISSING.

God, how had I forgotten what had happened here?

My breathing rhythm faltered, and I coughed when the chest tightening resumed.

The signs weren't old and faded, which meant it was happening again. Sure, this could have been some kid taken by an angry parent or stolen for human trafficking. But I didn't believe it was either of those.

I remembered going to bed at night when I was a child, fearful I would be the next kid from my school taken and found dead weeks later. I remembered my mother telling me that I was safe. I remembered Uncle Jack hugging me when I cried on his shoulder as a little girl, terrified that I would disappear like one of my friends had.

I'd only ever felt safe with him. Not with my mother. Not with my father.

I groaned, unable to stop the pain from coming. Breathing exercises wouldn't slow this freight train of grief that refused to brake.

There was only one thought in my mind: *Uncle Jack, why did you have to die?*

I buried my face in my hands and sobbed.

Chapter Eight

I wanted to strangle the person knocking on my hotel door. The racket made my headache worse, so I sat up in the bed, ready to inflict pain on the person at the door.

Goth lay on her back with only a piece of the sheet across her middle. She groaned and opened her eyes. "What is that noise?"

"Did you order food and then pass out?" I asked.

"No."

I got up, glancing at the clock on the table next to the bed: 2:19 p.m. I dragged on a pair of trousers and a button-down shirt while stumbling toward the door. I struggled with the latch and security slide before getting them undone. Realizing, as I turned the knob to open the door, I hadn't bothered to check the peephole to see who it was first.

Oh well.

I pulled the door open and stared at Deputy Lina. Did this woman ever change out of her uniform?

Lina's eyebrows went up.

I wasn't about to tolerate Lina's assessment of my current state. "What?"

"I'm checking in on you."

"Why?"

"Mr. Landry asked me to."

I wasn't inviting Lina in. "Why?"

"He said you missed your appointment with him, and he was worried about you. He said you weren't answering your phone or returning texts."

I didn't even know where my phone was. It was here … somewhere. "The appointment was today. I missed it. So what?"

"The appointment was yesterday."

I frowned, trying to piece together the events after my unraveling on the side of the road. I'd made it back to the city and called Goth. Green and blue pills with the yellow ones and beer, sex, shots, wine, more sex, and …

Everything blurred after that. Empty bottles and food cartons were in and around the trash bin, so Goth and I had eaten somewhere in that mix too. "The funeral was …?"

"Two days ago."

"Oh. I've been drinking and … um, drinking. I'll call Mr. Landry and reschedule with him for tomorrow."

"He was hoping you would come out today. I can drive you if—"

"No!" I softened my voice. "No." If Lina became my driver, I wouldn't be able to go my own way and leave when I wanted. "I need a shower and some time to clean up. I can be out there this evening."

Goth's voice came from the bedroom. "Is it food?" She emerged wearing a black camisole and matching panties. "Whoa!" she said upon seeing Lina.

Goth's eyes darted around, and I half expected her to bolt for the balcony to make her escape.

"She's a friend," I said.

Both Lina and Goth stared at me.

I wasn't even sure what I meant—the woman-now-deputy

I hadn't seen since I was six was a friend? Or the woman I met two, no, three days ago and didn't know her name was a friend? I didn't bother trying to clarify my remark, if it could be clarified at all.

I moved to close the door. "Lina, I'll call Mr. Landry and coordinate with him on when I'll be out."

"Janie," Lina said, "I'm sorry how things left off the other day. Anthony sends his apologies for being rude and prying into matters that weren't his business. I'm sorry too. I should have been more sensitive, given the circumstances."

I nodded. "I'm sure you both have done everything you could to help Uncle Jack's investigation. I'm sorry for being an asshole."

"I hope we can try again and catch up. Uncle Jacques was very fond of you."

"Thanks." Don't fall apart. *Don't* fall apart.

"I noticed that when you were leaving, you met Samuel."

"Yeah. Great kid. If I'm to meet Mr. Landry this evening, I should get in the shower."

"I'll see you around."

"Uh-huh." I closed the door and flipped the latches to secure it. I leaned my forehead against the door.

"Holy *shit*!" Goth said, then laughed. "I thought we were toast and getting busted for the pills. You're full of surprises."

I winced when she swatted my ass.

"Janie," Goth said.

"What?"

She smiled. "That deputy was pretty hot."

"Stop it." I headed for the bathroom.

Goth followed me. "Maybe I get rid of the pills and we invite her back."

"No."

"Where does she live? Maybe we go to her?"

I spun around, ready to shut Goth down, but the woman grinned. She was teasing me. I resumed my trip to the shower.

"Who is Uncle Jack?" Goth asked.

"I attended his funeral yesterday, um, two days ago."

"Oh. Sorry. And Uncle Jacques?"

"Same person."

"What?"

I turned the shower on. "When I was little, I couldn't pronounce Jacques, so he became Uncle Jack."

"The po-po is your cousin."

Lina was a deputy and not a police officer, so she wasn't technically the po-po. Except Lina *was* law enforcement. I decided to lump her in with the police. "No. Uncle Jack is an uncle in title only. He was a close family friend, but he is—was—Lina's biological uncle."

"Do you have biological family in Louisiana?"

I hesitated. "What's your name?"

"Why?"

"You do not get to ask these questions and pry into my life when I don't even know your real fucking name."

"Evangeline Guidry. Eva to many, but not gonna lie, I like Goth better." She stripped, maneuvered around me to check the water, then stepped into the shower.

Goth-Eva was naked and in the shower again. My annoyance with life evaporated, so I tossed my clothes to the floor and got in behind her.

Chapter Nine

M r. Landry had agreed to an early morning meeting the next day, so Goth stayed another night in the hotel with me.

After thinking of her as Goth for the last few days, calling her Eva felt weird. I refused to drink more than one glass of wine that evening at dinner. Neither of us took any pills. I liked that she didn't give me any shit for abstaining. We had had some time to talk instead of only getting trashed. I realized that I enjoyed Goth's company for more than just a romp in the sack … and it created tension in my head that I didn't enjoy.

I checked out of the hotel, figuring life would be a little easier if I stayed closer to Jardin for Mr. Landry's paperwork crap. Then I would head back to the city before flying out. That was the plan. Visiting the Martil estate was *not* on my to-do list.

I parked next to Mr. Landry's car in the driveway at Uncle Jack's little two-story home. The elderly lawyer remained in his car and waved to me with one hand while holding his mobile in the other.

Uncle Jack's house needed repairs and paint. I couldn't fathom why it was in such disrepair. His salary for taking care of the estate had been beyond generous. He could have owned a brand-new house twice this size, with a nice European car, too.

Sure, the European car would've been useless to him, but he could've afforded it without an issue.

I stepped out of my car, grumbling when the heat assaulted me upon leaving the air-conditioned vehicle. My sunglasses kept my eyeballs from being fried by the blinding sun, but I wished I'd packed shorts instead of only trousers. I didn't dwell on my choice of clothing too long because my eyes had fixated on one of the trees outside Uncle Jack's home. The myriad of bottles hanging from lengths of string tied in different places on the tree limbs captivated me. They seemed spaced far enough apart to not hit each other and shatter with stormy winds.

I thought there was a reason for the bottles, but I couldn't remember what it was … Something to do with good luck? Maybe a Southern culture thing?

Most of the bottles were blue, with some being smaller and of different colors. I couldn't recall if Uncle Jack had had these here when I was little.

I turned and spotted a pair of cobalt-blue bottles hanging from strings on either side of the front door. My attention had been focused on the house's peeling paint, so I hadn't noticed them.

Mr. Landry remained on the phone inside his car, engine running to keep the AC going. I was ready for him to end his damn call and get my meeting with him over with sooner rather than later.

Uncle Jack's home sat on the border of the Martil property, and I didn't need his house. Why would he give this to me? To incorporate it into the non-plantation's boundary? A few more acres wouldn't matter, except apparently it had to Uncle Jack.

My phone vibrated, so I pulled it from my pocket, noticing I didn't have enough of a signal to make a phone call out here. But texts didn't need much bandwidth to go through, and I half smiled to see a text from Goth.

How's it going?

I'm standing outside and melting. Louisiana really sucks, I replied.

Sometimes it does. Have fun turning into a puddle.

Thanks.

That was the end of the interaction. Goth had a twisted sense of humor that I appreciated.

I wanted to check work emails while I waited, but I couldn't do that with a crap signal. My phone was useless out here, so I returned it to my pocket. Mr. Landry emerged from his car holding two thick manila envelopes.

"Janette, good to see you again. Sorry about that. Urgent family call. Let's go inside." He fished a set of keys from his pocket and led the way.

"How are you able to use your phone out here? My signal sucks."

"Part of it will be your carrier," he said. "I paid through the nose to have a booster installed in the car. Too many dropped or missed calls when out in remote areas like this." He patted his forehead with a wrinkled handkerchief. "Whoo. Gonna be a hot one today."

"It's already hot as hell."

"Not yet, but it will be."

I hated this place so much.

I noticed a line of rust-colored dust on the step leading up to the small porch and another line of dust at the base of the front door. The wind had swept some of it away. I stepped over both lines so I didn't track it into the house.

Uncle Jack had been killed three weeks ago. The autopsy and investigation had taken some time to sort out before the funeral was arranged, which also took a while to get the masses of Montpeliers organized and present.

Once inside I removed my sunglasses. The silence in his home unnerved me. I fidgeted with my sunglasses while noticing the light layer of gray dust coating everything.

I felt like an intruder.

I remembered visiting Uncle Jack's house with my mother a few times as a child, and how he always had some new gift for me. My favorite had been a wooden puzzle box that I'd kept since the day he gave it to me.

The box was in Boston on my nightstand next to my bed. I wished I'd brought it with me now that I was stuck in Louisiana for a bit longer. Opening and closing the box, the feel of the carvings under my fingertips—those things calmed my mind when I was stressed. And the strain of being in Jardin with memories that refused to stay suppressed was creating all sorts of tension.

The only photos remaining on the mantel were of Uncle Jack and me together at different places in the French Quarter. The spots on the mantel free of dust indicated that other photos had been moved or taken since Uncle Jack died. Patches of brighter-colored squares and rectangles against the faded wallpaper were the ghosts of other framed pictures that were now gone.

I used the sunglasses in my hand to point at the rectangles on the wall. "Where are the pictures?"

"All other items of Mr. Montpelier's estate have been distributed to the recipients per his instructions," Mr. Landry said, sounding like a prerecorded legalese bot. When he turned to face me, he reverted to human form and smiled.

"Photos and other items went to various family members," he said. "The car went to a niece starting college soon. The old truck went to one nephew, and the tools went to a niece attending an automotive repair class at the community college.

Cash assets went to area charities. All that has been addressed. The last thing was the house and land going to you." He removed a set of papers from one of the envelopes. "These are the papers I need you to sign."

I went to the thermostat on the wall and adjusted it down. The air-conditioning had been left on, but I decided it was still too hot in the house. I welcomed the blast of cooler air.

I neared the table and the papers. "Are you sure this house wouldn't be better in someone else's hands? Surely he has a family member who could use it more than me."

"You were declared his heir and executor of the remainder of his estate. Everything left in and around this house is yours to do with what you will."

None of this made any sense. "What's the other envelope?"

Mr. Landry slid it across the table to me. Uncle Jack had sealed and signed his name across the flap closing the envelope.

"Whatever is in there is only for you," Mr. Landry said. "I don't know what's in it. It's remained sealed since the day he gave it to me."

It seemed a bit ominous for the contents to be so top secret. I decided to deal with it later. I signed the papers where Mr. Landry wanted, and then he left.

I was alone in the house with a mixed feeling of comfort and of being an outsider.

Wine was required for me to figure out what was left in the house and what to do with it. I grabbed the sealed envelope and left.

Chapter Ten

Upon returning to Uncle Jack's house from the store, I deposited the envelope on the counter next to my three bottles of red wine and new corkscrew. The cooled interior of the house was divine. I opened all the cabinets. I never expected to find an actual wineglass, so it was either a coffee mug or a Mason jar. I settled for a purple coffee mug, one I remembered seeing Uncle Jack drink from when I was little. It was chipped on the bottom and the handle had been glued back on at some point. Though there were plenty of mugs in the cabinet, this one had a lot of miles on it, so I assumed (pretended?) Uncle Jack had used it frequently.

I filled the mug to the top, then took a long drink from it. My thoughts drifted to Goth. I considered topping off the cup, but my gaze landed on the sealed envelope.

Might as well get this over with.

I reached for it, but someone knocked on the door.

I took my mug with me and wished I had checked to see who was there before opening the door. I was never this careless in Boston, but since arriving in Louisiana, my mind was too preoccupied with thoughts other than basic safety measures.

"Janie," Frank said, smiling. "I'm so happy to see you."

He wore street clothes, and his short-sleeved tee left his

arms exposed. For a man with such a wiry, lean frame, his muscles rippled when he moved. Although he was in his late fifties, I figured he was stronger than he appeared.

"Hi, Uncle Frank."

"I've really missed you. You look so much like both Katherine and Henry."

I nodded, though I couldn't recall my parents' faces anymore. Too much time had blurred those memories.

"May I come in?" he asked.

"This isn't a good time. I've got a stack of papers from the lawyer to sort through."

"I understand."

"Thanks again for your help at the funeral."

He smiled. "As I said before, anytime. Maybe I can take you to lunch or dinner before you leave."

"Yeah. We'll do that at some point."

"Great! One sec." He went to his dark-colored sedan and rummaged inside it for a moment. When he returned, he handed me a slip of paper. "That's my number. Call me whenever. I work at different times but have a flexible schedule, so we can even meet later for a beer." He glanced at the mug's contents. "Or wine."

"Sounds good. Thanks."

He gave me another smile, then went to his car. I leaned against the door frame. A hint of a breeze caused the blue bottles hanging near the door to sway. When Frank's car engine started, I returned my attention to him. He waved to me, and I mirrored the gesture before retreating inside.

Once in the kitchen, I dumped the mug's contents into my mouth, then refilled the cup. That's when I noticed the time.

Okay, maybe eleven in the morning was a bit early for pouring a bottle of wine down the gullet.

I corked the bottle.

The refrigerator was empty except for an open carton of baking soda. The freezer had a few microwave meals that didn't appeal to me. I wasn't hungry anyway and decided I would get food when I left to find a hotel or bed-and-breakfast to stay a couple of nights.

The sealed envelope continued to wait for me.

I snatched it off the counter. I took it and the mug to the couch and sat. After another gulp of wine, I placed the mug on the floor, then opened the envelope.

Dearest Janie,

I can't tell you how many times I have written this letter only to burn it later because I knew it would disrupt your life. The last thing I have ever wanted is to cause you any distress. I'm sorry I was never brave enough to tell you these things in person.

I'd love to ease you into this, but I know how much you hate idle chatter.

Janie, I loved your mother, and you are our daughter.

I scowled at the paper in my hands, then looked up. There had to be a hidden camera somewhere filming my reaction. This was some bullshit joke I didn't find the least bit funny. My hands shook so badly, I couldn't read the rest of the letter.

I placed the paper on the top of the envelope in my lap and took a drink of wine. A second gulp and the cup was empty. Now I was trembling *and* lightheaded.

This couldn't be happening.

A small part of my brain had a different reaction: relief, happiness, and something I had always secretly wished for— that Uncle Jack was my real father and not the cold-hearted bastard Henry Martil.

Denial, my savior, came to the rescue. No. This wasn't real.

About a year after Henry and Katherine moved into the newly built plantation house, I met Katherine. When Henry traveled for business, I'd check in on her since she was home alone much of the time. She had staff there who helped with the estate, but they always went to their own homes at night.

Our friendship grew and turned into an affair. When she became pregnant, Henry knew you were not his child. He loved Katherine, though, and kept her as his wife. She never told him who the father was, and she and I had to be careful and see each other only in public after you were born. Henry had too much money for me to go up against him for paternal rights.

I think Henry tried to love you, but he was distant with you. He became cold toward Katherine too. The Katherine you knew was withdrawn. She had some money, but Henry controlled everything, including her cash. She wouldn't leave Henry, though I begged her to grab you and go away with me. She was too afraid, and that made her even more unhappy. It tortured us both to not be a family together with you.

Nothing made me happier than to see you when I could. Nothing made me sadder than to see your mother so miserable. We tried to be together when possible, but her visits with you were always short, only an hour or so. It was when you and Lina became friends that things changed for the better. The playground became the haven your mother and I needed to be together and watch you play and laugh. Those were the days we felt like a real family, and I'll never forget them.

Janie, it nearly destroyed me when you were taken away. I went to Mr. Landry and told him the truth. I called your aunt in Boston, but she would not let me speak to you. I wrote letters to you, but they were returned. Those are included in the envelope. I even drove up to Boston to try to see you, but Kim sent me away with a promise of police involvement if I came back.

I had parked well down the street that day and wept when I saw you walking home after school. I knew by the slump of your shoulders that you were not happy there. Your aunt whisked you into the house as soon as your shoe had touched the front step. I think she suspected I was somewhere nearby. She wasn't wrong.

I prayed you wouldn't think I'd forgotten you. I continued to write; the letters were always returned unopened.

The happiest day of my life was when you called on your eighteenth birthday.

I stopped reading, this time to wipe away tears. Under Aunt Kim's care, I had believed that Uncle Jack had abandoned me, but one night I had overheard my aunt's muttering about "another birthday card for the brat from that asshole swamp rat."

There were a lot of swamps in Louisiana, but only a Jardin Swamp rat would know where to send me a card.

I had peeked around the corner to see Aunt Kim shrieking more curses to an empty office and waving a yellow envelope with an orange flap keeping it sealed. Kim scrawled something on the front of the envelope, then tossed it into her desk drawer. Late that same night when I crept into my aunt's office to check the desk, all the drawers were locked.

I had assumed the swamp rat was Uncle Jack, so I retained a sliver of hope that I might see him again … that he might rescue me from this hell. When I turned eighteen ten years later, I walked out of Kim's house at midnight and called Uncle Jack.

He broke into tears when I identified myself to him on the call. He told me that he'd tried to contact me and see me while I lived with Kim but hadn't been allowed. After being shit on by so many adults, I never truly believed him. I guess I believed him enough to stay in touch with him afterward, but trusting others had never been easy for me.

But now I had to know if that yellow envelope had been sent by Uncle Jack.

I slid off the couch to my knees and shook the contents of the envelope out onto the floor. I pawed through the envelopes until I found the yellow and orange one. The postmark date was a week before my eighth birthday.

Oh, God.

My eighth birthday was when I gifted myself a composition notebook and wrote everything down about Aunt Kim and her associates and friends. I also chronicled the various abuses and neglect I suffered over the next ten years under Kim's shitty care.

My phone vibrated against my leg, so I pulled it from my pocket. It was a text from Goth. I tossed the phone aside. I couldn't deal with anything else until I finished the letter.

> *Janie, after I hung up the phone from your call that day, I wept for hours. You may remember me crying when you visited me a week later, too. Fortunately, I managed to hold myself together better than I did after the phone call. You were in New Orleans for just*

two days, but those were the best two days I'd had in years.

I'm so sorry I couldn't tell you this before. I know I'm a coward.

The rest of the letters that I sent you over those years are in the upstairs room with the desk. In the bottom right drawer is a puzzle box for you, too.

I love you, Janie. I love you more than my own life. I know you have had unhappy times, and I hate that for you. I'm so proud of you and the woman that you became and the woman that you are. Take care, my daughter. You are stronger than you realize.

Love, Jack. (Dad. I regret that I never got to hear you call me "Dad.")

The letter slipped from my fingers. Tightness gripped my chest, but not from a coming panic attack. This was a pain unlike anything I had ever experienced. It continued to build and hurt more.

I pulled my knees close to my chest and wrapped my arms around them. It didn't make the pain stop. My mind ceased working. Time froze. I gasped for air, certain my insides would explode and I would die.

A couple of tears slid down my face. Then the floodgates opened. I became consumed by the grief I had managed to keep locked in a cage for so many years. Now that the beast was out, I could only weep.

Chapter Eleven

I returned the cards and letters to the envelope, carried it upstairs, and placed it on top of the desk. Seated in Uncle Jack's worn but comfortable desk chair, I slid it back to better access all the drawers. Only one had anything in it. I removed the box containing mailing envelopes organized by date with Return to Sender scrawled across the front of each one. I passed my fingertip over the writing, noting that it had been almost gouged into the paper. I'd always known Aunt Kim was a horrible person, but this latest insult had altered her status from horrible to fucking despicable.

A large wooden puzzle box sat in the bottom of the drawer. I lifted it and placed it on my lap. I rotated the beautifully carved wood, noting the perfection and symmetry of the fleur-de-lis, one on each side of the cube.

Uncle Jack created his boxes with a secret opening mechanism. Pressing on two corners at the same time caused the top of the box to open like a flower. But Uncle Jack's special skill was to make them so it wasn't obvious which corners needed to be pressed.

The tiniest of hinges and gears operated on the interior to control the top of the box. Pushing the top back down caused the lid to click back into place and lock. The only other way to get into one of his puzzle boxes was to smash it open, and I would never destroy something so beautiful.

I smiled and pressed the corners to open it … except it didn't open like my other one did. My smile vanished.

I pressed on the other corners, changed the sequence of how I manipulated the corners, turned it over in case the bottom corners were the secret. Nothing. I lost track of time while I struggled with the box.

Why the fuck did he leave this thing for me if I couldn't open it?

I gave up and placed the box on the desk. My stomach rumbled.

I checked the time: 6:30 p.m. Shit. I hadn't eaten all day … Wine for brunch wasn't food.

I headed downstairs and toward the kitchen, then paused when I realized the back door wasn't fully closed.

I hadn't heard anyone come in, but I'd also been immersed in learning who my real father was and getting my ass kicked by a puzzle box I couldn't open. I closed the door, then tugged on the handle to make sure it had latched. I flipped the lock.

I couldn't recall if it had been open like that since this morning.

Uncle Jack's house was at the end of a long dirt road and surrounded by woodlands on three sides and a marshy area leading to Jardin Swamp on the remaining side. No one in their right mind would come way the hell out here.

I turned back toward the kitchen, but someone stood in the entryway to it.

I yelped and stumbled back.

"Janie!" Lina said. "I'm so sorry."

I leaned forward with my hands on my knees and closed my eyes. I trembled while my heart raced. I needed a moment to calm down, but I couldn't slow my breathing. Dizzied, I shifted to lean against the wall, then slid down to my knees on the floor.

Lina was at my side. "I'm really sorry."

I managed to take a deep breath. I lifted my head and glared at Lina (while noting she wasn't in uniform for once). "Why are you in this house sneaking around?"

"I … no." Lina shook her head. "I called a couple of times and texted. When you didn't respond, I drove out to check on you. I knocked but you didn't answer. Your car is here, so I peeked in the front window. Your phone was on the floor, and I got worried. The door was unlocked and I called out for you. When I heard the back door click, I came through the kitchen. I didn't mean to startle you."

Lina had done more than startle me. I checked my hip pocket; my phone was indeed not on me.

I then remembered tossing it aside when Goth texted while I was immersed in Uncle Jack's letter.

Should I think of him as Uncle Jack? Should I refer to him as my father? Dad? Uncle Dad? Jack Daddy?

I giggled with that last one. I had too much adrenaline running through me, zero food, and what seemed to be a touch of delirium.

"Janie?"

I waved Lina off. "It's been a rough few days."

Most of the adrenaline had worn off, but a lot of noise remained in my head.

Uncle Jack being my father meant Lina was my cousin. Given the size of Uncle Jack's family, I now had a plethora of aunts, uncles, and cousins. Maybe.

I couldn't process all this information at once.

My stomach rumbled again.

"Oh! I brought you dinner," Lina said. "That's the whole reason why I came out."

"Thank you. I'm starved." I stood but kept my palm against the wall for a few seconds. Satisfied that I was steady, I left the wall and headed into the kitchen.

"You good while I run out to the car to bring the food in?" Lina asked.

"Yeah. I'm fine now." I was an absolute fucking liar.

Once Lina left, I kept my arms close to my body and rotated my hands to extend them—my discreet effort to assess how fine I really was. I frowned at my trembling hands, grabbed the purple mug from the counter, and filled it with water. I dumped the water into my mouth, wincing at the bitterness of the taste.

I downed another mug of water, and that one seemed less bitter. I chalked it up to the house being empty and old water in the pipes.

I stared at the mug in my hand. I didn't remember bringing the cup to the kitchen. I'd left it in the living room on the floor with my phone. I wandered into the living room while Lina came in through the front door carrying two full bags of food that smelled both Southern (fried and greasy) and heavenly (very fried and greasy). I bent to pick up the phone, and Lina froze.

"I didn't pick it up when I was looking for you in case … um," Lina said.

"In case?" I tilted my head. Oh. "In case it was evidence?"

"Uh."

"Crime scene evidence?"

Lina shifted her feet and cast her gaze to the floor. "Someone could have gotten inside while you were here."

"Who the hell is gonna come all the way out here to commit a crime, Lina?"

She brought her gaze up and I observed her. Lina remained calm, but I noticed she blinked frequently with this confrontation. Calm on the outside but rattled on the inside, at least a little rattled.

"It's training and experience," Lina said. "That's all."

I could've let this go, but it irked me that she'd been in the house without my knowledge. I pressed her. "Then why move the mug to the kitchen and not the phone if this was a potential crime scene or whatever?"

"I didn't touch anything when I came in."

I hadn't expected that answer. Maybe in my semi-drunken and unfed state earlier I had moved it on my way upstairs.

God, I wanted a massive glass of wine right now. But a deputy was standing in front of me. If I started drinking the way I wanted to, I would have to stay the night here.

No. Fucking. Way. I was getting a hotel somewhere tonight.

"I'm sorry," I said, realizing Lina continued to stand with her hands full while I romped with my random thoughts. "I'm really tired. I'm not thinking straight half the time." Most of the time.

I took a bag from Lina and carried the food into the kitchen. My mouth watered with the smells. I removed containers and half wished Lina wasn't here so I could shove the stuff into my mouth. Jambalaya, crawfish étouffée, deep fried and powdered beignets, and cherry cobbler. There was enough food for four people.

"You made all this?" I asked.

"I did the cobbler and jambalaya. My mama made the étouffée and beignets."

"This is amazing," I said.

"Hope you like it all. I wasn't sure if you were vegetarian, so if you are, I can run out to bring you something else since there is meat in the jambalaya and étouffée."

"No, no." I smiled. "Everything is staying. Thank you."

Another thought struck me: I wasn't a Martil anymore. I

was a Montpelier like Lina. Maybe. If Uncle Jack was indeed my father.

My maybe-cousin stared at me, and I turned to grab plates to hide the likely flush creeping into my face.

"Are you staying to eat?"

"No, I have to go. I'm on a late shift tonight. I'll catch you later."

"Thanks for the food."

"You're welcome."

Lina left, and I took a large bite of the cherry cobbler, closing my eyes and savoring the sweet and tangy flavors mixed in with baked flour and butter. I couldn't get a dessert like this in Boston unless I made it myself. And I couldn't cook or bake worth a damn, so this was one more thing I hadn't had outside of my rare trips to New Orleans to visit Uncle Jack.

I grabbed a dish towel and carried the food to the table. I sat and placed the towel in my lap, ate a few more bites of cobbler, then checked my phone. I did indeed have missed calls from a Louisiana area code with two different time stamps. I had never heard the phone ring, but given the lack of a signal, the calls had probably punted straight to voicemail. The texts from the same number confirmed that the missed calls were from Lina.

Hey, this is Lina. Wanted to check in on you and bring dinner by.

Mr. Landry told me you were at Uncle Jacques's house when he last saw you. Are you staying there?

Let me know where you are, and I'll bring food.

I'll take a drive out that way in case you're there.

Lina had always been kind to me when we were kids. I liked that she hadn't changed—except that she was now law enforcement, which conflicted with my tendency to abuse whatever substances I got my hands on.

Ah, yes. Substances. I snickered and filled my mug with wine.

I skipped the voicemails Lina had left, then sent a quick reply to Goth. I set the phone aside and stabbed my fork into the jambalaya.

Chapter Twelve

Between three and four in the morning had always been a perfect time to dispose of a corpse. Bars had closed, roads were deserted, sleepy towns were deep into their slumber, and no one was around to witness the act.

Farmers and other early risers stirred shortly after four. The occasional drive-through-the-night traveler passed on this road during the wee hours, but the killer knew his route and kept contingency plans for all possible scenarios.

He checked the time once more and paused, assessing for any hint of headlights approaching. There were none. His spot tonight was well off any main or secondary roads and hidden by trees. No cars had come by in over an hour. His eyes had had plenty of time to adjust to the remote area's darkness, and he could detect the shapes of objects nearby. Trees, stumps, moss, and other plant life that could be a tripping hazard would not be problematic tonight.

He never enjoyed this part of the process. His shoes for disposal work were a size and a half too small, and his heels ached while his toes remained pinched by the squeezing fabric. His long-sleeved shirt and trousers made the suffocating heat worse, but he had to be careful about trace evidence and his own DNA.

He tugged on his leather gloves, pulling them tighter over his fingers so he would have a secure hold when he lifted the body.

To conceal his movements within the dark void of the swamp's edge, he had removed the bulbs in his interior dome lights. The lights that automatically came on when he opened his trunk were also minus their bulbs. The only sound was the slightest squeak when he opened his car door. He made a mental note to address that noise with lubricant once he was home.

He opened the trunk and gazed down at the plastic-wrapped shape lying in his trunk. He'd been forced to hold on to the body longer than he wanted. An evening rainstorm two nights ago would have left too many tire tracks and footprints. The daytime temperatures would've dried the mud, but he'd had a prior engagement last night. Tonight was perfect and on a weeknight, so no risk of weekend revelers.

He hummed a hymn while he unwrapped the exterior layer of black plastic encasing the deceased child. Once that layer was peeled back, he placed the cans of paint he carried in his trunk on top of the plastic to hold it down.

He left the body wrapped within the clear plastic and lifted the corpse out. It was uncomfortable to hold near his chest. He turned, carrying it down the slope to one of the many creeks that fed the swamp.

When he stopped, he eased it to the ground, then gave the body a light shove. Gravity and physics did the rest. The dead child rolled the rest of the way down the slope and landed in the water with a gentle splash. He watched for a moment more until he was certain the body had floated into the current.

The clear plastic was a special type that would dissolve in the water, eliminating any trace evidence he might have transferred to the body while carrying it. He headed back up the slope. When his shoe slipped, he pitched forward and prevented his fall with one hand.

His gloved fingers sank into the softer mud, and he cursed under his breath. He straightened and was careful to not touch anything with the muddied glove while keeping his eyes fixed on the indentation his hand had made. He pressed his shoe into the space, erasing the handprint.

He resumed his walk up the slope, and once at his car, raked his glove through grass to clean it. Using his clean hand, he lowered his trunk lid with the same gentleness he'd used to place the body there a few hours earlier. The lid's latch caught, and then he returned to the interior of the car, sitting and using the same technique to close his door. He did everything with one hand now to prevent transferring any residual mud to the steering wheel or to his clothes.

He would vacuum the car later per his usual routine since he knew he'd tracked mud onto the floor mats, and he'd burn the gloves. He always had a plan for anything that could go wrong. He'd been doing this work for many years, and he had come a long way since his earlier mistakes back then.

He started the engine and put the car in gear. He couldn't prevent the tire tracks and footprints he'd left behind, but that was a lesser issue. His car was simple, nondescript, and his tires and shoes had been purchased from a big-box store where these same items were sold daily. Plus, his natural shoe size was larger than the shoes he wore.

The police didn't bother with the children vanishing. That had been another thing he'd addressed a long time ago. Money made those kinds of things disappear. The only problem he'd had recently was Jacques Montpelier. And that problem had been addressed and put in a grave.

He smiled when he turned onto the vacant main road.

The task was done. His somber mood had lifted.

It was time to celebrate.

Chapter Thirteen

I decided to tackle the puzzle box again. The wine had my head spinning, but I'd had only one mug of it with dinner—well, dinner that had been breakfast, lunch, and dinner rammed into one meal that had started with cobbler. I rested the box in my lap and turned it in my hands. The craftsmanship was incredible. I admired Uncle Jack's woodworking skills more than ever, recalling the small puzzle box I had kept with me since the day he'd given it to me—my fifth birthday.

Most kids clung to a stuffed animal or doll. For me it was the box. Solving the combination of pressure points on my box, then closing it again helped me survive stressful times. I sometimes hid little treasures inside it, like smooth rocks or trinkets, taking them out when my parents argued. Once I was in Boston, the treasures became coins I'd stolen from my aunt. As I got older, I took more of my aunt's money and some of her pills and hid them inside it.

This new box from Uncle Jack was larger, about twice the size of a cube-shaped carton of facial tissue. I wondered if he'd left something in it for me, and that piqued my interest and my desire to get the thing open. I shook the box, but there was no sound. I traced my finger over the tiny images of animals carved into different places of the box. I hadn't noticed them before since I'd been too captivated by the beauty of the fleur-de-lis carvings.

I worked on the box, losing track of time, and my frustration grew. Sighs became grumbling. Grumbling morphed into swearing out loud. Nothing worked to get the damned box open.

I pressed harder on the corners, then yelped when dark red liquid seeped out of the seams between the pieces. I flung the box to the top of the desk, where it flipped end over end twice before stopping.

I slid the chair back and stood; my trembling hands were painted red. A musky odor from my hands filled my nostrils. Blood.

Oh, fuck.

Blood streamed down the box's sides and pooled on the desk. The puddle grew until it neared the edge of the desk, then dripped, leaving red trails down the desk drawers. More pools formed where the drops fell on the floor.

The puddle changed into a hand-like shape that flowed toward me. I took a step back.

In a blink, the blood was gone.

My hands were clean. I neared the desk, poked a finger at the box, tipping it to see underneath, and there was nothing, no blood. I released a slow breath while staring at the box. It didn't move, and it didn't bleed.

What the hell had happened?

The box sat on the desk.

I'd deal with opening it tomorrow. I picked the box up, checking it once more for blood that wasn't there, and tucked it under one arm. I flinched when a shadow moved past the doorway.

I didn't make a sound or breathe. I didn't hear anything or anyone inside the house, only the pulsing rush of blood in my ears. No boards creaked or doors clicked shut. I inched toward the door since it was the only way out.

Sure, I could go out one of the room's windows, but I didn't think dropping from the second story to the ground below was necessary unless the place was on fire or there was an actual intruder instead of an overactive imagination.

My mind raced and I spun in a circle, taking a quick inventory of the room. No fire. No bleeding box. No shadows in doorways.

I hated this feeling of paranoia and started for the door. My legs buckled, but I managed to not fall. I took another wobbly step, then another.

I wasn't drunk enough to be walking like this.

I didn't know what was wrong with me.

I stumbled my way down the hall to the stairs and stopped. First my mind and now my balance was gone.

The smart thing would be to go down the stairs on my ass. The smarter thing would be to not attempt them at all, sit, call someone (if I had enough of a signal to make a call), and wait until help arrived. Or I could stay the night, sleep off whatever was wrong with me, and deal with everything tomorrow.

Yes. Deal with the shit tomorrow, or the next day. Or never.

I pulled my phone from my pocket. I wasn't sure how it was already four in the morning, but per the phone, it was. I could call Goth to come get me, but I barely knew the woman.

Lina was working. Wasn't it part of law enforcement's job to do wellness checks on people? I was *not* feeling well. That counted, right?

I started the text to Lina, but a floorboard behind me creaked.

I turned to stone.

I hadn't moved my feet since stopping at the top of the stairs.

Fuck the text. I decided to go downstairs and outside for a better signal to call 911 and try to explain to them why I was losing my mind and holding a bleeding box that wasn't bleeding anymore.

Angered now for being so fearful before, I spun to see what was behind me.

A looming black shadow rushed at me, and I leapt back.

I cried out when my back slammed onto the steps. I kept tumbling down the stairs, losing the box and the phone. Grabbing for the rail or wall or anything to stop my fall was futile. My chest and cheek crashed into the floor where I came to rest. I groaned but didn't try to rise, not yet. Everything hurt too much, but adrenaline kept my mind aware of my situation.

The steps creaked, and terror numbed all pain. I rolled over. The shadow raced down the steps. I raised my arms to try to protect myself from the impact of the shadow crashing into me, but it never came.

I eased my arms down.

There was no shadow, no creaking steps, and no one in the house.

My rapid breaths created another layer of dizziness. Standing wasn't an option, so I lay back on the floor. My vision blurred, but I managed to spot the box and my phone. The box was closer than the phone. I rolled to my side and groaned. In my disorientation, I pulled the box close, cradling it in my arm, and rested my head on the floor.

I blinked a few times while staring at the box. The animals carved into the box matched the ones Uncle Jack had given me for my birthdays.

I was too young to remember, but I had been told the elephant was his gift to me when I turned a year old. Then came the wildebeest, the impala, the cheetah, the ostrich, and the giraffe. I rotated the box, noting six animal carvings that matched my birthday gifts.

They were the directions on how to open the box.

Movement in my peripheral vision caught my attention. It wasn't the Shadow Man.

My dead childhood friend with flowing red hair sat on the floor in the corner of the room and waved at me.

"Hanna," I said.

Dead Hanna gave me a sad smile.

I closed my eyes.

I darted for the bathroom, but my stiff and sore body slowed my movements. My stomach splattered its contents on the floor in front of the toilet. A few more inches and I would've made it into the bowl. I ignored the mess for a moment to go to the sink. The cool water I splashed on my face felt divine, so I stayed at the sink for several minutes. My mind cleared enough to somewhat recall last night. My aches reminded me of my graceless trip down the stairs.

My back and ribs hurt the most. I twisted my upper body to try to stretch out the soreness and winced. I needed ibuprofen in my system before I tried that again.

Someone knocked at the front door. I didn't want any visitors. They knocked again. I wiped my face with a hand towel and took it with me to the door. I was at least walking now—not necessarily in a straight line, but upright and moving in a general direction.

I stopped and scanned the living room. Dead Hanna wasn't seated in the corner. I'm not sure what I would've done had she been there.

I turned the doorknob, noting that it was unlocked. Maybe someone *had* been in the house last night. But the Shadow

Man (Was it a man?) hadn't actually touched me. I had thrown myself off balance and down the stairs. And when the shadow came at me while I was on the floor, it never collided with me. It was simply gone a second later.

I realized I had opened the door while lost in my thoughts. My mind snapped to the present. "Uncle Frank."

"My God, Janie," he said. "You look awful."

He reached for me and I took a step back. He lowered his hand.

"I'm hungover is all," I said. "And I'm not trying to be rude. I don't like being touched." Unless it involved sex with a woman, then I was all for being touched … a lot.

He shoved his hands into his trouser pockets. "Thanks for telling me. Are you up for getting breakfast?"

Food now was not an option. "No, but thanks for the offer. Late lunch, maybe? I should have this headache under control by then."

"That would be great."

We hashed out the details of time and location, and then Frank left. I wished I hadn't made the plans with him, but he *was* my uncle … unless Jack was right about being my father.

I gazed up at the cobalt-blue bottles flanking the entryway. The sunlight striking their glass bounced beautiful rays of colored light off them. The sun also made me sweat. I turned to head back in.

The sound of tires crunching over Uncle Jack's winding driveway made me wonder if Uncle Frank was coming back. Upon spotting the approaching deputy car, the insides of my chest fluttered. I didn't have any drugs on me or in the house. Wine wasn't illegal, and neither were non-bleeding boxes, hallucinations, or falls down the stairs.

The tension in my shoulders eased when I recognized Lina as the driver. I wanted to go back inside into the air-conditioning, but I lingered at the doorway.

Lina parked, then was out of her car, wearing her uniform and sidearm.

I noted that my childhood friend looked damn fine in uniform.

I refused to let that thought go anywhere else. She was my cousin … might be my cousin.

"Well, you look like complete shit," Lina said.

"Feel like it." My possible cousin stood before me and I smiled.

"What?" Lina asked.

"Uh, random thought. It's nothing."

"I passed Frank on the way in."

"Yeah. He stopped by to see if I wanted to go for breakfast. I opted to meet him later."

"Good idea."

"You can come in if you don't mind the smell of puke. I have a little cleanup to do first."

"Are you still sick since the funeral?"

"No. A little too much wine last night."

I had zero explanations for why I had hallucinated last night and barfed all over the floor this morning. I had had the pukes after drinking too much before. Last night wasn't the same as those incidents. Something else was wrong. Maybe I *was* starting to go insane. Did insanity cause vomiting?

Shit. I was doing it again—lost in my thoughts while someone watched me stare into nothingness. I stepped aside. "Come on in. I have something to tell you, uh, after I clean the floor."

Chapter Fourteen

I emerged from the bathroom with a soiled towel and wasn't sure where to put it.

Lina placed the puzzle box and my phone on the counter next to her. She pointed. "Washer is behind that door."

"Thanks." I opened the side door and tossed the towel onto the top of the washer. "Any chance you know where Uncle Jack kept ibuprofen?"

"The cabinet to the left of the sink," Lina said. "Your phone was on the floor again. You seem to have a hard time keeping it on you."

Like my laptop, I kept my phone PIN protected, so even if my maybe deputy cousin had wanted to snoop on my phone, she couldn't. I said, "I'm not a fan of the leash it becomes."

"But on the floor? Put it in a drawer or something if you don't want to carry it."

"Yeah, that's a better idea."

"Why was the box on the floor too?"

"I, um. It was another rough night."

"I'm not judging you."

I was well acquainted with my aunt's scowls, grumbles, and slaps to the face for added emphasis when she showed me how she felt about me or anything I'd done or didn't do. I didn't give a shit about being judged or not by Lina. I *did* want Lina to stop asking so many questions, though.

"Didn't you work last night?" I asked. "Why are you awake now?"

"I did an evening split shift, so I wasn't up all night. I go back on duty in an hour. What did you have to tell me?"

"Oh, right. I learned yesterday that Henry Martil might not be my biological father." I paused, waiting for any kind of reaction from Lina, who merely nodded. "You already knew?"

"I've never been told, but I've suspected Uncle Jacques was your father."

"Why him?"

"The way he talked about you even though you didn't live here anymore. I always knew when you'd recently talked to him because he would be giddy for days."

"Oh." Damn. I suddenly wished I'd called him more often.

"Is it Uncle Jacques?"

"I don't know. If he is, you and I are cousins. DNA would prove it."

"You want me to get a DNA test?"

I nodded.

"I'm game."

"Uh, thanks." I had expected Lina to want time to think about it or even refuse. The quick agreement caught me off guard. "That's great. I'll check with Mr. Landry on how it will work and get back to you. I'll cover the cost. Did anyone else suspect Uncle Jack was my father?"

Lina shrugged. "Maybe. It wasn't something the family talked about at the dinner table. Why?"

"Just curious. I feel like I'm the last one to know anything."

"That must be frustrating."

Indeed, it was. My gaze landed on the puzzle box and I went to it.

"What's with the box?" Lina asked. "That's Uncle Jacques's handiwork, right?"

"It is."

"May I see it?"

I slid the puzzle box across the counter to her, then retrieved the bottle of ibuprofen from the cabinet Lina had indicated earlier. I clutched the bottle like it contained gold.

Lina traced her fingers over the carvings and smiled. "Do you know how to open it?" she asked.

"I haven't gotten it open yet." I wondered if Lina would notice that I hadn't given a straight answer. I popped three pills into my mouth, then scooped a handful of water from the tap to wash them down.

"Eat something soon so the pills don't irritate your stomach," Lina said.

I muttered an acknowledgment of her advice, then drank another handful of water from my palm. A civilized person would drink water from a cup. I was not bougie. I was a hungover-falling-down-stairs-hallucinating person. My palm substitute worked fine. I wiped the remnants of water over my face, enjoying its soothing coolness against my skin.

Lina slid the box back to me. "I never figured out how to open the puzzle ones without him having to show me," she said.

I removed what was left of the cobbler from the refrigerator, then dug in a drawer for a clean fork. "He's such a talented craftsman."

"He was."

I realized my verb tense error. Is. Was. Did it matter?

"Want some?" I asked, gesturing with the bowl of cobbler in my hand.

"No, thanks."

I ate the last few bites of the dessert, then put the empty bowl in the sink. Streaks of the red cherry filling left in the bowl resurrected the recollection of the bleeding box from last night, or this morning … whatever time it was. "Do you happen to remember the girl at our school, Hanna, who went missing?"

"I do. I mean, I don't remember what she looked like other than she had dark red hair. The reporters went nuts and swarmed everywhere when she vanished."

"The media never got worked up when a Creole kid disappeared or died."

"No, they didn't."

"That serial killer ever caught?"

"We couldn't confirm the other kids were killed by the same person. Well, I say 'we' meaning the police in general. By the time I was in law enforcement, kids vanishing and turning up dead, *if* they turned up, had stopped around five years prior."

"What about the girl on the billboard by the interstate?"

"She's from Destrehan, so I don't know all the details about her case. She remains missing."

"How long?"

"Almost two weeks."

"Shit. That's awful." Hanna's body was found a month after she disappeared. "Kidnapped by a family member?"

"All family have been cleared. Wait. Are you suggesting she's another Hanna or one of the other kids in the region who went missing?"

"Not at all." I was a total liar. "Curiosity, really. If a family member took her, there'd be a chance she's alive."

Lina shook her head.

"What?"

"She has diabetes and needs insulin. Time is running out if it hasn't already."

This was horrible news for the girl. "Fuck."

"It's not your town or your people. Why do you care?"

My mood shifted. "It's basic fucking humanity to care about

others, Lina. Jesus."

"I didn't mean it like that. I'm sorry. You live in Boston and well away from what happens down here."

I cooled my anger. "Not far enough away. I just … Since Hanna, I don't know. It hurts when a kid is gone. She was our friend."

Lina nodded. "Fortunately Jardin had only one other kid go missing after her. I was in the academy when it happened. I had this lofty idea that I would be the one to find and rescue the boy once I was out of the academy. Except some fishermen found his body a week before I graduated."

"Was his killer found?"

"No. I did some investigating on my own, but I didn't get far before the job took up most of my time." Lina checked her watch, then straightened. "I need to go. Work beckons soon. Do you need any other food brought by?"

I noticed Lina's glance at the wine bottles. They were the same three bottles that I had bought yesterday, with two unopened. "No, thank you. I have leftovers from what you brought yesterday. I'll get the dishes washed and returned to you, too."

"No rush. Give a shout if you need any info on where to get groceries or anything."

"I will, thanks."

Once Lina was gone, I returned my attention to the puzzle box. No signs of it bleeding. But why would there be? I had hallucinated that and the shadow stalking me during the wee hours of the morning. I'd slept on the floor because I was what? Too shit-faced to make it to the couch or a bed? And I'd seen my dead friend waving at me.

That wasn't a drunken stupor last night. I had no answers.

I wanted to open the box, but I opted to go for a reset on the day. Scrambling from the floor to the bathroom to vomit was hardly a great start. I fetched my clothes from the car, and on the way back in, I stopped. More orange dust lay on the porch by the door. I raked the toe of my shoe across it, mixing it with the dust that had been there yesterday.

Powderpost beetles up north bored into beams of old homes, leaving powdery wood dust on the ground as a sign of their activity. This was different, though. I crouched, my sore ribs protesting, and dragged my finger through the orange material. It had a gritty feel to it. There weren't any bugs on the porch, and I didn't bother searching any harder for the source of the dust.

A breeze whispered through the trees around the home, and one of the hanging glass bottles made a low-pitched whistling sound. I wondered if Uncle Jack had had to take the bottles down every time a big storm came through. A breeze causing the bottles to sway was different from a hurricane slamming them together. It wasn't my problem since I had no plans to stay long enough for a storm to roll in from the Gulf of Mexico.

I headed indoors. My mind was less foggy after my shower, and while I dressed, I ignored the bruises on my body, though the aches remained a frequent reminder of my fall. I considered texting Goth. After last night's freakiness, maybe a night away from all this crap would be good for me. Well, good in helping me unwind for a few hours and get laid. Horrible in me functioning the next day.

See how the day goes. Sort it out later.

With that plan in place, I worked through the sequence on the box, pressing on each animal carving in the order that Uncle Jack had given them to me for my birthdays. An internal mechanism clicked, and the pieces on the top of the box opened like a flower bloom. I peered down into the center to find a flash drive and something wrapped in paper secured to the bottom of the box with tape.

I removed the wrapped item and unfolded the paper. Inside it was a hand-carved lioness. I smiled and read the note Uncle Jack had written on the paper.

Dearest Janie,

I love you.

I hadn't ever allowed Uncle Jack to give me gifts since reestablishing contact with him when I turned eighteen. It disappointed him, but I had known nothing but cruelty during my childhood, and my denial bestie told me I couldn't be let down by others if I didn't let them get close. That tactic had kept me alive for many years, and I trusted it.

I rotated the lioness in my hand. Maybe I had been wrong all those years to deny him that pleasure, and now he was gone. My smile faded.

I placed the lioness and paper aside, then pulled the flash drive from the bottom.

Chapter Fifteen

I tried to call Goth while my laptop booted up on the kitchen counter, but my call wouldn't go through. I scowled at the single bar declaring my cell signal not worth shit. Good thing there hadn't been an actual intruder and a need for emergency services last night. I would've been fucked.

This was the price for living away from everyone else. Nice and quiet, but not worth it if you needed to make a phone call.

Uncle Jack was old school. He had a landline in the house, but I hadn't been thinking clearly last night. I lifted the receiver and heard no dial tone. The landline wouldn't have done me any good even if I had been thinking straight. It didn't matter. I refused to spend another night here, so I texted Goth.

I may be in the city tonight. You around?

I watched the phone's screen for a moment for a reply. Nothing yet.

I folded the little note from Uncle Jack and put it into my laptop bag, but I slipped the lioness into my pocket. The laptop was ready for my password, so I typed it in, then slid Uncle Jack's flash drive into the USB port. The usual windows opened, and I drilled down into the folder on the portable drive. There were numerous images of photos and copies of news articles and police reports.

My breath quickened when I went to the next photo and then the next. The dates marked on the pictures of the children dated back to a few years before I was born. I gasped when the image of Hanna filled my screen, smiling with bright green eyes and red hair.

I was beginning to believe Uncle Jack-Dad was the cruelest person ever. First the announcement that Henry wasn't my father, and now Uncle Jack's research (Was it called research?) into missing children over the last several decades. I clicked around in the files some more and found a folder labeled *Notes*.

Once in there, I opened the file with the most recent date stamp of three weeks ago and started reading.

I'm certain the killer taking the children is local to Jardin or Vacherie, but I can't prove—

My mouth opened for me to mutter one of my usual expletives, but I couldn't make a sound.

I skimmed over the rest of the note. I did a search within the folder for *Hanna*, and it pulled up one file within the *Notes* folder.

He'd made notes of Hanna's disappearance day, including the times when witnesses reported seeing her after school. My name was listed as a friend of Hanna. Lina's name was next to mine. I had been one of the last few people believed to have seen Hanna alive, and I shuddered.

I didn't want these memories. Not now. Having Dead Hanna haunting me was plenty of trauma all by itself.

Uncle Jack's notes on Hanna weren't a revelation. Hanna's disappearance had been documented by the media, and I remembered talking to the police who came to the estate to question me and my mother.

I resumed reading.

… I know Janie had a horrible life with her aunt in Boston. She won't talk to me about it, but she carries so much pain every day. A very small part of me is thankful that Janie did not grow up in this area. I fear she would have become like Hanna if she had. There is a predator here.

I decided to give the flash drive to Lina. Let her sort it out. I reached for the device to yank it out of the port, but my hand froze, poised above the flash drive.

Why did Uncle Jack leave this for me? Why hadn't he given it to Lina instead?

I ran a search for Lina's name, but the only mention was the entry listing her as Hanna's friend.

Could Lina be trusted? Or had he told Lina and she'd dismissed his claim?

I opted to hold off on contacting Lina. I needed more time with these files, and I wanted to cross-reference some of the information online. Uncle Jack had no internet service at his home, and my mobile signal wasn't enough to make a phone call. Using it as a hot spot was out.

I considered going to the estate. It wasn't quite as remote as Uncle Jack's house, so I should have a better phone signal there.

Another thought struck me.

Where was the computer that Uncle Jack used to make his notes and store them on the drive?

My initial attempt to sprint upstairs faltered, and I placed my palm against my sore ribs. The ibuprofen wasn't enough to erase all my stupidity last night. So I took the stairs one at a time to the second floor. I dug through the desk drawers. No laptop or computer tower. No tablet. Nothing. I went through the rest of the house but hesitated before entering Uncle Jack's bedroom.

It didn't matter that per the legal documents the house was mine now. I slowed my furious search and entered the room, respecting the space as his. The dresser had been emptied of clothing, as had his closet. A box labeled as tax documents sat in the corner of the closet. I didn't find a laptop, but I did find a glass Mason jar half full of an orange, grainy substance.

I unscrewed the lid, noting the unmistakable sound of the metal lid scraping against the glass. I shook some of the contents into my palm. It was the same gritty material I had found at the front door. I raked my palm over the edge of the jar to scrape the substance off my skin and back into the jar. I screwed the lid on and placed the jar back on the shelf in the closet.

My phone vibrated. I pulled it from my pocket and smiled to see Goth's text.

I have a couple of appointments with clients.
I wrap up by 8.
I'll let you know when I leave Jardin to head that way.

Plans to meet Goth made me feel a little more normal, given all the weird shit with Uncle Jack … assuming whatever this was I had going with Goth would be considered normal. Probably not.

I headed back downstairs, unplugged the flash drive, and stuck it in my bag. A quick time check indicated that I needed to leave to meet Uncle Frank. I packed my clothes and laptop and left the house.

Chapter Sixteen

Getting out of the car had proved easier than getting into it. Once parked at the diner, I took a few seconds to adjust my posture, making a mental note to never fall down stairs again.

The exterior of the hole-in-the-wall diner was run down, with peeling paint and a faded sign declaring they served breakfast all day. But the interior was almost full of customers.

All the tables and chairs were situated too closely to each other for my liking, but the smell of cooking eggs, bacon, and whatever else they had on the grill was intoxicating.

Uncle Frank was too tall for me to miss once he stood, and he waved. I wove through the seated patrons to his table. He moved toward me as if to hug me, then stopped.

"Sorry," he said. "I'm a hugger, but I remembered what you said."

"Thanks." I gave him a small smile, then eased into my seat, pleased to see a cup of coffee already poured and waiting for me.

He sat and tilted his head. "You seem stiff."

"I slept wrong last night." I placed the napkin on my lap, then straightened the utensils.

"Hungry?" He passed me a menu.

"Yes! I can feel my arteries clogging from smelling the food."

"It's always packed in here because it's so damn good. Oh. Sorry. I'll watch my language."

I waved him off. "Say whatever the fuck you want. I don't care."

His eyebrows flicked upward, and then he grinned. "You didn't grow up in Southern belle territory."

I laughed, then turned my eyes to the menu.

Frank listed the items he recommended, but I already knew what I wanted. We placed our orders, and I sipped my coffee. The bustling diner was a hive of activity and noise. A child in a high chair cried, a group of young men seated together laughed, grandparents and waitstaff bustled around the table where a boy had knocked over his glass of juice, and the general hum of background chatter filled the silence between my uncle and me.

"I'm glad we got some time together," he said. "I know you haven't seen me since you were a child, but it wasn't due to my lack of trying to see you. Your parents were protective of you, and then you were in Boston. When you were older, I heard Jacques was seeing you, and I asked for your number or for him to relay a message to you." Frank shook his head. "He said you wanted your privacy and that you'd reach out to me if you wanted to see me."

Once out of Aunt Kim's care (if it could be called that), I'd only contacted Uncle Jack. I had never tried to reconnect with Frank. I figured I owed him some sort of explanation, but I wasn't sure where to start. I took another sip of my coffee.

"Uncle Frank, I don't have a lot of happy memories of living in Jardin. Coming back here for Uncle Jack's funeral was, well, I tried avoiding that, too, but ended up here anyway. It was easier to leave everything here after being gone for so long. I hope you understand, and if not, that's okay too."

He nodded and leaned forward, resting his arms on the

table. "I understand. Did your parents ever tell you about your cousin? My daughter?"

I shook my head, realizing I knew nothing about Frank.

He started to speak, but our food arrived.

I stared at my plate. Hash browns like this didn't exist up north. New Englanders liked their chopped bits of potatoes that they called home fries. This diner served shredded potatoes that had been grilled to make the pile of hash browns crispy on the outside and soft on the inside. The one time I had tried to make them for myself, I set off the smoke detectors in the apartment. The few times I found a place in New England serving hash browns, it wasn't the same. Northerners tended to make them so they were more soggy than crispy.

My omelet was anemic. I had wanted to get one with spinach, jalapeños, tomatoes, and mushrooms, but this place didn't have spinach, jalapeños, or mushrooms. So I had gotten tomatoes and cheese thrown into it. At least it was semi-colorful. The aromas made me salivate.

Frank surveyed his own plate, mounded with pan-fried ham, toast, and poached eggs. He had a side plate of crispy bacon. "I can't eat here too often since none of it is healthy, but when I do, it sure is a treat. Dig in."

"You mentioned your daughter."

"We can eat while we talk. Go ahead and eat."

I took a bite of hash browns and closed my eyes. "God, that is amazing."

"Told ya."

I opened my eyes, forcing myself to slow down and enjoy the meal. I paused eating long enough to splash hot sauce on the omelet.

Frank chuckled. "Still some of the South in you."

I smiled and took another bite of my hash browns.

"Aisha, my daughter," Frank said between bites. "She was

three years old when you were born. My wife and I were living in Lafayette, and they were killed when a tornado flipped the car. I was away at work when the storm hit."

I stopped eating. I knew what it was like to lose family.

He continued, "I left Lafayette and have never gone back. I drive out of my way to go around the city instead of through it when I'm in that area. I do understand you not wanting anything to do with Jardin."

I put my fork down, wondering if I should ask the next question. I asked it anyway. "Considering the shit we've been through, you ever think our family is cursed? *We're* cursed?"

"I believed that for a time, yes. I don't know too many people who have suffered the volume of death—catastrophic deaths—that you and I have. Do you believe we are?"

"I don't know. Sometimes it sure seems like a viable answer to everything."

"I didn't mean to bring our time together down," he said, then resumed eating.

I lifted my fork and took a bite of my omelet. The hash browns tasted much better than the eggs, so I returned my focus to the heavenly potatoes.

"How are things in Boston?" he asked. "How do you deal with the cold weather?"

"Boston's fine," I said. "It's never hot there like it is here. Plows keep the roads clear, so getting around isn't an issue when it snows, unless it's a really big snow. And you figure out what kind of winter clothes work best to keep you warm. Fall is my favorite season, but it doesn't last long." I hated talking about the weather. It was such a banal topic, but I'd learned that Northerners tended to be fascinated by the climate and living in the South, and Southerners had the same fascination about snow and the North. It sure beat talking about dead family members.

We chatted about other benign topics while I increased my pace of eating. I was ready for this mini reunion to wrap up. I had things to do today.

Frank insisted on paying for the meal, so I didn't argue. I stood and scooted my chair closer to the table. I turned when a tiny hand patted my right hip. It took me a moment to recognize the boy with the beaming smile.

"Hi, Janie," he said.

"Samuel. Hi."

When his mother arrived, he said, "Mama, it's Janie."

"*Miss* Janie, to you, mister." She turned to me. "I am so sorry. He spotted you as soon as we walked in and ran straight for you."

"It's no problem," I said.

"You're leaving?" Samuel asked.

"Yeah," I said. "We're finished eating. Uh, Samuel, this is Frank, my uncle. And …" I didn't know the woman's name.

"Clara," the woman said.

"Frank," I said, "this is Clara."

With the introductions and pleasantries complete, I wasn't sure what to do next. I was relieved when one of the staff arrived to clear the table. I glanced around the diner. Our table was the only one coming available, and more people were filing in.

"Excuse me," I said to the man clearing the table. "Is it okay for them to have our table?"

"Of course. Y'all have a seat," he said to Clara.

"Was this your chair?" Samuel asked, touching the seat closest to me.

"It was."

He smiled. "I'll sit in your chair."

"It's yours now."

"We'll share."

"Sure. Yeah." I smiled at him. The kid was too sweet to not adore him.

"Thank you," Clara said.

"You're welcome. Have a good rest of the day," I said.

Samuel waved. "Bye, Janie."

Clara winced. "*Miss* Janie." She gave me an apologetic look, and I chuckled.

I headed toward the door with Frank. "Sorry. I met that little guy the other day, and he remembered me."

"He's clearly a fan," Frank said.

"I guess." I frowned when the heat smacked me in the face. My sunglasses were inside the rental car, so I shielded my eyes from the sun with my hand while heading down the steps.

"I'd like to do this again, Janie. Spend time with you, I mean," Frank said.

"Yeah, we'll figure it out."

He shuffled his feet, waiting. I figured he wanted a parting embrace, but I wasn't ready for that. I pulled my keys from my pocket, dislodging the lioness. It struck the sunbaked dirt parking area and bounced, landing at Frank's shoe.

He picked it up. "What's this?"

I extended my hand. "A gift from Uncle Jack."

Frank examined the lioness, and I tensed. I wanted it back *now*.

Frank smiled, then dropped it into my waiting palm. I clenched my fingers over the carved animal. I didn't know why I had reacted in such a way, but I didn't want anyone else touching the lioness. Maybe it was because it was the last thing Uncle Jack had given me … other than the puzzle box and flash drive. Maybe the answer was simpler and I was a weirdo about people touching me or my things.

"Thanks again for lunch, Uncle Frank."

"You're welcome."

I retreated to my car, grumbling at how hot it had gotten during my time indoors. The vehicle's air-conditioning couldn't cool me off fast enough. My sunglasses were hot to touch, so I held them in front of the vent to cool them before putting them on. I spotted Frank pulling out onto the main road in his sedan.

The lioness had not been harmed by the fall, and I tucked it back into my pocket.

I put the car in gear to back out, but motion in my side mirror made me hit the brakes. A child with red hair darted behind my car. The backup camera didn't show anything, nor did the proximity alert sound.

"Fuck!" I slammed the car into park and got out. I walked around the car and scanned the parking lot of several cars, trucks, and minivans, but there was no redheaded kid weaving between them.

Broad fucking daylight and I was seeing shit not there. I was losing my mind. I really was.

I muttered more curses while getting back into the car, grunting with the renewed pain in my side. I checked my mirrors and backup camera several times before easing the car out of my parking space and toward the road.

Chapter Seventeen

The car's tires ground over the gravel on the half-mile-long driveway from the main road to the estate house. I had to admit I enjoyed the tunnel-like view when passing under the towering oak trees with thick limbs, speckled with moss and reaching out over the road. No moss and no trees like this in New England.

My mind flicked to Boston. Did I miss it? No homesickness yet, so I guessed the answer was no.

I emerged from the trees, and the massive Greek Revival, square-shaped mansion loomed before me. The extended roof on the top of the second floor and the twenty-eight columns wrapped around the house created cover for the second-floor balcony and the ground level. I used to enjoy sprinting laps around the house on the second-floor deck and running my fingers along the thick, black wooden rail that kept me from toppling over the edge.

The wisteria plant that my mother had carefully cultivated to grow along the balcony was stunning this time of year. The six- to eight-inch purple blooms hung down from the vines. Some wisteria species stank like cat urine, but the variety that my mother planted and groomed had a sweet scent. It had covered only one corner of the house the last time I had seen it. Now it spanned the length of the front of the house and continued down the sides. Additional vines had been planted near some of the columns during my time away, and those added to the spectacular array of vines and blooms decorating the structure.

The front and rear of the house had wide double doors with an arched entryway in the center high enough to almost reach the base of the next floor up. One set of double doors with open shutters were on either side of the arched entry on both the ground and second floors. These double doors served as windows for the rooms as well as exits directly from the room to the outside. I'd been told the exterior of the home was modeled after a French design. I didn't know what that meant, but the house was beautiful and its symmetry perfect.

The third floor was smaller in size, thus bringing the topmost roof line angling in toward the center of the house, where it met to create a flat roof. Dormers with tall windows extended off the third floor and made me think of hooded eyes gazing down at me. There were no exterior doors on the third floor like the other two levels.

A deck sat above the third floor on the flat portion of the roof. It was a simple square shape lined by a black rail and was accessed via a ladder from a hatch within the third level. Mother had always called the rooftop deck a widow's walk, though to this day, I didn't know why. I had not been allowed on the roof without my mother, but I would sneak away and go up there alone anyway.

The winding road's final curve carried me well around the house to the side near the garage, and I parked next to the cars already there.

The sides of the house were much like the front and rear sides of the cube, minus the grander, arched entryways. Four sets of double doors with open shutters were perfectly spaced out along the sides of the house on the two lower levels. Like the front double doors, the side ones were also windows and entry/exit points from rooms within the house to the exterior balcony. On cold days, which were uncommon, I had liked sitting by those windows, warmed by the sunlight that came through them. All the shutters allowed for a quick closing up of the house to protect the glass and interior during a hurricane.

I didn't like the fluttering in my chest, and I coughed. My phone had a decent-ish signal, so I called Mr. Landry and left him a message asking about Uncle Jack's computer. It was already too hot inside the car, so I either had to get out, drive away, or stay in the car and die of a heatstroke.

I cursed under my breath and left the vehicle with my laptop bag. As I neared the house, I slowed. The scents of the wisteria and other flowers in bloom filled my nose, bringing back many memories that I had long ago buried—or thought I'd buried.

The gardens outside had always been my favorite place to be when I lived here. It gave me a place to escape to while my parents argued … a frequent occurrence. At night, when their shouts escalated and interrupted my sleep, I left my room for the roof. I learned to bring a sheet with me to the roof deck to help keep the mosquitoes from sucking me dry.

"Hello, ma'am."

I flinched at the man's voice so near. I hadn't seen or heard his approach. I turned to a young man who was no more than twenty-five. His angular features and muscular build reminded me of magazine photos of male models.

"My apologies for startling you." He paused. "Jane? I mean, Janie?"

I flicked my eyes to the sides, feeling a little trapped and unnerved that this stranger knew my preferred name. Not Janette. He'd called me Jane but then corrected himself. "Yeah?"

He flashed a broad smile. "I'm sorry. I should be calling you Miss Martil."

"Oh, no. Janie is fine. Do I know you?"

"No, ma'am. I'm Stephen Montpelier. One of Uncle Jacques's many nephews. I saw pictures of you at his house, and he spoke of you often. Lina pointed you out to me at the funeral, but I had already recognized you from the photos."

"Oh." I hadn't expected Lina's name to come up, but then, Lina and Stephen were cousins. The small-town-everyone-is-related thing was starting to cook my brain, especially now that I was part of the mass of Montpeliers—assuming Uncle Jack was right about being my father. Lina's DNA compared with mine would be the final verdict.

Shit. I'd forgotten to mention that in my message to Mr. Landry. Stephen watched me while fleeting thoughts wandered around inside my head. I wasn't sure what to say next, so I went with politeness.

"Nice to meet you, Stephen. You work here?"

"Yes, ma'am. I've been working out here with Uncle Jacques since I was thirteen."

"You're *that* Stephen," I said, nodding. "Uncle Jack told me about you helping him."

"Jack?"

"Speech impediment as a kid. I couldn't pronounce Jacques. And he wasn't my biological uncle."

Uncle Jack had been the primary caretaker for the estate, but the place was too big for one person to manage. Mr. Landry would've handled the paychecks out of the estate's funds, but I had remained so distant from everything happening with the Martil property that I had no idea how many employees *I* technically had on the estate payroll. "How many others work here?"

"Eight total. Well, seven now."

I nodded. I didn't want to get into the weeds about Uncle Jack-Dad's death. "Tell me about them and what all goes on day to day while we walk. I haven't been here in a while. And this heat is fucking killing me."

His face twitched.

"Sorry. I'll try to scale back on the profanity."

"Yes, ma'am."

"You can drop that formality too, please. Just Janie."

"Yes, ma'am … Miss Janie."

I resisted the urge to roll my eyes.

Telling a Southerner to stop being so polite was akin to asking them to remove their skin with pliers. Hell, Jardin's hospitality was as deep-fried as every other town in the parish. Correcting Stephen again wasn't a battle worth fighting today.

Chapter Eighteen

Stephen continued, "We keep furniture, paintings, and other items covered with sheets to help keep them clean and prevent fading when the sun comes in through the windows. When Mr. Landry said you were coming into town for the services, we uncovered everything in case you stopped by."

My gaze was on the wisteria vines. "You really didn't need to go to all that trouble for my sake."

"We didn't mind," Stephen said. "The house looks great with everything uncovered."

The house had nothing but rotten memories for me. Uncovering furniture wouldn't change that. "I'm sure it does," I said to be polite.

He had finished his updates by the time we reached the porch. The shade and a light breeze wafting through the columns made the humidity a tad less oppressive. Ceiling fans mounted on the porch's overhang spun in a slow, mesmerizing manner and kept the air moving. If it hadn't been so hot in general, I could've imagined myself sitting on the bench on the porch and even enjoying it. Not today, though.

Stephen left, and I entered through the front arched doorway.

The estate staff had kept everything maintained over the

years. The home's vaulted ceiling spanned the length of the center of the house. The interior mirrored the exterior to create an extended porch-balcony all around the inside where one could be on either of the upper levels and look over and down to the ground level. It reminded me of the balconies on Bourbon Street—without the drunken revelers.

The grandiose entryway had gray marble floors and paintings and photographs of landscapes and people on the walls. I sneered at the one photo of my father. He managed to stare down at me disapprovingly, even now. When I took a step to continue, I paused. I took a step back.

Henry's eyes seemed to follow me when I moved.

"Bastard," I muttered, then ignored his stern glare to return my attention to the house.

The long, winding staircase with gray marble steps led from the ground floor to the second level. Their beauty made me smile. A narrower but no less ornate staircase extended from the second floor up to the third, where it turned to go up to the roof. I promised myself I would go to the roof later.

Per my mother's stories, French mansions were modest on the inside, unlike their exteriors, but Mother had wanted extravagance inside, too. To me, the place seemed more like a hotel—a really nice hotel with a lot of marble, high ceilings, and different-sized chandeliers in several of the rooms.

I gazed up at the largest one in the center of the house. It was lit, and the giganto three-tiered chandelier was overkill but gorgeous. The light bounced off the pieces of glass and created a stunning spray of golden light in all directions.

I may not have been happy living in this house, but there was no denying the artistry that went into its design. I closed the door behind me and welcomed the air-conditioning inside, mentally thanking Mother for that modern feature in a house that was built to mimic plantation homes two hundred years older.

I recalled the lowest level's layout from memory. The parlor (that was never used) was the first room to my left. It had a fireplace, cushioned chairs, and benches near the walls, along with a few tables and bookshelves. It was well lit, and I had gotten yelled at frequently for rearranging the furniture in the room to create obstacle courses.

To my right was a combo pantry-laundry-kitchenette with its own refrigerator, sinks, and table that sat four. I always thought that was the most normal-looking room in the entire house. It had two sets of double doors that took you out to the porch and gardens, but it was cozy and welcoming.

I walked toward the center of the house, admiring the second- and third-floor balconies above me. When I reached the rear half of the lowest level, I stopped. To my right, behind more sets of double doors, was a massive, professional-chef-grade kitchen that connected to the normal-people kitchen and to the formal dining room (never used) that spanned two-thirds of the back side of the first floor. I recalled running laps in that room when it was too stormy to play outside. That got me yelled at too.

A lot of yelling in this house.

I turned left, walking beneath the winding stairs to enter the office. The heavy wooden door didn't creak when I opened it. I stood inside Father's office—rather, the office of the man I had believed was my father.

Henry. I decided to call him Henry. I had had no real relationship with him as a child even before he died.

The oversized wood desk and matching chair were almost in the center of the room and faced the two sets of double doors-windows facing the East Garden. A black marble fireplace (also never used) was behind the desk, and matching marble baseboards ran along the perimeter of the room.

Thick metal rods with heavy, dark green curtains framed the doors-windows. A white lacy fabric hung under them and obscured the views in and out of the room but allowed plenty of light in. I noticed a crack in the wall and peeling paint near the bottom edge of the curtain. A dead fly lay on its back on the floor. I realized that the exterior of my life seemed nice, similar to this house. But there were cracks and dead things inside. I discarded the gloomy albeit accurate thought.

A much smaller chandelier than what was in the center of the house hung from the flowered design in the middle of the ceiling. For an office, all this decorative crap was wasted.

I rotated in a circle. His office, though more like the size of a normal family's dining room, appeared smaller than I remembered. But then, I had been a scrawny kid the last time I was in here, and Henry had yelled at me to get out.

His office connected to a half bath in the back of the house, and that same half bath connected to the end of the formal dining room. Everything in the house screamed symmetry and perfection, but there was nothing perfect about the family that had lived here.

I deposited my laptop bag onto Henry's bare desk, then began going through the drawers. I wasn't looking for anything in particular. I knew nothing about Uncle Frank's history other than what he'd told me today, and I knew nothing about Henry's past either. They were two men from my childhood, and supposedly family, who were utter strangers.

The files were labeled by year from before my birth up until the year my parents died. They contained business documents and invoices for repairs on the house and work around the estate. I shuffled those aside to resume going through the rest of the drawers. Tax filings, banking information, a thick folder of the many papers that came with buying land and construction contracts, and some folders I would have to read through more to know what they were. Henry didn't throw anything away. It was all old and from before much of this stuff had become electronic.

Once I had everything out of the drawers and stacked on the floor around me, I frowned. Though I thought it silly, I dug around in the empty desk hoping to find a false panel or hidden cubby somewhere inside it. Uncle Jack hid flash drives inside puzzle boxes. I remembered that Henry hid things in his study upstairs, but my search of his office had been a waste of time.

I put the folders back into their drawers, then headed up the stairs.

Chapter Nineteen

I reached the second floor and took a left toward the east-facing part of the house. My parents' bedroom had been in the northeast corner of the second level. My insides twitched, and my hand stopped an inch before touching the doorknob.

I walked to the rail facing the center of the house. The rail separated me from a fall to my likely death. If the impact on the marble floor on the ground level didn't kill me, I would probably wish it had.

I found it odd that I was inside this stunning home and the incredible view of much of the interior and my thoughts had drifted to mutilation and death. Maybe that was because despite the beauty of this house, some of the people linked to it ended up dead.

I spun and headed into my parents' bedroom without hesitating at the door this time.

My bravado fizzled in an instant.

"Oh, fuck."

The room had not been changed since my parents died. It had been kept clean, but items had been left in place. One of Henry's ties hung from the corner of a mirror. The bed had its ornate posts and silken canopy over it.

I opened Mother's closet door. The racks remained full of

clothes covered in thin, clear plastic. Shoes were arranged in neat rows on the floor in the closet. Henry's closet revealed the same.

The estate had gone into a holding pattern until my eighteenth birthday. And my lack of interest in the estate had kept things frozen in time.

Shit. This was creeping me out, and my skin prickled.

I left the bedroom and strode to the other side of the balcony to take the winding stairs up to the third-level room that served as Henry's study. I opened the door and stopped. The third-floor rooms were narrower because of the roof's inward angle to create the roof deck above me. The exterior walls and sloping ceiling didn't diminish the study's impressive layout.

A bookshelf spanned the length of the wall with the dormers. Henry had a safe tucked behind books on one of the shelves. He kept cash in it, but I wondered if he had other things hidden, too. He had never let me in the room much, but that didn't keep me from snooping as a kid.

I wasn't ready to tackle the study yet, so I left it to take the narrow set of stairs up to the hatch to the roof deck. When I stepped out on it, I cringed with the heat. I shielded my eyes from the blinding sun with my hand.

A tanker, easily visible from this height, cruised the Mississippi River. The treetops and gardens surrounding the home took my breath away. I wanted to spend more time up here, but the heat chased me back inside.

I wiped sweat from my brow while I went back down to the third level.

How did people live in this shit?

When I arrived back at the study, I strode to the center of the room. The closed-up room was musty with the hint of stale cigar smoke. The room had always smelled this way ... maybe not as pungent, but the mustiness was ever-present, even when I was little. I wrestled with one of the three dormer windows to get it open and allow some fresh (although hot as hell) air in. The air-conditioning wouldn't fix the smell, but an open window might do it some good.

I knelt by the desk next to the overstuffed leather chair where Henry liked to sit and smoke his cigars, read, and gaze out the window. I twisted to squeeze under the desk and slid the top drawer out a few inches. I found the tiny slip of paper with the numbers to the safe taped between the underside of the desk's top and the first drawer. During one of my childhood "spy missions," I'd been under this desk, hiding from my pretend bad guys, and found the combination. It had taken me weeks to figure out that the numbers on the paper were reversed.

Maybe leaving the estate as it was hadn't been so bad after all. I committed the numbers to memory, slithered out from under the desk, then went to the floor-to-ceiling and wall-to-wall bookshelves. I removed several books to access the safe.

I spun the dial, then stopped. The books had been dusted, but the combination dial and handle on the safe's door were dusty. I raked my fingertip across the top corner of the safe, and the dust rolled into a thick ball under my finger.

Frozen in time.

I spun the dial around and was rewarded with a satisfying click when I grasped the lever. I glanced over my shoulder to make sure I was alone. Not even my Shadow Man or Dead Hanna were there.

I pushed aside four stacks of cash and removed a cardboard box a little smaller than a shoe box. I opened the lid to find a revolver lying on top of three notebooks. I used my thumb and forefinger to lift the revolver by the grip. I set the gun aside and pulled the books from the box. I put the revolver back in the box and returned it to the safe. I flipped through the first notebook, slowing to read a few lines.

Father was a poet? I never knew. Then I frowned; he was only Henry.

I slammed the book closed to flip through the next one. This one was more interesting and appeared to be an accounting of the cash in the safe. Sometimes there were deposits of ten to thirty thousand dollars captured with dates. Other entries showed withdrawals ranging from a few thousand to tens of thousands. I set that one to the side. The third notebook had notations that were gibberish. Letters, maybe initials, dates, numbers—but not numbers I recognized like the format of currency or phone numbers. I wasn't sure what they were, but if Henry kept them in the safe, they had meant something to him.

I put the poetry book back in the box with the revolver. I grabbed one of the stacks of cash before I closed the safe and replaced the books in front of it. I hurried downstairs to Henry's office and opened my laptop bag. I was running a little low on cash, so I stripped a few twenties off the top of the stack and put them in my pocket. I put the rest of the money and the two notebooks into my bag.

I tried to make a call to the hotel that I liked in the city, but the signal was shit. The only way I would get any research done was to go somewhere with decent phone service and internet. I stepped outside and walked around for a few minutes, stopping when my signal strength improved. I called and booked a hotel room for the night, then headed for the car.

Stephen rounded the corner of the house, heading toward me. "Miss Janie, anything you need or want done to the estate?"

I found a place in the shade under a tree instead of standing by the car and being burnt to a crisp by the sun. He joined me.

"Are you the only one who works here full-time?" I asked.

He nodded. "Everyone who works here has been doing it

for years. I think they like the place. It's quiet. But I'm the only one who was out here every day with Uncle Jacques."

"I need someone to look after things the way he did. If you want his job, it's yours."

"Well, I … yes, ma'am. I do."

"Hire people to help you, if needed. Full-time, contract work, whatever. Mr. Landry can handle everything on the payment side."

I dug into my bag and pulled out the cash.

Stephen's eyes widened.

I placed the money into his hands. "Take a quarter of that for yourself … a raise or bonus or whatever. Split the rest among the remaining staff here. I am grateful for how well y'all have taken care of the place, and—"

Y'all? Fuck me, I had gone Southern.

"Uh, anyway," I said, "the estate is immaculate. You all do nice work here."

"Yes, ma'am, Miss Janie. Thank you."

"Janie," I said.

He nodded and redness crept into his cheeks.

A bead of sweat trickled down the middle of my back. I needed to make this quick and retreat to air-conditioning. "My parents' clothes and shoes are still in their bedroom. Please have someone go through everything, checking pockets for anything in the clothes or left in any dressers, and I'll review those things later to determine if they stay or go. If the staff doesn't want or can't use any of the clothing or shoes, have it donated. They're not doing anyone any good sitting in closets."

"Yes, ma'am."

I decided to give up trying to get Stephen to drop the formalities and be on a first-name basis with me.

"Have a good day, Stephen. I may be back out tomorrow."

"Yes, ma'am."

I hurried to the car, dying for some artificially cooled air on my skin.

Chapter Twenty

The killer tossed the last parts of the dead man from the bridge into the river. He had been driving all over the state the last few nights making what he called "deposits" to rid himself of the corpse. The water's current would carry the final pieces far away from his dumping location, and once the clear plastic dissolved in the water, turtles, fish, and alligators would feast. Any parts that floated or ended up on land would be devoured by other animals.

The one time someone found and reported a severed foot, the killer changed tactics to thoroughly dismember the bodies and crush larger bones like the skull, pelvis, and femurs so they were unrecognizable. He also randomized his dumping spots and time line for disposing of the carcasses. The dismembering also helped him obscure the marks on their bodies where he had tied and chained them down while they were alive. *If* a part ever made it to a crime scene lab, determining a cause of death was unlikely. His work was brutal and messy but efficient at protecting himself from ever being caught.

He was pleased to have the remaining pieces of the drug-addicted homeless man out of his home and vehicle. The addict had been poor and needed more drugs, but he had shown no signs of a mental illness such as schizophrenia. His addiction hadn't stripped him of his ability to make decisions. His kind were more difficult for the killer to capture and yet the most pleasing to cull. The killer had to work a bit harder to convince the man that he'd pay him well for sex. Sometimes his pay-for-sex scheme failed, but when it worked, once the killer had them in his car, his prey would not escape.

The addict had eventually agreed, and the killer had brought him back to his home and added a sedative to his drink. Once the man was sedated, the killer dragged him down to the basement and put him in chains. This addict, like several others, had been the killer's special guest. They were the ones he tortured for several days before ending them forever. The knives and hammers he used on them were punishment for their sins. And when they soiled themselves, the killer sprayed them down with a hose. He never believed their promises to change if their lives were spared. Proclamations of repentance had come too late, and none escaped the sentence of death.

No one ever reported them missing. No one cared about the prostitutes and addicts that vanished. Long-term homeless people sometimes simply disappeared.

There was far more risk when he took them back to his home, so sometimes the killer took an easier path. It was shorter-lived satisfaction for his work, but it was satisfaction nonetheless. Those targets were the ones he found in the cities and whose bodies he left there. He'd give them drugs or buy them bottles of liquor and wait. Once they were fall-down intoxicated, he'd offer them more alcohol or drugs that he'd laced with his unique concoctions to cause an overdose. He'd leave them where they fell. The discovery of their bodies in an alley or behind an abandoned warehouse never made the news. They were just another addict overdosing or a drunk suffocating on their own vomit.

His other favorite targets were the homeless schizophrenics.

The killer used his homemade psychedelic mixtures on them. They were similar to the ones for the children, but the mixes for the children produced pleasing hallucinations. His potions for the people who didn't deserve to live produced terrifying visions. He'd kept meticulous notes and learned over time which concentrations worked the best to send them into an extreme state of paranoia, terrifying them until they threw themselves off a building or bridge or ran onto the train tracks or into oncoming traffic. He never had to deal with those bodies, and they were always ruled suicides.

When he couldn't get a photograph of one of his adult victims, he wrote down everything he could remember about them, things they'd confessed or told him during their time together.

Tonight, the killer arrived in New Orleans after midnight and parked his car. He'd purged the world of another sinner and degenerate. He now had an opening for another one in his cooler. He prowled the alleys and streets. One man lay on a bench, but he was too drunk to arouse. The killer moved on.

He spotted someone he recognized and tucked into a shadow, away from the lit portion of the street.

The Martil heir walked the city with another woman. They stood too closely together to be friends. His suspicions were confirmed when they kissed in front of an art gallery; she was a degenerate like the others.

He followed them for a while.

They talked during their wanderings, but neither appeared intoxicated. They didn't go into any of the bars, but sometimes they'd pause outside a bar to listen to the music from within or stop to drop a few dollars into the jar of a street performer.

He'd never taken two people before, and he wouldn't attempt it now. Too many mistakes could be made with a reckless abduction. He'd have to find someone else for entertainment tonight and purify the world of the heir's presence later.

I had never had a better evening in my life. Following dinner, Goth and I roamed the city, enjoying conversation, music, and art. The galleries and studios were all closed, but that didn't stop us from peering through the windows and admiring the works. I didn't mention that I had paintings in my own collection by some of the artists we admired on our walk. I loved my collection, but I didn't want to come across as bragging. Goth's knowledge of the various painters and musicians in the city impressed me. She knew her city, and I envied her a little. Goth had found her home. I had not.

On our stroll toward the hotel, I glanced down when Goth took my hand.

"Is this okay?" she asked.

"Uh, yeah. Yes," I said, and smiled.

The humidity had dropped to not-quite-swampy levels, and the breeze took a few more degrees off the hellish night air. And I declared bonus points for the evening because I hadn't had any hallucinations like last night.

Oh. Last night.

I dreaded having to explain the bruises on my body from my fall down the stairs. But once I got naked with Goth, there would be no hiding them. I wasn't sure why, but my pulse increased the closer we got to the hotel.

I thought of excuses or outright lies, but everything sounded feeble. Would Goth understand my bout of seeing shadow people, a dead girl, and bleeding boxes, and being frightened enough to fall down a flight of stairs? Hell, even I didn't understand. How could Goth? I decided I would tell enough of the truth … maybe.

We reached my room, and as soon as I had the door closed, Goth had me pressed up against it. But instead of frenzied attempts to get clothing off as soon as possible, I was surprised (and perhaps a little disappointed) when Goth took her time kissing me and moving her hands over my body. I began removing her shirt, and Goth caught my hands.

"There's no rush," she said.

I forced myself to slow down, but struggled each time Goth's hands brushed my breasts. I enjoyed the time we spent making out and forgot about the bruises until Goth paused after sliding my shirt off my shoulders. I followed her eyes to the dark, swollen area on my right shoulder.

"I, um, it—" I stopped when Goth's lips brushed the bruise. Goth worked my shirt the rest of the way off. She then relieved me of my bra.

She cupped one of my breasts in her palm and kissed my nipple. Her slow pace was wreaking havoc inside my brain and panties. I flinched when her hand touched the bruise on my side.

Goth lifted her head and examined my body. She touched the marks on my ribs as though her fingertips were made of feathers. No one had ever been so gentle with me, and a hint of tears burned my eyes when it happened. She never said a word and shifted downward to kiss my bruised side. That was my final undoing, and Goth owned me.

Chapter Twenty-One

I startled awake but wasn't sure why. I was in the hotel, and Goth was asleep and sprawled across the bed, sheets in disarray. Our evening had ended with phenomenal sex, but no drugs or massive quantities of alcohol were involved. Goth never mentioned the bruises or asked about them, saving me the awkwardness of explaining them. I appreciated her acknowledgment of them in her own way and moving on.

I ran both hands through my hair, thinking. I hadn't had another night involving the creepy shit I'd seen in Uncle Jack's house, but I was troubled for other reasons. I actually *liked* Goth. For the first time in my life, I was attracted to someone for more than a night or two of partying and sex.

Maybe it was simply a longer-term fling than my usual short-term ones. I wasn't ready to figure out what to do with this revelation. It wasn't like I was going to propose to her or anything. And I sure as hell wasn't moving to this humid shit-hole state. But Boston didn't beckon for my return. Work emails piled up, but I wasn't homesick for the city. Was I capable of homesickness?

I opted to sort it out later.

I rolled out of bed, dragged on some clothes, then dropped into the chair at the desk. I opened my laptop and pulled out the notebooks I'd taken from Henry's safe and the flash drive from Uncle Jack's puzzle box.

Once online I opened my email and calendar.

I owned and managed two small but active galleries in Boston. My parents' life insurance money had given me the means to open the first one. Art sales funded the second one. I couldn't paint a straight line or make anything but more lumps out of lumpy sculpting clay. I'd tried to be an artist. I'd dreamed of it my entire life. My own artwork improved as I practiced, but artistic skills were not mine to be mastered.

My eye for what I called "good art," though, was exquisite. I knew what would be popular, if a piece would sell quickly, or if a piece would sell in time and for a high price. That's where I made my killing in the art world—finding those hidden gems and turning a significant profit on them. My favorites I kept in my Boston residence. Okay, maybe I was a little homesick, but only for being surrounded by my collection.

Collectionsick? Was that a thing? I discarded the random thought.

I answered some emails and rescheduled appointments. I blocked another week off my calendar and extended the rental car reservation again. I did *not* want to stay in Louisiana for another week, but I blocked my calendar anyway. I finished up a few more work-related tasks, then glanced back to the bed. Goth was asleep.

I opened a search engine link on the laptop.

It took me a few tries searching for Evangeline Guidry, but when I found a picture of Goth showing in the results, I clicked on it. My mouth dropped open upon landing on Goth's website. I clicked through the photo gallery of her paintings and drawings. They were unlike anything I'd seen before, but the Crescent City's influence on Goth's work was undeniable. Some paintings captured bayou life with marvelous beauty. Other, more abstract pieces, caused a strange fluttering sensation in my chest. Admiration? Awe? Hope? I wasn't sure what I was feeling, but Goth's work, without question, made me *feel*.

The colorful interaction and mix of techniques such as brush strokes texturing thick layers of paints mixed with the hard lines created by a paint knife that then blurred everything down into a smooth arc of color captivated me.

I viewed a few more images and then did more searches for Eva or Evangeline Guidry. There were a couple of small posts about her from within the art community, but essentially, Goth was an unknown.

How the fuck could she be an unknown with this kind of talent?

I glanced back to the bed, and Goth was gone. I yelped to find her standing to my left.

"Fuck!" I held my palm to my heart. "You're going to give me a heart attack."

Goth pulled a chair over and sat next to me. "That's not all I give you." She pointed at the laptop with her chin. "I see you found me."

I stared at her for a few seconds before lowering my hand. Goth was naked, and my focus on the website wavered. "Uh, yes. I, um …"

"Don't worry about it. You'd be silly to not look me up, but I'm surprised it took you this long."

"You looked me up, too?"

"Of course. Wanted to make sure I wasn't sleeping with a psychopath." Goth shrugged. "It's awkward when that happens," she said, then winked at me.

I thought back to the night we'd met. Maybe Goth knew who I was and about my Boston galleries. It could have been a plan on Goth's part to get an angle on me for sales. Except I had been wandering the city before hiding in the back of the bar with my wine. My decision to fly to New Orleans had been last second. No one but Mr. Landry knew I was flying in for the funeral … except when he'd told Stephen that I was coming into town.

Plus, I didn't have an online presence like interviews or anything. All promotional crap about the galleries dealt with the art. I'd always declined interviews that would be in front of cameras to avoid that kind of attention. I also didn't want my face plastered all over the internet or social media. My marketing of the art I bought and sold focused on the art and artists. That's all.

"The good news, Bougie, is I don't think you're one," Goth said. "I had to dig to find shit on you, ya know? Your name, listed as Janette, was in the news when you were a child and your parents died. Then nothing until a few years ago when your name was mentioned in an article about Boston galleries. You're a Martil and there happens to be a Martil Plantation in Jardin, the same town you've been visiting. That's your family's place?"

"Yeah," I said, happy to keep the bit about the estate being *mine* out of my response.

"Big-ass house on that land. Lotta swampy stuff down that way too."

I nodded. "Fortunately it's not so close to the swamps that they have to shoo the gators off the porch every day."

Goth laughed and patted my knee. "You're funny. Good choice on going by Janie. You are not a Janette."

"I agree."

Goth rose and retrieved her clothes from the floor.

"You're leaving?" I didn't want her to go.

"I need coffee. Want some?"

The instant relief of knowing she wasn't leaving made me even more unsettled. I was *not* in love with Goth, but I had no words for these weird-ass feelings when around her.

I squinted at the time on the laptop: 8:30 a.m. How did that happen? Why the hell was I up now after only a few hours of sleep? "The biggest and strongest of whatever they make wherever you're going."

"Will do."

"I'll buy."

"I got it," she said, and was out the door.

I worked while she was gone and smiled when she was back. Goth had also gotten food, and my mouth watered. I ate the biscuit first, marveling at how a wad of baked dough could taste so good.

I spooned grits into my mouth and wondered who'd thought it was a good idea to grind up corn and declare it a viable food source in the Deep South. I stirred the grits, mixing the butter into them more, then took another bite.

"You act like you're eating glass," Goth said. "If you hate it that much, stop eating it."

I swallowed hard, then set my to-go bowl aside. I removed the napkin I'd placed across my thigh and wiped my hands. "It's the texture that gets me."

"You need to eat it with more cheese and with a biscuit soaked in it."

"I could probably do that."

"Nothing healthy about it, but it tastes great."

I glanced down at the notebook with the gibberish. I'd been able to read more of the notes and info in the books in the time between checking into the hotel yesterday and meeting Goth last night. But I hadn't figured out the numbers.

Goth checked the time. "I've gotta run," she said, and stood. "What are you reading?"

"A book I picked up from my father's things. I'm not sure what it is."

Goth extended her hand. "May I?"

I passed her the notebook.

Goth flipped through it. "I'm not sure what all the other stuff is, but the numbers are coordinates. Latitude and longitude. Usually you see those written out as DMS though."

"DMS?"

Goth moved to stand beside me. She pointed at a set of numbers. "This might be a date field, but the format is a little weird. These numbers are coordinates. It's in decimal form, but you can look online to see how to convert them to degrees, minutes, and seconds—DMS—if you want. Should be easier to view them that way, but you can plug these numbers in to see where they are on the globe."

I took the notebook back. "I haven't been able to figure out what those meant. How did you know that?"

"I got into cartography in junior high … until I got into girls," Goth said, and shrugged. "A fleeting hobby. Cartography, that is." She winked at me.

"Hey, I'd like to see your studio. I'm interested in buying some of your work."

"No!"

The sharpness of Goth's tone and her sudden scowl surprised me. "Sorry?"

"No."

"I'm confused."

"I don't need you to buy my stuff. I don't need your money."

"That's not what I meant." I left my chair, following Goth to the door. "I really like your work. I want to see more of it. The multicolored fleur-de-lis is fantastic. I'd like to buy it."

"It's not for sale."

"Okay. You have other pieces on your website that I like."

"None of it is for sale, not to you."

"Why not?"

"Because I said so."

Goth left and I stared at the closed door. What the fuck just happened?

Chapter Twenty-Two

I was too distracted from the fight or whatever it was with Goth to focus on any research. I replayed the conversation with her over in my mind. Had something in my tone made me come across as arrogant? I didn't think so. But I wasn't sure. Part of me wanted to call her. Part of me wanted to leave it alone. I had touched a nerve, that much was clear. I had no idea how or what I'd done to do it, though.

Figure it out later.

I passed the time keying in coordinates, realizing that they were all within Louisiana except for one in Texas and two in Mississippi. I went down to the front desk and got a tourist map of the state. I borrowed a marker from the man at the desk, then headed back to my room.

With the map unfolded and on the floor, I cross-referenced the coordinates on my laptop and placed a mark on the paper map. When I had them all done, a cluster of marks formed that orbited a pocket of southern Louisiana with Jardin near the center. There were some outliers, but there was a pattern.

But what did the dots mean?

I packed up and checked out of the hotel. Had the morning not gone to shit with Goth, I would've stayed there another couple of nights.

I drove to Uncle Jack's, washed my dirty dishes, and retrieved the food and wine, plus the unwashed (and now putrid-smelling) puke-cleanup towel from the top of the washer. I went to the Martil estate and parked the car.

Fuck. Back again.

I didn't want to be here, but Henry's study would make a nice place for me to spread out and dig further into the notebooks. I gathered everything I could carry from the car and lugged it inside and upstairs. On my second trip with the last of my things, including my clothes, I stopped in at the kitchen to put the remaining leftovers from Lina in the refrigerator. I tucked the wine and the purple mug I'd mooched from Uncle Jack's house into the cupboard.

I tossed my dirty clothes and the gross towel into the washer. Once back upstairs, I gazed at the bag on the floor containing my clean clothes. Was I *really* going to stay in this massive house tonight?

I texted Goth.

I'm sorry for whatever I said or did to upset you. Can we talk?

I waited, pacing while watching my phone for a full minute. No reply.

Fuck it.

I stuffed the phone into my pocket and grabbed my bags. I headed up to the second level, bypassed my parents' old room to go to the southeast corner of the house to my childhood bedroom. Upon opening the door, I gasped.

Nothing had changed since the day I'd left it other than it had been routinely dusted over the years. The twin bed with frilly yellow-and-green pillow covers and comforter seemed so tiny now. I took a tentative step into the room and stopped. Time had frozen in my parents' room, so I wasn't sure why I'd assumed things would be different in my room.

My skin crawled to be here. The hand-carved animals Uncle Jack had given me for my early birthdays remained in a neat line on my dresser. I had spent hours playing with them. I pulled the lioness from my pocket and placed it after the giraffe. I recalled leaving the animals behind because I had believed that I would be back soon. I was six, naive, and hadn't yet learned how shitty the world could be. Aunt Kim had refused to let me return or to have the carved animals shipped to Boston.

The anger inside swelled, but I refused to dwell on my aunt's actions. The horrible woman didn't deserve the time spent on rehashing shit memories from a rotten childhood.

"Miss Janie?"

I startled, almost dropping my laptop bag and clothes.

"Oh, I'm so sorry," Stephen said.

After a couple of deep breaths, my heart felt like it might stay inside my chest after all.

"I saw your car outside and wanted to see if you needed anything," he said.

"I'm fine!" I said more sharply than intended.

"Yes, ma'am. Lina mentioned she'd come by later if that's okay with you."

Great. Company.

Oh, shit. I'd forgotten to get Mr. Landry to set up the DNA test for Lina and me. Stephen stared at me.

"I have her number and will coordinate a time for her to swing by," I said.

"Okay. A few of us worked on your parents' room this morning. It's all cleaned out. We did find a few things in some of the clothes, like coins and keys that we left on the dresser before we donated the clothing. It's ready for you if you want to stay in that room while you're here."

"Uh, I think I'll find another room, but thanks for clearing it out. Do this one next if there are clothes and such in it," I said, nodding toward my old bedroom. "Leave the carved animals. I'll gather those later."

"Yes, ma'am. Since it looks like you might be staying, each of the bedrooms has a key to lock its door. It's in the top drawer of the dresser in the room. That same key locks the room's balcony doors, too."

I wasn't sure why I would need to lock my bedroom's doors if I was the only one overnighting in the house, but it didn't matter at the moment. "Thank you."

"Yes, ma'am."

I bristled at his repeated ma'am responses and wanted it to stop. But before I could bark at him, my phone vibrated with an incoming call.

He pulled a slip of paper from his pocket and passed it to me. "That's my number. Call or text me anytime."

"Thanks."

He hurried off, and I pulled my phone from my pocket, hoping it was Goth.

It was the estate lawyer. "Hi, Mr. Landry."

"Hello, Janette. I can hardly hear you."

"One sec." I raced for the outdoor balcony over the front of the house. My signal improved with my relocation, though I was back out in the smothering humidity. "This better?"

"Much."

I relayed all my messages to him that I'd kept forgetting, then wrapped up the call. It bothered me that Mr. Landry reported that Uncle Jack didn't own a computer that he knew of.

Uncle Jack didn't have cable TV or internet to his home. To me that was the equivalent of living in the Dark Ages. If he did have his own computer, had it been stolen? Did he go somewhere to use another computer? A library, maybe?

I refused to stay at the estate tonight. New Orleans would save me from this family drama horseshit. I would get my clothes from the washing machine tomorrow.

I escaped to my car, threw the bags into the trunk, and left the estate.

I was almost to the interstate when I saw the sign at the intersection again.

MISSING.

I pulled off the road into the same area where I'd had my panic attack the other day. This time there wasn't a meltdown, but the image of the sign with the little girl was stuck in my head. A heaviness grew inside my chest. Something solid and weighty resided there. It was the same feeling when I got the call from Mr. Landry that Uncle Jack had been killed.

This was pure dread. It was the only way I could describe it.

The police hadn't been able to sort out any of the missing children's cases spanning several years. Were they all really *that* incompetent? I considered Lina. She wasn't an idiot.

Were the dots on the map related to the children?

I wanted more information about Uncle Jack's research and the odd notes in Henry's notebooks. I had too much digging to do to keep running off and hiding in the city.

I wasn't hiding.

Okay. I was hiding.

I *really* hated Louisiana.

Chapter Twenty-Three

A sedan I didn't recognize was parked at the estate. I hauled my bags from the car, including some things I'd purchased on the drive back to help me set up in Henry's study. A broad-shouldered Black man in a suit sat on the bench by the front door. He stood and pulled a handkerchief from his pocket and mopped his brow. I couldn't fathom how the man hadn't died yet from wearing a suit in this heat.

"Miss Martil, it's a pleasure to meet you." He stuffed his handkerchief back into his pocket and held out his hand. "I'm Reverend Oakes."

I recognized him as the loud-voiced preacher at Uncle Jack's service. My hands were full. I wasn't putting the bags down to shake his hand, so I shrugged instead.

"Oh, of course. May I take those for you?"

"I've got them."

"I came to speak to you about a sensitive matter. Could we go inside?"

There was no way I was letting a minister inside the house. "I'm rather busy. What is it?"

He shifted his stance, but I didn't budge. I was not letting him in despite my own desire to retreat to air-conditioning.

He glanced around before speaking. "Were you aware that

you have, uh, unsavory types working here?"

My eyebrows went up. "Unsavory?"

"Homosexuals."

I laughed, and the minister frowned. This made me laugh harder.

"I'm serious," he said.

I sobered in an instant. "So am I. Get the fuck out of here. Unsavory types are welcome. *You* are not. Come back and I'll have you cited for trespassing."

I would've laughed at the horrified look on his face except I was too angry. I moved around him and fumbled to get the door open, but once inside I kicked the door shut with my foot.

"It's a sin!" he said from the outside.

"Fuck off!" I left the door and went to the washing machine. I placed the bags on the floor and flung my clothes in the dryer. I grabbed the bags again and headed upstairs. In my fury I took the steps two at a time and was gasping for air by the time I reached the study. I put the bags on the floor and needed a moment to breathe.

I peeked out the window and spotted the sedan leaving. Good riddance, asshole.

It wasn't the first time I'd heard some religious type berate others for being queer. It wouldn't be the last time, either. Some parts of the world remained stuck in their homophobic trenches, and the Deep South was no exception.

Resolving to *never* live here, I discarded the interaction with the minister and went to work.

I had bought larger, more detailed maps of Louisiana, Mississippi, and Texas. I also had markers, pushpins, and sticky notes. I rearranged Henry's study how I wanted it, took some plaques down, and hung my new maps on the wall in their place.

It took me an hour to transfer the coordinates' dots to the

larger maps, but I was pleased I'd taken the time to do it.

I checked the time, locked the study with the key I found in Henry's desk, then headed downstairs. It seemed silly to lock the door when I was the only one staying in the house, and I had no explanation for why I felt the need to protect (hide?) this research.

I sorted my clothes from the dryer and took them back upstairs to the guest room on the second floor I'd claimed for the night. I had double doors to take me out to the exterior balcony, an en suite full bath, and a king-size bed. I stood in the room for a moment, trying to recall if any of the second floor's three guest rooms had ever been used by my parents' friends. I had no recollection of any guests staying over when I was a child.

Once back downstairs, I ate some leftovers and drank the not-too-sweet, lemony tea left in the fridge by the staff. I pulled the purple mug from the cabinet and grabbed a bottle of wine. I paused long enough to check the time.

Lina was due to arrive soon, so I left the mug and bottle out on the table. I would get drunk today, no question, but I opted to hold off a little longer.

This house left me unsettled. My myriad emotions slammed into each other. Anger and frustration were at the top of my list.

I paced, agitated that Goth had not responded to me. I had never acted this way about any woman before. I had never cared about my prior flings. Why care now? I didn't have an answer … at least not one that I wanted to admit.

I headed out the side door off the kitchen to roam the gardens until Lina arrived, but I stopped upon noticing a line of rust-colored dust outside the front door. I hadn't noticed it there when I returned two hours ago. Maybe it had been there and I'd missed it. I stuck my finger in the dust, and it had the same texture as the stuff I'd found at Uncle Jack's house and in his jar.

Whatever.

My wanderings took me away from the big house. I paused at a tree near the vast swamp that separated the Martil property from Uncle Jack's land—now my land, too. Hundreds of cypress trees and gray moss that seemed to drip from the limbs limited how far I could see into the swamp. Cypress knees jutted up from the dark brown water, looking like bald, brown aliens emerging from the liquid. Depending on the angle, sometimes the water appeared black and gloomy.

I remembered Uncle Jack taking Lina and me in his small wooden pirogue a little ways out to fish while Mother watched from the shoreline. I wondered if he'd ever used his boat to pole or paddle across the swamp to meet Mother during their affair.

A log that looked about twelve feet long on the embankment several yards away moved, and I realized it was an alligator. It slid from the shoreline into the water, and I scurried away from the swamp's edge. I'd never been in any danger from the creature, but the thought of being so close to an animal with so many teeth and such power created a cold sweat.

My pace quickened while heading back toward the house, and I took another path that wound a few yards from the swamp's water, careful to watch for snakes and more alligators. I stopped at a tree with bottles hanging from its limbs by strings. Many of the bottles were blue like the ones in Uncle Jack's tree. I touched the strings, noticing the knots tied in them. Each string had nine knots, and some of them were so frayed, I wasn't sure how they hadn't broken yet.

I wondered if Uncle Jack had made this tree, too.

A noise like a child's giggle echoed through the trees. I thought I glimpsed a redheaded girl run by, but when I spun to look, there was nothing and no one there. The giggle sounded more distant now, like it was coming from within the swamp.

I shivered despite the heat. I didn't linger by the tree with the bottles any longer, and left. I considered leaving everything behind … Uncle Jack's research, the DNA inquiry, stalker shadows, Dead Hanna, the asshole minister, and this fucking heat to return to New England.

Hanna, though. The girl from Destrehan.

Fuck.

I'd stay a couple more days. Then I was out of here.

Nearing the house, I noticed Lina on a bench in one of the side gardens. I trotted to reach her faster, feeling guilty for wandering and making her wait. But as I neared, I slowed to catch my breath and wipe at the sweat now dripping from my face. I glanced back, realizing I hadn't covered *that* much distance. The humidity made everything so much worse. My stamina in this heat was rotten.

"Hey, sorry for being late," I said, slinging sweat from my fingertips. "I was walking around and went out too far."

Lina stood, smiling. "I didn't mind waiting. It's peaceful in the gardens."

"It is when it's not hotter than hell itself." I noticed two things: Lina wasn't in uniform, and she had barely broken a sweat. The first detail meant I might have a drinking buddy tonight. The second detail annoyed me. "C'mon. I have some iced tea inside."

"I'd love some."

Once indoors, I poured us both a glass of tea.

"I'll be right back," I said. I darted upstairs to the study, grabbed a piece of paper from my laptop bag, then relocked the door. I arrived in the kitchen as Lina was refilling her glass with more tea.

I passed her the slip of paper. "This is the info for the DNA test … if you're game."

"Yeah." Lina tucked the paper into her back pocket.

"What's the deal with the blue bottles hanging from trees? What are those?"

"Bottle trees. The bottles are supposed to capture evil spirits in them to prevent them from entering the house. When the wind blows over the tops and makes that low-pitch *oooooo* sound, that's proof the bottle has a spirit in it."

"Uncle Jack has bottles by his front door. Why?"

"Some people make wishes with them too."

"He believed in that sort of thing?"

Lina shrugged. "Some do it for the tradition or only the look. They can be very pretty. Sometimes the bottles are put on the limbs, sometimes they're placed upside down on a piece of the limb, and other times they're tied to the limb with thin rope or hung by a doorway."

"What's the difference between doing it those different ways?"

"I'm not sure. There are other practices where tying knots in strings has some significance too."

"I've seen the knots. Nine on each string. What does that mean?"

"I don't know. It depends on how the person practices their beliefs."

"Like religious practices?"

"Spiritual more than religious. Voodoo, spelled with four *o*'s, is the touristy, commercialized version. There's also African Vodun and Haitian Vodou. Voudou, spelled with *o-u* and *o-u*, is pronounced the same but has a different meaning. That one is tied to spiritual practices that are a blend of the others and some practices specific to our region. It's also zero tourism."

"I didn't know it was so complex."

"Most people don't," Lina said, then chuckled. "There's this whole history behind it all, and I don't know all the details. But the Louisiana flavors added over time give our Voudou its uniqueness."

"Interesting. So if a bottle tree is to protect the house, would someone ever make one off in the middle of nowhere away from a house?"

"Not that I know of. Some people have them for decoration and that's all."

I frowned, wondering why there was a bottle tree on my property that was so close to the swamp instead of near the house … not that I needed protection from evil spirits or anything.

"Why?" Lina asked.

"Curiosity. Are you off tonight? We can order food and have some wine," I said, gesturing at the bottle on the counter.

Lina's phone chirped. She pulled it from her pocket and headed for the side door. "Sorry, this is work. Here's hoping I can get a call to go through outside."

"Good luck." I left the table, taking my tea with me out into the vast openness of the lower level of the center of the house. I gazed up at the vaulted ceiling. This place was too large to be so empty. One person staying here was ridiculous, and no one living here was a waste of space. The house could be more than a place to dump money for the upkeep.

"Hey," Lina said, joining me in the foyer. Her shoulders were slumped and her eyes downcast. "I've gotta run. I was off work but now I'm not. A body has been found."

I figured the body belonged to a child—*the* child. The *MISSING* sign girl was now a recovery and not a rescue. I felt awful for the family of the girl.

Another one like Hanna.

I walked Lina to the door. "Do you know what this red-orangey dust is?" I asked, nodding at the gritty substance under Lina's sneakers.

Lina gazed down and shifted her feet so she wasn't standing

in the dust. "No."

"Good luck with the investigation. Ideally you'll find some evidence to help you catch the missing girl's killer."

Lina frowned. "I only said a body was found."

"Jesus, Lina. You didn't have to get into the details for me to know the body was probably the girl. Your mood change and body language after that call said it."

"Oh. I guess so. We don't know for certain it's the Destrehan girl, so don't go starting rumors."

Who the hell would I tell in this wretched state? I wanted to laugh at the absurdity of being told to not start rumors. Instead, I kept my laugh contained. "Bye."

I watched her leave, then closed the door. I was not thrilled about an evening here alone. My phone showed no message from Goth. I wanted to talk to her, but I didn't want to harass her.

I washed the tea glasses and filled the mug with wine. I drained the mug, refilled it, and took it and the bottle with me upstairs to the study.

Chapter Twenty-Four

I had stared at the wall maps for so long, my vision blurred. I rubbed my eyes but wasn't ready to quit. I didn't know what the dots from the coordinates in Henry's notebook meant. I used my laptop to dig through the files on Uncle Jack's flash drive. I opened the folder labeled with the same year that Hanna disappeared. There were four sub-folders. Three were labeled *confirmed* while the fourth was called *potential*.

I drilled into the folders and wished Uncle Jack had a less convoluted filing system. Hanna's picture was in one of the *confirmed* folders. I closed my eyes and shivered. Over time I'd forgotten exactly what Hanna looked like, other than the basics. The girl smiling in the school photo came with long-lost memories.

Hanna had a plush pig she always carried with her. It would get filthy when she had it on the playground with Lina and me. The next day, after having gone through the wash, it was back to being mostly clean except for a few permanent stains. Hanna rarely let anyone else hold the pig. The day Hanna disappeared, the pig was discovered in a wooded area near the playground.

I tried to remember more from that day.

Hanna was usually the one missing school because of illness, but on this day, Lina had stayed home with a cold. Hanna and

I had played together that afternoon until my mother picked me up from school. Hanna had been there with an older cousin when I left. Hours later, Mother received a phone call from Hanna's parents. The police stopped by later, asking about Hanna, and I told them she was at the playground.

The search for her had gone on for weeks with any hope for her safe return dwindling to near zero. Then her body was found by some hunters.

I opened my eyes to see a smiling Hanna on my screen. I closed the photo and then read through the other files inside the folder. I noted the article indicating where Hanna's body had been found, so I went to the maps and found a dot already in place. I noticed another dot matching the playground's location.

My gut knotted, bringing with it a wave of nausea. The coordinates from the book in the safe had already identified the locations of Hanna's disappearance *and* where her body had been found.

I rifled through Henry's desk searching for string or something to connect the two points. The nausea passed while I continued pawing through the drawers. I downed another mug of wine in my frustration after finding no string. I refilled my mug with the remnants in the bottle and drank that too.

Mother's sewing kit!

But first …

I skipped downstairs, opened a new bottle of wine, and carried it back upstairs, taking a few drinks directly from the bottle on my way up. I told myself that it helped calm my nerves after reviewing information about Hanna's death. Now standing in my parents' bedroom, I took a much bigger gulp from the bottle. I wobbled when I walked to Mother's closet that was now void of clothes and shoes and pulled the sewing kit down from the upper shelf. I rummaged through it to find a spool of thread.

A childlike giggle echoed out in the hallway.

My skin prickled, and I remained in the closet for a few moments, clutching the wine and thread. The noise didn't come again, so I inched out of the closet toward the door to leave the bedroom. I paused another minute at the doorway, gazing out across the second-floor balcony. Silence reigned, so I left, chiding myself for being ridiculous and jumpy.

Back in the study, I placed the bottle on the desk and used the pushpins to run the thread between the two points. I stepped back from the maps and wondered how many of the other points were connected. I turned to the laptop to continue my research but stopped to lean my palms against the desk. The buzzing in my ears and waves of dizziness almost buckled my knees.

Please, not this again.

I assumed this was my body protesting how I had been chugging wine like someone would drink iced water in a desert. I needed food. I left the desk and collapsed. I lay on the floor for a moment, waiting for the dizziness to pass, but it didn't go away. I used the chair and desk to get back upright. Hanna's picture was displaying on my laptop's screen.

"Janie," the photo said.

My eyes widened.

"Come outside to play." The photo giggled.

"Hell no!" I slammed the laptop lid down with trembling hands.

The buzzing noise was all around me now. I wobbled, dangerously close to toppling when I moved. Outside it was dark, and a reddish smoke the color of Hanna's hair filtered in through the open window. Whispers seemed to come from within the smoke. I lunged for the window and slammed it shut. The smoke swirled around my feet, and what sounded like hundreds of mingled voices within the smoke grew louder, calling my name.

I bolted for the door.

It was a clumsy escape, but I reached the hallway and yanked the door closed behind me. I slowed long enough to grope in my pocket for the key.

Because locking the door would keep the spooky smoke in the study. Sure. That would work.

It was obvious to me that I was losing my mind.

I locked the study door, tucked the key back into my pocket, then stumbled toward the stairs.

The stairs moved side to side, twisting and looping in on themselves. I closed my eyes.

"It's not real. It's not real," I whispered.

I used both hands to grip the rail and inched toward the stairs. But where would I go once downstairs? I was unable to walk, much less drive. Wine had never done this to me before, and I'd drunk countless bottles of the stuff over the years.

I crept forward, keeping my eyes closed, and stopped when the tip of my shoe reached the edge of the topmost stair. I risked opening one eye, then the other. The stairs were motionless, but the buzzing in my head worsened.

The hardwood floor softened, and my feet sank into it. I scrambled down the stairs, almost falling a few times before I reached the second floor. I moved across the balcony, using it to help keep me upright-ish until I reached the next set of stairs. I stumbled twice during my final descent, but I managed to recover some of my balance. When I reached the bottom, I sprawled on the marble floor.

"You don't belong here," the smoky Shadow Man said, swirling around but not touching me. "No one wants you here. No one wants you at all."

I struggled with my clumsy movements but got my feet

back under me. I wasn't sure how long I could remain upright, though.

Shadow Man was right. I didn't belong here. I didn't have a home.

"Do the world a favor and drown yourself in the swamp or throw yourself off the roof. Take a handful of pills and be done with it all," the shadow said.

Would the world be better off without me? I wasn't sure of the answer.

I fought to remain standing, but the expansive center of the first floor was void of any furniture except along the walls. I lunged toward one of the walls and crashed to the floor again.

Noise from outside the house startled me. A flash of lightning lit up the house, and I thought I saw a man within the shadow looming over me.

Then the power went out.

Oh, fuck me.

I remained on the floor, my limbs refusing to obey commands to roll over and stand. I didn't know where I would go once I was up again.

At least the shadow had stopped talking.

I pulled my phone from my pocket. The light from it was small and weak inside the vast, empty house.

I found the right button to use it like a flashlight and then passed the beam around me.

Shadow Man was gone. The buzzing inside my head was almost gone, but I remained dizzy.

Car headlights approached the house, and I managed to stand in the darkness. I bumped into the wall and other objects on my way to the kitchen, knocking the framed portrait of Henry off the wall. I winced when it struck the floor and the glass shattered. The wrecked portrait didn't bother me. The noise from the breaking glass had hurt my ears.

Upon reaching the kitchen, I placed my phone on the counter, then scooped water from the kitchen faucet. I drank several gulps of water from my palms. Once I splashed some water on my face, the dizziness eased a little.

Someone knocked on the front door.

Ghosts and shadows couldn't knock on doors, could they? Stairs weren't supposed to melt or twist, but they had a few moments ago.

I carried the phone with me out of the kitchen. I passed the light around. No talking shadows, no reddish smoke, and no melting floors. But lots of glass was on the floor where I'd clobbered the portrait.

The person knocked again.

Now I was angry on top of being frightened. "What?" I barked.

"It's Anthony."

Anthony? Who the fuck was Anthony? I searched my memory. Oh.

Pleased with myself for stumbling only once on my way to the door, I opened it to see Anthony's hulking form in full deputy gear. He held a flashlight in one hand, and his uniform was speckled with raindrops.

"I figured this wind from the storm might knock out your power," Anthony said. "I tried to get here before that happened to make sure you found the candles and stuff."

The light rain that Anthony had arrived in was the storm's foreplay. The sky suddenly opened up and dumped sheets of water on the estate. The old trees leading to the house bent and twisted with the gusts of wind. I saw them only when the lightning flashed, but the wind roaring through the leaves was an impressive sound. The porch protected us from the worst of the storm.

"How do you know where the candles are?" I asked.

"I'd come out here with Stephen and Uncle Jacques sometimes. These summer storms can be quick and rather violent."

Deafening thunder boomed overhead, and the wind shifted, pelting us with rain.

I stepped aside for him to come in.

He entered and passed his flashlight's beam over the floor. He stopped at the broken picture and glass.

"I knocked it off the wall," I said. "When the lights went out," I added.

"You seem a little unsteady."

"I had some wine while I was reading, and then the power went out. I'm drunk."

And hallucinating.

"As long as you're not driving," he said.

"No, not driving." I realized I wasn't even sure where the car keys were.

"C'mon. I'll show you where the storm stash is. Hurricanes like Katrina and Ida made Uncle Jacques stockpile a few more supplies than he usually kept in the house for future hurricanes and storms like this."

I felt like a puppy following him, but I appreciated his presence with my nonexistent Shadow Man lurking around. Anthony pulled candles and a lantern from a closet I would have never found by myself. He placed the candles on the kitchen table and lit them. I turned the light off on my phone.

I thanked Anthony several times but didn't ask him to stay when he mentioned leaving.

I carried my candle back to the kitchen. My shaking hands almost made the tiny flame go out, but once I arrived at the table, I sat. The darkness lurked at the edges of the light cast by the candles around me.

Now that I was alone, I wondered if that was the right thing to do. I didn't know why I was in such a rush to oust him when I liked him being there a few minutes ago. The house creaked and made noises when the storm wind lashed it. I folded my arms on the table and rested my head on top of them, resolving to stay awake until the power came back on.

I closed my eyes.

Chapter Twenty-Five

I knew I was dreaming, but I couldn't wake up. I stood at the bottle tree on the estate while multicolored fog swirled around me. Voices that I couldn't understand spoke. My feet were covered by grass and roots, attached to the ground.

I couldn't move.

The voices grew louder, and I heard my name this time.

A hand touched my shoulder, and I jolted awake from the dream, sitting up so quickly, I almost toppled from the chair.

Stephen jumped back away from me. "I'm *so* sorry, Miss Janie. I didn't mean to alarm you."

I glanced around. It was daylight, and I was in the kitchen, where I had fallen asleep (passed out?) on the table. The power was back on. The candles had melted into puddles of wax.

There was no Shadow Man. No red smoke. No melting floors. And one massive fucking headache. I touched the side of my head and groaned. I thought I would vomit, but that sensation passed.

"Miss Janie?" Stephen said.

I tried to speak, and my voice cracked. I cleared my throat and tried again. "Yeah?"

"Are you okay?"

I grunted in response to his question. My mouth was too

dry to moisten my parched lips.

Stephen filled a glass with water from the tap and handed it to me. I hated the way my hand shook when I took it from him. I drank slowly at first, then downed the rest like I was guzzling wine. Ugh. Wine. That had to be the reason for the rotten taste in my mouth. I placed the empty glass on the table.

"More?" Stephen asked.

"No, thank you." I stood and pressed my palms onto the table. I wiggled my toes, ensuring I had proper sensation in them before trying to walk. My ankles were swollen from having spent the night in the kitchen chair. I swayed when I left the table. Stephen was at my side, but I raised my hand. I didn't want to be touched.

My mood was awful, and I needed a shower. Possibly a bath instead. That might be safer than standing in a shower. I decided to figure it out once I got upstairs. Oh, God. Stairs.

"Uh, Stephen, may I bother you to come with me upstairs to make sure I get up them safely?"

"Of course, Miss Janie."

He hovered too much for my liking, but I at least knew that with his arm around me, my odds of a face plant into the floor were low. Once upstairs and outside my room, I rested against the door frame for support.

"Thank you," I said. "I can manage from here."

"Yes, ma'am. Um, may I ask why you slept in the kitchen?"

"I had some wine and came down for food, and then the power went out."

"One of the pictures was broken."

"I bumped into it when the power was out and knocked it off the wall."

"The folks who clean the house will be here today. We'll get the glass cleaned up, and I'll take the photo into town to be reframed."

"Hold off on the reframing. Put it aside in Henry's office, and I'll decide what to do with it later." Like burn it.

"Yes, ma'am. I'll have the staff clean this area last today so you can rest."

"That would be great. Does anyone among the staff have keys to the study upstairs? I found the key in the desk and have it. Are there other keys?"

"I have the only other copy but not on me right this second. Do you need it?"

"You can slide it under the door later."

"Yes, ma'am."

I nodded and then entered my room. I closed the door and leaned back against it, listening as Stephen's footsteps became more distant with each step. I slid down to the floor and dropped my head into my hands.

I wasn't sure what had happened last night. I felt awful, but there was a dark thought in my mind: Death. And this wasn't a flippant wish for death to escape my weird hangover. This was a much more ominous feeling that the world would be better off without me in it.

I rose and stumbled toward the en suite bathroom. On the way, I kicked my shoes off and emptied my pockets on the dresser. I finished stripping once I arrived in the bathroom. When the tub was full, I slid beneath the water, leaving only my face exposed. The water muted all sounds except my breathing.

Death. I shuddered.

I expelled my breath, then went completely under.

I woke to find myself naked and sprawled on my belly on the bed with the sheets knotted around me. I had no recollection of making it to the bed. The last thing I remembered was toweling off after the bath.

My headache had improved—it wasn't gone, but it was better. I rolled out of bed, pleased to have almost normal-sized ankles again. I dressed in clean clothes, brushed my teeth, and pulled my hair back into a bun. A fog lingered inside my head.

I grabbed my phone and keys, then picked up the key on the floor by the door. Stephen had brought me the copy of the study key as I'd asked. He was a good man.

Instead of going downstairs, I walked halfway around the interior balcony to my childhood bedroom. I took a deep breath before entering. All the carved animals from Uncle Jack remained on my dresser. I gathered them with care and carried them with me. Halfway down the stairs, I stopped. The steps weren't melting or twisting.

Of course they weren't!

The flood of embarrassment for being so silly about the damn stairs annoyed me. I continued down and headed into the kitchen to find an elderly Black woman surrounded by grocery bags. Food lined the countertop and covered much of the table.

"Mama Tess?" She was Mama Tess to everyone in Jardin, possibly everyone in the parish.

The woman turned and then squealed. Mama Tess threw her arms around me. "Sweet, sweet Janie!"

"Hi, Mama." I remained cocooned in the woman's arms.

"I'd recognize you anywhere, *chère*. Ole Jacques, bless him, was always showing me the latest picture he had of you, girl. I always wondered if I'd see you before it was my time to go. Where you been all this time?"

"Busy with life." So many lies buried in that one little sentence, it disturbed even me.

"I'm so happy to see you."

My hands contained the carved animals, so I couldn't hug her back without dropping them. Mama held me for a few more seconds, then released me.

"Uh, what are you doing here?" I asked.

"I wanted to come sooner, but my knees were hurting something awful. I've been checking in with Stephen to see when you were here, though." Mama waved her hand. "You come and go with the wind, don't you?"

"I guess."

"How are you feeling? Stephen told me you didn't sleep well."

I wanted to strangle Stephen. "He called you?"

"Oh, no, *chère*. I came by to visit, and he said you were sleeping. Last night's storm had kept you up."

Stephen had lied to cover for my hungover state. I would hold off on strangling him. "We don't get this kind of weather up north too often."

"I imagine not. Too damn cold. You can keep your snow!" Mama Tess laughed, then poured three glasses of iced tea.

We were the only two in the kitchen.

"When I came in here to make some tea for you, I noticed the empty fridge," Mama said. "So Samuel and I were makin' groceries while you slept."

I almost laughed. "Makin' groceries" was a phrase I had only ever heard in Louisiana, and it meant grocery shopping. I didn't know who this Samuel person was though. "Samuel?"

"Lina said you met him at the funeral. Sweetest boy ever. He wasn't feeling well today and didn't go to school, so I have him with me while his parents are at work."

"Oh. I saw him the other day too." I was about to ask where he was when he came in through the side door. His eyes were red and bleary, but he smiled at me. He approached, arms wide, so I shifted to deposit the carved animals to the table and empty my hands.

"Hi," he said, squeezing me around the waist.

I patted his back. "Hi, Samuel. I'm sorry you're not feeling so great." He wasn't the only one feeling like shit today.

"I'll be better tomorrow," he said. "The medicine always makes me bad for a day."

I didn't know what he meant. He released me, then sat in a chair, slumping like he was exhausted. Mama placed a glass of tea in front of him and he drank from it.

I surveyed the groceries on the counter. "How much was the food? Let me pay you."

Mama waved me off. "No need." She handed me a glass of tea, then gazed down at the animals on the table. "What have you got here?" Mama picked the elephant from the mix. "Jacques made these?"

I nodded.

"He always had such a talent with carving. Even as a little boy he carved the most delicate birds, flowers, and …" She smiled at the figure she held. "And elephants." She placed the animal back on the table.

Samuel eyed them with interest. "I like giraffes."

"Me too," I said. "Would you like to play with this one while you visit?"

He nodded and smiled.

I handed him the giraffe, and he took it into his hands like he was holding an egg.

I sat and lined the animals up, smiling to remember doing this exact same thing as a kid while Mother made breakfast. Mama Tess placed a muffin on a small plate before me.

"I know it's afternoon," Mama said, "but since you're only now getting up, it's basically breakfast. You're looking kinda ragged, girl. I'll make some coffee."

Before I could protest having Mama do more things for me, she was already on the task.

"Are you hungry?" I asked Samuel.

He shook his head while stroking the giraffe's long neck and body with one finger, petting it. My stomach rumbled, so I devoured the muffin, chasing it down with tea.

"Gracious," Mama said. "You were hungry. Want another muffin?"

"No, ma'am."

"I think you need another one."

Mama took the plate away, and I didn't bother arguing when the plate reappeared with a new muffin.

"Hey," I said to Samuel. "Do you want to keep the giraffe and take it outside to play in the shade?"

His eyes widened. "I can keep it?"

I hesitated a moment, thinking. Something about this felt right. I couldn't explain it. I'd gotten twitchy when Frank had held the lioness. But this was different. This honest, sweet child reminded me of how I used to be at that age ... before my parents died and before the world had started routinely shitting on me. "Yes, it's yours."

He smiled so widely, I noticed where he'd recently lost a tooth. He slid out of the chair, hugged me, then went outside.

Mama waited until the door closed. "You didn't have to give it to him."

I felt some semblance of contentment I hadn't felt in a very long time. "I don't mind. He's adorable and will take good care of it."

"That he will," Mama said, nodding. "What have you been up to since you've been here?"

The hamster wheel in my mind had a field day with that question. Sleeping with a stranger. Pissing off the stranger and wanting her to call me back. Yelling at a minister. Seeing dead children, shadow people, and melty floors. Getting drunk and falling down stairs.

"Digging through some of Uncle Jack's estate documents," I

said.

"Sounds boring."

Mama had no idea how un-boring it was becoming.

She stood and poured a cup of coffee. "Milk and sugar?"

"Just milk, please."

Mama Tess finished preparing the cup and placed it before me. She grabbed herself a muffin, then sat at the table again.

"Mama, was there anyone in Jardin that Uncle Jack didn't like? Or someone who didn't like him?"

"You mean his murder?"

"I don't know what I mean. I have so many unanswered questions."

"We all do, *chère*. I can tell you Jacques and Frank were oil and water." Mama sipped her tea, then shook her head. "Awful."

"The tea?"

"No, their constant arguing."

I cradled my coffee with both hands. "About what?"

Chapter Twenty-Six

I was more than a little tired after Mama Tess and Samuel's visit, yet grateful the woman had stopped by to chat and bring food. Samuel was an absolute delight to be around even when he felt like crap.

I wished Mama Tess had given me more to go on about Jack and Frank's bitter relationship. It boiled down to bickering anytime the two crossed paths, which wasn't a red flag for murder.

Mama's visit took my mind off the terrors of last night and my wrecked state this morning. She'd been a welcome distraction, but my anxiety was back. I distracted myself by finding an iron and ironing board, bringing them back to my room, and ironing my clean clothes. That task wasn't enough to switch my anxiousness off.

Pacing in my bedroom didn't help my preexisting fatigue. The carved animals, minus the giraffe, were lined up on the dresser, watching me wring my hands.

I had to deal with the study. My open bottle of wine was up there and needed to be poured out. I couldn't remember how else I had left the room other than in a hurry. I refused to unlock that door and go back into the room where nightmares and dead children lived.

My phone vibrated with a text alert, and I hoped it was Goth. I snatched my phone from the dresser and frowned. I unlocked the phone to read Lina's message.

Hey, you doing okay? Anthony said you were a little out of sorts last night.

I sighed, wondering how many other people in the parish were in my business.

I was. I'm fine now.
Was Frank ever looked into with Uncle Jack's death?
Mama Tess said they didn't get along.
He was and he had a credible alibi. Why?

Just curious.

I hoped that would be the end of it, but when the little dots appeared on my phone, signaling Lina was typing back, I groaned. I probably should've left that one alone.

Liar.

I grinned. Busted by the po-po for lying in a text message.

Sounds like we need to talk. I can't today. You around tomorrow?

Yeah. We'll sort it out tomorrow.

I slid the phone into my pocket and figured I had time to come up with a good enough excuse to avoid this conversation with Lina. In my haste to leave the room, I bumped into the dresser, and the elephant tumbled to the floor and bounced under the bed.

I knelt, groping blindly under the bed for the elephant,

but came up empty. I crouched lower, spotted the elephant and reached for it, then froze. A chalk-drawn image was on the hardwood floor under the bed.

Someone had been in my room. The staff kept the house spotless, and the white chalk was easy to see from this angle. "Goddammit." I stood, feeling a mix of fear and anger. Sure, it was possible the drawing had been there all along and I happened to find it today, but my hunch was that it had been made recently since there wasn't any dust under the bed.

I wrestled with the bed to drag it to the side. I picked up the elephant, then stared at the chalk image of a heart with curling lines coming off it. Two snakes were on either side of the heart and drawn in a way that they appeared more like a *2* written correctly and another one written backward to mirror it.

I put the elephant back on the dresser with the other animals and headed into the bathroom. I grabbed a washcloth, wet it, then wiped the drawing off the floor. I dragged the bed back into place, pausing to catch my breath.

I would put an end to this nonsense of someone being in my room and drawing shit under my bed. As Stephen had said, my room key was in the top drawer of the dresser. I snatched it from the drawer. I gazed back at the carved animals, then put the lioness in my pocket.

I flipped the lock to the balcony doors, then left the bedroom, locking it behind me this time. I stepped out onto the interior balcony running the length of the home and gazed up, able to view the door to the study from where I stood. That room could wait a bit longer.

I wanted some fresh air but didn't want to be out in the gardens where I could be seen. I headed downstairs to the first level, then to the rear of the house to the creaky old door that would take me down another level to the basement.

Except when I opened the door, it didn't make a sound. I

guessed Uncle Jack had fixed that noisy door at some point in the last decade or so.

I headed down the stairs. There was something both comforting and unnerving about being *under* the house. Except this house was a sham. It wasn't a home to anyone. It was a big fucking house on a big fucking plot of dry land—with a lot of swamp bordering it. I forced my bitterness aside.

From the bottom of the stairs, I groped on the wall for the light switch, wincing when my fingers brushed feathery cobwebs. I finally found the switch and flipped it on.

The tomb-like darkness of the cellar disappeared, but I tensed anyway. Veils of cobwebs hung from the ceiling and corners, wafting with my presence and the stirring of the musty, stagnant air. A distinct dampness closed in around me. I didn't see any actual spiders, but shit, this place was creepy. Dusty chairs and benches lined one wall in the corridor that led to the next area of the cellar containing old tools and a long table serving as a work station.

I passed through a set of double doors to another room with empty shelves. To my left was a set of doors to my father's— *Henry's*—wine collection I had forgotten existed. Three long racks full of wine bottles positioned on both sides of each rack spanned the length of the room. On the back wall was another rack.

I wound around the racks, admiring Henry's collection. Every bottle was covered by a layer of dust. I pulled a bottle and wiped the dust from the label to read it.

Well done, Henry. I returned the bottle and checked a few others. I wouldn't need to buy wine for a very long time with this exquisite stash. And *maybe* I'd sip this stuff instead of guzzling it. Maybe.

With a promise to come back this way to bring a bottle or two upstairs later, I zigzagged through the wine racks until arriving at the other end and at a heavy wooden double door that I had always struggled to open as a child. It opened now with no squeaks or straining. I was now in the so-called servants' passage that would take me out to the gardens on the back side of the house.

My parents had never had servants of any kind. This was another ridiculous thing my mother had built to make the house a plantation replica.

I flipped the light switch near the door, plummeting the wine racks, storage, and work areas back into darkness. I had enough light in the corridor and headed down it, noting cobwebs and trickles of water rolling down the stone walls in the dark passage. The tunnel was cool and damp. It wasn't cold enough to make me shiver, but I shivered anyway.

A giggle echoed from behind me. I spun around. I was alone, and the sound didn't occur again.

I was losing my damn mind.

I neared the growing natural light where the exit was to the rear gardens. I stopped when I heard adult male voices. There were two distinct voices mingled with some laughter. The unmistakable scent of marijuana reached my nose. I resumed walking, the shadowy corridor concealing my presence. Once I rounded the final turn, I saw Stephen kissing another man who was lankier and slightly taller than him. Their lips parted, they smiled, kissed again briefly, and then Stephen took a drag off a joint.

I stepped into the light, and Stephen gasped. He stepped back, away from the man, and moved his hand with the joint to behind his back.

"Miss Janie!" Stephen said, his voice wavering.

I strode up to him and held out my hand. "Give it up."

He stammered for a few seconds, then hung his head while he passed the joint to me. "I guess I'll be looking for new employment."

I took a long pull off the joint, savoring the musty smell and burning in my throat. I held the smoke inside my lungs a few seconds, then blew it out. I examined the joint between my thumb and forefinger. "Why would you need new employment?"

"Uh. I, uh, assumed," Stephen said.

I shook my head. "No, don't do that." I had another pull off the joint, then offered it to the other man, who took it. Stephen continued to stare at me.

"That's good weed. Got more?" I asked.

"Um, yes, ma'am," Stephen said.

"Please stop with the formalities, Stephen. We're smoking a joint together, for Christ's sake."

"Yes, ma'am," Stephen said.

The other man chuckled when I rolled my eyes.

"Who are you?" I asked him.

"Mike."

"Good to meet you, Mike. Are you and Stephen a couple?"

"Yes."

Stephen groaned, and I tilted my head. "What's wrong?"

"I'll definitely need new employment now," Stephen said.

"Nonsense," I said. "Mike, if you're not going to smoke that thing, then give it back."

Mike grinned, had a hit, then passed it to me. I smoked it once more, then gave it to Stephen.

"Loosen up, Stephen. I don't give a shit that you have a boyfriend, are making out with him, and are having a joint while on the clock."

"You … you don't?" he asked.

"I can't get any queerer myself."

His eyes widened, and I snorted. Tension in my muscles left. "Damn, that's *really* good weed."

"I grow it myself," Mike said.

"Nice. Do you work here?"

He nodded. "One of the gardeners, part-time."

"Do you have a second job?"

"I work at the hospital. It's nothing glamorous, being in the laundry department, but I enjoy it."

"Good for you. If you want to work here full-time, you can."

"I appreciate that offer," Mike said. "I'd like to think about it if that's okay with you, ma'am."

"Oh, God, not you too," I said. "Stop the 'ma'am' bullshit. You don't have to come on full-time if you don't want it. Decision is yours, but the offer is there."

Stephen's hand shook a little when he smoked the joint.

"Stephen," I said. "Work it out with Mr. Landry to come up with a title or whatever for Mike so it's not you, a supervisor, in a relationship with an employee kind of thing. Okay?"

"Yes, Miss Janie."

I turned to Mike. "Make him stop doing that."

Mike and I both laughed. Stephen managed a chuckle, and then he had the final smoke off the joint so there wasn't any more left. He stubbed it out on one of the rocks that made up the wall of the passage.

"This place sucks," I said.

"It's a beautiful plantation," Mike said.

I frowned. "It's not a plantation and never was. It has *zero* historical value other than being a knock-off design of a real plantation house somewhere in Georgia. This house was built thirty years ago because my mother had this fascination with Southern living in a giganto house and fancy gardens like something out of a magazine. My father happened to buy the only remaining dry piece of land in the midst of a fucking swamp to build it for her." My words were full of anger, but the pot was working its magic.

I burst into laughter, and Stephen and Mike joined me.

"I'm going to change the name of this place. It won't be Martil Plantation anymore," I said.

"What will you call it?" Stephen asked.

"The Swamp House." I waved my arm. "Home to oak trees and gators."

"And mosquitoes," Mike said.

"Yes!" I suffered another bout of giggling.

When it passed, I wiped tears of laughter from my face. The sadness and darkness that had plagued me earlier was gone, and I hoped it would never come back … except the pain always returned once the alcohol and drugs wore off.

"How long are you here?" Mike asked.

I shrugged.

"You have a girlfriend back home?" he asked.

Stephen scowled at Mike. "Do *not* get into her personal affairs."

"No," I said.

"One here?" Mike asked, his eyebrow going up.

Stephen grumbled at Mike.

I ignored Stephen. "Um, no?"

Mike smiled. "Sounds like something to me."

"No, not really."

"Uh-huh," Mike said. "I'll bring you some more weed when I come tomorrow. I gotta get back to work." He kissed Stephen. "I'll see *you* later."

I smiled, glad that they seemed happy together. The Deep South had a long way to go before it fully accepted queer people. New Orleans was much more progressive, but Jardin … My smile faded. Being queer and being open about it while living out here couldn't be easy.

My thoughts drifted to Goth. I checked the time and

decided to head into the city tonight. "Bye, Stephen. Thanks for leaving the extra key to the study."

"You're welcome, Miss Janie."

I gave up on correcting him and headed back into the passage, through the heavy door, and snagged a bottle of wine. I grabbed a second bottle before heading back up to my room to pack. Once done, I sprinted upstairs, darted into the study, snatched my laptop, laptop bag, and notebooks from the desk, and scurried back out. I realized I had held my breath for the duration of my time in the study.

I locked the door again, my hands shaking a little with the key. Once the lock clicked into place, I hurried back downstairs, gathering my things and rushing outside.

Lina headed toward me, but I had already frozen in place. A line of police cars and other vehicles, some hauling canoes and pirogues, approached the house. I stared as they all found places to park.

"Janie, I tried calling ahead of time but I kept getting punted to voicemail," Lina said. "We'd like to use your property for official purposes. Your land borders the area of the swamp we need to search." She paused. "We found only a partial body at the other site."

My mind seized with this information, my chest tightened to the point that I didn't have time to prepare for the onslaught of anxiety, and I forgot to breathe.

Chapter Twenty-Seven

I hadn't passed out, but my mind refused to process most things, including motor function.

Lina caught my arm. "Shit. Sit here."

I sat on the bench on the porch and leaned forward, resting my elbows on my knees and my head in my hands.

"What's wrong?" Lina asked.

It took me a moment to find my voice. "Them. The cop cars."

There had been a search of Manchac Swamp to recover my parents' bodies. Police had pulled up to the house when I was a child to let my sitter know that I was an orphan. My heart beat faster with the memories. Seeing a somewhat similar procession and a body being involved had tripped my panic switch. I was trapped by this house. Trapped by horrible memories and the terrifying hallucinations that happened to me at night.

"What about them?"

I lowered my hands. "It's dragging up memories from when my parents died. It's freaking me out."

Lina's eyes widened. "Oh, shit. I never even considered that. Janie, I'm really sorry. I'll, um, I'll get rid of them."

I was sweaty and shivering. "No. I'll go inside."

I stood, swayed only a little, and flinched away from Lina's offered hand to steady me. I didn't want her assistance. My agitation level was on screech.

I grabbed my things, and she followed me inside to the kitchen. I put my bags on the floor. I almost dropped the two glasses I'd taken from the cabinet.

Lina eased them from my tenuous grasp and poured us both some iced tea, and I leaned against the counter while I drained the glass.

"Better?" Lina asked.

"Sorry about that."

"No need to apologize." Lina eyed my laptop bag and pack on the floor. "Where were you off to?"

"New Orleans."

"Are you sure that's wise?"

"What do you mean? I don't have to stay here while y'all search the swamp, do I?" *Y'all* ... again. Fuck me. I promised myself I would forever purge that word (if it was a word) from my vocabulary.

"No, you don't need to stay. We needed a good place to launch the boats somewhat near the designated search area, which is actually about a mile by boat from here. I suggested this place as a location to park and launch from. I didn't think it would be a problem, but I'm sorry. I should've asked you first."

I fidgeted with my empty glass. "Why shouldn't I go to New Orleans?"

"You smell like weed. I don't care if you smoke it, but you shouldn't drive high."

"I did smoke some earlier, but I'm not high."

"You almost passed out."

I was shaken and shouldn't be driving anywhere, but I was *not* staying here tonight. "Can you give me a ride to Uncle Jack's house? I'll stay there tonight and y'a—*you* and the other po-po folks—can use the land and the house however you need to help with the search."

"Sure. I can give you a ride."

"Can you grab someone else to follow us over and bring my car, or however you want to arrange drivers? I don't want to be without transportation if I do need to leave for something."

"Of course. I'll take care of it now."

"I've got to head upstairs to grab something, and then I'll be back down and ready."

Lina picked up my bags and left while I headed upstairs.

With others in and around the house, surely the red smoke and Shadow Man wouldn't be waiting for me in the study, right? I unlocked the door. Everything was as I had left it. No smoke. No shadows. I grabbed the purple mug and the open bottle of wine from the desk, then headed back out, pausing to lock the door again.

Once back in the kitchen, I poured the wine down the drain.

"Hope that wasn't a good wine," Lina said upon entering.

"No." I shook the last drops from the bottle and set it aside on the counter. "My stomach didn't like this kind at all." Might have been the truth. Sorta. I took some food items from the refrigerator and placed them in a paper bag. I rinsed the purple mug, then added it to the bag of food. "I'm ready."

"Isn't that Uncle Jacques's mug? Well, *was* his mug."

"Yeah. I borrowed it from his house before."

"It's your house, Janie. Your mug now."

I shrugged and headed for the door. I wasn't having this conversation with her.

Lina drove my rental car, and I hopped out of it once she had parked it at Uncle Jack's house. I grabbed my bags and headed for the door while Lina's coworker sat in the deputy car, waiting. I stopped at the front door and groaned. I'd left the key to Jack's house at the estate.

"Everything okay?" Lina asked.

I grunted some semblance of an affirmative. It was the Deep South. Not too many things stayed locked up tightly, so I figured there had to be a spare key close by. I glanced down and frowned. More red dust was at the threshold, though the wind had blown much of it away. I lifted the welcome mat.

A key lay under the mat as I had hoped, but it was on top of an odd design drawn in white chalk that was hidden under the mat. There was a heart with a snake drawn over it, all on top of two lines drawn like a cross with curving lines coming off the sides of the heart.

"What the fuck is this?" I muttered. I picked up the key but kept my eyes on the design. "More of this Voudou-y bullshit?" I glared at Lina, not angry with her but angry in general. "Is that what this is?"

Lina shrugged, which only irritated me more. I raked my shoe through the design and scattered it and the rest of the red-orange dust away from the door. I flung the mat back down, then unlocked the door. I picked up my bags.

"You'll be okay out here by yourself?" Lina asked.

"Yes!" I stepped through the door, then paused, chiding myself for being a jerk. I softened my tone. "I'll be fine. Thanks for the ride."

"You're welcome." Lina handed me my car keys. "Maybe have a rest. Relax a little. Smoke some more weed," she said, then smiled. "I'll text you when we clear out after the search so you can return without all the extra people around."

"Thanks."

Lina left, headed for the cop car, and got in. She and the other deputy left, and I was relieved to be alone. But the old house creaked when I closed the door, and I didn't want to be alone anymore. Damn ghosts.

I pressed my forehead against the closed door. It was all in my head. It had to be.

I turned and leaned my back against the door. The living room lay before me with the kitchen on the other side of it. The memories of sitting on the floor and reading Uncle Jack-Dad's letters were both disturbing and a comfort.

Why did he have to die?

I slid down the door until my rump touched the floor. I pulled my knees up to my chest and curled until my head rested on my knees. I stayed that way until my bladder screamed to be emptied and my ass had gone numb.

I carried the bag with food to the kitchen. Once everything was in the refrigerator, I used the toilet (noting I was using the toilet for something other than vomiting *this* time). I headed outside, toward the swamp. The idea that part of the missing girl's body was somewhere out in the dark water, among the cypress knees, and possibly inside an alligator's belly, was morbid … yet intriguing. Maybe it was my recent preoccupation with death that made it all weird.

Both Henry and Uncle Jack had data on missing children and where their bodies were found … if found. The smart thing would be to turn everything over to Lina. I didn't need the memories or the photos and research of dead children. I absolutely didn't need Hanna's photo talking to me again.

I found a bench on a side part of Uncle Jack's yard with a nice view of trees, moss, and the swamp in the distance. I sat on the bench and imagined Uncle Jack sitting next to me. It was a silly thing to imagine, but it brought me a measure of peace in its own way. I could've done this with him when he was alive had I not been so hell-bent on avoiding Jardin.

Sunset arrived with a fiery glow in the sky. Darkness settled over the property while the sun continued to sink below the horizon. I listened to the insects and frogs and whatever else was calling among the trees and plants around me. No phantom, giggling children disturbed my peace while I made a mental list of things to do for tonight and tomorrow.

Tonight's list was short: eat, skip the wine, sleep on the couch.

Tomorrow's list seemed easy at first, but then it got complicated: a couple of errands, sort out final paperwork crap with Mr. Landry, New Orleans, find Goth and …

And what? Tell her I miss her?

Tell her I'm a fucked-up mess in the head and I went into the city to find her because I'm a stalker?

I snickered. First part of that was true, no question. Second part, eh. Maybe.

I slapped at a mosquito biting my neck, ending my time on the bench, and retreated to the house.

Chapter Twenty-Eight

I had already wandered through the artists' stations for over an hour, considering my attempt to find Goth a lost cause. I hadn't suffered any hallucinations last night, but I also hadn't slept much. I had stuck to last night's plan, for the most part: eat and lay off the wine. The sleeping part was a fail since the couch wasn't that comfortable, but I couldn't fall down Uncle Jack's stairs again if I didn't venture up the damn things. My errands and time with Mr. Landry had taken longer than expected, so I was extra tired now.

I was wrong to come to New Orleans to look for Goth. I decided to leave, go to a hotel, and get some sleep. What was I doing out here anyway? I didn't know what to say to her if I did find her. This was stupi—

I spotted someone carrying a small print of a painting that was unmistakable as one of Goth's. I approached the man.

"Excuse me," I said. "Your print is amazing. Did you buy it from an artist here?"

"Yeah."

"Could you tell me where the artist's booth is?"

"Back that way," he said, pointing. "Not on the corner but close to it. Best hurry. She was starting to pack up."

"Thanks so much!" I left him, chiding myself for walking

only the interior of the square. I weaved my way through the vendors and shoppers to the periphery. I spotted Goth and froze.

I wanted to talk to her, but my feet wouldn't move. My throat seemed to slam shut along with the functioning parts of my brain. I tried to think of something clever or witty to say to Goth to get her speaking to me again.

My palms became sticky. I had never been this hung up on a woman before.

Goth paused in packing her things to speak to some shoppers, likely tourists, who appeared to be asking for directions. She smiled when she spoke to them. They replied and she nodded. She said something that made them all laugh. After a few more moments of talking, the shoppers left.

I continued to stare at Goth.

I wanted to walk away. I wanted to stay.

I was jerked from my inner conflict when I realized Goth was watching *me*. I swallowed hard and forced my feet to move.

My mind became an abyss; I could think of nothing to say to her.

"You stalking me?" Goth asked.

"Yes," I said. "Sorta."

"You're not very good at it, ya know. Standing over there like a statue and looking like you might shit yourself."

"The looking like I might shit myself is my specialty." I shrugged. "It's a skill."

Goth laughed. "Well, since you're here, you can help me wrap up."

I accepted the offered truce with a smile. I grabbed or moved whatever Goth told me to touch and only when instructed. The paintings were small and were displayed alongside prints of the larger paintings that I had seen online. It was a smart way for Goth to easily transport her art to smaller displays like this, but I wished others here recognized the true extent of her talent.

Money didn't motivate Goth or her art. That was clear. But I had a ton of questions about her artistic process. A sense of desperation welled up inside my chest and mingled with the tightness that came with fear and eventual panic. I was dying to see Goth's studio, but I also felt like I was barefoot and tiptoeing around shards of glass.

I was more desperate to keep my helper job, and being near Goth made me happy. I didn't want to do anything to be sent away, or worse, have her walk away from me again.

When we finished packing, Goth watched me for a moment.

Shit. I was under the microscope now. I shouldn't care what she thought of me, except I did.

All I managed to say was "Um."

"Um?" Goth asked.

"Can I buy you a coffee?" I asked. There were a million other things I could've said, but the one that tumbled out of my mouth was about fucking coffee.

"Coffee," Goth said.

"Uh, yes?"

"You don't sound sure."

I shuffled my feet and stared at the ground. "I didn't want to overstep and offend you again." I brought my head up. "I'm sorry for doing so before."

"Do you know why I was offended?" Goth asked, folding her arms over her chest.

The truce was over, and I didn't have a great answer. Except, I did have part of one. "You don't need me or anyone else to rescue you. I acted like a savior swooping in to buy up your art to make us money. You don't need me. You love this and being out here among people. I saw your prices. You don't sell your stuff to make a killing. You want your art, which is by default a part of you, to go to other people's homes and make them happy."

Goth lowered her arms and gathered her things. My chest tightened with panic to the point that my breath caught and I coughed. I was losing her.

"I saw you interact with some of the tourists," I said. "You're a kind person and love it here. My arrogance was, well … I'm an ass, and I am sorry, Eva."

Goth flinched. "Ew. Eva. That sounds weird coming from you."

"Me calling you by your name sounds weird or my apology sounds weird?"

"Both."

"I, uh, can try again with the apology … Goth."

"You can work on it while you help me carry this stuff."

"Sure. Yeah." The truce was back in place, and I breathed again.

I gathered the things she told me to carry, and we started walking, mostly in silence, along the streets. We reached a building, and I followed her up a set of stairs and carried a portfolio sleeve in each hand.

I was breathing hard and sweating an embarrassing amount. Attempts to breathe more slowly and less gaspy-sounding almost made me pass out, so I stopped trying. Goth wasn't out of breath despite carrying more stuff than I was.

Each stair creaked with every step in the aged building. The lack of air-conditioning in the stairwell was suffocating. Goth rounded the landing and started up another flight. She paused and leaned over the rail. "You gonna make it?"

"Yeah," I said between gasps.

Goth took a few steps down to meet me on the landing. She took both sleeves full of prints from me.

"I can carry them," I said.

"And die in the process."

I needed a minute to breathe and stall. "This explains your muscular build. You carry this stuff out to the square and back by yourself."

"Every day." Goth resumed her ascent.

I made my feet move faster to keep up. "You're out there during the day and then do bigger sales after?"

"Yep," she said without slowing. "If someone really wants the painting instead of a print, we make an appointment for them to see the original."

I was brimming with excitement to be headed to Goth's studio; I resisted the urge to giggle. When we reached the apartment, I stepped in and stared at the empty walls in the space.

No paints. No easels. No paintings. There was a chair in one corner with stacks of books next to it and potted plants everywhere else. But there *was* air-conditioning.

Goth set her things down and leaned the portfolios against the wall. "What's wrong?"

"I thought we were bringing these things back to your studio."

"Why are you so intent on seeing my paintings, Janie?"

Lie. Just lie. "Because they make me feel."

"Feel what?" Goth asked.

"I don't know. Seeing your prints and photos on the internet elicited a reaction unlike anything other art has done for me."

"Uh-huh."

"I-I can't explain it."

Goth watched me for a moment. She sighed and gestured for me to follow her. We left the tiny living room (though it was more of a plant room) to an even smaller room with a bed on an old iron frame, a bedside table with a book and a lamp, and a rack with clothes on hangers up against one wall. Goth stepped into the closet crammed full of canvases and flipped through them. She slid one out.

My mouth dropped open.

"This is the fleur-de-lis one you wanted to buy, right?" Goth asked.

I nodded.

She lifted the broad canvas and moved it away from the closet. She placed it on the floor and leaned it against the wall. "There. Have a look."

I approached the painting, then sat on the floor in front of it. That gave me the most on-center view of the work. I marveled at the lines and elegance in the piece. The colors seemed to swirl like they were alive and moving. I wondered if I was hallucinating again but decided I wasn't. For such a simple shape as the French flower, it moved me.

"*What* is happening here?" Goth asked.

I pulled my eyes from the work to where she sat on the floor next to me. "Huh?"

"You haven't moved or spoken for twenty minutes."

"It hasn't been twenty minutes."

"You didn't budge when I sat next to you. You haven't spoken and have barely blinked or breathed since parking your ass in that spot."

I wanted to deny the accusation, but I figured Goth had no reason to lie. "It's captivating."

"You want this one to sell?"

"No! Never. I wanted to buy it for me."

"To collect."

"No. Yes. I mean, yes, I collect, but this is different."

"How?"

I wondered if I had the vocabulary to put what I felt

into words. Goth waited, so I gave it a try. "The colors and lines draw me in, like I'm mesmerized. Caught in a web. Yet at the same time, I don't want to look away or escape. And contentment. It's like being held captive and happy to be trapped." I shook my head, the heat of embarrassment creeping into my face. "I'm sure that makes no sense whatsoever."

"What else in your collection makes your eyes practically bleed from staring at it for so long?"

"Nothing."

"Huh." Goth fell silent for a while to gaze at the painting. "Then you can have it."

"I can buy it?"

"No."

"What?"

"You can have it."

I frowned. "I don't understand."

"You. Can. Have. It."

"But …"

"Jesus, Janie. It's a gift."

"Why? Why give this to me when I offended you about it before?"

"I'm not offended now. If you want it, it's yours. It's not for sale for you to buy. It's a gift."

"*Why?*"

Goth grumbled and stood. I got to my feet too.

"It's not complicated," she said, her voice sharp.

I seemed to have a knack for pissing Goth off. I didn't know what to say, so I remained silent.

Goth relaxed her shoulders. "When was the last time someone gave you something for free? A gift. No strings attached or any underlying motive. A present."

"Does someone giving me something because they died count?"

"No."

"Does a coffee mug for Boss's Day count?

"No."

"Okay," I said. "My uncle gave me a hand-carved wooden giraffe when I turned six."

"Six years old?"

I nodded.

"Well, that explains a lot."

I scowled at her. "Meaning?"

"That you have no clue how to accept a gift from someone because it's been forever since you've had one … which is its own tragic thing, but we're not dealing with that right now. When was the last time *you* gave someone a gift?"

"Oh." I paused, realizing my blunder. I knew how to give gifts but didn't know how to receive them. "Yesterday."

"What was it?"

"I gave my hand-carved giraffe to a little boy."

"The same one you were given when you were six?"

I nodded.

"That was a kind and generous thing to do."

I shrugged. "It felt right."

"So does this." Goth took my hand. "The painting is yours. And you owe me a coffee."

Coffee. I felt like I could handle that task since my head was spinning over the artwork. We headed for the door, but I stopped. I took another look at the fleur-de-lis and remembered what it was like when I received the carved animals from Uncle Jack and seeing Samuel's face when I gave him the giraffe. "I love it. Thank you."

"You're welcome. And, uh, confession. I lied when I said you were sitting for twenty minutes. It was actually a full hour."

"No way."

"I sat in my chair and read while you went into your trance.

I got tired of waiting after an hour and moved. You never noticed me sitting right next to you, so I interrupted your whatever state you were in."

"Oh."

"And you should probably know that if I hadn't run into you today, I'd planned to reach out to you tonight anyway. But you pulled the stalker thing and saved me the trouble." Goth grinned.

"Ah. So I'm troublesome now?"

"You're always troublesome. I got angry, ran away, and gave you the silent treatment." Goth shrugged. "I probably could've handled that better. I … I kinda like having you around."

"Only kinda?"

"More than kinda."

I liked having Goth around too, and kissed her. Coffee would wait.

Chapter Twenty-Nine

I used the napkin to wipe at the powdered sugar on my fingers and scowled at the results. I changed napkins and managed to move the sugar from one part of my hand to another. Goth's snicker brought my head up.

"Bougie's getting her ass kicked by a beignet," Goth said.

I put the napkin down. I wanted to protest, but couldn't.

Coffee had ended up waiting until this morning. I had a great evening with Goth, so my promise of buying coffee was a little late in being fulfilled. She didn't seem to mind the delay since we sat at the small table together and were so close, the sides of our legs touched.

"Uncle Jack and I used to come down here when I was in town," I said. "He said he only ate beignets with me. I don't know if that was true or not, but it was always nice to visit with him, though I never figured out how to eat the damn things without getting sugar all over me."

"He sounds like a great uncle," Goth said.

"Yeah. There's a chance he's my father. He said he was in a letter."

"Any reason for him to lie?"

I shook my head. "Not that I know of. I'm waiting on test results to confirm it, though."

"Will it change how you feel about him if it comes back that he isn't your father? Or if he is?"

"No, but it would provide a few answers to things if it's true."

"Answers like what?"

I paused, thinking. My life was always so convoluted and complicated. My time with Goth was so simple … and happy. Sure, the sex was fantastic, but Goth felt like a safe person—someone I trusted. I barely knew her, but she had been an anchor for me even during this short time in Louisiana. I wasn't sure why it seemed that way, but all of the weirdness in my life disappeared when I was with her. I wondered if that would change if I dragged her into my madness in the estate house … in the study.

"You don't have to answer if you don't want to," Goth said. "I'm not trying to pressure you."

"I know. I was thinking about something else." My heart beat a bit faster while the nervousness built inside my chest. I picked up the napkin again, twisting it. "Um, any chance you could skip being in the square today and you'd want to come out to Jardin?"

"To your place there?"

"My mother's place, but yes. There are some things I'd like to show you that would be too hard to explain without seeing them."

"Sounds mysterious."

I twisted the napkin tight enough that it tore. I placed the pieces on the table. "Somewhat, yeah."

"I'm game."

"Really?"

"Yeah. I need to be back here tonight to meet a buyer, so I can drive and follow you over."

"That's fine."

Goth placed her hand on my knee. "You don't need to be nervous around me. I don't bite. Well, I do," she said, and winked at me. "But in a way you seem to rather enjoy."

I nodded and smiled, noting Goth's ability to turn me on in an instant.

"Want to leave after we finish breakfast?" she asked.

"Sure."

I parked my rental at the estate and shifted in my seat to try to see Goth's face while she parked her little gray sedan behind me. Her eyes were on the gardens and not on the house. We got out of our cars.

"*Please*, can I come out here sometime to paint these trees and gardens?" Goth asked.

"Whenever you want."

"Sweet. Thanks!" She headed for the gardens, and I followed.

Goth turned, faced me, and walked backward. "Mind if I take photos while I'm here?"

"No, not at all." It was clear that Goth didn't give a shit about the house.

She fished her phone from her pocket and pointed it toward me. "Smile."

I blinked instead.

Goth frowned at the photo she'd taken. "Bougie, we gotta work on you smiling for photos." She continued into the gardens.

Mike was working on something by the shed and waved. I waved back and kept walking. Goth muttered when she walked around the various plants, pausing to examine lighting and angles before taking a photo, then moving on. Sweat trickled down my back, and I scratched at the remnant mosquito bite on my neck. The artist in Goth had taken over, and I enjoyed watching her work. I would pay to watch her paint, but I would take this for now.

Goth spotted me and stashed her phone in her pocket. She hurried back to me, taking my hand.

"I'm *really* sorry about that," she said. "I sorta forgot myself and got lost in the beauty here. I can do photos another time."

"Did your artist brain overload?" I asked, not bothering to hide my smile.

"It did. I'm sorry."

"Don't be. I didn't mind. But I would love to watch you when you paint."

"Why? Seems like that would be boring to watch."

"Not for me. It's part of how I like to stalk people."

Goth laughed and squeezed my hand.

I took her through the gardens, showed her the swamp (where she *had* to take a few more pictures), then showed her the bottle tree.

"This is amazing," Goth said, staring at the bottles swaying in the gentle breeze that I wished would blow harder to cool me off. "The light is *perfect* with this colored glass."

"Take photos if you want," I said.

"I do want to, and I want you in them."

"Why?"

"Trust me."

I didn't understand why I needed to be in the photos. "But …"

Goth positioned me where she wanted me, had me shift my feet a little to the left and then back to the right. A step back. "There!" she said. She worked her phone and instructed me on what to do, how and where to stand, and such.

I obeyed but felt silly. Goth finished and took my hand

again. We headed back toward the house where Mama Tess had three glasses of iced tea already poured.

"Janie!" Mama said. "Who is this? Oh, you're beautiful." Mama threw her arms around Goth before either of us could speak. "I'm Mama Tess. You feel free to call me that. Welcome to the family."

Goth's brow crinkled.

"You've been adopted," I said.

Mama Tess chuckled. "I'm everyone's Mama."

"I'm Eva," Goth said. "Nice to meet you."

Mama released her and held her at arm's length. "Just *beautiful*."

"Thank you," Goth said.

"Janie," Mama said, waggling a finger at me. "You haven't eaten nearly enough of that food I brought over. A stiff wind will knock you over, girl."

"I went into New Orleans last night, Mama."

"To see her?" Mama glanced at Goth, winked at her, then shifted her focus back to me.

"Yes, ma'am."

"Good! You make a lovely couple."

"Uh."

"I saw you two holding hands in the gardens," Mama Tess said. "It made me happy to see that. Like when Stephen and Mike think they're sneaking in a kiss when no one can see them. I'm glad you've been staying out here so Stephen can be around another rainbow."

"I, uh, didn't know you knew."

"Lord, girl, I'm not blind. Old as hell, but not blind." Mama Tess laughed.

I glanced at Goth, who grinned at me. Mama handed us each a glass of tea.

"Janie, dearest," Mama said, gesturing for us to sit with

her. "Stephen has the face *and* the body of a god. Even married women lose their minds when they're around that gorgeous a man. Some men do too. You don't even blink when his name comes up. I knew. Mm hmm. I knew," she said, then drank from her glass.

"How is Samuel?" I asked.

"He's better and back at school," Mama said. "Carries that giraffe with him everywhere, even to bed."

"I'm glad he's feeling better."

Mama was here to chat, and Goth and I would not escape it. I slid a chair closer to Goth and sat.

Goth took a sip of tea. "Wow. This is amazing."

"Damn right it is," Mama said. "Eva, what do you do in the city?"

"I'm an artist, and I sell my paintings in the square."

"Wonderful! Where ya from, *chère*?" Mama asked.

I remained silent, drank my iced tea, and enjoyed learning more about Goth by way of Mama Tess's interrogation. I smiled when Goth cracked a joke that made Mama Tess laugh to the point of tears. I wondered if Goth was one of those people who made friends with anyone. I realized I liked her more than a little but did not appreciate the ridiculous fluttering in my chest that this thought created. At least I didn't start coughing.

Chapter Thirty

Goth and I walked Mama Tess out, and once Mama's car was on the long driveway to leave the estate, I grabbed my things from the car before Goth and I headed back in. I walked up the stairs with her beside me.

"I'm quite happy to have been adopted by Mama Tess," Goth said.

"She's the kindest person on the planet. Never married. Never had kids. She claims half of Jardin as her own."

"And the other half?"

"She hasn't met them yet."

Goth laughed. "Sounds about right. So, you're not related to her."

"Uncle Jack and Mama Tess were cousins. I'll know if I'm related to her once I get the results of the DNA test."

"Gotcha. You're doing better on these stairs than you were on mine."

"Far fewer steps, and the balcony stroll to get to the next set gives me time to breathe."

"And admire that chandelier," Goth said, nodding at the massive centerpiece of the house.

"Mother loved that thing."

We reached the third floor, and I pulled the key for the

study from my pocket. Goth leaned over the rail and gazed down.

"Wow, quite the view from up here," she said. "Quite the fall, too."

"I wouldn't recommend making a leap from up here. The marble floor below won't be a soft landing."

"Not at all." Goth straightened. "You grew up in this house?"

"My first six years; that's all."

"Hmm."

"What?" I asked.

"It seems kinda sterile. I mean, it's big with plenty of room for a kid to run around in, but …"

"It doesn't feel like a home."

"Yes!" Goth said. "That's it."

"It wasn't a home." I unlocked the study and entered. A shiver rippled through me to be back in this room.

Goth glanced around the room, then went to the maps with pushpins and thread on the wall.

I closed the door and flipped the lock. A locked door would keep Dead Hanna and Shadow Man out, right? I shook my head, hating this foolishness and my fear of things that didn't exist. I opened my bag and pulled out Uncle Jack's notebook of coordinates while noting Goth was watching me.

I decided to get it over with. "Here's the quick version of my past. My father built this place for my mother. I was born. My father was a cold, distant man, and my mother suffered from unhappiness and depression when I was a kid. I had a few friends. One of them was kidnapped and later found dead. My parents died not too long after in a plane crash in Manchac Swamp, and I got shipped to Boston to live with my mother's sister, who was an absolute fucking horror. I turned eighteen, left my aunt, inherited all this crap," I said, waving my hand.

"And I refused to ever come back … until I found out Uncle Jack had died. He was murdered. It remains unsolved. And he may be my biological father."

"Fuck, Janie. That's a lot of hard shit to go through."

I held up the notebook with the coordinates in it. "This book you've seen before. The coordinates."

"Yeah."

"The points on those maps match up with what's in this book."

Goth shifted her gaze to the maps. "Do you know what they mean?"

"Blue pins are where the kidnapping of a child took place. Black pins are where the body was discovered."

Goth faced me, her mouth slightly open.

"Not all blue pins have a matching black pin because those were ones where a body was never recovered."

"Awful. How does this impact you?"

"Let me back up a bit," I said. "Uncle Jack left some things for me in his will, including handwritten letters. In them he tells me about his affair with my mother and that I'm his daughter."

Goth nodded.

"He also left me a puzzle box that contained a flash drive. The documents on the flash drive are research. He thinks someone local to Jardin, or in the immediate vicinity of Jardin, is involved in all these kidnappings and killings," I said, gesturing to the maps.

"Whoa," Goth said.

"If Uncle Jack suspected someone in particular of being the killer, he didn't mention it in any of the files."

"What do you think?"

I sat on the desk. "I like to see things for myself, so I did the test with my DNA and the DNA from one of Uncle Jack's nieces."

"The cop?"

I nodded. "I don't know how I'll react if he is indeed my father. Hell, I don't know how I'll react if he isn't. I'll sort that mess out when I need to. But I'll know if Uncle Jack really is my father or not once those results are back."

"What about the rest?"

"That's harder to prove. I have more digging to do, but I'm on limited resources out here except for notebooks and the flash drive. I can do phone calls if I'm outside or halfway hanging out a window, and even then, the reception can be sketchy."

"You mentioned there being more than one notebook."

I slid off the desk and grabbed the other one from my laptop bag. I passed it to Goth. "It's a money ledger of sorts of the cash my biological father, Henry, kept in the safe … I think. I don't yet know exactly what it is."

Goth flipped through the pages. "Some of these dates go way back. Cross-referencing the dates with the children might show some correlation."

"Didn't think of that. Great idea."

"Is there a particular reason you haven't given this to your cop cousin—your *maybe* cop cousin?"

"Several."

"Do you trust her?"

"I don't know. Family ties get weird in the South."

"God, do they!" Goth said, then chuckled. "It's okay. I know what you mean." She handed the ledger back to me. "There's something else you're missing here, Bougie."

"What?"

"I'm not making accusations …"

"Fine. What is it?"

"Jack has his info on the flash drive. Henry had the notebooks of money movements and coordinates of the children from where they were taken to where they were found. Jack thought it was a Jardin local killing the kids."

I nodded.

"What if Henry is the killer?"

"You think it's Henry?"

"Or Jack."

My anger flared. "Uncle Jack would never—" I stopped when Goth held her hand up.

"You like to see things for yourself. You just said it. Remove the history you have with these people and examine what you have in front of you. Maybe only one of them is the killer. Maybe they both are. Maybe none of them are."

I opened my mouth to argue but snapped it closed. I didn't have enough information to make any kind of real conclusions at this point. I was going off only what Uncle Jack had said and hadn't been looking at things without Uncle Jack's opinions in the mix. "Shit. You're right."

"Also consider the implications that *you* have all this information with you and no one else."

"What? Like I killed these kids? Some of these dates were before I was born."

"I know. All I'm saying is that you need to think of how things can get misunderstood or misconstrued. Jack left you information but didn't give it to the police. He didn't give it to his own cop niece."

I groaned and closed my eyes for a moment. Fuck! Goth was right again.

"Why was it important for you to show me this?" Goth asked.

I hesitated, considering my answer. I could lie, but I didn't have a good one ready to use. "Because I'm the only one who knew this crap, and I guess I wanted an ally."

"You have one. I can't help you with the research though. I

have to head back to the city soon."

"I know. I'm not asking you to stay out here and get in the middle of this with me. I'm glad someone else knows about this too."

Goth took my hand. "Are you in danger? Does having this stuff put you in danger?"

"No, I don't think so …"

"But?"

I cast my gaze down, feeling the tightening belt across my chest again. "Do you believe in ghosts or that places can be haunted?" Oh, God, what was I doing?

"I mean, in general," I said. "Not like this place." I despised the nervous laugh that escaped me, wishing I appeared more confident in whatever silly game I was trying to play now to prove I was sane. I was on the verge of coughing.

I removed my hand from Goth's to fold my arms across my chest … my meager attempt at self-protection. "I do mean this place. I don't know if it's my imagination fucking with me or this place is straight-up haunted like Uncle Jack's house."

"Interesting," Goth said. "Question first. Why did you lock us in this room?"

"You noticed that?"

"Yep."

"It wasn't to murder you."

"No, I know. Besides, if you came at me to kill me, I could take you." Goth grinned.

"You'd kick my ass for sure." I took a deep breath and sobered. "Sometimes when I'm in this house by myself, I see things like smoke and hear voices. Sometimes the voice is a child's. I'm sure it's me being overtired or something and blowing things out of proportion."

"You do realize you're gaslighting yourself?"

"Yeah. But I'm also trying to make sense of things that

make no sense."

"Can you understand what the voices are saying? Do they tell you to do things?"

I nodded.

"Do you do what they tell you to do?"

"No."

"What do they say?"

"The, uh, most recent one advised me to kill myself."

"Jesus Christ, Janie. Don't listen to that one. Ever!"

"I obviously *didn't*."

"When did that happen?"

"Two nights ago."

"What about the child's voice? That one tell you to kill yourself too?"

"No. That one asked me to play with her. And sometimes she smiles or waves at me but doesn't say anything."

"The child. She's your dead childhood friend?"

I didn't want to, but I nodded anyway.

"Any of this happen before you left Boston?"

I shook my head. "I'm sorry I asked you out here and dragged you into the muck of my family drama bullshit. The ghosts are nothing. It's probably the wine causing the weirdness at night."

"The police will have access to resources you don't. They can probably put this whole side investigation thing to bed in a snap."

"Maybe. I'll think about it. You didn't answer my question about ghosts, though."

"I don't know that I would say I believe in ghosts," Goth said. "I do believe the Universe is sometimes trying to talk to us but we're too stubborn to listen." She checked her watch and sighed. "Shit. I hate to leave, but I have to get on the road."

"It's okay. I understand." I took her hand and walked her

downstairs.

Once outside, Goth took a few pictures of the wisteria vines and blooms before stashing her phone again. "Sorry," she said. "I promise I'm done."

"I don't mind. I really don't."

"Thanks."

Lina drove up in her personal vehicle while we headed for Goth's car. She parked and met us before Goth got into her vehicle.

"I remember you," Lina said, smiling at Goth.

"Nice to meet you," Goth said, extending her hand. "I'm Eva."

"Lina," Lina said, shaking Goth's hand. "Pleased to meet you officially this time."

"Yeah. It was a little hectic in the hotel room before," Goth said, grinning.

My face felt like it was on fire (worse than it was from walking outside into Louisiana's heat) while Goth practically admitted to the police what she and I had been up to the day Lina had showed up. The alcohol and sex weren't illegal, but the pills we had taken and had in the hotel room when Lina came knocking sure as hell were.

"Janie," Lina said, "is this a good time to pick up our text conversation from the other day?"

My mind raced. I had no clue what Lina meant. "Oh! That. Uh …"

"It is," Goth said. "I'm headed out anyway. Lina, Mama Tess left some tea in the fridge."

I picked up where Goth left off. "I'll meet you inside," I said to Lina.

Lina nodded, then left.

I was unamused with Goth's tactic. "I wasn't ready to talk to her yet. Why did you throw me under the bus with her?"

"I needed to get rid of her."

"Why?"

"She didn't need to be around to watch," Goth said.

"Watch wha—"

Goth planted a kiss on me. Her soft tongue so deep inside my mouth took my breath away. Once the initial surprise had passed, I reciprocated, and we made out while leaning against Goth's car.

"Let's get in the back seat," I said. I wanted to be naked with her *now*.

"We'll die of heatstroke having sex inside the car."

"We have plenty of bedrooms in the house. We can use one for a while. Hell, we can use them all. I'll get rid of Lina."

Goth laughed, then gave me a quick kiss. "Sounds like you two have stuff to discuss." She pulled a small, clear plastic baggie from her pocket that contained one pill. "Want this?"

"Jesus, giving me drugs with the po-po here." I wasn't about to refuse though. I slipped the baggie into my pocket. "Thanks."

"Have a good night," Goth said. "I'll check in with you later."

I kissed her, not ready for her to go. My mind filled with a hundred excuses for why Goth should stay or I should go with her, but the only word that came out was "Okay."

I watched Goth's car drive away and wished I was going with her. Instead, I trudged back toward the house.

Chapter Thirty-One

I popped my head into the kitchen. "Give me two minutes. I'll be right back," I said to Lina.

"No rush," Lina said while topping off two glasses of iced tea.

I didn't want to have this conversation about Uncle Jack's death, but Lina was here now. I didn't have much of a choice since I had opened the topic with her yesterday. I darted upstairs and went to the study. I made a quick pass through the room. Everything was how I had left it when I had walked Goth out.

What exactly had I expected? Dead Hanna and Shadow Man moving shit around while I was gone? Pleased that no one was around to see my insanity in action, I locked the door and headed back down.

I dropped into the chair opposite Lina and took my glass.

"Are any other searches needed in this area for the girl?" I asked. "Do I need to plan to vacate again?"

"No. I really am sorry about that."

"It's okay. You didn't know." My thoughts were on darker matters. Whatever parts of the girl's body hadn't been recovered yet were apparently gone forever. Not only had she been taken and killed, but her body had been torn apart too. Sadness for the girl and her family weighed on my mind.

"You asked about Uncle Jacques's case," Lina said.

I almost appreciated the topic change ... almost. "I'm not implying that you and others didn't do your jobs or that you aren't continuing to investigate, but ..."

"But you want to make sure we *did* do our jobs and *are* continuing to investigate."

"Yes."

"Uncle Jacques was killed well outside of my parish, so I don't know everything. Frank was investigated, given his turbulent history with Uncle Jacques. He was confirmed to be out of state at the time."

"Confirmed how?"

"Debit card transactions."

"He could've given his card to someone else to use to make it appear like he was away."

"Yes," Lina said. "That is true but unlikely."

"Why unlikely? Did you confirm it with video that it was him making the transactions?"

"We didn't need to. A witness confirmed he was in the store and made the purchases."

"What kind of store? One that sees only a few customers a day? Or one that sees tons of customers and there is no way in hell someone would remember one shopper from the next, especially days later when the po-po show up asking for a positive ID?"

Lina took a deep breath.

I was pushing too hard on this. I had no business telling Lina how to do her job any more than Lina had telling me how to buy and sell art.

"I'm sorry," I said. "I have too many questions about everything."

"The questions you ask are valid. You might make a half

decent 'po-po' yourself."

"Never."

"Janie, Frank is your uncle. Do you want him guilty for this?"

"I don't *want* him guilty."

"You can see him as a murderer?"

Murder was indeed different from bickering.

"Or are you wanting someone to blame?" Lina asked.

"I don't know," I said, slouching in my chair and not touching my tea. "Yes. I want the asshole who killed him to burn," I said, somewhat surprised by the surge of anger from within.

"So do I."

My heart sank. "I am sorry, Lina. I wasn't the only one to lose him, but I'm acting like I was." My eyes stung, tears threatening to come. "You don't deserve my harassment or badgering. I have no right to tell you how to do your job."

"Apology accepted." Lina offered me a smile, then sipped her tea.

The silence after made me squirm, so I sat up and drank some of my tea though I didn't want any. It gave me something to do.

"You sticking around for a bit or heading back to Boston?" Lina asked.

The paperwork with Mr. Landry was done. I had no reason to stay … Well, I had *one* reason. But that didn't involve papers and lawyers or DNA tests. The dead children mystery had my interest piqued, but even that wasn't enough to keep me in Louisiana. Or was it? No question though, Goth had sent my world into a spin. "I have some things to sort out here."

Lina grinned. "Like Eva?"

"That sorta happened. I didn't plan for … to … um." My face felt like it was on fire.

"You didn't plan to like her as much as you do."

"Yeah. That."

"She's got the Gothic look down, and she seems nice."

"She is," I said, nodding.

"Wow. Everything about you brightened a little talking about her. You *really* like her."

"Well, no. Not like that." Yes, exactly like that. I wasn't ready to handle such thoughts.

"What is it?" Lina asked.

I blinked, returning my focus on Lina. "Huh?"

"You zoned out for a sec."

"Oh. Um." I tapped the side of my head. "I get sidetracked by random thoughts in here. Attention span issues."

"So I'm boring you."

"No!"

Lina laughed. "I'm messing with you."

"Do you want to stay for dinner?" What I should have asked was if Lina wanted to go *out* for dinner. My cooking skills were quite limited. I could handle heating up a can of soup or something—provided there were directions on the can.

"I can't tonight, but thanks for the offer. We'll do dinner before you leave. I promise."

"Sounds good," I said, except I noted sadness inside me. Did I want to spend time with Lina or did I mostly not want to be alone? That question didn't have an answer yet. "May I ask a few more questions about Uncle Jack? I promise I won't be a jerk about them."

Lina nodded, and waved her hand. "Go ahead."

"Were you able to retrace his steps before he went to New Orleans East?"

"Mostly, yes. There were a few gaps in the time line but nothing significant enough to cause alarm."

"Did he ever go to a library or somewhere to use a

computer?"

"He liked going to the library, but that was for reading. After he died, I returned a book to the local library and one to the public library on Loyola in New Orleans."

I figured the libraries had to be how he got access to a computer to create the files on the flash drive since there was no sign that he'd owned a computer. I wanted to visit the libraries to see if the staff could confirm that Uncle Jack used their devices. "What were the books about?"

"Uh, one was on popular ghost stories from around Louisiana. I remember that one only because I flipped through it and read one of the stories. The other one was fiction, a crime novel, I think. I don't remember. You're digging for a lead based off his reading preferences?"

"No. I was curious." Blatant lie. Okay, mostly a lie. "I knew him, but I didn't *really* know him, if that makes any sense."

"He had his eccentricities, sure. I don't know that anyone in the family knew the real Jacques. He was very private at times."

I wished I had not been so selfish with my time and visited him only when it was convenient for me. He also hadn't told *me* that he was my biological father, so I knew the blame didn't rest entirely on my shoulders. I wasn't ready to confront any of those feelings yet anyway, so I switched topics to the banality of things to do in Jardin. I had no intention of loitering in Jardin and getting to know the town, but it was better than talking about a dead girl's body parts in the swamp and my murdered uncle-dad.

Later, I walked Lina out. I watched her drive away, then pulled my phone from my pocket, wondering if I would appear as desperate as I felt if I called Goth now.

"Janie?"

Mike carried a pack of cigarettes in one hand and glanced around me before making eye contact.

"Lina is gone, right?" he asked. "Like gone and not coming back right away?"

"She's not coming back tonight," I said.

His shoulders relaxed and he handed me the cigarette pack. I opened it. Four neatly rolled joints were inside the pack.

"You're a lifesaver, Mike."

"Rough day?"

"More of a weird day. Want to light one up with me?"

"Tempting. I'm meeting Stephen soon."

Shit. I couldn't even bribe someone to hang out with me with marijuana in hand.

"There's a disturbance in the Atlantic," he said.

I blinked. "I don't know what you mean."

"Probably nothing other than a storm system that will turn into a hurricane and swing over to pop Florida, but you never know. It could come this way. Hurricanes Katrina and Ida didn't fool around when they clobbered us before."

"Something like that keeps you alert if there's even a hint of a threat, yeah?"

"Exactly. I've gotta run, but I'll keep an eye on the storm and update you."

"Thanks. And thanks for these," I said, raising the cigarette box.

"You're welcome."

I checked the time. It was too late to visit the local library, so that had to wait until tomorrow. I considered lighting a joint now but opted to hold off.

I remembered something from Uncle Jack's notes. The prior disappearances had gotten almost zero media coverage and only a short stint of police investigation. If Henry had been involved, he had the money to make those things go away. Well, I had the money to make media things happen. I had enough of a signal to make a call, and Mr. Landry picked up on the second ring.

"Hello, Janette. What can I do for you?" he asked.

"Hey, do you know if there is a reward for info on the dead Destrehan girl?"

"There is. Her parents didn't have much money so a local group that searches for runaways and other missing kids put up five thousand dollars for info on her whereabouts when she first disappeared. That's what I heard from one of the TV reports. Why?"

"This group that searches for kids, do they investigate the disappearances or only help search for them?"

"I'm not sure, but I can find out."

"I want to throw some money at this. The girl's killer needs to be found, and more cash may loosen up some tongues. Can you up the reward to a hundred thousand dollars? Make it anonymous. Under no circumstances does my name or the estate get released as the donor."

"Understood."

"And if the family agrees, pay all the expenses for her funeral. Anonymously."

"I'll make it happen."

"Thank you, Mr. Landry."

"Anytime. Do you want to come pick up the DNA results or do you want me to bring them to you?"

"Oh, uh. Those are back already?"

"Any divorces with paternity claims, I always use a certain lab for those types of tests. They know me well and tend to expedite the results."

"Great. I'll swing by your office tomorrow if that works for you."

"It sure does. I look forward to seeing you again, Janette."

I hung up. If there was a group of people that searched for missing children, that was worth checking into, too … not to give them Uncle Jack's research, but to ask a few questions about their work. I also wondered if I was ready to find out if Uncle Jack was really my father. I wasn't sure, but my stomach rumbled, redirecting my thoughts.

I headed inside, grabbed a quick bite to eat, then found the purple mug. I filled it with wine from one of the bottles I had taken from the cellar yesterday. I took a sip. "Damn, that's smooth." I headed upstairs to try to learn a bit more about the ledger and the dates the children had gone missing.

Chapter Thirty-Two

Stealing supplies from the hospital was not all that difficult. Had the killer been going for narcotics, that would've been different. He could get those on the streets easily enough, so stealing drugs from the local hospital wasn't worth the risk. But no one monitored the clear bags used for storing soiled bed linens and towels before they went into the wash.

The hospital used clear plastic bags that dissolved when thrown into a washer. The hot water cleansed the linens and eliminated the plastic … the same plastic he used to wrap the children before placing them into a body of water. The plastic kept trace fibers and other evidence off their bodies after he washed them. Then the plastic dissolved while the body was in the swamp or river. Animals helped that process along when they tore into the plastic to get at the flesh.

He had the perfect system, except he was running low on the clear bags. He strode into the hospital, said "Hello" to the security guards at the front desk, and continued on his way. They knew him, so there was no need to slow and show the credentials clipped to his shirt.

The killer walked through a couple of departments where he was also known. The hospital had security cameras, and none of his movements would create suspicion.

He headed toward the morgue and the bowels of the facility where the soiled laundry was moved into the wash and clean laundry moved out. The noise from the machinery obscured any sounds he made. The killer ducked behind a corner when one of the laundry staff entered with a cart full of dirty laundry brought down from the hospital's patient care units.

The staff person left the cart and headed back out, grabbing a cart laden with clean laundry to bring back up to the units.

The man pulled on a pair of vinyl gloves from one of the many racks on the wall containing boxes of different-sized gloves. He opened the door to the storage room and removed a roll of unused bags. He closed the door and removed the folded gift shop bag from inside his shirt. The bag was tattered on the corners from overuse and being folded in half. He decided to stop back through the gift shop to buy something and get a new bag the next time he was here for an errand other than a supply run.

He removed the purple tissue paper from the inside of the bag and unfolded it. He peeled his gloves off and dropped them into the bottom of the gift bag. The roll of plastic bags went in next and sat heavily in the bottom.

The killer pulled a clean hand towel from a stack of folded laundry. He placed it over the roll of bags, then arranged the decorative tissue paper over it so it showed out the top of the bag like it was a gift. He weaved his way through the lower level of the facility, worked his way back up to the main level, then left.

Another successful supply acquisition was cause for celebration, and removing a sinner from the streets of New Orleans was what he'd do next.

The killer moved through the city's streets, patrolling near the alleys and under bridges where he knew addicts and degenerates loitered. He'd changed into frayed clothes since leaving the hospital so he'd blend in. No one would bother trying to mug him if he looked poor like the others.

He kept a subcompact pistol inside his waistband in case someone got stupid. He hadn't needed to shoot anyone with it yet and had flashed it once a few months ago when a drug-addled idiot wouldn't leave him alone. The addict had retained enough wits to recognize the weapon and be on his way. The killer didn't plan to ever use the weapon, but he would, if needed. He paused, watching a man and woman step into an alley.

He tucked into a shadow near a pile of garbage that also reeked of excrement. The man and woman had something in their hands, but the killer couldn't tell what it was until they brought their hands up near their faces and snorted whatever drug they had. They repeated this process two more times, and giggled together in their stupor.

The man handed something to the woman, and she turned and hiked her skirt up over her ass. She leaned her palms against the wall, and the killer watched the man unfasten his trousers, then proceed to fuck her.

Watching them have sex didn't arouse the killer at all. He didn't know what drug or drugs they had taken, but he'd watch and wait. He was unsurprised when the sex was over after a few minutes.

The man pulled his trousers back up, and the woman tugged her skirt down, then turned to face him. He leaned in to kiss her, but she walked away.

"Bitch," the man muttered.

She flipped him off and never slowed her pace.

The man stumbled while he headed back toward the

street … toward the killer.

The man would've been a potential target, except he headed toward the street and people. The woman walked deeper into the alley and away from others.

The killer hunched his posture, shuffled into the alley, and followed the woman at a distance.

She staggered a few times, and the killer increased his pace. She stopped to lean against a wall, and he approached.

"Are you sick?" he asked.

She eyed him. "You're a big fella."

He didn't respond.

"I'm not sick," she said. "I could use some fun." She traced a finger down the front of his dirty shirt.

"I have pills and crack to create some fun." The crack was far from pure, and he'd laced it with a few other things that would stop a horse's heart.

"I'm in. I'll even give you a free fuck for the crack."

He tried to smile like this tempted him, but in truth, his stomach clenched with nausea. The killer pulled three pills from his left pocket, took the smallest one for himself, and popped it into his mouth. It was a pill for heartburn and nothing more. He offered her the other two, which were impure narcotics.

"Aw, a gentleman." She took the two pills and swallowed them without hesitation.

He removed his lighter and crack pipe from his other pocket. Thunder rumbled overhead and the first raindrops fell.

"Ladies first," he said.

She took the pipe between her lips and he flicked the lighter, holding the flame under the bulb. She breathed deeply, sucking the vapor into her lungs. He didn't stop her when she kept going, taking in more of the poison.

Her balance wavered, and he held her up.

"That's good shit," she said, slurring her words.

The rain fell harder, soaking them both.

"More?" he asked.

She nodded and he helped her take another drag from the pipe. Ear-splitting thunder cracked overhead and she winced. The killer didn't move. She coughed a few times, and her knees buckled. She clung to his trousers.

"I can … I can give you a blow job. In a minute. I need …" She gasped for air. Her eyes widened. "I can't …"

The killer dropped to his knees and stared into her eyes. She was terrified and he smiled, genuinely this time.

Rain fell in sheets now, creating streams in the alley. The killer noted how the rain cleansed the filthy alleys in the same way he cleansed the streets of human filth.

She choked on her vomit, and he turned so it didn't spatter on him. The killer gripped her hair and shoved her face into the shallow stream. She would've died on her own anyway, but he was ready for this to end. No one would question how she'd managed to pass out and drown in an alley flood once they got a toxicology report back. The pills alone could've killed her. The mixture he'd made with the crack … She never had a chance.

Her struggle was short since she was already succumbing to the pipe's vapors. He left her facedown in the stream and pressed the pipe into her hand. He pulled his phone out and took a picture of her. Lightning flashed and lit up the alley. He was alone, and once the alley was submerged into darkness again, he left the corpse behind.

Chapter Thirty-Three

I immersed myself in Henry's notebook of coordinates and the notes from Uncle Jack's flash drive. Uncle Jack didn't have coordinates documented like Henry did, but I had enough details to add different-colored pushpins.

Henry's coordinates were blue for abduction site and black for where the bodies were found, with a thread connecting them. Those I had already set up, and Goth had seen them. I needed to take things a step further.

Uncle Jack had stored screenshots of articles he'd gathered online from news outlet websites or he had digital images from newspaper articles. I guessed he'd gotten them from library archives. The library in New Orleans was far bigger than the local one. I scribbled a note on a piece of paper to visit both libraries. For Uncle Jack's info, I used a yellow pin to mark abduction sites and red for body recoveries, using thread to connect them.

The last yellow pin I stuck into the map was the Destrehan girl's street since she was believed to have been taken during her walk home from school. Per Uncle Jack's notes, her name was Letitia Clark. I ran thread to two red pins since most of Letitia's body had been recovered from two different locations. Nausea washed over me to stick the red pin so close to the Martil estate.

I stepped back and eyed the maps. The blue pins were clustered within a fifty-mile radius of Jardin, with a few outliers. The yellow pins all had dates of disappearances after Henry and my mother died. Up until his own death, Henry had tracked the children with coordinates in a notebook tucked in a safe with a revolver and a lot of cash. Uncle Jack had tracked his research on a flash drive … up until *his* death.

I shivered to realize there were more yellow pins than blue pins. Whatever had been going on and whoever was taking the children, there had been an uptick in disappearances since my parents had died—per Uncle Jack's records.

My shoulders and neck ached, and my wine sat untouched on the desk. I picked up Henry's ledger, stifled a yawn, then put the ledger down. I pulled Goth's pill from my pocket, put it on my tongue, then downed it and the wine in a few gulps.

I locked the study, headed downstairs to retrieve the rest of the bottle, pausing to grab a handful of crackers and sliced cheese from the groceries Mama had brought over.

Crackers, cheese, and wine. This was living it up, right? I chuckled while I chewed and trudged back up the stairs to the study.

I refilled the mug and finished off my snack. A decent dinner would be better, but it would involve labor and cooking that wasn't about to happen.

I pulled up a spreadsheet on my laptop and entered all the abduction and recovery dates, color-coding them to match the pins on the maps. I created a formula to auto-calculate the number of days between disappearance and recovery. I also created a formula to determine the number of days between each subsequent disappearance.

Other than the outliers where a body wasn't discovered at all or ones that weren't found for several months, one to two weeks tended to be the time it took for a body to turn up.

Henry's dates showed anywhere from six to ten months between disappearances. Uncle Jack's dates started off around five months apart then decreased to five to six weeks with the more recent disappearances. If this was all the work of the same person, they were taking kids more frequently now.

Would another child be taken within a month, since Letitia had disappeared almost three weeks ago?

"Shit," I muttered, hoping the increased reward would bring in tips to get the killer caught soon. My heart beat a bit faster, and I welcomed the energized state that Goth's pill created. I grabbed Henry's ledger and flipped through it. I added the dates and payout amounts to my spreadsheet, and I noticed the pattern.

There were five-thousand-dollar amounts on the fifteenth of every month. There were also payouts of ten- to fifteen-thousand-dollar amounts within a week of a disappearance. The payout the week Hanna had been taken was fifty thousand.

The monthly payments could've been recurring bribes. Or maybe Henry was being blackmailed, and that was his payment to keep things (what things?) quiet. Given the volume of cash around her disappearance, I figured Hanna had been the only White kid of the lot. Unfortunately, that made sense.

I jotted another note to confirm if the other missing kids were people of color.

But who had received all that money? Were the payouts still happening and being paid by someone else with Henry dead?

I was at a loss and paced.

I stopped. The financial records were in Henry's office.

I drained my mug, refilled it, then headed downstairs. I stopped on the second floor, turned, and went back up. I grabbed the wine bottle from the desk, locked the study behind me, then started back down again. I might have been the only person in the house, but I had this nagging feeling that I was wading into murky territory the more I poked into the details. And some jackass had drawn a chalk image under my bed. Locking the doors made me feel a little safer.

Digging into Uncle Jack's data was harmless and only Goth knew about it. Harmless. Yeah. It'll be fine.

I stumbled when I reached the bottom floor. Might be a little drunk.

I gazed up through the center of the house. Nothing was melting or bleeding or twisting. The floor wasn't sinking. I grinned to realize that in my stumble I hadn't spilled a drop of the wine. Not drunk enough. I snorted a laugh.

Once in the office, I stopped. The scowling portrait of Henry glared at me.

I strode up to the portrait sitting on the floor and leaning against the wall. I wanted to know what he'd been up to with the cash. I wanted to know if he was somehow involved in Hanna's death. The portrait's eyes followed me when I moved. "Asshole." I flipped it around so it faced the wall.

I left Henry, pulled everything out of the desk drawers, and stacked file folders in piles on the floor by year. I lifted the stack from the year my parents had died and dropped them onto the desk. I rifled through the folder. Taxes, checking and savings account summaries, house repair receipts. Nothing showed anything remarkable.

I flipped through more pages. I found a record of a twenty-thousand-dollar cash withdrawal from a savings account three weeks before my parents died. Half of that amount matched what I had found in the safe.

Where did the other half go?

I got to the month Hanna had gone missing and found a house repair receipt for fifty thousand dollars. I revisited the house receipts to review them again and found another repair for fifteen thousand.

Uncle Jack had always taken care of the estate. I wondered if he was the one getting the payouts. Except I didn't want to believe that Uncle Jack was involved with making kids disappear.

I remembered Goth's words about drawing my own conclusions. I was the executor of Uncle Jack's estate, so I needed to review *his* records to see if he'd deposited any of the cash.

A more prominent question rattled around in my head. What if Henry's receipts were bullshit, and there were never any actual house repair costs that matched the ledger payouts? The receipts could be a cover for something else.

Cash wasn't traceable if there were no bank records. So why would Henry keep the ledger and create fake receipts?

My mind was going in circles, and I had more questions. I drank the wine, then topped off my mug, noting a thunderstorm outside that was picking up momentum. Wind gusts pelted the windows with rain, creating a rapid ticking noise when the drops collided with the glass.

I lost track of time going through the rest of the files, separating out suspicious repair receipts and large bank withdrawals. Once I had finished, I put all the folders back into the desk and picked up my segregated stack.

I carried my now-empty wine bottle and mug back to the kitchen. I held the papers against my body with one arm while I used my free hand on the rail to help steady myself on the stairs.

Outside the study, I fumbled with one hand to remove the key from my pocket. The papers slipped from my grasp and scattered on the floor.

"Goddammit."

I bent to pick them up and toppled to land on my hands and knees. I remained where I was for a moment.

My vision blurred. I gasped when my hands sank into the floor. I yanked them free of the floor and landed on my back. A couple more feet and I would've tumbled down the stairs to the second level. But I wasn't sinking into the floor anymore and considered that a good thing.

I gathered the papers and got them safely locked inside the study.

My watch indicated it was three o'clock in the morning. I was drunk and hallucinating. I picked my way down the stairs to the second floor and wobbled to my room. I flopped onto the bed on my back. Thunder cracked and lightning flashed, illuminating my room for an instant.

The ceiling moved and swirled above me. I was mesmerized until it transformed into the shape of Letitia's face. My chest tightened, and I didn't move.

"W-what do you want?" I asked.

The face smiled at me, and then it snarled. I flung myself off the bed.

I jolted awake with my heart pounding, lying on my back on the bed, and desperate to catch my breath.

Was I really awake now?

I had been awake, but I had fallen asleep. Or had I?

Maybe I had slept and hallucinated in the dream. Was that even possible?

The ceiling was its usual flat, unremarkable surface. I stumbled to the bathroom and splashed water on my face. I was too dizzy to go anywhere else, so I sank to the floor, rested my head against the tub, then closed my eyes.

Chapter Thirty-Four

My stiffness eased somewhat after a screaming-hot shower in the morning, but my stint of sleeping on the bathroom floor had not been kind to my body. Once showered, dressed, and coffee in hand, I headed to Uncle Jack's house.

I stood from his desk and massaged the back of my neck with both hands, cursing myself for allowing the snarling Letitia dream/hallucination to chase me into the bathroom for the rest of the night.

I had found both of Uncle Jack's library cards and had them in my laptop bag. The one for the "local library," as Lina had called it, wasn't in Jardin. It was in the next town over. It didn't matter, because I was going to visit it anyway.

Since I was here, I wanted a look at his bank records and figured they were in the boxes with the tax documents in his bedroom closet. I pushed his bedroom door open and stalled at the threshold, wondering if I truly needed to enter.

Had he and Mother had sex here? Was this where I had been conceived? Did he have other women over?

I shook my head to clear the wandering and useless thoughts, then stepped into the room. I stopped short upon seeing a framed photo of Mother on his bedside table. I hadn't noticed it the last time I'd been in his room.

He'd loved her.

My eyes burned, and then the tears fell. I brushed them away. It shouldn't be so fucking hard to find love and keep it.

My mother and Jack had lost their love between Henry's overbearing bullshit and then Mother's death. The two people on this planet I had loved were my mother and Uncle Jack. Both were dead.

I needed to end this thing with Goth. She'd likely end up dead too if I didn't.

My mood was simple: Fuck it all.

I returned my attention to the closet. I knelt and slid the box labeled as taxes away from the wall. It had receipts and tax records from the last five years, which wasn't what I wanted. I pushed some clothes hanging in the closet aside and found a door about two feet wide and four feet tall. I opened it and used my phone's flashlight to shine it into the space. Numerous boxes were stacked with ranges of years written on the outside. I pulled a few of the boxes out and placed them on the floor in his bedroom.

I went through several of the file folders and bank records. No unusual deposits with amounts or dates correlated with Henry's ledger. I wanted more time to go through them, but I had too much to do today. I hauled the boxes out to the car and into the trunk. Back inside, I closed the hidden door in the closet, shuffled the clothes back to conceal it, grabbed my keys and laptop bag, and locked the house behind me.

Frank waited by my car.

"Good afternoon, Janie," he said.

I checked my watch. Shit. I hadn't meant to spend that much time in the house. Of course, I could've had an earlier jump on the day had I not gotten smashed on wine last night and overslept. No one to blame for that but me.

"Hi, Uncle Frank."

"I was hoping to treat you to lunch today."

"I'm sorry, I can't. I have a to-do list longer than my arm."

"Anything I can help you do?"

"No, but thanks for the offer. Rain check on lunch?"

"Of course."

"Great." I managed a smile, then got into my rental and drove to the nearby library Uncle Jack had frequented.

Once inside the small library, I slowed to observe the interior. Uncle Jack came here. I wanted to see the things he saw when he visited. There were posters about historical society meetings, a neighboring parish's fair, and a sign-up sheet for a bake sale to benefit the library. There was no need to ask for help finding the front desk since it was only a few paces from the entrance. I liked the idea of being in a place that Uncle Jack had visited.

The older White man with gray wisps of hair on his head frowned at me from behind the counter.

I strode up to him and smiled.

"Hi, my name is Janie, and I was hoping you could print out a list of books checked out from here by Jacques Montpelier." I presented him with Jack's library card.

"You're not him, so you don't get anything, miss."

My pleasantness vanished. I reached into my laptop bag at my hip and produced the formal document saying I was the executor of his estate and had power of attorney. "Jacques is dead, and I'm his executor."

"You're too young to be an executor of anything."

"Jesus Christ," I said, trying my best to not lose my shit on this idiot.

"Do *not* take my Lord's name in vain."

"Do *not* fuck with me."

He gasped at my outburst. "You horrible, disrespectful child."

"These are the legal documents that grant me access to his accounts, including this one at this library. Give me the list."

"No woman should ever have control of a *man's* estate," he said while he keyed things into the computer next to him.

I rolled my eyes but remained silent. This wasn't the first time some asshole with a Y chromosome had belittled me for being a woman. It wouldn't be the last.

The printer hummed while it warmed up, and then it spat out the pages I wanted. He handed them to me.

"Are you going to address his overdue fees, too, Miss Executor?"

"How much?"

"Three dollars and thirty cents."

I had four ones, but I pulled out a ten-dollar bill and handed it to him.

His scowl deepened while he passed me my change.

"I'd like a receipt," I said.

He grumbled while he clicked a few things on the computer, and then the printer cranked out another page. He gave it to me, and I was pleased to see a pending balance of zero. This jerk wasn't going to be able to alter the records to resurrect Jack's fines now that I had this paper.

"Do you have a computer here that patrons can use to research things on the internet?"

"No. We had one but it's been broken awhile."

"How long is 'awhile'?"

"Since last summer. The bake sale is to raise money to buy a new one. Unless, Miss Executor, you want to buy one for us."

I didn't bother responding and left.

Once in my car with the air conditioner running, I scanned the list of titles. Most everything Jack had checked out at this library were area history books, including the ghost stories one that Lina had returned.

Another dead end. My middle growled with hunger, and I put the list and the receipt into my laptop bag on the passenger seat.

Food and coffee. Then Mr. Landry.

Chapter Thirty-Five

The exterior of Mr. Landry's office building was nondescript: plain, off-white in color, and bland. The interior was far more interesting. Mr. Landry's assistant escorted me down a hallway. I'd never been here, and I found the design welcoming. Large glass panes allowed me to see into the larger conference room and a couple of smaller meeting rooms. The interior windows had built-in blinds, adjustable to block anyone from looking into the rooms, but today they were all open and the rooms were empty.

The reception area, rooms, and office in general were modest in appearance. The furniture was simple but well built. Chairs had leather seats that looked like they would be comfortable. Louisiana- and New Orleans–themed art hung on the walls. The brightly colored works were a nice contrast with the darker furniture and desks. There were no plaques, awards, or any other things of that sort on the walls or shelves. I liked that he kept the décor modest and not flashy.

"You can wait in here, Miss Martil," the assistant said, gesturing to the meeting room. He was a young, lanky White man whom I hadn't met before. "Mr. Landry will be with you in a moment. May I bring you something to drink? Water? Hot or cold tea?"

"Water would be great, thanks," I said.

"Would you like a cup with the bottle of water?"

"No, thank you. The bottle is fine."

"Yes, ma'am."

He disappeared, and I sat at the table, placing my bag in the seat next to me. The chair was indeed as comfortable as I'd assumed. I examined the artwork on the wall. The pieces were nice but nothing of interest for buying and selling in my galleries. I was more impressed with the icy-cold air-conditioning in the building. I would *almost* need to wear a sweater or other layer if I worked here. Compared with Louisiana's daytime temperatures, I was in Antarctica, and I loved it. A twinge of longing for a Boston winter pricked my chest. Maybe Boston was a version of "home" for me after all.

The young man reappeared with my bottled water. "Here you are. May I get you anything else? Is the temperature to your liking? I know some people find it a bit chilly in here. I can raise the temperature if needed."

"It's perfect. Thank you."

He nodded, then disappeared again. I wondered if he could go teach the library jackass what hospitality, customer service, and general decency were. I would've happily purchased a new computer for the library had I not encountered the horrid human working there.

I took a drink from my bottle and pulled my phone out when it vibrated. I opened a text from Goth to find a picture of a painting in progress. I tapped the image to fill my screen and gaped at the colors and beauty in each stroke that had created vibrant purple wisteria flowers, making them appear to be dripping down the canvas.

Goth had mastered the impasto painting technique. She used thick layers of paint, making the sharper lines woven into the paint with palette knives visible. It was like Goth carved the paint, bending it to her will in a way that I longed to observe in action.

That is GORGEOUS! Truly gorgeous.
I can't wait to see the finished product.
Thanks! I'll show you gorgeous.

A picture of me standing near the bottle tree appeared on my screen. I had never spent much time in front of a mirror examining my looks. I figured I had a decent enough appearance, but in Goth's photo, with the light and colors the sunlight cast on me, I was indeed stunning.

That is beautiful.
You're killing me, Bougie. YOU are beautiful. When do I get to see you again?

I smiled, wanting to see Goth again too.

Soon. I'll be in touch.
Meeting with the lawyer today.
Have fun!

I wanted to spend more time with the photo of the painting, but Mr. Landry emerged from his office. I tucked my phone away and sipped my water. I stood when he entered, and we went through the usual greetings.

He handed me a slip of paper. "This is the contact information for one of the ladies running the search group. Her son went missing years ago and was never found."

"That's terrible."

"She's quite pleasant, and if you call, mention my name. I told her I knew someone who might be interested in helping her group." He held up his hands. "I know that's not what you said, but I wanted to create an 'in' for you," he added quickly. "I figured you would want to talk to her yourself."

"Yeah, that's fine. Thanks." I put the slip into my bag.

He reached into his gnarled, leather messenger bag to pass me a sealed envelope. "The DNA results," he said.

I took the envelope and slid it into my bag. "Thanks."

"Oh. I thought you'd read the results right away."

"So you could put the question to rest about whether Uncle Jack was my biological father? To finally know whether he told you the truth?"

Mr. Landry stared at me. "Uh …"

I sat. Seemed like Uncle Jack's letter saying he'd told Mr. Landry about being my father was true, given the lawyer's stunned reaction. I needed to confirm some additional bits of information. "You may want to sit, too, Mr. Landry. This isn't a quick visit." Once he was seated, I continued. "How were Henry and Katherine's wills structured so I inherited everything?"

"Henry listed Katherine as his primary beneficiary, and Katherine had him as her primary. Henry had the higher net worth of the two, but Katherine wasn't a pauper when the two married. Her father had left her some money when he passed. Not a ton, but some."

"Who was the secondary beneficiary for them?"

"They both listed you as the recipient of everything if they both died."

"Tertiary?"

"If you died before you were eighteen, everything was to be sold off, with portions of cash given to the caretakers of the estate and the rest distributed among a few charities they'd specified."

This seemed odd. Henry had a brother, and Mother had a

sister, yet they got zip? "Nothing going to Uncle Frank?"

Mr. Landry paused.

"What?" I asked.

"He, um. Henry …" Mr. Landry took a deep breath. "Henry's first will after he and Katherine married included Frank. That was before you were born. Later, Henry and Katherine both updated their wills to specifically exclude Frank from receiving anything. They both had explicit clauses in their wills to indicate that Frank didn't get a penny."

"How much later was that change made?"

"A few months before they died. I don't know what had happened, but the day Henry came in here to make the changes, he was furious. Katherine seemed as confused as I was, but she didn't argue or protest taking Frank out of her will too."

"And Katherine's sister, Kim?" Speaking my horrible aunt's name roiled my stomach.

"Kim was included when it came to who would care for you if your parents died before you were eighteen. She wasn't to ever receive money as an inheritance. She received a monthly stipend for your care, and that would go away when you were eighteen unless you decided at some point to either have her adopt you or remain with her after your birthday."

I barked a laugh that startled the lawyer. The mere thought of having my aunt from hell adopt me or of willingly living with her after I turned eighteen was absurd.

I wasn't done with my questions. "Uncle Jack said he couldn't go up against Henry and his money to get paternal rights to me. But once Henry and Katherine were dead, why was I not given to Uncle Jack?"

"You are a Martil, Janette. The wills spelled out where you were to go. That was part of the stipulation for you to inherit everything."

"If Uncle Jack told the truth, a paternity test back then

would have confirmed him as my father."

"I couldn't give you to Jacques. Katherine insisted that Henry was your father, and the documents forbade genetic testing before you were eighteen."

"Forbade? What kind of fucked-up mess is that? You went along with that horseshit and kept me from Uncle Jack so I would get the fucking money?"

"Yes, but you were in good hands, Janette. Kim took care of you."

Rage swelled within me and my heart pounded, not from anxiety but from pure fucking hatred. My hands trembled and I tightened them into fists. Both Mr. Landry and my parents had left me in the care of a monster over some goddamn money.

"Janette?"

I calmed myself a little. "Kim took the money and kept it for herself and the people reporting back to you. The only time I wasn't wearing rags to school was when she made a trip to a donation center to buy more clothes. If they were too small or too big, it didn't matter. I wore them anyway. When I complained, I got beat and locked in a closet. Every card Uncle Jack sent to me got returned. *That* is what was in that sealed envelope he left me. Years of cards sent that had 'Return to Sender' gouged into them."

Mr. Landry's face paled, but I wasn't finished.

"There were two caseworkers and a Boston lawyer in the mix."

"Yes. They were obligated to report back to me on your well-being. They sent copies of your report cards and school photos and only spoke of how well you were doing."

"They fucking lied. Anything less than an A in a class was another beating and … other abuses." I wasn't ready to get into those details with him. "I wasn't allowed to spend time with friends … not that I had any. Being the raggedy-dressed orphan in a rich-kid school made me stand out in a bad way. Were they mandated to put me in that fancy place?"

"Yes."

"Not surprised. If they could've gotten away with it, they would've thrown my ass into public school and kept the private school tuition for themselves."

Mr. Landry reached into his bag and pulled out a notebook. He grasped his pen. "Tell me more."

"Not now. Pull all the financial records and any other correspondences you had with them. Everything. I want everything."

He looked up at me, tears in his eyes. "I'm so sorry, Janette. I had no idea."

"Did Uncle Jack tell you he flew up to see me, and Kim sent him away?"

"Yes."

"And that didn't seem off to you?"

"At the time, no. It's not unusual for a family caring for an orphan to be protective of the child."

"Why didn't you call and talk to me yourself? Or fly to Boston to see me instead of relying on the word of others you didn't know?"

"I ... I, um." He shook his head. "I should have. I'm sorry I didn't. I trusted them as professionals, and ..." He closed his eyes, and a tear slid out the corner of his eye and down his wrinkled cheek. "I failed you."

I remained angry, but neither of us could change the past. "Fix it for me now. Pull every last document I'll need to sue the shit out of those assholes. This is about ruining them forever ... and taking the money back."

He nodded, writing again. "I'll destroy that lawyer. He'll never practice again."

"I want them *all* destroyed. Get the documents."

"Anything else I can do?"

"Yeah. I need a will."

He stopped writing.

"If I die, my personal liquid assets get split. Half gets equally divided up among the caretakers of the estate."

Mr. Landry resumed writing, and I continued.

"The other half goes into the estate itself for upkeep, to continue paying the workers, and to convert the place into a nonprofit safe house for young people being abused or in need of a safe place to live—any color, male, female, trans, gay, straight, whatever religion, or no religion. *Anyone* is allowed … provided they aren't assholes to other workers or residents. Zero tolerance for racism or homophobia or any other version of assholery. The estate is to be self-sufficient and *not* affiliated with any religion or political party, ever. *No one* working or staying there gets to shove their beliefs down someone else's throat. Period. A polite, open discussion is one thing, but someone trying to manipulate another is not tolerated. Any of that shit and they get immediately booted out. Understand?"

"Yes," Mr. Landry said while writing.

"Make that a written agreement for employment or staying there so no one can claim ignorance as a reason for being a dick to someone else."

He nodded.

"Tutors, job training, paid tuition, food, clothes, employment, and whatever else they need, the estate covers it. Louisiana, in general, isn't exactly known for its tolerance of others. Install cameras and hire security to protect those living and working there. This is to be a *safe* place for everyone. If for some reason the estate can no longer sustain itself, it will not take money from any donor or group to keep going. Sell it off and donate that money to other charities with the same ideals."

"Do you know your total net worth, Janette?"

"I know about what my personal net worth is."

"What about the value of the estate and the combined investments Katherine and Henry had that they left you?"

I shrugged.

"Obviously it's not important to you. The estate will have no issues being self-sufficient for a very, *very* long time."

"Good. Get some goddamn internet and a good cell signal set up out there."

The older man chuckled, nodded, and went back to writing his notes. "And your Boston assets?"

I hadn't really thought about those. I would change the will later if needed. "Sell the art and galleries and split that money among those employees. Sell the apartment and everything in it and roll that into the funds for the estate here. Neither Frank nor Kim gets a cent from my shit or the estate's. Ever."

"Anything else?"

"For now, no."

"You want the will done right away?"

"Yes."

"If you want to grab something to eat or have an errand, I will have the draft ready for you in a few hours. We can fine-tune the details for your final review and signature later. I can bring the draft to you to sign when it's ready."

"That won't be necessary. I'll be back shortly before you close. One more question. Why was Kim designated as my caretaker and not Frank?"

"I don't know the specifics or why, but Henry was adamant that you were to never be under Frank's care. That was another specification in his will."

"In the version right before they died?"

"No. As soon as you were born, Henry and Katherine updated their wills to include you as heir and specify Kim as your caregiver."

"What did Henry have against Frank?"

"I don't know."

"Okay," I said, then stood.

He stood too and wrung his hands. I realized I had wrecked this man's world. He'd cared for me from afar, and it was clear he had had no knowledge of the horrid conditions my aunt had kept me in. My heart softened, and I hugged him. He sniffled and squeezed me.

"Thank you for your help today," I said, releasing him.

"I'll take care of everything you asked for and have the will ready. The other papers will take a bit more time to retrieve."

"Oh. Can you also dig up comprehensive financial documents from my parents for as far back as you can get them? Henry kept records of things that I found in his office, but they look incomplete in places." I didn't mind lying about that last part. I wanted to know if Henry had other accounts or done other transactions whose records weren't kept at the estate house.

"I'll get everything I can find."

"Thank you. Sorry, one more thing." I pulled the library card from my bag and handed it to him. "Buy this library a new computer and make sure they know it is a gift from the Jacques Montpelier estate." No sense letting library patrons go without a computer because of the asshole librarian's issues.

"I'll take care of it."

Mr. Landry would walk through fire for me; I knew that now. He had been a victim of my aunt's bullshit too.

Chapter Thirty-Six

After striking out at the New Orleans library, I left to meet Goth. I was out of breath by the time I reached her door. I took a moment to wipe sweat from my face before knocking.

Goth opened the door and smiled. "You made it up and didn't die."

"Barely. Where's the elevator in this place? I refuse to do those stairs again."

Goth took my hand, and we left her apartment. She led me down a long hall, a couple of turns, and another hall before we both stood before an elevator. Goth pushed the button to call the elevator car.

The sound of metal grinding against metal made me wince. Something, I guessed it was cabling, whined while it hoisted the elevator car up. It made a loud *thunk* when it stopped, and the doors screeched when they opened.

"Oh, damn," I said. "I'll take my chances with the stairs."

Goth laughed. "I thought that would change your mind. C'mon. You wanted to see where I paint."

I walked with Goth back down the way we came, my confusion growing with each step. It seemed like we were going back to Goth's apartment until she stopped at the unit next to hers. She released my hand to get her keys from her pocket and unlock the door. I followed her in, my eyes widening.

Six various-sized canvases rested on six easels around the room. Drop cloths taped together covered the entire floor. Paint speckled the drop cloths, and the paintings were all in different levels of completion. Paint tubes, mixing palates, brushes, paint knives, and cups were neatly arranged on a cloth-covered table in the center of the room. The counters in the kitchen area off to the side were also covered with cloth and more brushes. I moved around the room, spending time with each canvas before ending at the one with the wisteria blooms.

"They're all incredible," I said.

"Thank you," Goth said, smiling.

"So you rent your apartment to live in and rent this one as your studio?"

"Makes for a short commute."

I paused, understanding how my remarks about buying and selling her art had pissed her off.

"What's wrong?" Goth asked.

"I, uh, realize how much of an asshole I can be. When I made you mad and you stopped talking to me, I get it now. I had treated you like a starving artist, and you're doing fine without some arrogant turd acting like they can swoop in to rescue someone who doesn't need rescuing."

Goth shrugged. "I'm not angry anymore."

"Yeah, but I understand my error much better now, and I'm sorry."

"It's all good."

"Thanks." This apartment had the same floor plan as the one Goth lived in, so there was another room beyond the living room that served as her painting area. "What's back there?"

"C'mon."

I followed.

"More painting supplies and a futon."

We arrived at the room. It contained a few small tables, paint tubes, brushes, and stacks of blank canvases. The futon was upright in couch form with five books stacked next to it and a bottle of water next to the books.

"No plants?" I asked.

"Nah. I keep the rain forest next door where there is better natural light for them."

"You sell in the square during the day and paint after?"

"Usually, yeah. I sometimes sleep here if I'm painting late into the night."

"Because it's too far to walk next door to go to bed?" I asked, grinning.

"When I only want to sleep for an hour before getting back at it, yeah."

"You're quite the book hound, huh? You have books squirreled away everywhere."

"I'd rather have books than a TV. Do you want to watch me paint?"

"Of course!"

"The wisteria one work for you?"

"Yes!"

Goth chuckled. "My God, you are so frickin' giddy."

I sobered. "I'm sorry."

"Don't be. It's cute as hell."

Goth moved a wooden chair. She instructed me to sit, then put on a paint-riddled apron and prepped her paint. I watched her work and remained silent. Goth made several broad strokes with the paint knife, setting up the background layer, then transferred globs of purple paint onto the canvas to create the next wisteria bloom. I stared, mesmerized by Goth's movements and how she brought the flower to life. I remembered to blink when my eyes burned.

Goth stopped painting. "How is this not boring?"

"It's fascinating."

Goth shrugged and set her brush and paint knife aside.

"What's wrong?" I asked.

"Seems like we could do other things with our time." Goth closed the distance between us and kissed me.

I stood, clumsily kissing her while I moved, intent on taking her to the back room to the futon while my phone vibrated in my pocket.

"Do you need to get that?" Goth asked.

"No."

"You sure?"

"Yes."

Goth reached into my pocket to remove the vibrating distraction. "Landry," she said.

"The lawyer. He'll leave a message."

Goth pressed the option to answer the call, then handed the phone to me.

I frowned but took his call. He updated me on some of his progress while Goth rummaged in the refrigerator. I tried to pay attention to his updates, but I had sex on my mind. When I ended the call, Goth returned from the kitchen with two bottles of water and a bag of sliced carrots.

"How is your lawyer guy?"

"He's working on some things for me and wanted to give me an update. I have to swing back by his office before he closes to pick up papers."

Goth checked the time. "So you need to get on the road soon," she said, and handed me a bottle of water.

I considered putting Mr. Landry off until tomorrow.

Goth snapped off a piece of carrot into her mouth. She held up the remnant chunk of carrot. "Want some?"

I wanted to take her to the futon. "No, thanks."

"How is your research going?" Goth asked.

I grumbled.

"Uh-oh. What's wrong?"

"I keep ending up with more questions than answers. Uncle Jack did his research at the library here. The local one didn't have a computer that worked, so he came to the city. I got lists of books he checked out at both libraries, but nothing stands out from either list. The staff let me use the same device he used. I checked the downloads folder and the recycle bin and got nothing."

"Browser history?"

"A script runs daily to wipe them. He used the microfilm and microfiche archives, but I'd be starting from scratch to try to retrace everything he viewed on them. And I'm not sure that would be useful anyway since he already had pertinent images from his research on the flash drive."

Goth munched on another carrot. "What else?"

I fidgeted with the water bottle before opening it and taking a few sips. Goth ate her carrot in silence (except for the crunching sounds). My stalling wasn't getting me anywhere—not when Goth had the patience of a stone.

"I got the DNA results back, but I haven't opened them," I said.

"Open them when you're ready."

I had expected at least a little bit of prodding to read the results, but Goth didn't seem interested in pressuring me.

"My parents' wills were a convoluted mess, and I need to sort through that nightmare. I'm digging through their financials and found boxes of records at Uncle Jack's house. Those are in my trunk, and I'll go through them later. I found some correlations in that money ledger with dates of when kids went missing. Henry had home repair receipts, some of them for large sums matching the payouts in the ledger."

"Bribes?"

"Maybe," I said, then shrugged. "I don't know yet."

"The place I had lunch at today had TVs on. It's all over the news about the girl who was found dead. Big reward posted, and there's a public memorial for her tonight in Destrehan."

"Yeah. I heard about that."

"You're going?"

I nodded.

"Is Lina going with you?"

"No."

"Do you want me to go with you?"

I lost my voice for a moment. Goth's offer was small yet full of kindness. "I, um. Thanks for the offer, Goth. I appreciate it. I really do, but, um, I'm not sure I'll be in a good headspace with the memorial. I won't be good company." I checked the time and winced.

"You need to go."

"Yeah."

"If you change your mind about the memorial, let me know. I'll go with you, crappy company and all."

I smiled and hugged her. "Thank you. In the midst of all the rotten shit going on in this world, you're like a goddamn beacon of light."

"Nah. You give me too much credit." Goth put her bag of carrots down and took my hand. "C'mon. I'll walk you to your car."

Chapter Thirty-Seven

I was short on time after retrieving my new will from Mr. Landry. I stopped in at a florist shop to place a last-minute cash order to be delivered to Letitia's service. Instead of using my cell phone, which would show as a Boston number, I claimed a dead battery and borrowed the florist's phone to call the woman from the search group.

I gave her a false name and asked her a few questions. Her son had disappeared on one of the dates matching Uncle Jack's records and was one of the yellow pushpins on my maps that had no thread or red pin—he'd disappeared and never been found.

The group was limited in what they did for research other than talk to people door-to-door and post signs. She expressed her disappointment with the media and police efforts to find her son years ago and their ongoing poor efforts for those more recently taken. Other parents with missing or dead children helped with the searches and fundraisers, but they'd never gotten enough attention to their cause ... until this new reward from an anonymous donor.

She asked about my interest in their group, and I lied about being a cousin to one of the children taken when I was also a child. Since the group didn't have anything regarding evidence about the children, they weren't a resource to corroborate Uncle Jack's research. I promised the woman a donation, then hung up.

With my flower order placed, I left the shop, called Mr. Landry from my car, and left him a message asking him to give the group an anonymous ten-thousand-dollar donation. I used the time I had left to find some food and then headed to the service.

I stood on the levee with a few hundred people gathered for the memorial. A minister and others leading the ceremony stood on a small elevated platform while I remained at the rear of the crowd.

A large picture of the girl rested on an easel, and flowers were everywhere around the platform. I overheard some conversation about Letitia. She'd wanted to grow up to be a veterinarian. I couldn't remember if Hanna had ever declared what she wanted to be when she grew up.

A few people spoke to the crowd, sharing their memories of Letitia. One woman, the girl's aunt, tried to speak, but she fell apart with grief. My own aunt would never have shed a tear for my death. The loss of all the cash inflow with my demise, sure—Kim would have done lots of wailing and gnashing of teeth over the loss of the money—but if I had died, it would've been a non-event.

Someone with a deep voice spoke from behind my left shoulder. "You taint this place with your presence."

I turned to find the minister from Uncle Jack's service loitering next to me. "Fuck off," I muttered.

"So full of sin. Sinners burn in hell."

"Louisiana *is* hell," I said, then walked away.

He clung to his precious Bible and moved into the crowd toward the front.

People passed candles, creating an eerie glow on the levee.

There were more people than candles but enough flames to be a fire hazard. The smaller children were given battery-powered plastic candles that flickered like the real thing. A booming voice erupted from the platform, and I looked up, though I already knew the source.

The minister started his show and carried on about the sins of the world and blah blah blah. He was easy to tune out.

I wondered why I'd bothered to come … except I knew why.

Hanna.

My friend had died, and my parents didn't let me attend any services, saying I was too young to understand. Maybe that was true. All the churchy crap would've been beyond my understanding, but it didn't mean I didn't comprehend what it felt like to lose a friend. I sure as hell knew what it felt like to lose my parents and be taken from my home and remaining friends not too long after Hanna's death.

My parents had made some shit decisions, no question. I tried to remind myself that the past wouldn't change, but I harbored so much anger and resentment for, well, almost everyone.

The killer was displeased by the attendance at the memorial. Letitia was a sweet girl, but neither her nor her family were prominent enough in the community to warrant this kind of turnout. Some people came to spectate and pretend to care. Some came because it was a version of a social event. Family members wept. Others had speaking parts during the service.

He could not understand why the Martil heir was there, though. She was a loner and coarse with almost everyone she met … except Samuel. He'd seen her when she first met the boy at Jacques's funeral.

That's when he knew which child he'd take next. The boy was sick. That was no secret in the community. The killer had helped organize some of the fundraisers created for his medical bills. The child was suffering and costing other families money by continuing to exist.

He'd begin organizing his plan tonight to take Samuel soon. Since Letitia had been dead and deposited in the swamp, he was eager to save another child from their maladies. Samuel would be perfect.

Chapter Thirty-Eight

My mind wandered during the service. I was pulled from my thoughts when someone came to stand next to me. I knew it wasn't the minister, because that jackass remained up front. My gaze traveled upward, following the linebacker-sized body until I met Anthony's eyes.

The group moved forward to gather closer to the portrait and platform and sang. I remained where I was, and so did Anthony.

"Why are you here?" he whispered.

"That's not your business."

"You don't live here. This has nothing to do with you."

"Paying my respects to a dead child is a crime?"

He fell silent. Police or not, I wasn't letting him intimidate me.

"Why are you here?" I asked. "You don't live in Destrehan either."

"I'm working. Looking for anyone suspicious hanging around somewhere they shouldn't be. And I run into you."

"You're saying I'm now a murder suspect?" I barely managed to contain my laugh and was thankful for the volume of singers drowning out our conversation.

"Everyone's a suspect," he said, and I scoffed at him.

"Bullshit. You were all interested in my well-being during that storm, but now you're up my ass for something you *know* I didn't do. Lina skulking around out here too?"

He grumbled, then left me. I watched him move along the periphery of the larger group until he disappeared into the darkness. My interest was piqued, though. I glanced around at the others who, like me, were hanging back from the masses.

I recognized Mike and Stephen at the edge of the larger group near the platform. They weren't holding hands and stood far enough apart so they looked more like friends than lovers. I felt bad for them having to hide who they were in public.

I noticed one man moving with a quick stride away from the group and toward the long line of vehicles parked on the side of the road. He had Frank's build, but it was too dark, and he was too far away for me to be sure. Destrehan wasn't that far from Jardin, so it didn't surprise me to see a few people I knew. Southern communities tended to band together when tragedy struck.

I stayed a bit longer, wishing I had been able to attend Hanna's service. Maybe me being here was a way of doing that now. I wasn't sure.

A pair of women with tears on their cheeks approached the singing group, one of them carrying a stuffed pig. My throat closed, and I coughed a few times. The belt around my chest tightened with a quickness I had not expected.

Fuck. The panic attack was coming hard and *fast*.

I hurried toward my car, parked what seemed like half a mile from where I was. I tried to slow my breaths, but this was a losing battle. The panic attack would hit me full on. I jumped into my car and locked the doors. I coughed a few more times, and my head swirled. Dizziness and the inability to take a deep breath threatened to make me pass out.

I squeezed my eyes shut, and images of Hanna, Uncle Jack,

and Mother collided in my mind. The visual of Hanna's stuffed pig came next, and I broke. Tears flowed down my face, and I sobbed into my palms.

By the time I had myself pulled together enough to drive, many of the other vehicles had left.

When I arrived back at the estate, I hurried inside and snatched a bottle of wine. I grabbed the purple mug, gave it a quick rinse to remove most of the other night's dried-up wine stuck to the bottom, then took it with me upstairs, drinking from the bottle on my way.

I reached my bedroom, filled the cup, drained it, then filled it again. I checked under the bed, pleased to find it free of any chalk drawings on the floor.

The carved animals watched me from the top of the dresser. I opened the puzzle box and placed the animals inside. I pulled the lioness from my pocket. I wasn't feeling so brave or strong tonight. I placed the lioness inside the box, then sealed it again.

A few more tears fell, and I slammed more wine down my throat. My phone vibrated; it was a text from Goth.

Hey, checking on you. I'm sure tonight was difficult.
Call or text anytime if you want.

I tossed my phone aside. I was in no mood to communicate with anyone. Hell, it had been hard enough to read Goth's text. My vision blurred when I reached for the bottle of wine.

Maybe I'd had enough. Maybe I'd go to the cellar and drink myself to death. Maybe I would fall down the stairs on the way to the cellar and be done with life that way. I *had* options.

My stomach roiled, and I scrambled for the toilet, reaching

it in time to empty myself into the porcelain bowl instead of onto the floor. I heaved several more times before staggering to the sink to wash my face and rinse my mouth.

God, did my head throb.

I eyed the bottle of wine. I could start over with the drinking and probably puke again, but would that be such a horrible thing? I wobbled, then stumbled, and almost made it to the bed before I fell. I dragged the blanket off the bed, wrapped myself in it, and closed my eyes.

Chapter Thirty-Nine

As much as I had wanted to get a start on digging through Uncle Jack's files, it took me a bit more time to get moving in the morning. I'd barfed up all the wine last night, so I didn't have a hangover, but my mood was shit. Stephen, Mike, and some others were busy in the gardens, mowing and trimming the greenery. It was that noise that had awakened me. I couldn't blame them. They were only doing their jobs. My unraveling at the memorial service was more the cause of my rotten mood today than the noise outside. Sleeping on the floor hadn't helped, either.

I dumped the remaining wine in the bottle down the sink and washed the mug from last night before placing it in the drain rack. I ate a muffin while the coffee brewed. Once the coffee was done, I poured a cup and headed outside. I dropped my ass onto one of the benches near the front door, noting the slight crinkling sound of the folded envelope containing the DNA results in my front pocket since I remained in yesterday's clothes.

I decided I would read the results today ... at some point.

My mood managed to sour even more. The humidity wasn't so bad as to make me start sweating right away, but the air was heavy and damp. I didn't want to be drinking a hot liquid on a hot morning, but I needed to wake up more before I tackled the day.

Granted, I didn't know what I needed to tackle (other than opening the envelope), but I would figure that out later. Seeing Goth again was high on the "to do" list. I'd never replied to her text from last night. I pulled my phone out and sent a quick apology for ghosting her. Goth's reply of "It's all good" made me smile.

I tucked the phone away and sipped my coffee while watching the sheriff's car head toward the house. Once parked, Lina was out of the car and headed my way with quick, determined steps.

"We need to talk," Lina said.

"Good morning," I said, though Lina wore a deep scowl. I took another sip of coffee, pleased that I wasn't the only one off to a rough start. "Want some?"

"No!" Lina said, then softened her tone. "Thanks, though."

I rose from the bench and led Lina inside to the small kitchen. I might not have grown up in the Deep South, but I knew the rules. I poured out my coffee, then poured two glasses of iced tea, handing one to Lina before I sat at the table.

"What's on your mind?" I asked.

"Are you behind this reward?"

Oh, this was going to be fun. "Reward for what?"

"For information on the girl's disappearance and death. It's exorbitant."

"Exorbitant? How could any amount of money be worth more than a child's life?"

"Stop fucking with me, Janie. Did you increase the amount for the Destrehan girl?"

"Her name is Letitia."

"I know what it is! Did you increase the reward?"

"No."

"Did you have someone else do it for you?"

"No."

Lina shifted in her seat, then took a long drink from her tea. "Fine. Be difficult."

"How am I being difficult? You asked me questions and I answered them."

"With lies."

"Don't take this shit out on me. What are you really pissed off about?"

"The money is drawing a lot of attention. Local media picked the story back up—"

"Which they had no business dropping in the first place."

"Yeah, true, but they've got it back. Other outlets statewide have picked it up too. We have people hounding us every time we turn around. The tip line has completely blown up, and we don't have the staff to follow every call coming in."

"And that's my fault?"

"No, but you should've warned me you were upping the amount."

"Would that have changed things with the investigation?"

Lina turned her glass in her hands before taking enough gulps to drain the contents. "A little warning would've been nice is all."

"A warning that I could not have given you since I wasn't involved." Sure, I was lying my ass off, but it was fun. I *maybe* felt a little guilty that Lina's work life had become more problematic as a result of the higher reward, but finding Letitia's killer was more important than Lina's comfort. Period.

"Where were you yesterday?" Lina asked.

"Errands."

"Are you being evasive on purpose?"

"Are you interrogating me on purpose?"

Lina sighed. "I'm sorry. I didn't mean that to come across as an interrogation."

"Except that's what it was. More accusations than anything else." I stood and grabbed the pitcher of tea from the fridge, topping off Lina's glass.

"I came by yesterday and you weren't here. Stephen didn't know where you were."

"Because he didn't need to know that I was running errands. I stopped in to see Mr. Landry in case you need to confirm that with him." I pulled the folded envelope from my pocket and tossed it onto the table. "But maybe that will serve as enough proof. The DNA test is back."

Lina picked up the envelope and unfolded it. "You haven't opened it yet."

"No. Was waiting to do that with you." Another lie, but whatever.

"Why?"

I shrugged. "Misery loves company?"

Lina slid the envelope across the table to me. "I'm here now. You can open it if you want."

The belt of anxiety tightened around my chest, and I coughed. I cleared my throat to try to hide the cough but figured the deputy seated across from me knew I was nervous. I sat again and forced myself to pick up the envelope and open it. I unfolded the letter, unaware that my mouth had dropped open while reading until I tried to speak. "Um."

"What's wrong?" Lina asked.

"Well, we are not cousins."

"Oh, shit, Janie. I'm sorry. I thought for sure Uncle Jacques was your father."

"He is my father." I passed the paper to Lina.

Lina's hands began to tremble as she read the results. This was the problem with DNA tests. Sometimes it dug up things no one wanted dug up.

"Fuck," Lina said. "Half sisters?"

I inwardly smiled.

"No," Lina said. "This can't be right."

Denial. I knew exactly what denial looked like.

"Yep. Half sisters," I said. "I guess the people who mistook us for sisters when we were little weren't so wrong after all."

The side door opened. Mama Tess strolled in carrying a tall paper bag.

"Two of my favorite people in the same room!" Mama said. "Where's Eva?"

I rose and took the bag from Mama Tess. "She's not here today."

"Pity. I could've had three of my favorite people in the same room," Mama said before kissing me on the cheek. "Lina, everything okay, *chère*?"

"Mama, sit with us," Lina said. "We … *I* have questions."

"Don't badger her like you did me," I warned Lina and then placed the bag of groceries on the counter.

Mama Tess sat, and I prepared her a glass of tea. Lina didn't wait for me to sit.

"Mama," Lina said. "Who are my parents? My *real* parents?"

"Oh!" Mama's eyes widened. "This conversation might be best to do later. I don't think—"

Lina waved the paper. "DNA results. Janie and I are half sisters, so don't bullshit me."

Mama's expression changed from one of surprise to a mild glare. "Careful with that tone, Lina," she said, her own tone laced with warning.

I enjoyed watching this event unfold. Sure, Uncle Jack was confirmed as my father, and I'd have to sort through that later. But this ire in Lina was intriguing. And instead of Mama wilting under pressure, she bristled and put Lina in her place. Ah, the Deep South and respecting your elders crap.

Lina relented as I had expected.

"I'm sorry, Mama," Lina said. "I'm confused and want answers."

"Well, it's not some conspiracy against you," Mama said. "Lina, Jacques is your biological father. His brother—your father—was pretty much sterile, so Jacques served as a donor. Your mother didn't cheat on your father. They continued to try to get pregnant and also used Jacques's sample, so no one really knew who your biological father was … until today."

Lina fell silent and leaned back in her chair.

"The man you grew up with raised you as his daughter, Lina. Don't forget that. You were and always will be *his* daughter."

Lina didn't speak, and I sat.

"Jacques is your father too," Mama Tess said to me.

"Yeah. He and my mother did have an affair."

Mama nodded. "I didn't know until after you were in Boston. Jacques was a mess. I had suspected he and your mother were close. He was a broken man after she died and you were gone. He'd had a rough night and told me about being your father."

"Rough night? How?"

"He was in jail and called me to get him out. Small town, and everyone knew he'd been arrested during a bar fight with Frank."

"Oh, shit. You said they argued a lot. That's different from it getting physical," I said.

Lina sat up. "What did they fight about?"

The cop was back in the conversation, and I didn't mind.

"I don't know for certain," Mama said.

Lina tilted her head.

"Don't you give me that look!" Mama said. "He didn't tell me why they fought … well, not exactly. Jacques had been drinking and went to the bar since Frank liked to hang out there. Jacques picked the fight, accusing Frank of killing Henry and Katherine for their money, which was absurd since everything went into a trust for you, Janie. Anyway, both men took a beating, but since Jacques started it, he went to jail. Frank didn't press charges, and Jacques called me early in the morning to ask for a ride home. He told me about the affair during the drive."

"What do you think about his accusation against Frank?" I asked.

"I don't know that Frank would kill his brother and sister-in-law," Mama said.

"The plane crash was deemed a piloting error," Lina said.

I nodded. "It was. But that doesn't mean there was never a bribe or cover-up to hide the truth."

Lina shook her head. "Are you always so cynical?"

"Are you always so gullible?" I asked.

"Okay!" Mama said, and stood. "You two sure have the bickering like sisters mastered. Janie, I brought some more food for you. Try to eat it this time before you wither away into nothing." Mama Tess left, having never touched her tea.

I poured the glass out, then starting putting away the groceries. Lina remained seated and seething.

"Want anything to eat?" I asked.

"No." Lina headed for the door, then paused. "But thanks for the offer."

I was alone again. Uncle Jack was no longer an uncle. He was confirmed as my father, and I had no idea what to do with that information now that I had it.

Chapter Forty

I paced in the kitchen, then went outside. The heat almost chased me back in, but I needed to walk off some of this nervous energy and think. I headed out into the gardens. The sun beat down on me, causing me to change course for areas with more trees. Thoughts bounced around so quickly that I couldn't grab onto one long enough to think it through.

I stopped at the bottle tree and opted to sit on the ground beneath it. The slightest of breezes made the bottles sway a little but not enough for them to touch each other. Occasionally there was an *oooooo* sound when the breeze flowed over the top of a bottle, and it made me smile—not because of the supposed trapped evil spirit inside, but more because this was probably Unc—Jack's—handiwork I sat under. That brought my mind into focus.

My identity had shifted, and I wasn't sure what that meant. Mother was half Creole and half Black. I never knew Henry's genetic makeup, but he must have had Black heritage, given the texture of his hair and color of his skin. I considered myself biracial like Mother, and I even had light brown eyes like her, except mine had flecks of green in them.

But Jack was my father, and this changed the game. Jack's father was White and his mother was Black. Jack had had dark hair, dark skin, and beautiful hazel-green eyes—the same eyes as Lina. I had always assumed Lina's and Jack's eye color was similar because she was his niece. But that had changed too. Granted, I didn't remember what Jack's brother or Lina's mother looked like, but it seemed Lina's eye color had been passed on to her by Jack.

My situation was the same. The man I had believed to be my father was not. The man I had called an uncle all my life was my biological father. And the inexplicable green in my eyes was now explained: Jack.

This meant I was not biracial. I was Creole, Black, and White. Of course, being Creole meant I was a mix of Spanish, French, and African peoples. But this new information about Jack stunned me.

I wondered if I should get a comprehensive DNA test to learn more about my true ancestry, but I figured that might be best left alone. With my luck I'd find out that I was also part llama or something.

A pang of guilt stuck me for being harsh with Lina.

Half sisters. Shit. Never saw that one coming … and neither had she.

I sent Lina a text.

> *I'm sure this new information is baking your brain like it is mine.*
> *I'm sorry for being an ass earlier.*

I didn't wait for a reply and stuffed the phone back into my pocket. I dropped my head into my hands. The emotional roller coaster of the last few weeks had been brutal. Throw in some research on dead children and body recoveries, of course I would start hallucinating. All the stress and then being in Louisiana and surrounded by this insanity explained Dead

Hanna and Shadow Man.

It was stress. That's all.

This brightened my mood, and I made a mental list of everything I wanted to do today. The first was a phone call, and Goth picked up on the third ring. But instead of hearing her voice, I heard a few things fall over and Goth swearing.

"Fuck. Hang on a sec, Janie."

I winced, figuring I had interrupted Goth while she was painting, but then I heard other voices and a distant siren. Goth was in the square selling her art.

"Okay. Sorry about that," Goth said.

"If I'm interrupting you, we can talk later," I said.

"Nah. I'm clumsy and knocked a bunch of things over going for my phone. What's up?"

"Read the DNA results with Lina this morning. Jack is my father, and he's her father too. We're half sisters."

"Oh! That was unexpected, right?"

I chuckled. Unexpected was an understatement. "We were both surprised. It's taking some time to sink in."

"Does this revelation make you happy?"

"I'm not sure. Maybe. It's weird."

"The tectonic plates have shifted under your feet, so it's understandable to need some time to sort it out."

"I'm glad Henry isn't my father. He wasn't a kind man to me, but given what I have learned about him, I guess he didn't hate my existence, since he kept me in the will. I wish I'd known about Jack before he died. I wish he had told me years ago. It would've changed things, and—"

"Hey! You can't change what's already happened."

"Yeah. I know," I said, sulking.

"You *can* learn to live with it and change how you do things going forward."

"I guess so."

"I'm not trying to dig into your life, but it seems like you've been living on your own and by your own rules for a long time. Some of the rules have changed. You lost the last person you considered family and have gained some new ones. Lina's your half sister. You two have some catching up to do."

"Yeah." I had a half sister, and I smiled.

"Keep moving forward."

"Yeah." I was about to invite Goth out to the estate, but a voice asked her a question.

"Hang on," Goth said. After a few seconds, she spoke to me again. "I've gotta go, but we'll talk again tonight."

"Sounds good."

I ended the call and stared at the phone, delaying doing the rest of my mental list. I headed back toward the house, retrieved my keys, then started bringing everything in from the car. It took a few trips to bring all the boxes of records from Jack's house upstairs to the study. I grabbed the envelopes from Mr. Landry from the car, one of them containing my new will. I pulled the empty water bottle from the driver's-side door.

A golf-ball-sized red flannel pouch with a string tying it closed was also in the cup holder. I had never seen it before, and removed it. My skin crawled and my heartbeat ticked upward with the thought that someone had been in my car. I considered tossing it, eliminating it from my life the way I'd wiped the chalk drawing under my bed off the floor.

I decided I would do better at locking doors, including car doors.

I pressed the fabric between my thumb and finger and felt something hard and something softer inside the pouch. I didn't know what it was and carried it with me back inside, now that the car cleanup task was complete.

I tossed the empty bottle into the recycling bin in the kitchen and grabbed a glass of iced tea. Once in the study, I locked the door behind me and placed the pouch and my glass on top of the desk. I eyed the pouch, then untied the string.

I spread the flannel open. I had no idea what lay before me. Particles of the orangey dust I had found near doorways were in the pouch along with two small flowers with slim, white petals. I recognized a bay leaf and a sprig off a cedar tree. There was also a fine, red powder. I touched my fingertip to it, then sniffed it. It smelled spicy, like some kind of pepper, but I wasn't sure. I probed the contents more with my finger, and a clear residue remained on my fingers after touching the flowers. I sniffed it, then rubbed my thumb against my fingertip.

It was oily with the scent of lavender. I lifted the single strand of black hair from the mix of items. It was the right length to be one of mine, but it could have been from anyone.

The largest item in the pouch was an oval charm with a loop on the top so it could be worn on a necklace. It was metal, heavy like pewter, and had a person on it who resembled an image of one of the Catholic saints. I had been dragged to mass as a child, but I didn't know the specifics about any religion. I did know that I wanted nothing to do with them.

I flipped the charm over, but there was nothing inscribed on the back. I set it aside on the desk to look it up later, then re-tied the pouch with the rest of the contents inside. Whoever was putting the dust by the doorways had to have left this pouch too. I wasn't frightened by the pouch showing up in the car door, but the bullshit of someone fucking with me was getting old and irritating.

I took a long drink of tea before diving into the boxes I'd taken from Jack's house.

Chapter Forty-One

I stood among the numerous boxes from Uncle Jack's house. Dad's house? No. I wasn't ready to call him Dad yet. Jack. I would refer to him as Jack.

I muttered a string of profanities. I wasn't sure why I was aggravated by *not* finding anything incriminating in them. Jack's financial records showed nothing unusual. The large deposits were always the same date and same amount, matching the payments from the funds for his job overseeing the estate's upkeep in my absence. Every three months he'd move the same amount of cash from his checking account to a savings account that did nothing but receive the deposits. It never had any withdrawals on it.

I left the boxes for the two envelopes on the desk near the flannel pouch. I placed the one containing my will aside. I'd already reviewed and signed it yesterday when I'd picked it up from Mr. Landry. I opened the second envelope and removed the copies of the wills and documents he had compiled on Henry, Katherine, and Jack. He'd said he'd have the rest for me later.

Jack's files confirmed that the savings account number matched the account Mr. Landry had converted into a fund for his designated charities.

Instead of fixing his own house, he set money aside for those who needed it more. He couldn't have been killing kids with that kind of generosity.

Unless he did it out of guilt.

Fuck. That was possible.

Though I tried to remove my personal feelings from the situation, I did not see Jack as a murderer.

I packed up Jack's boxes while lost in my thoughts.

Henry's shady payouts disguised as estate repairs didn't make him a murderer either. Could he have been the killer up until the date he'd died, and then someone else took over? Or did he have a helper who became the new killer? Maybe there were always two killers and Henry happened to be the one paying to keep things suppressed. Or Henry was doing suspicious shit with his money that had nothing to do with dead kids.

If the payouts were bribes, who continued paying them after Henry was gone, and what were they for?

That's where the paper trail ended.

I stacked the boxes by the door, then grabbed my keys. I shuffled the boxes to the balcony, locked the study, then headed down the stairs with the first box.

Stephen called to me from the ground-level entryway. "Miss Janie, can I carry that for you?"

"I've got it," I said, though he was sprinting up the stairs to meet me on the second floor.

"I'm happy to help," he said, arms outstretched to take the box.

I had several boxes to move back to the car. "Tell you what. I'll bring them down and hand them off to you here. Stack them by my car, and I'll load them into the trunk from there."

He nodded and took the box from me.

"Thank you," I said.

He had already started back down the stairs. "Anytime!"

I went back up, grabbed the next box, and Stephen was waiting for me by the time I made it to the second floor again. We repeated the handoff process until the last box was out of the house. I went to the car, wincing with the intolerable heat. Beads of sweat formed on my face and back. Stephen's skin showed a hint of glistening. I'd start melting soon.

He helped me load the boxes into the trunk, and I was grateful he didn't ask about the contents. I closed the trunk once we were done.

"Thanks again," I said.

"You're welcome. Anything else I can do for you?"

"No, Stephen, thank you." I wiped at the sweat trickling down my face and wanted to scratch at the beads sliding down my back. "I truly don't know how anyone lives in this shit."

"It's easier if you've grown up in it."

Though living with my aunt had been horrible, I wasn't sure if growing up in the balmy South would've been better. No. Hot weather would've been better than her abuse.

But if I had grown up here, would I have become one of the dead kids?

"Miss Janie? Are you okay?"

My eyes snapped into focus on him. "Yep. I was distracted for a sec. Want some tea?"

"No, ma'am. I'll get back to my other duties."

I parted ways with him, happy to retreat inside. I downed a glass of iced tea, then refilled it before heading back upstairs. Once locked in the study, I went to the maps on the wall.

Jack had also been alive during the dates of kids disappearing, but he could not have killed Letitia from Destrehan. She had gone missing after Jack was killed.

Unless she wasn't reported missing until after he was dead.

If that was the case, Jack could have killed her, but the body didn't turn up until after his funeral. Maybe Jack had a helper who dumped the body after he was killed. Maybe the helper killed Jack.

Could Jack have been murdered by someone who found out he was killing children?

Or was he murdered for confronting someone else about killing the children?

Perhaps he simply was in the wrong place at the wrong time and got mugged.

"Fuck!" I stopped pacing and lowered my head into my palms. My head pounded, and I was hungry, too. I didn't believe the time, but the darkness outside the windows didn't lie.

I headed downstairs with the empty tea glasses from the study and put them in the sink. My mind went down more rabbit holes while I washed the glasses.

Per Mama Tess, Frank and Jack had a long history of dislike with no one seeming to have an explanation for it except for Frank, since he was the only one alive.

A knock at the door yanked me from my thoughts, and the glass in my hand slipped and clattered when it bumped against the bottom of the sink.

I carried the dish towel, drying my hands on my way to the door. I opened it and smiled upon seeing Stephen and Mike.

Mike extended his hand, palm up, holding three rolled joints.

"Oh," I said. "You are a prince!"

"Or princess," Mike said.

I laughed, hugged them both, then ushered them inside. "Come in. I was about to throw something together for dinner. Hungry?"

"We ate earlier," Stephen said. "But don't let us stop you."

"I won't. I'm starved."

I opened a bottle of wine, pouring them both a mug and filling my purple mug.

"Honey, we gotta get you some wineglasses," Mike said.

I chuckled. "Coffee mugs work."

"It'll be a struggle to get more low-rent than that, Janie," Mike said.

"Babe," Stephen said to him, "she's our boss."

"Nonsense," I said. "None of that employer-employee shit tonight." I placed the bottle in the center of the table between them. "And Mike's not wrong. My wine mugs are indeed low-rent." I wasn't sure why I was so thrilled to have company tonight. Researching murders had never done anything to brighten my mood, so I assumed their presence was the reason for my elation … That and we were going to get high together, too.

I threw a frozen meal into the microwave, and we chatted about the town and drank while I ate. I opened another bottle of wine, and then we headed up to the rooftop deck.

We shared a joint, and I welcomed the wave of relaxation washing over me. I would've enjoyed it more, except the tingling in my feet and the buzzing noise in my ears caused some alarm.

"Does the weed make you hear sounds like bees?" I asked.

"Um, no," Mike said. "But some folks react differently."

"It's in my head then." I giggled, then dissolved into laughter.

Stephen giggled too.

I sobered when the tingling traveled up my legs and started in my hands. The buzzing grew louder. Sweat formed on my brow. The nighttime temps were much cooler than daytime ones, but it wasn't hot enough tonight to make me feel this awful.

"You don't hear that?" I asked.

Mike laughed, then quieted. "You're serious?"

I wiggled my fingers. "Any tingling for you?"

"No," Mike said. "Have you smoked one of these before?"

"Not since we shared the one the other day."

"The one we smoked, the ones I gave you before, and the one tonight are all from the same batch of plants," Mike said.

"Did you put anything else in them?" Stephen asked.

Mike glared at him. "I would never do such a thing. That you have to ask—"

"I'm sorry," Stephen said. "I was clarifying."

"Bullshit. You accused me of doing it."

I tuned out their arguing, wobbling when I stood. Wine. Weed. Maybe the combination was the problem. Except a reddish fog rolled in over the estate grounds, covering the gardens and moving up and over the larger trees, engulfing them. The fog thickened and morphed into blood-red smoke when it neared the house.

I leaned against the rail and gazed down.

"What's wrong?" Stephen asked. "Are you sick?"

He was at my side, and Mike stood at my other side, bookending me.

"No?" I wasn't sure if that was the correct response. "Do you see the fog?"

"It's not foggy," Stephen said. He glanced at Mike, who agreed with him.

"Smoke?" I asked.

"Something's on fire?" Stephen asked.

"No." I winced and lowered my head into my hands when the buzzing worsened. When I opened my eyes, I was lying on my back on the roof deck with Stephen and Mike hovering over me. The bloody smoke rolled up the roof to the deck, flowing over both men.

Dead Hanna stood at my feet; she smiled at me.

I scrambled back from the dead girl. The deck rail prevented me from falling off the roof.

Only you can see me, Janie, Dead Hanna said.

"No," I groaned. "I don't want to."

"Miss Janie, what's wrong?" Stephen asked.

Stephen was shrouded in red smoke, but it was his voice amid the buzzing loud enough to make my head vibrate.

"She's here," I said. "You see her, right?"

"No, ma'am," he said.

How could they not see her? She was right there! The men were red smoky outlines, but Dead Hanna's form was clear, looking exactly like she did when we were children.

A palm touched my forehead. "Stephen, she's burning up. She's having some kind of reaction to the weed."

"But we aren't," Stephen said.

"It doesn't matter. *She* is."

Dead Hanna neared. *Janie?* She extended her hand to me.

A whimper escaped my throat, and I curled into a fetal position, tucking my head into my arms. Dead Hanna's ghost had never threatened me before, but I was losing my shit. I didn't know what was real and what wasn't anymore. "Stay away."

"Us?" Stephen asked.

"Her. Make *her* stay away."

"Shit," Mike said. "Let's get her downstairs."

"Does she need a hospital?" Stephen asked.

"No!" I said from my tucked position. "No hospitals." If I went to a hospital, they would never let me leave.

"Okay," Mike said. "We'll take you to your room."

"Can I keep my eyes closed?" I asked.

"Of course," Mike said.

The sound of hundreds of little feet crawling over the deck began. Then the crawling was *on* me. I cracked one eye open and gasped. Spiders were everywhere. Both my eyes were now open and wide. The spiders were on the deck, on my legs, on the two men. I tried brushing them off my arms, but they came right back. "Get them off!"

Mike's shadowy form leaned close to me. "Close your eyes. Good. I know it seems like something is on you, but you're safe, Janie. We won't let anything hurt you. I promise."

I squeezed my eyes shut and tried to ignore the sensations on my skin and the sounds inside my head.

They helped me off the roof deck and down the ladder to the third floor. Once indoors, they guided me down the next set of stairs to the second floor where my bedroom was. Only then did I open my eyes. Dead Hanna was gone, but the buzzing remained and the floor became liquid, pulling my feet into the wood. I gripped Stephen's arm.

"The floor is melting." My trembling worsened when blood dripped from the ceiling and streamed down the walls.

"Close your eyes," Stephen said.

I did, and he put his arm around me to guide me to the bed.

Someone put a cool, damp washcloth on my forehead.

"I'm sorry," I said.

"It's okay," Stephen said. "You're having a weird reaction to the weed. We'll stay until this passes."

Weed had never done this to me before. Sure, I'd had odd things happen lately when drinking wine, but they had drunk the same wine as me.

I was going insane. That much was clear.

I lost track of time in my misery, but the men stayed with me and I fell asleep.

Chapter Forty-Two

I woke with Mike sleeping next to me and Stephen asleep in a chair near my bed. My rotten evening had ended, and I felt shitty. I slid out of the bed and tiptoed to the bathroom.

Stephen woke and checked on me while I washed my face. I assured him and Mike that I was fine now and apologized for last night. Stephen wanted me to be seen by a doctor. That wasn't happening. I did give the cigarette pack containing the joints Mike had given me back to him.

Once the men were gone, I showered and left the house in search of hot food that I didn't have to cook. My mind remained foggy, but I was certain coffee and food would fix that.

My middle rumbled as soon as I walked into the diner Uncle Frank and I had eaten at before.

Uncle Frank. He wasn't my uncle—not biological, at least.

Before I could get too mired in those convoluted thoughts, I was seated at a table for two, had placed my order without needing the menu, and was sipping on my coffee. My stomach complained more with each passing minute.

I glanced around the diner, pleased to see a mix of families, couples, and solo patrons like myself.

The door opened and three deputies strolled in. Some of the

customers and staff waved or shouted a greeting to them. Most of these people were locals, and the cops were frequent fliers here. I had second thoughts about my choice of places to eat. The three men each wore a different uniform, indicating they were from three different parishes. An empty table for four was next to me, and there was one on the other side of the room.

Please don't seat them here.

The host greeted them, then gestured in my general direction.

Fuck.

The two White deputies were about the same height and build. They appeared to be related, and one had bushy eyebrows and the other had a mustache. Eyebrows said something that made Mustache chuckle. The third, a tall Black man, stifled a yawn.

Night-shifters. During my early years of college, I worked nights to go to school during the day. My inheritance was enough that I didn't need to work, but I had wanted to make things happen on my own terms instead of cruising through life on my dead parents' money.

These men were coming off night shift, and their feet dragged a little when they walked. I squirmed when they sat so close to me, and I kept my eyes on my coffee cup to avoid drawing attention to myself

"Mornin'," the Black deputy said.

"Good morning," I said, then returned my attention to my coffee.

"Fonty is already trying to get some," Eyebrows, who was seated across from Fonty, said. Mustache sat on the other side of Eyebrows and laughed.

"Ignore these jackasses," the Black deputy said.

I read his name tag. Fontenot. The other two had name tags with Broussard on them. They were indeed related, and I opted to ignore all three men.

Eyebrows yawned and then said, "I'm ready for this tip line bullshit to be over. So many calls pouring in all hours that we gotta pull extra shifts and work places we don't normally work."

"Mm hmm," Mustache said. "The dead girl is dead. We ain't gonna find her killer."

I clamped my teeth together, willing myself to stay quiet, but I failed. "Shouldn't you at least *try*?"

The three men stared at me, and I stared back. I wasn't backing down or going to be the first to break eye contact now. I would *not* wither under their gazes.

"You a cop too?" Eyebrows asked. "You know what we go through on a daily basis?"

"Nope. But catching killers is part of your job, is it not?" I asked.

Eyebrows snorted, shook his head, and returned his gaze to his menu. "Civilians always think they know how to do police work from watching shit on TV."

"That's right," Mustache said.

"We *are* trying," Fontenot said. "It's hard to chase down every tip, especially when the political entities are getting in on things and making life more complicated."

"How complicated do you think the dead girl's parents' lives are now?" I asked.

He fell silent.

"Have any tips proved useful?" I asked.

Fontenot shrugged. "A few of them are of interest."

"That's more information than you had before, right?"

Eyebrows leaned toward me. His voice was low and menacing when he spoke. "Why the fuck you so interested in this? You the media? Trying to angle your way into some flashy story to make this a bigger deal than it is?"

"A dead child *is* a big deal," I said.

A woman arrived with my plate and a glass of orange juice. Eyebrows straightened and cleared his throat. My appetite was gone, but I forced myself to take a bite of toast. It settled into my stomach like a brick, but I refused to retreat from these jerks.

The deputies placed their orders, and I continued eating, though in my peripheral vision I could see Eyebrows glaring at me.

"You never answered my question, little girl," Eyebrows said.

"Keep talking down to me and I'm not answering shit," I said before taking a bite of my omelet.

He scoffed at me, but Fontenot grinned.

"Fellas," Fontenot said, "she's not from 'round here, in case you haven't figured that out yet."

"With her uppity attitude, it don't matter where she's from," Mustache said.

I bristled at the uppity remark. Asshole.

"Where you from?" Fontenot asked.

"Boston," I said.

"See?" Eyebrows said. "Damn journalist poking her nose where it doesn't belong."

"I'm not a journalist," I said. "I don't work for any of the media."

"Then why you here? Go home," Eyebrows said.

"I hope to leave this humid shit state very soon," I said. I scooped up a bite of hash browns. "But I will miss these." I put them in my mouth and smiled. Damn, they were good, and my appetite had returned.

"Why you worried about the dead kid?" Eyebrows asked.

"Why are you *not* worried about the dead kid?" I asked.

"You really expect us to drop everything we're doing and put every officer in the state on the case for some girl God left in the oven too long?" Eyebrows asked, and Mustache grinned.

"Maybe the feds need to come in to take care of what you can't," I said.

Eyebrows growled. "Maybe that's your problem. Your brain got a little fried when you were left in the oven too long, too. Guess God shoulda done us a favor and left you in till you burnt to a crisp."

"Ah," I said. "I get it. You wannabe tough guys hide behind your guns and badges and pretend you're doing the world a favor." I scowled at Fontenot. "And you're okay working with these racist assholes?"

Eyebrows reached for my arm, and I wheeled on him with my fork, tines out.

"You gonna stab me with a damn fork, girl?"

"Don't think for a second that I won't. Try to touch me again and see what happens."

A few patrons near us had stopped eating to gawk.

Mustache grumbled, but Fontenot laughed, breaking some of the tension.

Eyebrows leaned back in his chair. "What's so funny?"

"You fellas picking a fight with the wrong woman this morning," Fontenot said.

I was done with them. I ate the last of my hash browns, finished my coffee, then slapped a twenty-dollar bill on the table. It was more than enough to pay for such an inexpensive meal in the South. I stood to leave.

"Run back to Boston, little girl," Mustache said.

"Gladly," I said. "Far fewer assholes there." Sure, that last statement wasn't true. Massachusetts residents were often called Massholes by other New Englanders for a reason.

My body was rigid with anger by the time I got to my car. I started the engine, appreciating the air-conditioning, then took a few deep breaths. But the rage continued to simmer. I had a good signal, so I called Mr. Landry.

"Good morning, Janette. I made that donation to the search group as you requested, and the library computer is ordered."

"Thank you, Mr. Landry. I would like you to increase the reward for the girl, Letitia, to five hundred thousand."

He paused. "Sure. I can do that."

"Maybe more cash will get any witnesses talking."

"It's worth a try. Anonymously?"

"Yes, please. Any way to spark national media coverage on this?"

"A half a mil will shake things up, no question. I have some contacts I can use to make sure word gets around if needed, but I don't think it will be necessary. That money will perk up some federal ears too. It's not a federal case, but the hefty cash reward will draw attention."

"Good. I read the DNA results, and Jack is my father. What needs to happen for me to change my last name to Montpelier?"

"I can get that paperwork started right away for you. Anything else?"

"That's it."

"I'll take care of everything."

"Thanks so much. I appreciate all that you've done."

"Let me know if there is anything else you need."

"I will. Thank you."

I hung up. I couldn't win the fight against the bigotry that was alive and well in the South, but I could increase the reward. I knew not all cops were racist dickheads, but the two in the diner made me question that assumption. I would need to borrow numerous people and their fingers to count the number of times I'd heard racist bullshit hurled at me during my lifetime, but I'd stopped counting a long time ago.

Eyebrows was a bully, and Mustache was his groupie. Both

were genuine assholes. Fontenot, if he had any self-respect, needed to grow a pair and ditch those jerks.

The higher cash payout and national media attention would blow up the police tip line even more, but I didn't care. I was not going to let Letitia be forgotten or have her murder brushed aside. The Broussard deputies would be even more miserable with this change, and I was okay with that. Sure, it would likely make Lina's life worse, too, but I was at peace with what I'd done. Anyone who got their ass in a wad over more pressure to find a child's killer could go fuck themselves.

Chapter Forty-Three

Once done lugging Jack's boxes into his home, I headed back to the estate. Frank paced on the porch. I parked and stayed in the car with the engine and air-conditioning running. I had a decent signal so I called Goth.

Our time on the phone would be brief since Goth was at her booth in the artists' square, but I called anyway and was pleased when she picked up. I apologized for not getting back to her last night and gave her a quick update on recent events while not admitting my role in the reward offers.

"How are you feeling?" Goth asked. "Any hallucinations?"

"Oh. Um." I considered lying. I lied to everyone. But I didn't want to lie to Goth. "I smoked some weed with Stephen and Mike last night, and that didn't go well."

"They hallucinated too?"

"No, only me. There was a weird fog-smoke-whatever that was the color of blood. And there were buzzing noises and spiders everywhere."

"Any voices?"

"Yeah, but not the one before that told me to kill myself. The one that spoke this time, a girl, said I was the only one who could see her. That was all."

"Was the girl someone you knew?"

"She was my friend who was kidnapped and killed when I was a kid."

"Shit. Understandable if that weirded you out."

"It did. The guys stayed with me until it stopped. We drank the same wine. Smoked a joint from the same batch of plants. They'd already eaten when they arrived, so I had a frozen dinner. That is the only thing I did differently from them."

Goth fell silent.

"What?" I asked.

"Well, I'm wondering if these events are your mind trying to open up to other things. Like this girl, was she threatening?"

"No."

"Talk to her if you see her again."

I considered her suggestion. "I can try if I'm not freaking out. Hey, how is it that you can talk about this so calmly while I'm busy thinking I'm losing my sanity?"

"You're not insane, Janie. I don't know what's happening, but you're not losing your mind."

"How do you know?"

"There are a lot of people in this city with mental health issues like schizophrenia and such. I'm not a psychiatrist, but I don't get the insanity vibe from you."

"Do you believe in curses?"

"I think there are things in this world that we cannot presume to understand. Do you think someone is putting hexes on you?"

"No. Maybe. I keep finding weird things like orange dust near doorways and a chalk drawing under a welcome mat. I put my shoe through it to erase it. There was another one under my bed that I washed off the floor."

"Creepy that someone did that in your bedroom."

"And I found a pouch in the rental car. It had a necklace charm, some flower petals, and other plant pieces in it."

"Was it red?"

"Yes! How did you know?"

"It's *gris gris*."

She had pronounced it *gree gree*, and I was baffled. "What is that?"

"*Gris gris* is like a good luck charm, if you believe in things like that. Maybe the prior renter of the car left it in there, or someone put it in your car for good luck."

"What about the dust and chalk drawings?"

"I'm not sure, but I can ask around. Do you have any photos of them?"

"No."

"Grab pics if you see any more of them and send them to me."

"Okay."

"I've gotta run."

"I want to see you again. Soon."

"You will."

"Good," I said, smiling. We said goodbye, and I hung up.

Frank remained on the porch, so I got out of the car.

He approached and I stopped, wishing I'd stopped in the shade instead of under the sun. I suddenly didn't know how to address him. Frank? Uncle Frank though he wasn't my uncle? Should I tell him he's not my biological uncle? "Hi."

"You did this cash reward thing, didn't you?" he asked.

That was not the greeting I expected. "What?"

"Did you do the big reward?"

"I am not the only person in this crappy state who has money. There are other people on this planet who give a shit about disappearing children."

"Not in Jardin!"

"You mean people in Jardin don't have money or people in Jardin don't give a shit?"

Frank worked his jaw like he was grinding his teeth. A vein on his forehead bulged.

"Why are you angry about the reward?" I asked.

He took a deep breath and calmed. "I know what happened to the girl was terrible. Word travels fast around here."

Not fast enough for Letitia to have been found before she died.

"It's going to make real estate hard to move with the media flooding the area." He held up his hands. "I know I'm being a selfish bastard saying that. I know. I'm sorry I vented my frustration out on you. Keep the reward in place."

"I didn't have anything to do with the reward."

He nodded. "I'm sorry I blamed you. Do you want to get lunch later?"

"Thanks for the offer. I had a big breakfast not long ago."

"Some other time," he said, and smiled.

"Yeah."

"I best get going. It was good to see you."

"Yeah. You too."

He left in his sedan and waved at Lina as she passed him on the driveway. Christ, this place was a revolving door of visitors today. I stepped into the shade under the porch and waited for my next guest.

Lina parked, then joined me. "Hey, can we go in?"

"Sure." I opened the door, and Lina followed me. "Tea?" I asked.

"No, thank you."

I headed to the kitchen and poured myself a glass. "I'm pretty sure I'm going to have withdrawals from Mama's tea once I'm back in Boston."

"You'll survive without it."

I was surprised at the bitterness in Lina's tone. "What's wrong?"

"You upped the reward again."

"We've been through this already."

"Play the dumb card, but I know you did it. My boss knows you did it, Janie. He's up my ass to get you to call it off. The media is everywhere. We have cameras in our faces and reporters badgering us with questions every time they spot someone in uniform. They're not only local reporters now, either. More have come in from out of state. We can't investigate like this, with that money attracting so much attention."

"Who posted the reward?"

"It was done anonymously."

"Yet you and your boss *know* it was me. How is that?"

Lina folded her arms across her chest. "We just do."

"How? Magic? Some Voudou shit? Crystal ball? Explain to me how you have this divine knowledge."

"You're obsessed with Letitia and were asking about Hanna."

"I'm not obsessed."

"You went to Letitia's service. Anthony told me you were there."

"Oh, so me being there is suspect, but Anthony being there isn't?"

"Stop fucking spinning this around!"

I smiled. I had Lina pissed off.

"What's so funny?" Lina asked.

"For the police in this area, you're sure doing a shit job of being public servants. Too worried about where reward money is coming from to actually care about finding a child murderer."

"That's not true."

"Isn't it?" Now I was pissed. I set my glass on the counter. "I ran into three cops this morning. All of them ranting about the tip line overloading them. Fuck you, Lina. Fuck your boss, and fuck those other guys. A child is killed and the police are too busy whining to do anything else with their time. Why can't the police be appreciative of someone wanting to help by offering a bigger reward?"

"Five hundred thousand dollars, Janie. We have idiots from out of state calling in now. Bullshit psychics calling and telling us where the body is when we've already recovered it! Most of it. Animals got what we couldn't recover so these 'psychics' are useless."

"Your point?"

"The money doesn't make our jobs easier, and now the feds are asking questions."

"Good. Maybe the feds won't tuck tail and run from the tip line."

Lina glared at me. "That's not fair."

"Fair? Hanna being murdered wasn't fair. Letitia being murdered wasn't fair. *You* getting leaned on by your boss? Aw. Poor, poor you. You're alive when others aren't! Stop being so goddamn arrogant, Lina."

"Arrogant? Me? There isn't a person on this planet more arrogant than you."

"Get out."

"See? There it is. You don't get your way, so you kick people out." Lina pulled a folded piece of paper from her pocket. "Still believe Frank could have killed Jacques?"

"I never said he did."

"You were so desperate to know before. Well, he didn't." Lina unfolded the paper and slapped it on the counter.

I picked up the paper. It was a picture of Frank on a surveillance camera paying for things in a store. The image had a date and time stamp matching the time frame of Jack's murder.

"I went to that store myself," Lina said. "I lied about my role in the investigation and got the manager to give me this image from their footage," she said, tapping the paper in my hands. "Frank wasn't anywhere near Uncle Jacques when he was killed. He *didn't* kill him."

"Could the picture have been altered?"

Lina sighed. "Jesus, you don't give up on the conspiracies. I was there. I watched the manager pull up the recordings and watched it play through until Frank showed up on them. It wasn't altered. Not so smug now, are you?" She turned to leave, then stopped. "Regardless of what you think of me, I do care about finding Letitia's killer." She slammed the door closed behind her.

I stared at the picture of Frank smiling at the clerk. It wasn't that I *wanted* Frank to be guilty. I wanted some goddamn justice for once. Jack deserved that. I crumpled the paper and flung it into the trash bin.

Chapter Forty-Four

Both Stephen and Mike checked in on me during the day while they worked at the estate. I assured them that I was fine now and dismissed last night's events as a weird reaction to smoking pot. After Lina's visit, I spent much of the day pacing (sulking).

Frank didn't kill Jack, so I was back to having more questions and very few answers. The sun sank, the staff went home, and I was alone again. I decided to go into the city, gathering my things to pack an overnight bag, but I was interrupted by a knock at the door downstairs.

I headed down, noting no melting floors or bleeding ceilings on my way, and opened the door to find the blockish form of Anthony there, not in uniform. I had to admit he was much more imposing dressed as a deputy.

"Hello, Anthony. What brings you here tonight?"

"I came to apologize for the way I acted the night of the memorial."

"Okay."

"It's a lot of stress, this job. I didn't need to take it out on you. I'm sorry."

"Apology accepted."

"Do you know anything about this reward?"

I rolled my eyes. "It's not me. Goodbye!" I closed the door, then headed back upstairs, where I had my bag packed in record time. Back downstairs, I yanked the door open and yelped when I saw someone standing there.

My phone clattered on the floor, and the bag slipped from my shoulder. My heart rate was out of control even though I'd realized it was Lina. I leaned forward with my hand on my chest.

"Shit, Janie," Lina said. "I didn't intend to startle you like that."

I righted and took a deep breath. "Anthony send you since I chased him off?" I retrieved my phone from the floor but didn't pick up the bag.

"Anthony?"

"He was here a few minutes ago with a fake apology and asking about the reward. You put him up to that?"

"Me? No. I haven't talked to him since this morning, and that was about work."

"Then why are you here?"

"Wait." Lina's brow furrowed. "I didn't pass anyone when I drove in. Are you sure he was here that recently?"

"Yes, I'm sure!" I hadn't kept track of the time while packing, but not much time had passed. "Why are you here?"

"There's been a development."

"What the fuck does that mean?"

"Can I come in?"

"If it's to accuse me of the reward again, no."

"It's not."

I stepped aside. "Come in."

Lina did and paused, observing my bag on the floor. "Where are you off to?"

"New Orleans."

"To see Eva?"

"Yes. Maybe. If she's free."

"And if she isn't?"

"Get fucked up in a bar and sleep it off in a hotel."

"You seem like you're in a hurry to leave."

I realized what was happening. "*Stop* interrogating me!"

Lina held her hands up in surrender. "I'm sorry. I don't mean to. Can we sit somewhere to talk?"

I used my foot to push the bag aside, then closed the door. I considered going to the kitchen, but that seemed more like a place for friends and family to hang out. And I wasn't feeling too friendly toward my half sister. I led Lina to Henry's office and dropped into one of the cushy chairs in the corner of the room near a small table with a lamp and a book on it. I placed my phone on top of the book.

Lina sat too, but she remained perched on the edge of her seat.

"What's wrong?" I asked.

"A local boy was reported missing two hours ago."

I sat up.

"We don't know that he's been kidnapped," Lina said, "but we haven't ruled that out."

"Why come to me with this? You should be looking for him."

"We are, and I'll be back out searching, too, as soon as I leave here. I wanted you to know."

"Why?"

"Because once it's official that he's not with friends or another family member, we'll announce it to the media, and a reward would be good to announce at the same time. You don't need to deny the one for Letitia. You're not as good of a liar as you think you are, and a reward for a missing child is exactly the kind of generous thing you would do."

"I'm not generous."

"You very much are, Janie. You're a protector. You look out for others."

I tried to look out for others when I could, that part was true. Lately, I was busy some nights fleeing a Shadow Man. I couldn't protect myself, much less anyone else. "I disagree."

"When we were kids, my parents were poor. In the winter, you always gave me your sweater or jacket and told your mother you'd lost them. When I outgrew my shoes, you'd give me yours and come home in your socks and tell your mother you lost the shoes when you got stuck in some mud. She knew you were lying because she'd see me in your clothes and shoes, but she didn't care either."

"I don't remember that."

"I do."

I remained silent.

"I can't elaborate, but we did have a couple of encouraging tips come in around Letitia's disappearance."

"Tips like what?"

"It's complicated, and I can't say anything more."

"Bullshit. What tips?"

"I can't say anything else. Don't harass me about it!"

I wanted to strangle her for being so evasive.

Lina took a deep breath and returned her voice to a normal volume. "I won't tell anyone you're behind the rewards. We may not find Letitia's killer, but this early in the game, we'll have a better chance with this missing boy. If we can't find him right away, well … We'll need all the help we can get, and tip lines can help."

"You hate the tip line."

"I didn't want to admit that we, law enforcement, needed outside help. You were right. I was arrogant."

"One million."

Lina's eyebrows went up.

"If he's declared missing, announce a one mil reward for him and announce an increase to one mil for Letitia."

"That's, uh, significant. Thank you."

"Keep it anonymous."

"I will."

"What's his name?"

Lina's eyes glinted with the hint of tears.

I leaned forward. "What's his name?"

"It's Samuel."

"Samuel? Little guy from the funeral who hangs out with Mama Tess when he can't go to school? *That* Samuel?"

Lina nodded.

"Fuck!" I sprang to my feet, desperate to do something.

Lina stood. "Janie, wait. We're doing everything we can to find him. He's a sick boy and—"

"What do you mean he's sick?"

"His body doesn't make enough platelets, and he's got something else wrong with his blood. He's going to need medical care for it, so we need to find him."

I closed my eyes for a moment, feeling rotten and helpless. I opened my eyes. "The medicine that made him feel bad. He'd had a treatment when he felt crappy and was here with Mama."

"Yeah."

"Shit. What can I do?"

"Nothing for now."

"I can help search."

"We have plenty of searchers, but I'll let you know if we need more. I promise, I will."

"Mama?"

"She's heartbroken and has some of our cousins staying with her."

"He's from Jardin."

"Yeah. In our own backyard."

"Like Hanna."

Lina nodded. "I appreciate your generosity. I really do. I hate to drop all this on you and leave, but I need to get going."

I walked her out to her car. "Did you tell your parents you know about Jack?"

"Yeah, but I told them it didn't matter to me. My dad is my dad, regardless of genetics. I haven't decided if I'm going to tell anyone else."

"No one else needs to know we're half sisters. I'm changing my last name to Montpelier. I'm fine with others knowing Jack was my father."

"That's great." She paused. "I'm sorry about our argument earlier today."

"I'm sorry, too. I guess we both have some work to do to figure out how to act like siblings."

"Having time to visit without missing children always seeming to be part of the discussion would help."

"I'm sure it would."

Lina left, and when I returned inside, I picked up my bag and carried it back upstairs.

I tossed it into my bedroom, then went up to the third floor to unlock the study. The maps were always the first thing I saw when opening that door. I locked it behind me. I placed a purple pushpin for this new and pending case in Jardin next to Hanna's blue pin and wondered if I could've prevented Samuel from being taken.

It didn't matter that he hadn't been declared a victim yet. I figured he would be. The time frame fit. I opened my laptop and added the date to my spreadsheet, wishing I could do more for him.

Samuel sat on the twin bed with a plush teddy bear, holding it by its arms and making it dance on his pillow. He giggled drunkenly. His eyelids drooped while he played with the toy.

"Are you tired?" the killer asked.

Samuel nodded.

"You can pick out your pajamas for bedtime if you want," the killer said.

"I'll stay dressed. I'm going home soon."

"Of course you are. We'll stay here while your parents are gone on their trip."

"To find me a new doctor to make me better?" Samuel asked.

"Yes."

The killer patted the pillow with his gloved hand. "Put your head here and rest."

The boy did. "I have a pet giraffe."

"People shouldn't lie. It's wrong."

"I'm not lying," Samuel said, frowning.

The killer didn't have time for this. The child declaring he had a giraffe as a pet was absurd. Perhaps it was the concoction talking instead of the boy lying. None of it really mattered though. The man would end the boy's life in time, and pet giraffe or not, the child's suffering would be over.

"Do you want me to read you a story?" the killer asked.

Samuel pointed to a book on the shelf. "That one."

The killer touched the book with the green spine. "This one?"

Samuel nodded. "Why do you wear gloves?"

"To keep you safe. It's like being in the hospital when the nurses and doctors take care of you. They wear gloves to keep you from getting any infections."

"But they take them off."

"In time, yes. And I will too." The man was annoyed that

the boy was not more sedated. He considered dosing him again, but Samuel released a noisy yawn.

The boy settled more snugly into the bed and pulled the comforter up over his fully clothed body. He tucked the bear next to his cheek.

With no other alternative since Samuel continued to watch him, the killer opened the book and began reading.

Chapter Forty-Five

I sat at my little table in the corner of a dive bar. I sipped at the beer I didn't like, but this place didn't serve wine … or at least not any kind of wine I would consume. I might guzzle a bottle like I didn't care, but I did have some semblance of standards regarding what I poured down my throat.

A few men and one woman had eyed me from the moment I'd walked in, so I moved the extra chair at my table to another empty table. I didn't want any company.

A pool table was on the other side from where I sat. The *clack* when the balls hit each other was always followed by a mix of cheers and jeers. The three televisions in the establishment were on, with two showing a baseball game and the third on a cable news channel.

I took a sip of the beer, winced before swallowing, then read the scrolling news feed across the bottom of the screen. The volume was low, but a reporter on the screen spoke with an image of Samuel in the background. My heart sank. The next image was about a reward.

My gut knotted, thinking about him and his family.

I wondered if I should turn over Jack's research to an investigative reporter. This was the kind of thing they lived for, right? I wasn't sure. I'd only seen stuff about investigative reporters on TV shows, so there was no telling how inaccurately they might have been portrayed. Lina was an option, but I couldn't bring myself to show her the study. Jack had kept Lina out of the loop, and I didn't know why.

I wanted to text Goth, but didn't.

The news flipped over to a weather report and someone gesturing to a mass of weather sitting over the southern portion of the Gulf of Mexico. The scrolling feed declared it a tropical storm. The disturbance Mike had mentioned before had moved from the Atlantic into the Gulf and had strengthened.

A hurricane was the last thing I wanted to experience if it turned into that and tracked toward Louisiana.

I hoped it headed to some other state and not here.

I couldn't bear to take another sip of the skunky beer. The woman who worked there and had brought me the bottle approached.

"Ready for another one?" she asked.

"No, thank you." I pulled a twenty from my pocket and handed it to her. "I'll settle my tab now."

"Okay. I'll be right back with your change."

"No need," I said.

"You sure, hon? Beer ain't that expensive here."

"You can keep the change."

"Thanks. You, uh, interested in hanging out a bit longer? I can go on my break, and we can have some fun before you go."

Normally, I would've been tempted by this type of offer. I'd never had a problem with a casual hookup where no names and only bodily fluids were exchanged. And this woman was good-looking, too. But my mind wandered to Goth.

"You are an attractive woman, and I appreciate the offer. I do, but I need to get on the road."

"If you change your mind, we close in an hour," the woman said. She picked up the barely consumed beer and left.

I checked my watch, not realizing I'd loitered in the place for so long. It was after midnight. I headed for the door but glanced back at the TV. It was back to the report on Samuel, and they also had a photo of Letitia displayed.

I climbed inside the rental car, considering this newest development and Samuel's missing status becoming official.

Samuel and Letitia had made national news. That was a good thing, but it had taken money to get them the attention they deserved. Missing Black kids didn't make the national news unless they were part of a wealthy family. Hanna had made the headlines even with her family being lower income, but she was a gorgeous White child with beautiful red hair. Of course, Hanna's killer was never found either. And that was a part of the bigger issue.

I realized that my fear when seeing Letitia's face on the *MISSING* sign was a recurrence of the nightmares I'd had when Hanna vanished.

The killings hadn't ever stopped. I had been whisked off to Boston, but kids continued to be hunted and killed in this region.

That's what Jack's research was really saying. And the data I had pulled together confirmed it. But neither Jack nor I had proof of *who* had been killing them. I had some data points in Mississippi and Texas from Jack's documentation. If those missing kids were lumped in with the Louisiana ones, it would make it a matter for the FBI.

But I had no proof that these multi-state kidnappings were linked.

Henry had been doing something shady with his money, and I wondered if he had ever lived near the towns where the other kids had vanished. I needed to talk to Frank.

I sat in my car outside the gate blocking the driveway to Frank's house. I noticed the camera perched on one of the brick columns supporting the gate hinges. I considered calling him. My insides were a nervous mess sitting here. Maybe it was the shitty beer wreaking havoc on my intestines.

Once I exited the car, I approached the black iron gate. I pushed on it and it squeaked, but it showed no signs of opening for me. I chided myself for even coming.

Frank's place was large, so he must have been doing well with his real estate sales. I walked around the gate and followed the brick wall for a few feet, but I was forced to stop when I got beyond the light the car's headlights cast.

The flashlight on my phone guided me. Part of me questioned what the hell I thought I was doing out here. The other part of me wanted some goddamn answers.

I found a place in the brickwork big enough for the toe of my shoe, so I tucked the phone away and clambered up the wall. Once on top, I straddled the brickwork and removed my phone again.

Mosquitoes flew around my head while I passed my light over the shrubs on the other side of the brick wall.

Shit.

These weren't mere shrubs; they were holly bushes and full of sharp pointy things on their leaves that would shred me. I could jump and clear them, but I'd have to go through them to climb back up the wall to leave. I'd come here to talk to Frank, not get eviscerated by needle-laden bushes. I decided to go back to the car and call him.

When I shifted my position, the phone slipped from my grasp and got lodged in the middle of one of the prickly bushes.

I tilted my head skyward and groaned. Fuck.

A quick mental list of options all involved me getting stabbed by these fucking bushes.

Frank's gate had to have a buzzer or something near it for me to reach him that way. I would then have to suffer through explaining why he needed to get my phone from the bushes for me.

I slid off the wall to head back toward the car, keeping my fingers on the bricks. I stumbled a few times in the darkness before reaching the edges of the area that was well lit by the car's headlights.

Something rustled behind me. I stopped, but nothing moved or made a sound other than the nighttime insects. I continued toward my car. A dark shadow appeared in my path, and I screamed and leapt back, falling on my ass. I scrambled back when the shadow neared.

"Janie, I'm so sorry," Frank said. "I didn't mean to frighten you. But what the hell are you doing out here?"

I needed a moment. I'd been certain the Shadow Man had found me, but it was only Frank. I took some deep breaths to get myself under control and was grateful for the darkness concealing the flush I knew was in my face. I stood and tried to think of something clever to explain my presence. Nothing came to mind.

"I have some questions I wanted to ask you," I said.

"*Now?* At this time of night? Have you been drinking?"

I headed for the car so I would at least be in the light when we talked. He followed. "I don't know anything about you or Henry, and I got curious."

"What do you want to know?"

"Where did you and Henry live before coming to Jardin?"

"We grew up in Texas."

"Where? What towns?"

"Arlington at first, then Nacogdoches when we were in our early teens. Beaumont in our late teens. After that was Louisiana. I moved to Baton Rouge and Henry went to college in New Orleans. We moved to Jardin after Henry and Katherine married ... Well, I was in Hammond initially, then Jardin. Why?"

"Did either of you ever live in Mississippi or another state?"

"No. Henry traveled overseas sometimes for business. Before you were born, Katherine traveled with him, but once the big house was completed, she stopped traveling as much."

I made a mental note to recheck the maps for any pushpins of disappearances near the cities he'd mentioned.

"It's late, Janie. Is that all?"

"Did Henry own any properties outside of Louisiana?"

"No."

"Outside of Jardin?"

"No."

"Have you bought and sold real estate only in Louisiana?"

"I'm licensed to sell as a listing agent in Louisiana, but I can buy and sell in any other state with another agent. I flipped a house in Mississippi once."

"Where was that?"

"Natchez."

"When?"

He shook his head. "What's really going on here? Your questions are far too specific for mere curiosity."

I opted for a partial truth. "Some of the documents from Mr. Landry about the estate look odd."

"Meaning what?"

"They're about repairs to the estate, but Mr. Landry wasn't aware of anything like that happening. I thought maybe they were for some other property my parents owned."

"No," Frank said. "They weren't for estate repairs. Um, I

guess it doesn't matter now that Henry is dead, but he had a side business."

"Doing what?"

"Black market stuff. Antiquities. He had a crew of thieves that traveled the globe stealing from collectors and smaller museums. He'd sell on the black market."

"Wh-what?"

"He had his legitimate businesses and trades, but he did this on the side. More for the thrill, I think. A few times he got close to being busted and he paid off a cop or someone else. He must have pulled that money from his private account and covered it with a fake receipt for the house."

"Oh, shit." A tiny part of me was relieved to hear this. Henry was a thief, liar, and black market man and not a child murderer … maybe not a child murderer.

"I tried to talk him out of that line of work, but he refused to stop."

"Do you think his illegal side job had anything to do with the plane crash?"

"Not that I know of. The investigation said—"

"Piloting error, yes. I'm sorry to have bothered you."

"No bother," he said, then smiled. "Would you like to come inside?"

"I should go to bed. But thanks for the offer." I shifted to head to the car but stopped. "Shit."

"What's wrong?"

"This is gonna sound weird. I hadn't seen your place since I was a kid and with my parents. I climbed up the wall over there," I said, pointing. "I was trying to get a better look, and I dropped my phone into the bushes."

"Instead of using the call button," he said, gesturing to the box mounted a few feet below the camera, "you climbed the brick wall and dropped your phone?"

"I can get it if you let me in."

He punched in a number on the gate's keypad. It clicked when it unlocked, and he pushed it open a little. The high-pitched squeak it made when it opened made my skin crawl. I slipped through and went for my phone.

The flashlight on my phone was still on and led me straight to it. I incurred only a few scrapes from the holly leaves when I pushed the little branches aside to retrieve it. I panned the area with the light.

The house was too far away for my meager light to show much of anything. At least a football field of open lawn lay between me and the house. A few lights on the house showed the basic shape of the home, but that was all.

The gate squealed, then clanged shut, and I rushed back to it.

Frank stood on the other side. "Sorry! It slipped out of my hand." He fumbled with the key pad.

I coughed twice. I did *not* like being inside these brick walls and iron gate. He got the gate open on the second try, and I slithered through it as soon as it was wide enough. An involuntary shiver coursed through me, but I was free.

I realized that when I'd been busy climbing the wall and dropping my phone earlier, I'd never heard this noisy gate open or close when Frank had gone through it.

"Is there another entrance?" I asked.

Frank continued to hold the gate open. "What do you mean?"

"When you startled me earlier, I never heard this gate's hinges."

"Oh," he said, then smiled. "I have a small wooden door over there," he said, pointing. "It's concealed by shrubs. I use it to go in and out unless I'm driving and use this gate." He gave the gate a little shake, and I winced at its high-pitched squeal.

"Maybe oil those hinges?" I said.

He shrugged. "I used to, but they'd start squeaking again within a week. I gave up. Sure you don't want to come in?"

"I should go." I held up my phone. "Thanks for letting me get this."

"No problem. Feel free to come back during the daytime, and I'll show you around."

"Thanks." I headed for the car.

"Have a good night, Janie."

I wasn't sure how to address him. "Good night."

Chapter Forty-Six

I stood before the maps with a mug of coffee in one hand and a sticky note in the other. Last night I'd scribbled the names of the towns Frank had mentioned on a notepad, then gone to bed. I was thankful I hadn't had any issues with Shadow Man last night … other than mistaking Frank for the Shadow Man outside his gate.

The floors didn't melt. The walls didn't bleed. I realized how odd it was that my definition of a "good night" now revolved around not seeing madness come to life or having a dead girl trying to chat me up.

I found the towns on the maps and added pink pushpins at those locations. They were all within a twenty- to thirty-mile radius of a documented abduction. I didn't know if that distance meant something significant or not.

A few abduction pushpins were in the proximity of pink ones, but several vanishings had no pink pin within their area at all. The killer, if it was Henry, could have traveled to those abduction-pin areas, but I couldn't prove it.

I did the math to figure out the approximate years Henry and Frank had lived in the cities. There was some correlation to the list of dates for missing kids from Jack's data, but it wasn't enough to link Henry to them. This additional dead end caused me to take a break, so I locked the study and went to my bedroom.

I was out of my depth as an art dealer digging into suspicious financial records that may or may not have anything to do with vanishing children. Sure, Frank had said Henry sold antiquities on the black market and paid folks off with bribes. But there were a lot of entries of outgoing money in Henry's ledger. He had to have been up to more illegal shit without anyone knowing, given that volume of cash outflow.

I felt a bit more awake after a shower and wrapped a towel around myself. I dug through my bag and frowned. Almost all the clothes were dirty. I sniffed a few articles from the dirty pile and picked the ones that stank the least of sweat. I ironed my selection, then dressed. Upon examination in the mirror, I was pleased with the look of my pressed shirt and trousers. As soon as I walked outside, I'd be sweating in them anyway, so I tried to ignore the current odor clinging to the fabric.

Someone slipped a piece of paper under my door.

Instead of picking it up, I opened the door to find one of the younger women who worked in the house. I had been introduced to everyone who worked there, but I could not come up with a name.

"Oh, I had hoped to not disturb you, Miss Janie," she said.

"You didn't," I said, stooping to pick up the paper.

"Mr. Stephen asked me to bring that to you. A courier arrived with boxes from your lawyer, and Mr. Stephen had them delivered upstairs to the study."

I had a moment of panic, then recalled that I *had* locked the study when I left it.

"They're stacked outside the study door," the young woman said.

"Oh, perfect. Thank you." I searched my mind for a name and couldn't recall hers.

"You're welcome. Would you like us to fix you some breakfast?"

"No, thank you. I'll eat later."

"Yes, ma'am." The woman nodded, then left.

I closed the door and read the note from Stephen. It said the same thing the young woman had told me.

I carried my dirty clothes and coffee with me to the study and set them on the floor to deal with the boxes first. Some were labeled *Henry*, one *Katherine*, and a few said *Joint Accounts*. I unlocked the study, dragged the boxes inside, then relocked the door. They'd have to wait.

I gathered up my clothes and coffee cup again and headed downstairs. With the clothes in the washer, the next stop was the kitchen.

I either ate out or got takeaway food in Boston, so cooking was not something I'd bother to do this morning. I pawed through the cabinets and refrigerator, settling on a somewhat stale muffin.

While I ate, I watched the people working around the house. Stephen pulled a few weeds from around the bushes in the East Garden. Mike followed with a wheelbarrow and rake, collecting the uprooted weeds Stephen had tossed aside. Someone else mowed around the prominent oak trees on the estate. I left the window and finished my muffin, chasing the last of it down with the remaining bit of lukewarm coffee.

I cleaned up what little mess I'd made while a fresh pot of coffee brewed. My thoughts drifted to Goth, so I sent her a text.

I'd like to see you again. Soon.

I'd like that too. Sex with you is off the charts good.

Goth was turning me on with simple text messages now. God, I was helplessly attracted to this woman even when not in her presence.

Of course, I like you for more than just sex.
I miss you.

I froze, unsure how to respond. There was a lot to unpack in her little three-word sentence.

Did I miss the sex? Did I miss Goth? Did I miss both?

I missed both, no question. But if I had the chance to see Goth and no sex happened, would I be happy with only seeing her? That was a question I could answer.

My hands shook when I typed out my reply:

I miss you, too.

I hesitated another few seconds, held my breath, and decided to be brave and send it.

Before I hit the button, Stephen distracted me when he burst through the side door to the kitchen. His eyes were wide.

"Miss Janie, I need you to come with me."

I muttered something of an affirmative while shoving my phone into my pocket and abandoning my coffee and the text reply. I couldn't keep up with his long strides, so I sped up to a trot.

When I rounded the side of the house, Lina in full po-po gear was near her deputy car with Mike. Their bodies were tense, arms were waving, and it was clear they were in some sort of dispute. Stephen sped up, so I broke into a jog.

Lina spotted me, and I swear she rolled her eyes a little. Other estate workers looked on from a distance.

Stephen put his hand on Mike's shoulder. "Calm down, babe."

"No!" Mike barked. He shrugged away from Stephen's

touch and turned to me as I arrived to join the group. "Lina's saying I killed those kids!"

That, I was not expecting. Lina giving him shit for growing weed, sure. But *this*?

"I didn't say that," Lina said.

Mike trembled. "You did!"

Lina started to speak and I held my hand up. "Wait." I turned to the workers and raised my voice so they could hear me. "Go back to work." I had no idea what most of them did at the estate, but they knew their jobs and dispersed. With the gawkers gone, I turned my attention to Mike. "Stay here with Stephen. I'll talk to Lina."

Lina sighed audibly. I was stepping into her territory again, and I didn't want another argument. I nodded to her and started walking. She followed, and we stopped when we were several paces from the men. I kept my voice low.

"What's happened?" I asked.

"We had a lead to a car and a partial plate number off the tip line. It led to Mike's car," Lina said.

"Only a partial plate number though."

"Stop fucking around. This is serious."

"I know how serious this is. Tell me more." I'm not sure how I managed to remain calm, but I did. There was no way in hell Mike would've killed Letitia or taken Samuel.

Lina continued, "His tire treads match ones we have on record from a dump site two years ago. We also found mud on his car that is in the lab to see if it matches a sample we got off a body last year."

"Mud and tires?"

Lina lowered her voice. "I shouldn't be telling you this, but a dissolving plastic was part of the trace evidence found on Letitia's body. It's the kind of plastic used by hospitals when doing laundry. The bags dissolve in the wash. Mike works in the laundry department at the hospital, and they use those bags."

"He's not the only person who works in that department."

"I know."

"You're arresting him?"

"I'm not arresting him. I have asked him to come in with me for questioning."

"You badger. You don't question."

Lina glared at me. I'd hit a nerve, that was clear.

She spoke through clenched teeth. "I won't be doing the questioning."

I softened my tone a little. "Who?"

"Feds."

"Fuck."

"Yes, fuck."

Mike hadn't done this. I knew that just like I knew my own name. Well, I was a Montpelier and not a Martil like I'd thought. Fine, bad example.

"Mike works two part-time jobs," I said. "His shoes and tires will be from a common big-box store like everyone else around here who's on a limited income."

"He's not being arrested."

"Except you show up in your cop car and want him to go with you. He was gonna ride in the front seat with you or what?"

Lina fell silent.

"Uh-huh," I said. "You may not be arresting him, but his being in the back seat won't look so benign to others."

"At the station when they talked about bringing him in, I insisted that I be the one to pick him up instead of the feds or some other deputy. I didn't think it through far enough. I get it. I'm sorry."

"I'll drive him, and I'm calling Mr. Landry. Mike isn't speaking to anyone, including you, without representation."

"Good. Do that. I don't want him guilty for this, Janie. I swear, I don't. But we do need to clear up a few things about items we found."

"Clear it up when he has a lawyer with him. Do you know what the link is between the kids yet?"

"Other than them being Black or Creole, no."

Except Hanna. I wanted to pace but managed to remain motionless. I figured Mike and Stephen were watching us. I didn't want to appear as agitated as I felt. "There has to be something else. Samuel came to the house with Mama Tess when he was out sick. What did Hanna have? She was out of school a lot at times."

Lina shrugged, then narrowed her eyes, tilting her head.

"What?" I asked.

"I don't remember what Hanna had, but you're right. She had some sort of illness. Letitia had diabetes."

"The other kids?"

Lina had her phone out and started texting somebody.

If the kids all had some kind of ailment, that might also link them to the hospital … and to Mike who worked there. The po-po would want to talk to him even more now. I hadn't meant to make things worse for him. Lina remained glued to her phone.

"Lina."

She looked up.

"What are we doing?"

"Call your lawyer for Mike," she said.

I pulled my phone and called Mr. Landry while Lina headed for her car. My estate lawyer didn't do criminal cases, but the man had contacts who did. It was a short call with Mr. Landry, and then I rejoined Stephen and Mike.

Lina drove away, and the men stared at me.

"What happened?" Stephen asked.

"The three of us are going to visit Mr. Landry, and I'm driving," I said. "He's arranging for Mike to have a lawyer who deals with this kind of crap."

"I didn't do anything wrong," Mike said.

"I believe you, Mike. Don't speak to anyone, not even Lina, about the investigation or missing children without your lawyer. Understand?"

"I can't afford a lawyer."

"I've got it covered."

"But—"

"I've got it covered," I said more firmly. I couldn't shield Mike from the coming police questioning. I did have money and resources that could help protect him from a biased legal system, and I was going to use it.

Mike nodded. "Thank you."

"You're welcome. I suspect we're in for a long day, and there's a fresh pot of coffee ready in the kitchen. I'll get my keys and meet you there before we go."

Chapter Forty-Seven

The sun had set by the time we returned to the estate. No one spoke on the ride back after the extended stay at the police station. As much as I hated the estate and my history with it, I had to admit I was somewhat glad to be back.

"Thank you for everything you did for us today," Stephen said.

I hugged them both. "You're welcome. Go home, get some rest, and don't speak to anyone. Call the lawyer if the police come back around. If anyone else bothers you or you are uncomfortable staying at your home, come here."

He nodded and they left.

I needed something to take my mind off the hell Mike had gone through today. I hadn't been in the room with him, but Stephen and I had spent the day pacing while Mike was interrogated.

I was hungry and tired. Sleep was tempting, but I knew I'd lie in bed with my mind racing. Samuel remained missing.

I headed into the kitchen, poured a mug of wine, grabbed a handful of crackers, then headed upstairs to the study. Once the door was locked behind me, I put the remaining crackers and mug on the desk. I pulled the lid off the box for my mother first. The reams of documents inside them made my heart sink. Of course, I'd asked for this. Digging through decades of financial records wouldn't be quick or easy, but it would take my mind off other things.

I found nothing of interest in Mother's box, so I set that one aside. The boxes with her joint accounts with Henry were benign. My vision blurred, so I ate the rest of the crackers and drank the wine. I didn't want to trudge back downstairs for a refill.

I opened the safe, avoided the revolver like it would melt my skin if I touched it, and removed the poetry book and the remaining bundles of twenties totaling a few thousand dollars. I threw the cash into my laptop bag, then dropped into the chair at the desk with the book.

I read a few of the poems and decided Henry's flavor of poetry wasn't to my liking. But someone else might love them. Maybe Mother liked Henry's poems. Maybe she'd never known he was a poet. I wouldn't ever have those answers, so I flipped through more of the poems. The last half of the book's pages were empty, but writing in the very back caught my attention when I went to close the notebook.

I scanned the notes in the back of the book. There was a list of names, dates, and cash amounts. I carried the book with me to the stack of repair receipts I'd set aside the other day. The dates and cash payouts matched the notes in the book, but there weren't any names on the receipts other than the companies listed as having performed the repairs.

I wanted pictures of the receipts. That's when I noticed the missed call and two texts from Goth. Shit. I backspaced through the unsent "I miss you, too" text.

I promise I'm not ghosting you. We ran into some serious issues at the estate this morning, and I've been tied up all day. I'll call you tomorrow.

I waited for the little dots to appear and indicate Goth typing a reply, but nothing happened. I figured I'd pissed her off again, but there was nothing I could do about it tonight. I returned to my task.

When I checked to make sure I had the whole page of the first receipt in my view on the phone, I noticed two letters at its bottom left. I reviewed the other receipts, and they, too, had a pair of letters in the lower corner.

I flipped to the back of Henry's notebook. The letters on the receipts correlated with the names in the book.

Holy shit. The receipts had been marked with initials.

A chill coursed through me.

I took pictures of the pages in the book, then locked it in the safe and took more photos of the receipts. I grabbed my laptop, locked the study, then headed downstairs and outside.

Once parked on a bench by the front door and under a light, I checked my phone's signal. I had enough of one, so I set the phone to be a hot spot and connected my laptop. My searches were agonizingly slow, but I was able to confirm that none of these construction companies or contractors existed. My search on the names from the back of the poetry book yielded disturbing results.

The people I found were a mix of local and state law enforcement. I also found a judge, two people with local news outlets, and one reporter who covered news statewide. Most of the people had already died, but one stood out because there was an article about him in the Jardin news archives from when he'd gotten a big promotion.

Hudson Stark was a sheriff. He was Lina's boss.

Fuck me.

I started to call Lina but stopped. Maybe this was why Jack had never involved Lina. If he knew about her boss and had told her, she would've been in danger. I wondered why Jack had had to make this all so damn complicated. I wished he'd included a list of names with his other research, except maybe he didn't know the names and had never involved Lina because he, like me, wanted more information before pulling her in.

That had to be it. He had missing pieces too. He'd suspected a local for the killings, but that was all.

Hell, I couldn't prove anything yet either, other than that Henry was paying people and using fake construction receipts to explain the cash flow out of his accounts before his death. But his payouts didn't mean he was paying to cover up bribes for stolen antiques or murdered children. Sure, the names, dates, and cash amounts in the poetry book matched the receipts, but it didn't mean they were for making missing kids stay missing.

I wasn't sure if I wanted to keep digging into this. Hudson Stark had received money before his promotion and before Henry died. Someone else might be paying Stark. Or maybe this was all truly in the past and had nothing to do with Letitia and Samuel.

I did not call Lina.

I disconnected my laptop from the phone signal. I might find more information in Henry's boxes in the study, but those boxes didn't matter to me anymore.

Henry was dead. Mother and Jack were dead. All three were connected to me, and I wondered how big of a black cloud followed me everywhere I went. Not allowing anyone to get close had perhaps been my way of telling myself that I was protecting others. Or I was just a shit human who didn't allow others into my life—truly into my life.

Goth was a fling that would end because I would leave for Boston soon. I had a half sister who was safer not knowing any of this.

Flying out tonight was a viable option.

Finish my laundry. Pack. Bail. Goth and Lina would both be better off without me here.

It was time to leave this bullshit for someone else to sort out.

I paced under the porch light. My existence was built on lies and perhaps murder. Henry wasn't my father. Frank wasn't my uncle. Jack *was* my father. And my mother was … I didn't know how else to categorize her other than as an unhappy woman. Henry was a criminal, and I wondered if that was what had gotten him killed instead of a piloting error. Was Mother's death an accident too? Or was it intentional?

I half wished I'd gone down on that plane with them. None of this would be a bother now if I had. My eyes burned with tears.

My phone vibrated, saving me from the desire to start crying. My heart sank to see who was calling.

The killer remained in the shadows, watching Janette Martil pace on the porch. She'd been doing something on her computer, and he was desperate to know what it was. The one time at Jacques's home that he was able to sneak in and access her laptop, she had it locked with a password. He'd tried a few times to get around it but did not succeed. Her phone was PIN-protected, so he'd never been able to get into it, either.

He left the tree, inching closer toward the porch. She was alone, and he could make her disappear. She abused alcohol and drugs on the regular. Lina would look for her for a time, but the killer was too practiced in his art for anyone to find the Martil heir until her corpse turned up.

Lacing her designated wine mug with a mix of psychedelics had been the easiest task of all. She was unpredictable, but when it came to drinking, she was a creature of habit. She'd clean the kitchen and wash her mug, and he'd slip in to apply his custom blend to its interior. The more she drank, the more she dosed herself, sending her mind into a hellish altered state.

Pride always swelled within him to watch her unravel and become terrified of things that weren't there. His mixes were perfect for visual hallucinations, and though he didn't know what she saw when he approached her in her altered state, she never recognized him.

The mug she drank from tonight had already been treated. Her mind would soon descend into hallucinatory madness.

The attention from the reward and media presence were annoying. But when federal agents showed up, he was forced to make a move. Planting additional evidence at Mike's apartment had been easy. Next he had made an anonymous call to the tip line, giving enough details to send the police in Mike's direction.

The biggest problem with his plan to frame Mike was Janette Martil. She was up to something, digging through boxes of papers and keeping the study locked. He had a key to the estate and Jacques's house, but he didn't have keys for the estate's interior rooms. He needed to know what was in that study. He'd get it out of her, though.

He smiled. She deserved the suffering he would inflict on her. No one would hear her screams in his basement. He picked his path through the shadows, noting the last one that he'd emerge from, likely startling her. She'd recognize him and lower her guard, and then he'd pounce.

The killer quickened his pace, nearing the porch, but was

forced to stop when her phone rang and she took the call. He ducked back around the corner of the house, watching and listening.

"What's wrong?" I asked.

"Oh, we're, um, okay," Stephen said. "Mike is finally sleeping. I wanted to let you know that the storm has moved into the Gulf."

"Yeah, I saw that on the news last night when I was at a bar."

"It's now tracking for New Orleans and is projected to make landfall in a few days as a category three storm."

"Ah. *That* I didn't know. If it heads this way, *no one* stays at the estate. Whatever happens to it happens. If the house gets wrecked, so be it. Structures can be rebuilt. People cannot be replaced. No one, not even you, Stephen, are to stick around to try to protect this place. Do you understand?"

"I do. We'll close all the shutters to protect the glass in the windows and doors, but no one will stay on-site during the storm."

"Good. Thank you. Let me know if it changes course, please."

"I will."

"Are you going to be able to sleep tonight?"

"I think so. I wanted to call you first. I figured you'd be up."

"I am. Get some rest if you can. Good night, Stephen."

I hung up with him and stared at my phone for a full minute. It was time to end this thing with Goth.

Goth answered on the second ring. "Hey. I got your text. I hope things are okay. What's up?"

I'd expected to get punted to voicemail, so I wasn't prepared when she picked up. "I, um. We …" I coughed a couple of times.

I'm going back to Boston, and we're done. It was a simple sentence.

I coughed again. "I'm, uh."

I don't want to see you again. An even simpler one.

Goth remained silent and patient, which irritated me.

I couldn't end things with her. I didn't want to. "I heard this hurricane is headed for New Orleans. Leave the city and come here to ride it out."

"A hurricane party?"

"Sure."

Goth chuckled. "You don't know what a hurricane party is, do you?"

"No."

"I'll teach you. I have some stuff to take care of here first, but I'll come to you if it is indeed hitting the city. If it swings your way, you can come here to get away from it."

"Sounds good."

"How are you?"

"Oh, um. Complicated."

"Your research?"

"Yeah."

Silence fell between us.

"We can talk about it later," Goth said. "Or not at all."

"At the hurricane party. We'll do it then."

We said our goodbyes, and I picked up my laptop and headed back to the study.

Chapter Forty-Eight

Stephen called me again. Reporters loitered outside his and Mike's apartment, and I told them to stay inside. While talking to them, I carried my laptop and things inside and up to the study. I spent the better part of an hour talking to them, calming them both down.

They promised they would try to get some sleep, and we hung up. I was wide awake, though.

I lost track of time while digging through Henry's boxes of documents. I was hungry again, and my phone battery was almost dead.

I left the study to grab my phone charger from the car but opted to get food first. I took a few bites of some shrimp creole something-or-other Mama had brought the other day. I chased that with some of the wine I'd previously brought up from the cellar.

This new wine was oh-so-tasty, so I refilled my purple mug. I took another bite of food and chewed while I read the wine's label, hoping there were more bottles of it in the cellar.

I cleaned the kitchen after my minor refrigerator raid, then headed out to the car. I grabbed the cable from the center console, then stopped.

Another red flannel pouch sat in the cup holder of the door.

I growled and snatched the pouch from its hiding place.

Good luck or not, I didn't want people messing with my shit. I slammed the car door closed. I shoved the cable and pouch into my pocket, returned inside, then grabbed my mug and bottle of wine.

Once locked inside the study, I took a long drink from the mug. I plugged in my phone, then opened the pouch. It had the same contents as the first one, so I threw it into the trash bin by the desk. I didn't know if it had been there before I'd driven Stephen and Mike to the police station. I wondered if Mama Tess was behind the *gris gris*. It didn't matter. I'd tossed the damned thing.

I rummaged through the stack of documents that I'd set aside from Henry's boxes. They had bank transactions of large sums, so I'd pulled them out for a closer look.

I dropped into the chair and flipped through the pages while my head swam from chugging the wine. My liquid self-medicating had the desired effect and relaxed my body. I opened my laptop and compared the transaction dates on the pages with my spreadsheet. Some matched. Some didn't.

I grabbed a highlighter from the stash of office supplies I'd purchased the other day to flag entries on the paper documents. I didn't know the source of the large deposits, but they always landed within a week or two of the larger withdrawals that I did have in my spreadsheet. Henry brought in chunks of cash from somewhere not captured in the financial documents within a week before the payouts started. Every time.

I unplugged my phone from the charger and walked to the window. I called Lina, planning to leave a message, but she picked up.

"What?" Lina asked, her voice low and sounding like she had gravel in her throat.

I checked the time. "Shit. I'm sorry. I didn't realize it was so late. I lost track of time. I can call you tomorrow."

"I'm awake now. What is it? Do you need a ride home from a bar or something?"

"What? No. I'm at the estate. I found some records that I'm pretty sure are part of something illegal that Henry was doing before he died. Frank said Henry bought and sold stuff on the black market, but I'm not sure that's all he was doing."

"That was a long time ago. No one will press charges against a dead man."

"It involves some living people too … prominent people."

"Can we look at it later? I'm exhausted."

"Yeah. Sure."

"I'll come by midmorning."

"See you then."

Lina ended the call, and I had a pang of guilt for disturbing her. I fixed that problem by draining my mug, refilling it, then taking another long drink from it. The intoxication felt great until the unwelcome buzzing in my ears started.

Shit.

I left everything in the study, locking the door behind me. I made it to the second floor before my legs turned to lead weights. Walking was difficult, and I used the balcony rail to lower myself to the floor.

The lights flickered, or I thought they flickered. A shadowy figure ascended the steps. My arms wouldn't cooperate when I tried to crawl toward my bedroom. I was closer to the double doors that led out to the exterior balcony, and I managed to scoot and slide in that direction.

The shadow neared, and my breaths quickened as I recognized the floaty outline of Shadow Man.

I rolled to my side and reached one hand up to open the door. My fingers failed to grip the doorknob, though. I tried again and managed to turn it a little.

Shadow Man grabbed my foot and dragged me away from the door while I screamed. My palms slid across the floor like the rest of my body.

"It's time to die," Shadow Man said.

"No," I said, shaking my head. This wasn't how hallucinations worked. At least, I didn't think this was how they worked. Seeing and hearing shit that wasn't there was one thing. But being *attacked* by your hallucination? Was that normal?

Panic took over, and I thrashed against the shadow. My hands landed against something instead of passing through the impossibly strong Shadow Man. My limbs worked somewhat, and it was enough to break free.

I lumbered toward my bedroom, bouncing off the walls and the railing on my way. Shadow Man was unstoppable and came after me again. I lunged for my room, slammed and locked the door. The knob rattled, and the pounding on the door frightened me so badly that my knees buckled, and I fell. I remained on the floor and tucked into a ball, trembling.

Shadows didn't pass through doors, but they did drag me across a floor. My heart almost leapt from my chest when someone (something?) pounded on the double doors that would take me from the bedroom out to the exterior balcony. The curtains over the glass-paned doors quivered with the banging.

Next came the unmistakable sound of breaking glass. A shadowy hand moved the curtain aside and groped for the latch to unlock the exterior door. I used the bed to haul myself up. I yanked the iron off the ironing board, spun, and smashed the hand with it.

A distorted howl erupted, and the hand disappeared. I clutched my ridiculous weapon against my chest and staggered backward until I bumped into the opposite wall. Fingerlike blood spread across the ceiling and dripped down on the bed, the floor, and me.

I moaned but didn't move.

I waited. My tears stopped and dried on my face. Blood covered everything, but the shadow didn't return. I kept the iron and crawled into the closet. I huddled into a corner with the iron and its cord in my arms and shivered.

Dead Hanna sat in the opposite corner, smiling.

"Leave me alone," I told her.

We're friends, she said.

I tucked myself tighter into the corner, turned so I couldn't see her, and wept. I don't know how long I cried. I didn't care. I had been chased by a hallucination that wanted me dead, and my only company in the closet was a fucking ghost. This was the extent of my life on this planet: an unwanted and unloved orphan, a miserable existence escapable only with alcohol and drugs, now insane and alone except for Dead Hanna. My death would make all this go away.

Janie, Dead Hanna said.

I remembered Goth's suggestion to speak to the ghost the next time I saw her. I peeked over my shoulder but remained folded in the closet corner. "What?"

You can sleep now.

"Sleep? Permanently? Like you?"

No, silly.

I flinched when she reached for me.

She patted my shoulder. *You're safe.*

I shook my head.

Sleep.

I had no explanation for it, but exhaustion crashed over me, and I couldn't keep my eyes open.

Chapter Forty-Nine

A noise jolted me awake and I would've toppled except the closet wall kept me seated upright. Dead Hanna was gone. Everything hurt, joints refused to move, and it took me a moment to work the stiffness out of the rest of my body before I could exit the closet.

The knock came again.

"One second!" The pounding inside my head made me regret the outburst.

I tossed the iron onto the top of the bed, then reached for the doorknob.

I hesitated.

The blood that had coated the room and had covered me was gone. It no longer stained my clothes, nor was it running down the walls and dripping from the ceiling. Last night I'd been terrified. Now, in the daylight, I felt a bit braver. Except once I spotted the glass on the floor from the exterior door, my insides loosened.

I hadn't hallucinated the glass breaking. Unless I was hallucinating now. That was a possibility, since the communication between my eyes and brain seemed to scramble on a regular basis.

"Janie," came Lina's voice from the other side of the door.

"Are you okay?"

I was *not* okay.

I opened the door. Lina was in civilian clothes, and her eyes widened.

"Jesus, Janie. You look awful."

"Rough night."

"I texted and tried to call you this morning."

I reached for my pocket to find it empty. "Uh, left my phone upstairs last night. Sorry. Could you, uh, do me a favor and let me know if you see anything on the floor by the doors that go to the outside balcony?"

"Why?"

"Do it, please."

Lina furrowed her brow but took half a step into the room and tilted her head. "Glass."

I released the breath I held. "I don't know for sure, but someone may have tried to break in last night."

"What do you mean you're not sure?"

I sighed as an answer since the words to explain my madness didn't exist.

Lina entered the room and approached the exterior doors. She was careful not to step too close to the glass when she peeled the curtain back. "What time last night?"

"I don't know. I hit the wine kinda hard after I talked to you, and left my phone in the study. Maybe it was me being drunk and clumsy and I broke it, right?"

"Were you outside on the balcony?"

"No."

"Do you have any cuts on you?"

I checked my arms and hands to be sure. "No."

Lina pulled her phone from her pocket. "I'm calling this in."

"Wait. What?"

"The doors are locked. The glass is on the *inside* of your room, so the force came from outside. You have no cuts on you, and there is blood on some of the broken glass in the pane."

I started shivering and backed up against the wall for added support since my legs felt more like goo than muscle and bone.

"What did you do when this happened?" Lina asked.

I pointed to the iron on the bed. "I took that and hit the shadow with it."

"You hit the what?"

"Um, it was late, and I was drunk. The hand that came through the glass and tried to unlock the door looked shadowy." I hoped that feeble explanation would suffice.

Lina examined the iron. "There isn't any blood on it that I can see. Interesting choice of weapon, though."

I had no answer for that one. A lamp or a chair would've worked as a weapon, too, but I had used the iron.

Lina glanced at her phone.

"Wait!" I said. "There's more that I need to show you."

"Linked to this break-in?"

"Maybe. Probably not. How the fuck should I know? If you're going to get more police out here, let me show you the other stuff first."

Lina returned her phone to her pocket. "You are more complicated than our father's puzzle boxes."

"Give me two minutes to wash my face and wake up a bit." I groaned when a muscle in my back spasmed.

"What's wrong?"

I rubbed the sore spot while I headed for the bathroom. "I freaked out last night and slept in the closet."

"Much better hiding places in this massive house, but I guess it worked."

I wanted a shower but settled for less. I washed my face, brushed my teeth, then ran my fingers through my hair. My eyes were puffy, bloodshot, and there was no hope of fixing that anytime soon. I recalled what Lina had said. She'd referred to Jack-Jacques as "our father." I liked the sound of it.

Lina's attention was on the large puzzle box on the dresser. "Did you ever figure out how to open this?"

"Yeah. C'mon." I left the room, leading Lina upstairs. I appreciated the silence as we headed up. I needed to gather my thoughts despite being hungover and a mental train wreck.

Once outside the study, I pulled the key from my pocket.

"You don't have your phone, but you have the key to this room?" Lina asked.

"I already said it was a rough night." I took a deep breath to steady what was left of my nerves. "I need to explain a few things before we go in. Jack didn't leave me just his house when he died. He left me a flash drive inside that puzzle box. The drive had a shitload of documents on it. Research. He used the library in New Orleans and saved the files and his notes to the drive. He suspected someone local to Jardin or in the immediate area was killing these kids."

"Not this again."

"Shut up!" I winced and touched the side of my head. "Let me finish," I said. "I took his data and applied it to some maps with pushpins and thread. I found patterns. The dates of disappearances correlate with the dates of payouts I found in Henry's documents. I'm not certain they're linked, but I don't think it's a coincidence."

"Why didn't Jacques come to me with this? And what about the people you said were alive and involved in whatever Henry was doing? How does this link back to someone local?"

I held up my hand. "I'm getting there. I know you have the proof that Frank didn't kill our father, but with last night and other weird shit happening to me, I—"

"What kind of weird shit?"

"I swear to God, Lina. Shut the fuck up for one minute, and *then* I'll let you pepper me with questions!"

Lina pressed her lips together and nodded.

"I don't know who killed Jack, but I think him digging around in this stuff got him killed. No! Not one word," I said when Lina opened her mouth to speak. "The information I have is dangerous. I think Jack didn't give it to you because he didn't have enough proof yet. Before you ask, no, I don't know why he gave it to me instead. Your sheriff appears to be involved. Jack didn't know that, but he may have suspected it and didn't involve you."

I took a deep breath to try to steady my twitchy insides. It didn't work. "Knowing that much, do you want to know more?"

"I have a hard time believing that—"

"Do you want to know more or not?"

"I want to know more."

My hand shook when I unlocked the door and allowed Lina to enter first. Once we were both in, I locked the door behind us.

"What are you doing?" Lina asked.

"It's, um, a precaution." It was paranoia, no question. "Look at the maps," I said, pointing.

Lina moved closer to them, and I explained the colored pushpins while I pulled up my spreadsheets on my laptop and gathered my other documents.

"Yeah, there are definitely clusters of disappearances," Lina said, her eyes on the maps. "Each blue and yellow pin is a missing child?"

"Yes."

"The one purple one?"

"That's Samuel."

"Shit. That's a lot of kids."

"Uh-huh. This book," I said, holding it up, "is Henry's ledger, and it was in a safe in this room." I passed it to my sister, who opened it. "The wonky-looking numbers are coordinates, and they correspond to many of the disappearances that Jack also discovered." I pointed to the laptop. "This spreadsheet, the blue rows are ones that Henry had documented that weren't on Jack's list. The yellow rows are ones Jack captured, and in green are the ones they both had documented. Henry tracked the disappearances and payouts in the book and had fake receipts for house repairs that matched the payouts. Of course, his data only goes up until he died."

I slid the receipts to be in front of Lina. "Each receipt has initials in the bottom corner."

"How do you know they're initials?"

"I'm getting there. Jack's documentation didn't go as far back as Henry's, but Jack's continued where Henry's left off and up until Letitia's disappearance. You said the abductions had stopped by the time you were out of the academy."

"Yeah."

"They never stopped, Lina. The killer expanded their range. Some of these disappearances happened before you and I were born. Before *Mike* was born."

Lina nodded.

I pointed to the spreadsheet again. "This column shows the number of days between each disappearance. Before we were born, there were longer stretches of time. This date, the one with the fifty-thousand-dollar payout—"

"Hanna. I'll never forget the date she vanished."

"The disappearances stopped in the Jardin area, but Jack found more outside of this region and even this state. I don't know enough about those to know why he thought they were linked, but he included them in his research. The kids are going missing more frequently now. This last entry is Samuel."

"The killer has escalated."

"And this column," I said, pointing, "is how much time between disappearance and when a body was discovered."

"Oh, shit."

"We have three, maybe four days to find Samuel."

Lina reached for her phone again.

"Wait," I said.

"There's *more* to this?"

I moved the books from the shelf and opened the safe. "There's a revolver in there that I don't want in this house. I don't know if it's part of all this shit, but it might be. Maybe you can do ballistics and fingerprints and stuff? I only pinched the edge of the grip to move it out of the way the first time I saw it. I haven't touched it otherwise."

"Good."

I handed Lina the poetry book. "This book is crap Henry wrote, but flip to the very back. Dates, payouts, and full names of people. The dates and payouts match the fake receipts. And the names match the initials written on the bottom of the receipts."

Lina took the notebook back to the desk and compared everything herself. I tried to remain patient while I waited, but I paced while chewing on a fingernail. I wasn't sure what I'd do if Lina dismissed everything as paranoia.

Minutes passed, and the wait was killing me. I bit my nail too hard, and it bled. I stuck my hand in my pocket and gnawed a nail on my other hand.

Lina looked up. "Fuck, Janie. This is insane. You've been doing this the whole time you've been in town?"

"Well, not the whole time, but once I got the flash drive out of the box, yeah. I wanted to give it to you sooner, but I couldn't understand why Jack would leave you out of it. I wasn't sure if he trusted you. I only found the notes in the poetry book early this morning. I researched the names online and found your boss."

"I would've come over last night if you had told me it was this urgent."

"I didn't know what I had. The money that was paid out could have been for anything. Frank said Henry hired others to steal antiquities and sold them on the black market. Maybe that is part of it, but the dates of money going out of Henry's account always fell within one to two days after a disappearance." I pulled up another tab on my spreadsheet showing the data points in a graph. "X-axis is by date. Y-axis is cash. Black dots are disappearances. Red dots are withdrawals from Henry's account up until he died." There was no denying the pattern. "This one is Hanna."

"Why was so much more paid for her?"

"She was the only White kid who went missing. Remember all the attention from that? I'm betting the killer opted to stick to kids of color afterward."

"Because the media never latched on to a Black or Creole kid disappearing like they did a White one."

"Right."

"Did you find any links to who the killer might be?"

"No. But the disappearances continued after Henry and Jack died."

"You suspected our father?"

"I was able to rule him out as being involved."

"How?"

"I went through his financial records. He wasn't paying anyone off after Henry died, and he had no suspicious deposits coming in. I needed to be sure, so I checked his records. If it makes you feel any better, I looked into my own mother too."

"Who's paying people off now?"

"I'm not sure." I showed Lina the other documents I had on

Henry. "Mr. Landry dug up decades of account information. There are large deposits made a week before the phony house repairs were logged. I don't know where the deposits are from."

"Do you know who tried to break in?"

I avoided mentioning that the Shadow Man had been *inside* the house before going outside to try to get at me from the exterior balcony. "No."

Lina stared at me for a moment. "Is that all? Can I call this in now?"

I nodded. "Best reception is to open that front window and stand as close to it as you can without falling out."

Chapter Fifty

I wanted to fly back to Boston, but the incoming weather shut the airport down. I had kept myself busy by doing laundry and packing once Lina and the rest of the police had left yesterday with the revolver, their samples of blood from the broken glass, and all the documents I had acquired. They left my maps and pushpins after taking numerous photos of them. The FBI arrived, too, and I was thankful Lina handled that part.

Mike had been with Stephen the night of my intruder, and neither of them had cuts on their arms or hands. They had been confined to their home with the media outside their door. It had been a handy development that the media had time-stamped photos of them looking out their windows, confirming they'd never left their apartment. For now, the police were less interested in Mike.

With nothing else to do today, I helped Stephen, Mike, and the others prep for the storm by moving hanging plants indoors and running errands to get water and food supplies and to fill up gas tanks. It was enough to keep me occupied though my mind was elsewhere.

The hurricane gained speed and was due to make landfall earlier than expected, of course. It was on track to pop New Orleans, and Goth had promised she would meet me at the estate tomorrow ahead of the worst of the weather.

Nighttime arrived, and I was terrified that Shadow Man would return. Stephen and Mike stayed with me at the estate, and I didn't mind their company. I didn't sleep much, though my body screamed with exhaustion. I'd passed on weed and wine and was pleased I had had no visits from Shadow Man or Dead Hanna.

By morning, I welcomed the distraction of doing more work around the house.

Thick clouds rolled in ahead of the hurricane, and the wind shifted. I loved the lack of humidity and the constant breeziness. Sure, a deadly storm was headed toward the state, but I appreciated the nicer weather even if it would be nasty later tonight.

That evening, I picked at my microwaved dinner and sipped my iced tea. I checked my phone again. Goth said she'd text when she got on the road, but I hadn't heard from her yet. The city didn't have a mandatory evacuation order, but Goth wasn't inclined to ride it out. Plus, the storm's track had shifted westward some. Jardin wasn't taking a direct hit, but it would get more weather than previously expected.

I put my leftovers into the fridge and wiped down the counters. I tried to wash off the ink staining my fingers. Since I had touched the revolver in the safe, the police had taken my fingerprints to know which ones on the weapon were mine.

Larger operations had fingerprint scanners, but smaller outfits like the sheriff's office carried ink pads and fingerprint cards. It made me miss the city a little bit more. I gave up on the ink stains and went outside.

The wind had escalated, producing impressive gusts. No mosquito would stick around long enough to bite someone with this wind, and I decided that not everything about an approaching hurricane was horrible. I figured I would change my mind later when it got bad, but for now, I didn't mind what the storm was dishing out.

Stephen and Mike sat on a bench on the front porch, holding hands.

"Miss Janie," Stephen said, sitting up straighter. "Do you need anything? We can come inside if you like."

"No, no." I sat on the bench with them. "I appreciate the two of you sticking around. I find I don't much like being alone lately."

"We don't mind," Mike said. "We both owe you big-time."

"You don't owe me anything," I said. "Stephen, we're cousins. I got a DNA test, and Jack was my father."

He smiled. "Welcome to the family."

"Thanks. Call me 'Miss Janie' again, and I'll skin you alive."

Stephen laughed. "I'll do my best to remember, *cousin*."

"Do you want Jack's old house?"

Stephen leaned forward. "His house?"

"Yeah. He left it to me when he died, but it was really so he could give me all the research he'd been doing. I don't need it. You can have it if you want. Mr. Landry can flip the paperwork to transfer it."

"You're giving us Uncle Jacques's house?" Stephen asked.

I chuckled, realizing I had been equally as dumbfounded when Goth had offered me the painting. "If you want it, it's yours. It needs some work."

Stephen and Mike shared a glance and then stared at me.

"We'd love to have it," Mike said.

I smiled. "Then it's yours." I enjoyed seeing the elation in their faces, but my own happiness faded when Lina in her deputy car came barreling down the driveway. She had never driven that fast on the driveway before, so I knew it was bad news.

Lina parked and hopped out of her car. She was on the

porch moments later.

I was on my feet. If she was coming to resurrect shit with Mike, I was ready to fight. Sure, she'd kick my ass, but she was *not* taking Mike to jail for something he didn't do. Lina's shoulders sagged. She walked with purpose, but sadness was etched into her face with deep frown lines. My readiness to battle her waned. "What's wrong?" I asked.

"The gun had fingerprints on it that match ones from the cases of four dead children from three decades ago," Lina said. "Ballistics are expected back soon. The blood on your door matched DNA recovered from three victims from two decades ago. The feds found an overseas account belonging to Henry, but it has had transactions since his death. They found some other leads based off what you had, got a warrant, and went to pick up Frank for questioning."

"*Frank?* You mean my non-uncle Frank?"

"Yes. He's gone, but they found Samuel. He's alive."

Stephen and Mike murmured their relief that the boy was alive, but I wasn't sure how to respond. I was thrilled that Samuel had been found, but the thought of Frank being the kidnapper, probable killer, and on the run made me cough. When my chest relaxed enough that the coughing ceased, I found my voice. "How is he? Samuel?"

"At the hospital. He'd been heavily sedated, so he's getting checked out, and his parents and Mama Tess are with him."

"What's next? What about Frank?"

"He won't get far," Lina said. "Police and feds are searching for him. Mike, I'm sorry you had to endure all the questioning. You've been cleared. The FBI found a stash of muddied shoes and hospital laundry bags at Frank's."

Mike groaned. "I knew he never liked me, but *this*?"

"There isn't time to try to make sense of what Frank did. I'm certain he picked you to take the blame because of your connection to the hospital," Lina said. "Stephen, you and Mike, clear out. Go home and ride out the storm."

"What about you?" Stephen asked.

"Janie and I are going to my house until they have him."

"Would it be safer for you two to sit tight at the police station or something?" Mike asked.

"Um, no." Lina's gaze shifted to her feet. "When the feds approached Sheriff Stark, he shot himself. He's dead."

"Fucking hell," I said. "I'm sorry, Lina. I didn't mean—"

Lina touched my arm. "It's not your fault, Janie. It's not. None of it is. Okay?"

I nodded, but my gut remained twisted in a knot.

"C'mon," Lina said. "Pack your things, and you two," she said to the men, "scoot on out of here."

"We can all stay together," Stephen said.

"I've got this," Lina said.

Stephen relented, and he and Mike hugged me, then left. I headed upstairs to finish gathering my things with Lina right behind me. The darkness of the house with all the shutters closed made the entire place feel like the walls were closing in on me.

I had a fleeting thought. In all the efforts to prep the house and property for the storm, we'd forgotten to take the bottles down from the bottle tree by the swamp. The glass would be shattered in the storm. I couldn't do anything about them now.

I brought my things down and left them in the entryway of the front door. "I can't leave yet."

"Why not?"

"Goth—Eva—is coming here. She left the city to come here to meet me. I'm not leaving."

"We need to go."

"Not yet."

Lina growled, then stepped outside with her phone. I

checked my phone again. I tried calling Goth but reached an automated voice saying the call couldn't be completed. The storm was already knocking out power and would likely topple some cell towers.

The wind gusts escalated, stripping more leaves off the trees.

Chapter Fifty-One

I checked my phone again; I had zero word from Goth. My signal now fluctuated between super shitty and nonexistent with the weather. Standing outside didn't help improve my signal but did get me buffeted by building gusts of wind. Green leaves that had been ripped from their limbs tumbled around my feet and whipped past my head. The rain, thus far, had been light to moderate, but while the clouds darkened, my mood matched the sky. I wanted word from Goth. I wanted her off the roads and somewhere safe. I wanted her with *me*.

That last thought made me cough.

Lina cocked an eyebrow at me, and I pretended my full attention was on my phone.

"Anything?" Lina asked.

"Not yet. I don't know what time she left the city." I decided to make some use of the time while we waited for Goth. "I can't wrap my head around Frank. How is he involved in this? How could he want to kill children?"

"I don't know."

"He told me his wife and daughter were killed in a tornado, flipped their car. He used to be a paramedic. He *saved* lives."

Lina shook her head. "They weren't killed by a tornado, Janie. His daughter had leukemia and lived in hospitals for two years before she died. His wife left him and lived on the streets. She overdosed one night."

I couldn't speak. Frank had been lying to me as much as I'd been lying to him.

"That's what Mama told me years ago," Lina said, shrugging.

"Henry and the black market?" I asked.

"Another lie, is my guess."

"So Henry knew what Frank was doing and paid to keep the police and media away from it all?"

Lina nodded. "Seems so."

"The plane crash?"

"That investigation has been reopened. Looks far more suspicious now, given this new information."

"Fuck. I had no idea."

"I wish you'd told me sooner."

My mood shifted. "Bullshit. You wanted nothing to do with me asking about the missing kids."

"I know, and I'm sorry. I am."

I relented and checked my phone again.

"Anything?" Lina asked.

"No."

"We can't wait around here. It's too isolated. Once Frank is in custody, I don't care where you go. But for now, I want you somewhere safe. Come with me back to my place. Send Eva a message to meet us there instead."

"I'm taking my car. If I need to leave to get her, I will."

"That's fine, but we should go."

Lina told me her address. I sent the text to Goth, then got into my car.

The drive took longer than expected. A few limbs were already down from the wind, forcing us to maneuver around them and sometimes to go off the paved areas of the road. I wished I had rented an SUV, but there was no way for me to have known a trip south for a funeral would turn into a serial killer investigation with a side of hurricane.

Fucking Louisiana.

The already blustery wind threatened to turn violent while the early, more minor bands of weather from the hurricane passed over the region. Soon there would be no question that the storm was unleashing its worst on us.

I followed Lina through a little neighborhood of single-level, simple homes. A few houses had decorative fences or trimmed hedges. Most were bland, nondescript places in the early stages of disrepair with peeling paint, a few places of wood rot, and shingles with curved corners. This was a neighborhood for the working class. She'd been right, though. It *was* less isolated here.

I parked next to Lina. Her house had a newer roof and coat of paint on the exterior than the other homes.

It rained much harder now. The noise of the drops striking my car's roof was almost deafening. Once Lina had her front door unlocked, I left my things in the car and darted for her tiny porch.

Lina's keys *clinked* when they landed on the table by the door. My eyes were on my phone while I followed her.

The short dash from the car to the front door had given us a decent pelting by the wind-driven rain. My phone remained void of any contact from Goth. I slid the device into my back pocket and wiped water from my face.

"You good here?" Lina asked. "I'm going to change into a fresh uniform. I'll have to eventually leave for work, but Frank won't know to look for you here."

"Yeah, you do your thing," I said, waving her off. Lina left and disappeared into a room in the back of the house. I turned in a circle, taking in the surroundings.

Lina's home was sparsely furnished with one plant in the corner of the living room. Goth's apartment rain forest made Lina's single plant appear pathetic and lonely. A few pictures dotted the wall. All were of family members, including one of Jack. I neared the one of Lina and me as children, our arms draped over each other's shoulders and broad smiles on both our faces. God, we were so small back then.

Jack's daughters. I wondered if he always knew he had two daughters.

I didn't remember that photo being taken, but it made me smile.

If Lina was leaving soon, I decided I should learn my way around the home now in case the power went out. Maybe a bathroom visit was in order sooner rather than later since chances of a tree limb taking out a power line were high. No power in rural areas meant no well water and no flushing toilets.

I headed down a side hall, noticed the kitchen on one side and two doors on the other side. Movement behind a door beyond the kitchen informed me where Lina's bedroom was. I didn't want to snoop, but I did want to locate a toilet. I eased open the first door enough to glance in.

On the top of a dresser, a lit red candle burned safely within a tall, cylindrical glass holder and sat before a framed image of a woman with a snake.

I opened the door more.

To the left side, another dresser was covered with a white cloth. On it were two white candles with framed black-and-white photos of two older couples between them. Fresh-cut flowers with tiny white petals, the same as what I had found in the flannel pouches, lay on the cloth next to a stick of incense and a small bowl of water. A bowl of dirt sat next to the water.

A chalk drawing covered a portion of one wall. It was a triangle with curling lines off the sides and a straight line extending from the top point. The straight line then bifurcated into curled lines. It reminded me of a scorpion. There was another drawing of two straight lines with what appeared to be asterisks around them and on the line between the curving body of a crudely drawn snake like it was wound around the straight line. A picture of a Catholic saint hung below the drawing. It was the same saint on the pendants in the pouches that had been left in my car.

I began trembling. A voice somewhere in my head screamed at me to leave. But I couldn't tear my gaze away from the things in the room.

The candle flame wavered with the air disturbance from my movements. The eerie glow the candle cast over the other items on the altars caused my skin to prickle. My scalp itched, but I tried to ignore it.

Morbid curiosity overrode my instincts, and I stepped into the room.

The bottom of my shoe scraped against something, and I glanced down. I stood in the middle of a chalk-drawn image of a heart and snakelike lines similar to the one I'd seen under the doormat at Jack's house. A line of orange dust at the doorway was now mixed in with the white chalk. I'd dragged my shoes through the dust and mingled it with the chalk when I'd waltzed into the room like a damn moose.

A modest bookshelf sat on one side of the small room. Books occupied two shelves, while the other two shelves held different sizes of colored candles. Among the candles was a clear bag containing strands of black hair. A larger image of the woman with the snake was on the other wall. Another altar flanked the center one with the red candle and contained more photos, a cloth doll, a braided piece of some kind of plant, and pouches made of red fabric—flannel.

My mind felt as frozen as my feet. I tried to process

everything I saw in the room, but I didn't know what I was actually seeing. I couldn't trust my eyes and head to inform me of reality. They'd both been fucking me over for days now with seeing Dead Hanna and Shadow Man. Okay, Shadow Man turned out to be a real person who could bleed, but I had no explanations for Dead Hanna.

There was only one explanation for this room: Lina had been part of this crazy shit from the beginning.

I swayed with an onset of dizziness. I flung my hand out to steady myself and flinched when my hand landed in a bowl, tipping it over.

My fingers were covered in orange dust, and my breaths quickened. I coughed and needed to get the hell out of this house. I spun to leave, but Lina stood in the doorway, trapping me inside the room.

Chapter Fifty-Two

Lina was in uniform and armed, but she held her hands up in a gesture of peace and calmness. "I can explain."

I wasn't buying it, and Lina reaching for me only made my inner voice scream louder to run away.

I recoiled from her outstretched hand, but I had nowhere else to go except deeper into the room and closer to the altars. I hugged myself instead, wishing I could make myself smaller and escape this madness.

Lina inched closer. "The media and bullshit ghost tours would have everyone believe Voudou is evil and used only to harm others, but it's not. What we do is also for good."

I nodded toward the framed photos. "You're worshipping them."

"No," Lina said, shaking her head. "It's about reverence, Janie. Not worship. The couples in the photos are my great-grandparents. *Our* great-grandparents. I honor them."

"You've been fucking with me all along. You planted that dust shit everywhere as what? A curse?"

"The brick dust on the threshold or on the steps is for protection. It's not for harm."

I shrank into a corner when Lina neared.

Lina reached for the shelf holding a couple dozen books.

She pulled one with a red spine off the shelf and flipped through a few pages.

My eyes wandered over the altars. The symbols mixed in with the candles, pictures of people, and chalk-drawn symbols on the walls and floor were too much. I was trembling again.

Lina tapped my arm, and I flinched. She flipped the book so I could read it. She pointed to a paragraph header: *Protection Spells.*

I blinked to refocus my eyes when the dizziness hit.

Maybe I could pass out while the feds hauled Frank off to jail and wake up when this was over. But if I passed out, Lina might sacrifice me or some shit.

I managed to read a few lines of the book, confirming Lina's claim for how the brick dust is used and where it is placed for protection.

I shook my head. "You flat lied to me when I asked you before what it was."

"Like you haven't been lying your ass off since you stepped off that fucking plane."

Fair.

"One book," I said. "What about the others? Do they say how to use it for other purposes? And what is this?" I pointed to a symbol on the center altar. "You drew that at Jack's house under his doormat."

Lina cast her gaze downward for a moment before meeting my eyes. "Yes. You weren't meant to find it, but I drew it in case you stayed there again. It's called a *vévé.*"

"And this?" I pointed at the chalk scorpion on the wall.

"Another *vévé.* It represents a spirit, Monsieur Agassou. I petition him for protection."

I wasn't buying any of this shit. "The bottle trees and the knots in the strings. You lied about not knowing what they were."

"Yes."

"The drawing under my bed?"

"A protection talisman, a Marie Laveau one."

I rubbed the side of my head, hoping the headache forming there would go away. "The red fabric, the flannel. I found two of those fucking things in my car with the same flowers as you have here and pendants of that guy." I pointed at the photo of the saint under the crude snake drawings.

"Our ancestors were persecuted if caught practicing Voudou, so they mingled their practices with Christianity. That is Saint Patrick, and he represents Damballah Wedo, the father of all the loas."

"Who? The what?"

"Janie," Lina said, then paused to take a deep breath. "This isn't the time to get into all of that. Everything I've done was meant for good. The pouches, those are *gris gris*. Charms and such for—"

"Protection?"

"Yes."

"Fuck you."

"It's true. I swear."

"The strand of hair in the pouches I found, did that come from this bag?" I glanced at the bag on the bookshelf.

"Yes."

"Whose hair is it?"

Lina dropped her gaze to the floor again.

"Fuck me. It's mine."

"Putting something personal from a person inside a *gris gris* bag provides protection specific to that person. When I went to the house to put more brick dust down, on one of those trips, I went inside and took the strands from your brush."

"Is that when you drew that shit under my bed too?"

Lina nodded and brought her eyes back up.

"Un-fucking-believable."

"The other things with *gris gris*, the bay leaf, the cedar, the cayenne pepper … they're all for protection. Except the pepper—that's for chasing off your enemies."

"*What* enemies? Why do you think I need so much protecting?"

"You were hunting a serial killer!"

"And the feds are going to get him. It's over."

I realized something else, and my fear switched to boiling anger. "You didn't know what I was doing until I told you." I paused, thinking. "Or you knew all along. You're part of this."

"Of killing children? Jesus, Janie, listen to yourself. I'm not."

"How is it that your house is the nicest one in the whole neighborhood? Taking bribes to cover up their disappearances?"

"Now you're being stupid."

"Maybe *you're* why I needed protection."

"How can you say that?"

"You've been dosing me with whatever shit you probably brewed in here to make me hallucinate. I thought I was losing my goddamn mind, but it was *you*."

"I would never do that."

I needed to get away from my so-called sister, so I pushed past her, left the room, then turned down the hall to head to the front door.

Lina trotted behind me. "Janie, wait. I can show you more books."

When Lina grabbed my arm, my chest constricted and I panicked. I spun and shoved her away from me … *hard*. Lina stumbled backward and crashed into a wall. She winced and slid to the floor.

I bolted for the door but slowed long enough to grab Lina's keys from the table. I thought this was a good idea until she snagged my hand. I wrestled the door open with my other hand.

We were both blasted by gusts of wind.

I turned my back to the wind and kept my head down. That's when I noticed the remnants of orange dust at her doorway. I'd been too busy looking at my phone to notice it before when I'd entered.

Lina lunged for her keys again. She jarred them loose from my hand, but I managed to swipe my foot at the keys, kicking them outside into the darkness and foul weather.

"You're my sister, Janie. I'd never do anything to hurt you."

I sprinted to my car. My breaths were loud and ragged. I was hyperventilating, and the sensation of a belt across my chest worsened. A panic attack now was a death sentence. My life depended on me keeping my wits. I locked the car doors and shuddered when Lina fought with the handle.

"You're misunderstanding all of this."

I wasn't misunderstanding anything. Maybe the orange dust was for protection, but all the other shit? Lina drawing things under my bed, stealing my hair, and hiding flannel pouches around me? Fuck that. Lina wasn't an ally.

My entire body shook, and I dropped my own keys when I pulled them from my pocket. I groped around my feet, found them, and managed to get the key into the ignition to start the engine.

Lina backed away from the car when I put it into gear. My sister's hair and body were soaked. I had been too occupied with escaping her to realize that it had gone from heavy to torrential rain in such a short time. I, too, was drenched.

"Please let me explain," Lina shouted over the howling wind.

I stomped on the gas, sending the car into a lurch backward. I yanked on the steering wheel and spun the car around before changing gears and stepping on the gas again. I wish I could say this was a savvy move with the car like something seen in a movie. Since so much water pooled on the driveway and road before finding a storm drain, I had caused the car to hydroplane versus some fancy maneuvering. None of it mattered. I left Lina standing in the storm outside of her evil home.

I wanted to drive like my rear bumper was on fire, but with the standing water and inability to see much through the glass though my wipers were slinging rain on their fastest setting, I had to slow down or end up in a ditch.

Goth. Fuck.

Once the house was out of sight and well behind me, I stopped the car. All roads were deserted except for me. The smart people stayed home. I was not smart. I had become entangled with Lina's treachery, so I was now driving in a hurricane. I tried calling twice and sent texts to tell Goth to *not* go to Lina's address and to instead meet me at the estate. I wasn't sure what we'd do from there, but I wanted to know Goth was safe and then we would figure out the rest. First, I had to get far away from Lina.

The storm battered the car on the drive, and I swerved to avoid a falling limb that missed my hood by inches. I kept going until I arrived at a downed power line.

I knew the standard rule to never drive over power lines was in place for good reason, but I needed to escape all this insanity. The risk of frying the car and myself was a gamble.

The darkness all around me and the car was unnerving. I was so tiny and insignificant. The storm didn't give a shit about my circumstances or why I was running from Lina, my past, and my annoying emotions that insisted on bubbling to the surface at inopportune times.

No lights came from any of the homes on this stretch of the road, so I hoped that the power was out and the line across the road was dead.

I closed my eyes and stepped on the gas pedal. I both felt and heard the light thump of the front then the rear tires crossing the downed line.

I lived.

I opened my eyes, considered that bit of survival a small victory, then resumed the drive to the estate.

Chapter Fifty-Three

Frank stood at the window, looking out through the gap of the exterior shutters that had been closed for the storm. He used his bandaged hand to push the lacy curtain aside a bit more. He'd missed his chance to kill Janie the other day, and now the police were everywhere looking for him.

He'd lost Samuel to them, and that infuriated him the most. His chance to release the boy from his illness was gone.

The Martil Plantation was a good place to hide. The estate was massive, the staff were all gone, and Janie had a tendency to return here. Anthony had told him that Janie was with Lina, but Frank knew Janie. She'd come back, and he'd be ready for her.

A dark gray car pulled up next to the deputy's car already parked at the estate. It was the woman he'd seen with Janie in the city.

If she lived in New Orleans and had driven here through the strengthening storm, the drive would've been absolute hell with the wind and rain. He watched her while she sat in the car for a few extra moments.

The storm had shifted farther west than the original predictions had called for, and he figured she'd been caught driving in weather she would never want to drive in again. She checked her phone, and the killer smiled. There would be no calls or texts going anywhere tonight with some of the towers already down.

She peered up through the windshield, and the killer's eyes drifted upward too. Despite being able to see the outside only through the narrow space in the shutters, he could tell the sky was darker than anything he'd seen before, and the wind blasted the house.

The woman left the car, clutching only her phone and keys while she dashed for the porch.

The wind and rain lashed at her as she banged on the door, keeping her head down.

"What do we do?" Anthony asked him.

"Answer it. Be calm."

"Yes, sir."

Frank left the window for the kitchen doorway to watch.

When Anthony opened the door, the woman slipped in and then spotted the deputy closing the door behind her.

"Oh! Hi. I was expecting Janie," she said.

"You are?" he asked.

"Eva. And you?"

"Anthony. I'm Janie's friend. Why are you here?"

Frank growled. Anthony's tone was too sharp, and the woman's brow twitched.

"She offered for me to come out here to escape the storm, except I left New Orleans a bit too late and got caught in some of the mess."

Anthony frowned.

The woman's hands twitched. Frank observed her body language, realizing that she knew something was off with this situation. Anthony's behavior would cause her to bail, and it was too late for that.

"Ya know, I'll leave." She grabbed the doorknob. She got the door open an inch, and then Anthony's giant palm slammed the door shut.

He tried some semblance of a smile and kept his hand on the door. "No need to go."

The woman backed away from Anthony, and Frank needed to intervene. The house had multiple exits, and she would find one if she wasn't stopped now.

She sidled around Anthony, keeping her eyes on him, and when she had a few paces between them, she tried to bolt but came up short when Frank stood before her.

Frank sneered at her, and she lunged to slip around him.

Anthony's hand clamped down on her upper arm. She spun and landed a solid punch to his jaw.

Anthony smiled at her.

"You're not leaving," Frank said, smiling.

"Who are you?" she asked.

"I'm Frank." His smile vanished. "Take her to the kitchen."

She thrashed against the big man, kicking and kneeing, and even went after his eyes with her fingernails. Anthony held her arm and swatted her attacks away from his face.

"She's stronger than she looks," Anthony said.

Her black combat boots squeaked against the marble floor while he dragged her toward the kitchen. When they reached the doorway, she gripped the door frame with her free hand. He gave her arm a rough yank, and her fingers tore free from her meager anchor.

Frank grinned. This was going to be fun. "She's a fighter."

Anthony grumbled in response.

Everything she tried to escape Anthony had been unsuccessful because she'd been battling him with pure panic. Frank was intrigued when she snapped out of panic mode.

Anthony shifted his body to avoid her incoming kick.

It was a feint, and it worked. She planted that leg, then

brought her other knee up into his groin.

Anthony released her, and Frank laughed. She was a fighter *and* smart.

She broke away from Anthony, but he used his foot to swipe hers out from under her. She slammed to the floor, and her head struck a cabinet.

Frank dragged her semiconscious form toward the table. "Get up, you idiot," he said to Anthony.

The deputy groaned but got to his feet.

"Put her in the chair," Frank said.

Anthony did as instructed and held her upright. Frank placed his finger under her chin and turned her head. The cut on her head from the collision with the cabinet bled, but it wasn't all that deep.

She moaned and winced upon opening her eyes.

Frank knew she'd have a significant headache, but he didn't care. Her eyes widened when he pulled a long, broad knife from the knife block on the counter. She squirmed, but Anthony's hands kept her in the chair.

Frank placed the knife on the table next to a black case that was already open and had multiple compartments within it like a fishing tackle box.

He picked up two vials from his case, read their labels, then placed one on the table and returned the other to the case. He continued this process until he had three vials on the table near the knife.

"You're here and expecting Janie," Frank said, his eyes on the vials. "Now that I know she's coming, I'll do to her what I'm about to do to you."

Anthony chuckled.

She tried to go for the knife, but Anthony's hands gripped her so tightly that she cried out and stopped moving.

Frank used droppers from the three vials to drip their

contents into a fourth vial. When he was done, he returned the three vials to the case, then shook the fourth vial. It was only then that he focused on her.

"Who are you to Janie?" he asked.

"Her friend."

Frank sneered. "Not only does Janie lie, but she surrounds herself with liars. I've watched the two of you. You're her lover."

The woman remained silent.

He snarled at her and leaned in so close that he was less than an inch from her face. "You are both an abomination."

"And you aren't?"

The stinging slap he delivered to her cheek angered her more than frightened her.

"Fuck you," she said.

He slapped her again.

She strained against Anthony's grip and roared, "*Fuck you!*"

Frank ground his teeth together. "Hold her mouth open," he ordered Anthony.

Anthony's movements were so quick, she didn't have time to react. He released her arms to drop down behind her. He threw one beefy arm around her, pinning her spine to the chair and squeezing her arms to her sides. He had his chest against the back of the chair and gripped her so she couldn't take much of a breath. He grabbed her jaw and forced her head back. His fingers pried her mouth open.

She tried to squirm and bite at Anthony's fingers, but she stopped. Frank had the knife in one hand and his vial in the other. He pressed the tip of the knife to her throat, and she flinched.

"Fight this," he said, "and I'll get to watch you slice your own neck open."

She stilled.

Frank dumped the vial into her mouth. He knew it had a

bitter taste and wasn't surprised when she gagged.

"Swallow it," Frank said.

She resisted. Frank nodded to Anthony.

The big man's hand closed her mouth, and he pinched her nostrils shut. "Swallow it and then you can breathe again," Anthony said.

She jerked her head, but he held her.

"Swallow," Anthony said into her ear.

She did, and when Anthony released her face, she gasped for air. Anthony shifted his position to stand behind her again, forcing her to remain in the chair.

"You're thinking that you have bought yourself some time to figure out an escape," Frank said. "You are wrong."

She blinked several times, and Frank grinned. He knew his mixtures well. Her vision would be blurring now, and she'd be unable to focus on anything. Within a few more minutes her muscles would relax and she'd lose voluntary control of her body. She'd continue to breathe and remain conscious, but she'd feel paralyzed.

He waited while his concoction took its hold on her. She tried flexing her fingers, but they were sluggish to respond. Numbness would travel up from her fingers and toes, and her arms and legs next.

"What did you do to me?" she asked.

"A special blend to take the fight out of you for a while," Frank said.

Light flashed into the house through the front-door windows, illuminating the darker interior of the house since all the exterior storm doors had been closed to protect the glass. The light lingered too long to be lightning.

"Someone's here," Frank said. "Probably Janie. If it is, grab her. If it isn't, get rid of them."

"Yes, sir," Anthony said.

Frank changed places with Anthony, and he kept the woman in the chair by pressing down on her shoulders.

She struggled, but her efforts were feeble. "No!"

Frank lowered himself, tightening his grip around her chest and clamped his bandaged hand over her mouth. He hissed into her ear. "Quiet now or I'll cut Janie open in front of you."

A whimper caught in her throat.

"Shh," he said. "Be a good girl and stay quiet."

Chapter Fifty-Four

My heart leapt when I spotted Goth's car parked at the estate. Next to it was a deputy's car, and it wasn't Lina's. Anthony was here too, and my body relaxed some. I would tell him what Lina was doing, and he'd protect Goth and me from Lina. Frank wouldn't be stupid enough to come to the estate with a deputy parked at the house. Other than the storm and a lunatic sister, I couldn't have asked for better circumstances.

A violent clap of thunder overhead made me wince. If the storm cells spawned any tornadoes in Jardin, I didn't want to be in the car. Anthony, Goth, and I would all be safer in the bowels of the estate house. I abandoned the car and sprinted for the porch. I was soaked once more but didn't care.

I paused at the front door long enough to check for brick dust. If there had been any, it had been washed away. Good!

The wind shifted, driving the rain sideways at me. Hundreds of tiny needles pelted my skin, so I threw the front door open to escape the onslaught. "Goth!"

Anthony stood before me.

"Whoa." I released a nervous laugh. "I didn't expect you to be right *there.*"

"Come on in out of the weather," he said, ushering me away from the door. He wrestled with it against the blustery wind before slamming it closed.

My eyes scanned the lower level before I turned my gaze upward in case Goth was on an upper level. I didn't see her anywhere. "Where's Goth?"

"What?"

"Eva. Her car is here. Where—"

"Oh, yes."

I waited for more, but Anthony fidgeted instead. A bead of water rolled down the side of his face. His fingers brushed his service weapon while his other hand adjusted his duty belt. Something about him was wrong … off. This whole night had been a disturbing sequence of events, and his oddball behavior annoyed me.

He'd never acted like this before. There was a rancid odor in the air, I was soaked and cold, and where the fuck was Goth?

Anthony remained silent, and I dismissed the warning alarms going off inside my head and moved past the nervous deputy. "Fuck this. Goth!" I would tear this place apart to find her myself.

Goth's voice came from the kitchen. "Janie!"

"Shut up." Despite the growling nature of the second voice, I recognized it.

Frank.

I spun to alert Anthony of the intruder, but my head rocked to the side. Severe pain ricocheted inside my brain, tripping a cognitive circuit breaker I didn't know existed.

I knew I was falling but couldn't stop it. I must have blacked out for a few seconds, because I was aware that I was on my back with no recollection of striking the floor. I was swallowed by a dizziness and nausea unlike anything I'd experienced before. I wanted to vomit. I wanted to close my eyes and wait for it to all go away. But Goth was in danger. Hell, we were both in danger. Frank had Goth, and that worried me more than anything else.

I had to do something other than lie on the floor. My jaw ached, and my head pounded. When I moved, I groaned with the increased pain it caused.

Anthony saved me the trouble of rising by dragging me by the ankle across the marble flooring to the kitchen. He released me, and my leg struck the floor, jarring me more. Though my movements were clumsy, I managed to roll to my side.

Goth sat—was being forced to sit, rather—in one of the kitchen chairs. Frank had one arm wrapped around her neck. But something was wrong with her. She struggled against Frank's grip, but she was too weak to get him off her. Goth should have been able to beat the shit out of Frank, but if Anthony had gotten to her like he'd done to me, Goth could not fend them both off.

One of Goth's arms slid down to her side, limp and unmoving. Her head lolled forward, and that's when I noticed the blood on the side of her head. Anthony, Frank, or both of them had already hurt her, and I wanted to kill them both.

"That's it," Frank said into Goth's ear. "Give in to it. Let it take you where it wants."

An opened black case with a glass vial next to it was on the table. He'd drugged Goth. That explained her weakness and inability to escape.

"I could've handled Janie easily enough," Anthony said, "but you let this one scream."

"You can't do a goddamn thing without someone telling you what to do," Frank said. He loosened his grip on Goth and allowed gravity to take her to the floor. He examined his bandaged hand. "Bitch bit me right on my cut before the mushroom cocktail kicked in."

A bright red stain spread across the bandage. Frank had been the one to break my window. Frank was my Shadow Man.

Goth's eyes were tear filled and wide with fear. "Janie?"

I didn't know what to say. Telling her everything would be okay was a blatant lie. Help wasn't coming. The feds were chasing Frank, but they were hunting in the wrong places. Anthony, the fucking law enforcement himself, was a minion. And Frank was using a mix of psychedelic mushrooms to drug his victims.

Goth and I were fucked.

"I'm sorry," I said to her. "I didn't know they were here."

"Well, we are," Frank said, then laughed. "Pick her up," he said to Anthony while waving at me.

From my spot on the floor, I squirmed away from Anthony when he approached, but he was on me in an instant. He gripped my arms and hauled me to my somewhat-functioning feet. He thrust me into the chair previously occupied by Goth.

Anthony leaned in close. "Where's Lina?"

Frank placed the vial from the table into the case and pulled out different ones. I noticed the eight-inch chef's knife on the table.

"Where is she?" Anthony asked, giving me a rough shake for added emphasis. "Is she coming here?"

My eyes met his, and several realizations occurred at once. With him so near, the stink of sweat filled my nose. I had mistaken the moisture on his face for rain, but it was sweat. His eyes were wide and his pupils large. He resembled a wild animal, and that made me shiver.

"If she comes, we'll deal with her," Frank said.

Oh, God. I had completely fucked up. Now Lina was in danger too. Anthony didn't want to know where Lina was to help him. He needed to know she wasn't coming so he wouldn't have to kill her.

The gears of panic kicked in, and my breaths quickened. I coughed a few times. Frank didn't have a choice but to kill Goth and me. He'd kill Lina, too, if she showed up.

Lina had been telling the truth, and I had accused her of poisoning me. I'd been horrible to my sister, who was not part of Frank's web. Lina's keys were somewhere in the void of darkness. I had escaped who I thought was an enemy only to roll right up into the clutches of true evil. I wanted to scream, but I needed to stop freaking out first.

Frank would kill us all.

"Work called her in," I said, my voice wavering with fear.

"She's at work?" Anthony asked.

I nodded.

"Does she know you came here?"

"Yes, but she won't come."

"Why not?"

"It doesn't matter," Frank said. "Hold her head and open her mouth."

Anthony ignored him. "Why not?" he asked again.

"We argued, and I said some shitty things to her. She got called in, so she's there now and is mad at me."

Anthony nodded, and his blood-constricting grip on my arms relaxed enough for my fingers to stop tingling. "This storm will keep her busy for a while."

He loved Lina, that was clear. He didn't want to kill her.

My flicker of hope that I might turn him into an ally was dashed when he refocused on me. His eyes were hard, boring through me while he gripped my lower jaw in his bear paw of a hand. My gaze turned to Frank. He neared with two vials in one hand and an eyedropper in the other.

"I have the perfect blend for you, dear niece," Frank said. "Open your mouth."

I clamped my teeth together. Anthony dug his fingers into my cheeks, working them until he caused enough pain that I opened my mouth.

Frank grinned and filled a dropper full with brownish liquid. "Ready for another trip, Janie?"

I jerked my head aside, escaping Anthony's grip for a moment. Whatever Frank gave me would fuck me up soon, no question. I needed time I didn't have, and Anthony had my head trapped again.

"Stop struggling and open your mouth," Frank said, then glanced at the knife on the table. "Or I'll cut your girlfriend's face off."

I couldn't move my head within Anthony's powerful hands and arms. I squirmed in the chair but wasn't going anywhere without my head. Clawing at Anthony's arms did nothing to loosen his grip on me.

Frank set the vials down and picked up the knife. He pressed the blade against my neck. "Or shall I cut your face off first?"

All my squirming ceased.

"That's better," Frank said. "Stop fighting."

"Janie," Goth said from her immobile state on the floor. "Do it."

"Yes," Frank hissed. "Do it."

I didn't have to try hard to imagine the terror of his victims when he hovered over them with his lecherous grin. I shuddered but opened my mouth.

Frank chuckled. "Ah, that threat gets 'em every time." He swapped the knife for his vials again, emptied the contents of the eyedropper into my mouth, then refilled the dropper from the other vial. He squirted that into my mouth too. His grin vanished and he leaned in closer to me. "Make no mistake. That threat wasn't idle. I need information from you, and you don't need the skin on your face to speak. Swallow."

My mind reeled while the somewhat viscous and bitter liquid slid down my throat. Anthony kept my head motionless.

Seconds ticked by, feeling like hours until Frank nodded and Anthony released me.

I bolted from the chair, spitting the remnants of what was stuck to the inside of my mouth onto the floor. Anthony laughed when he caught me before I made another step. "Not so fast."

"Spitting or puking won't help you now," Frank said while he placed the vials back into his case.

"What was in that?" I'm sure there were far more intelligent questions to ask him, and I'd never really given a shit about consuming foreign substances to get high, but this was different.

"Psychedelics of a few varieties, extra concentrated, of course. And a few other things to keep you under control."

"You gave this to the kids to kill them?"

Frank fastened the final latch on his case with disturbing calmness. "What I did with the kids was a mercy, Janie. The others," he said, shrugging, "less so."

"The others?" I was stalling yet morbidly curious.

"The addicts, the homeless, the *homosexuals*. The torture and pain helps free them of their crimes. They repent before they die. Most of them. I've been cleaning up New Orleans for years," he said, seeming to beam with pride. His smile vanished. "Let's go," he said, scooping the case to carry it under his arm before strolling out of the kitchen.

Anthony gave me a rough yank, startling me from my Frank-induced trance to hear he'd been, in his mind, euthanizing children while torturing others in the city. Goth and I were on his extermination list. He'd already been fucking with my mind, dosing me with shit—something else I'd wrongly attributed to Lina.

My struggles against Anthony were futile. When I realized I was being dragged away and leaving Goth to lie in a paralyzed state, my stomach heaved with fear. I vomited.

Anthony never slowed his pace.

I spat the remnants of bile from my mouth. "Goth!"

Anthony stopped. "Keep fighting me and I'll kill her now."

I blinked back tears and acquiesced.

"Good girl," he said, then resumed hauling me toward the stairs that Frank ascended.

Chapter Fifty-Five

Anthony shoved me from behind. "Move faster." He hadn't pushed me hard enough to make me fall, but I stumbled forward as if he had. I was stalling any way I knew how, and falling to the floor seemed like a good way to gain a few more seconds. Except Anthony snatched me back up and forced me onto the stairs.

I had to find a way back to Goth. There had to be something we could do to escape this nightmare. I realized that the only time my hallucinations hadn't lasted forever was the night I'd taken one of Goth's pills while doing research. Goth likely had pills on her now, and I wanted them.

Frank, almost on the third floor, glared down at Anthony and me. "*What* is taking so long?"

"We're coming," Anthony said. "Maybe you should've drugged her *after* we were already upstairs."

"You forget your place, Anthony," Frank said. "When we're done, you will dispose of the two bodies but for half of what I usually pay you. You're *my* employee. Not the other way around."

Anthony growled a deep, guttural sound that made my blood go cold. Sure, Frank's proclamation that Goth and I were "bodies" was terrifying, but Anthony's simmering rage beneath the surface of control made everything worse.

And I had thought Shadow Man breaking through my window was terrifying. This was much worse. I understood now how some people soiled themselves with fear. Panic tickled the edges of every thought, and I figured my bladder and maybe bowels too would empty once I tipped into the realm of pure terror.

I should not be finding humor in anything right now. Maybe it was the mix Frank had given me. Maybe my mind was already gone, because the idea of pissing and shitting myself made me chuckle. I tripped on one of the steps, for real this time, and fell forward.

Yeah, probably Frank's drugs.

My toes and fingertips tingled.

Definitely the drugs.

Anthony had me up and moving again.

"I can pay you more than he can," I whispered. "Let us go, and I'll make you a rich man, Anthony. There's two million dollars in rewards if you turn Frank in. I can add to that number."

"Shut up," he said. He squeezed my arm so hard, I almost screamed.

That ended any attempt to get him on my side. Whatever control Frank had over him was far more powerful than money, though Frank did pay him.

The lights flickered, and I stopped. I remembered how, when I was a kid, the lights behaved when a tree limb rubbed a power line during a storm. It created an almost strobe light effect inside the house. The limb would either take the line down or cause something to overload and cut power to the house. The flickering stopped for a few seconds, then started again. I waited for my chance.

The power went out, submerging the house in complete

darkness. I jerked free of Anthony's grip and sped down the stairs. I knew this house well enough to navigate it at night.

But my knowledge of the house's layout faltered in the utter blackness, with the storm shutters closed. I misjudged where the last step was and crashed to the floor. I'd developed somewhat of a habit of falling down stairs since arriving in Louisiana.

"Fuck!" Anthony said, and the big man's feet stomped down the stairs after me.

"What now?" Frank shouted from somewhere higher on the stairs.

"She slipped away, but I'll get her."

I scrambled to my feet and headed for the kitchen, desperate to reach Goth before Frank's concoction prevented me from being able to do anything. My feet and hands tingled more. It wouldn't be too much longer until the drugs reached my limbs.

"Janie?" Goth said.

"I'm here." I rolled Goth to her back. It was dark, and my vision had begun to blur, but the fear on Goth's face was unmistakable. Her eyes were wide, and sweat beaded on her forehead. I touched her cheek. "Are you hurt anywhere other than the cut on your head?"

"No, but I can't move."

"Stay calm." My words were absurd. I was on the verge of losing my own shit. My hands shook while I patted down Goth's jeans. I felt what I wanted, then shoved my hand into her pocket.

"What are you doing?" Goth asked.

Anthony and Frank were shouting at each other now, but I was too busy to listen.

I snatched the baggie of pills from her pocket. I shook them out of the bag and into my palm. Willing myself to not drop them, I passed my fingers over the pills, counting them.

Between my deteriorating vision and the darkness, I trusted my fingers over my eyes. "How many of these can you take at once without dying?"

"Uh, three? Maybe."

Frank's voice boomed from the interior of the house: "Watch the door to make sure no one is coming up the road, like your cop cousin."

"Yes, sir," Anthony said.

One set of footsteps, heavy and clunky, moved within the vaulted foyer, while another set created a rhythmic beat as they came down the stairs.

Frank. Shit.

"Anthony, don't just stand there," Frank said.

"You told me to watch for Lina."

"Check the breaker box."

I had five pills and used my finger to shove three of them into Goth's mouth.

"Under the tongue for faster absorption," I said.

Goth nodded and worked her jaw to bite the pills, then slide them under her tongue. I tossed the remaining two pills into my mouth, chomped down on them, and winced at the bitterness. I slid the pieces beneath my tongue before hiding the baggie back inside Goth's pocket.

Frank neared the kitchen.

I didn't know if Goth's pills had enough stimulants in them to counteract Frank's concoction, but it was worth a try. My head spun, and Frank's drugs caused buzzing sounds in my head. The noises escalated until they were almost deafening.

I leaned down to Goth's ear. "When you can move again, get out of this house and hide from them."

"Help me up. We can both go now."

"His brew is already working on me. Leave as soon as you can."

"What about you?"

Frank was only a few paces away from us now.

My lips brushed her mouth, and I wondered if it would be the last time. "I don't know. I'll—"

Frank jerked me up by the back of my shirt. I wobbled with the sudden motion.

"No!" Goth's outburst earned her a kick in the ribs from Frank. She cried out but couldn't move or even hold her now-bruised side.

The lights came back on.

I lunged for the knife on the table, grabbed it, and spun. Frank shoved me backward, pinning my back against the table, then ripped the knife from my hand.

Frank brought the blade down, and I attempted to roll to avoid it. The knife sliced through my shirt and into my upper left arm. I screamed when the sharp, blinding pain tore through my flesh.

"Always be ready to have your weapon used against you," Frank said. He yanked me up from the table and rammed the blade deeper, sending the tip through the back of my arm.

I almost vomited again. My knees weakened, and the torment threatened to make me pass out.

"Janie!" Goth said.

I struggled to focus my thoughts. I had the pills under my tongue. Frank was occupied with me, which meant he couldn't harm Goth. I had to get him as far away from her as possible, but I didn't know how. Frank could've stabbed Goth and me to death right there, but he didn't.

Anthony entered the kitchen. "It was a tripped circuit breaker that took the power out."

Frank dug his fingers into my arms, forcing me to remain upright. I groaned and closed my eyes, but I opened them again when he gave me a rough shake.

Frank wasn't another hallucination. Neither was the kitchen knife buried up to its hilt in my left arm. The blood running down and dripping on the floor was quite real. He jerked the blade out of my arm.

I was aware that this time I really was going to pass out, because my world went darker than the house when it had been without power.

I stirred. Though disoriented, I knew I was lying on the floor and Frank was looming over me. I tried to slither away from him, but he dropped his knee onto my chest. Frank pulled hard on the ends of the dish towel he'd used to tie around my upper arm. I cried out and tried to escape the agony.

"Leave her alone!" Goth said.

"Shut up before I gut you," Frank said to her, then returned his attention to me. "Can't have you bleeding to death before you give me what I want."

I didn't know what he wanted. I didn't care. He seemed to have forgotten about the knife that was now on the floor next to where he knelt. I was thankful he hadn't used it on Goth yet. Yet.

"Let's go." He hauled me up, but my knees wouldn't hold me.

I tried striking him with my good arm, but he batted it aside with ease. My legs didn't work, so Frank dragged me along. I tried to stop him, but my limbs became weaker when the tingling changed to numbness and migrated up my arms and legs.

"Want me to take her?" Anthony asked.

"Like you did before?" Frank sneered at Anthony, and the giant deputy shrank away from him like a scolded puppy.

I had the sudden urge to pee. I was helpless to stop Frank from doing whatever he wanted, but I remained aware of everything.

My mind screamed with rising panic and my chest was constricted. If I coughed, I risked losing the pills under my tongue.

I was going to die tonight. I was not going to see Goth again, and Goth might die too. Frank would kill Lina if she showed up.

If I had stayed secluded and friendless in my shit little world in Boston instead of flying to Louisiana, everyone would be safe.

Well, everyone but the children and adults Frank would continue to murder.

My stomach clenched. If I puked, I would lose the happy-face pills in the upheaval. My vision blurred to the point of blackness, and my limbs became useless.

I tried to remain conscious, but I wasn't sure why. So I could see what was coming? So I could watch what Frank would do to me?

I moved my legs enough to get my knees under me to try to stand while Frank continued to drag me, but my strength failed. The mushroom mix-extract-whatever-it-was took over, and while my body slid across the floor toward the stairs, I closed my eyes.

Chapter Fifty-Six

My world was sideways, and I wasn't sure why. The chairs and desk weren't upright like they should be, and pieces of paper strewn about stood stiff and vertical, almost suspended in the air. I assumed I was hallucinating until I realized I was lying on my side on the floor in Henry's study. Frank had hauled me up three flights, and I had no recollection of it. The desk, chairs, and mess on the floor were all obeying the laws of gravity. Frank had ripped everything off the walls and tossed everything, including me, to the floor. He was frustrated and pacing, which made me smile.

I shouldn't be smiling, though.

Frank had Goth and me trapped in this godforsaken house. But he was agitated to the point of swearing and picking things up to throw them again. In my inebriated stupor, I laughed.

He wheeled to face me, and I sobered in an instant. I shrank away from him … Well, I tried. My limbs wouldn't cooperate. My left arm protested the most, and upon seeing the blood on my arm, the towel, and the floor, I remembered why. I moved my tongue. The pills were gone.

Fuck.

If I had swallowed them, they'd take longer to work—if they worked at all against Frank's poison. In my compromised state, I could have spit them out.

Stay calm. Breathe.

Frank grabbed the front of my shirt, pulling me up to a seated position.

I could not move my body, but on the inside my chest tightened, I needed to cough (mostly because my heart seemed lodged in my throat), and my pulse had to be beating faster than a hummingbird's wings.

His face almost touched mine, and his eyes were full of hate. "Your maps of everything—where did you get the information? Where is it now?"

I cut my eyes toward the wall where the maps had lived. Only the corners remained attached to the wall. The maps were in pieces, and pushpins and thread littered the floor. Fist-sized holes speckled the walls.

My head drooped toward my chest, and my left arm ached and burned. The numbness in my limbs was gone, though everything continued to tingle.

Goth's drugs were working. Sure, Frank was scaring the shit out of me, but Goth's pills had my heart on overdrive. The pills had dissolved.

But were two pills enough for me to regain control of my body?

Another question: Where the hell was Anthony?

Frank grabbed my lower jaw and forced my head up. "Where is it?" He trembled when he spoke.

He'd lose all control soon, and I didn't want to be anywhere near him when he did. I moved one of my legs while his eyes bored through my skull. My leg felt rubbery, but it moved when I wanted it to.

"Jacques was digging into the kids," Frank said. "He somehow left you his research. I want it now."

As soon as I gave it to him, he'd kill me. I didn't have it

anyway, and he'd kill me for that, too. I had to stall him. To what end, I didn't know, but I wanted Goth to have time to escape and maybe warn Lina.

"Safe," I said.

He released my jaw and drew his hand back to strike.

I turned my head and closed my eyes. "It's in the safe."

"Where?"

I risked opening my eyes, and Frank lowered his fist. I almost pointed, but I wanted him to believe I remained paralyzed. I flicked my gaze toward the wall of books. "Bookshelf."

He left me and flung books off the shelves. I needed other ways to delay him while my chest felt like it had a jackhammer inside it. The pills were working but maybe too well. I tried to control my breathing, but it did nothing to slow my drug-induced rapid heartbeat.

Telling him the info he sought was in the safe was not my best move, but at least the gun that had been in there was already in police possession. I worked my legs and arms while he was occupied with raking books off the shelves and onto the floor. If I could move parts of my body after only two of Goth's pills, Goth should be in better shape by now with three pills on board, right? Assuming three pills didn't make Goth's heart explode. I didn't want to know what three pills felt like.

Thousands of spiders crawled up through the cracks in the wood flooring, and I gasped.

They aren't real. Don't fucking move.

Frank had paused his destruction and laughed. "The hallucinations have started. What do you see?"

He created an opportunity for me to delay my death, so I did.

"Spiders." I shuddered when they came up through the cracks like black water flowing over the floor. "*So* many."

Frank grinned. "The amount of alcohol and whatever other shit you take to make your miserable life more tolerable made it hard to find the right blend. Getting you to consume it without knowing was far easier."

My curiosity overrode some of my fear. "How?"

"We're all creatures of habit, Janie. And you do love your wine."

"You laced the wine?"

Frank laughed and shook his head. "No. I watched you pick that one purple mug out of the many available to you. When you did happen to lock any doors, I already had keys and slipped in and doctored the mug. You even took it from Jacques's place when you came here. Maybe that thing has some sentimental value for you from when you saw him as a kid. Don't know and I don't care. But you and that stupid mug made my task of fucking with your mind far easier."

Frank had been watching me since the day I'd arrived in Jardin. I didn't want to have this conversation anymore.

"You were supposed to be on that plane with your parents, so I fucked with you for fun at first. One night when hunting in New Orleans, I spotted you with that woman. You're not worth shooting and wasting a bullet. But dosing you to try to make you kill yourself was indeed entertaining."

Frank's form blurred and dissolved into a dark shadow with smoke swirling around him.

"'Do the world a favor and drown yourself in the swamp or throw yourself off the roof.' You said those words to me," I said.

"But you didn't listen," Frank said. "Your snooping around my house alerted me that you were digging into shit that was none of your business. Jacques had asked me some of those same questions about where Henry and I had lived. Like him, you'll end up dead too, dear niece."

My stupidity was going to be the cause of my death today. I

groaned and hung my head.

"Don't bother sulking now." Frank and his swirly smoke resumed throwing books to the floor until he found the safe. "What's the combination?"

"I don't remember." I loved lying to him.

He stalked toward me, hands clenched into fists. He'd beat it out of me. He was unhinged and desperate. The FBI, along with the local and state police, were after him.

"The desk. Top drawer on the right," I said. "Remove it. The combination is taped to the underside of the desk between it and the drawer."

Frank changed course and went for the desk. He yanked the drawer from the desk, dumping its contents out. He knelt, spotted the paper taped to the desk, then ripped it off. He carried it to the safe.

I had more strength now and brushed the nonexistent spiders off my leg while Frank's back was to me.

I knew how this would go. Frank wouldn't be able to get the safe open with those numbers. He'd beat me until I told him the numbers were reversed. He'd open the safe and find it empty, and that would be the end of me.

"Henry was cutting me off from the money overseas," he said while turning the safe's dial. "He said I was out of control and refused to keep paying the bribes." Frank laughed.

"Why would Henry help you kill so many children?"

Frank turned to face me. "He did the covering-up part. Henry didn't have the stomach for the dirtier work, but he had plenty of cash to keep things quiet. Guilt will make you behave in ways you never saw coming."

"Guilt from what?"

"We had a younger brother, Mahlon. Mother put Henry in charge of watching us while we played at a creek, except Henry was busy reading his book when Mahlon went under.

I mean, what else can you expect but a disaster when a child is put in charge of other children?" Frank shrugged. "It wasn't Henry's fault, but he bore the brunt of the shame and guilt, and I used it. After Mahlon, Henry always swore he would never let anything bad happen to me. When I made some mistakes with my earlier children, I went to Henry and worked that guilt, and he paid to keep me safe … keep me out of prison."

I was glad Henry was dead. The bastard had helped a murderer, repeatedly. "But when he was going to stop the money?"

Frank returned his focus to the safe. "I'd already rigged his plane to take him and you and Katherine down, but you couldn't fly. Ear infection or some shit. Otherwise I would've inherited everything with the three of you gone."

Frank didn't know about the will.

"Why did you and Jack argue so much?"

"He was convinced that I'd killed your parents. He wasn't wrong, but he had no proof. Jacques was always after me for one thing or another. Stupid bastard. He was like a nagging fly until I got rid of him."

Frank swore and tried the combination again. I rolled to my knees and got my feet under me. Frank cursed at the safe, and I lunged for the door.

My balance failed and I stumbled. Frank abandoned the safe and stomped after me.

I righted enough to keep moving and had made it to the door when Frank tackled me. We rolled out of the study to the landing before the stairs. He pinned me on my back.

"Anthony!" Frank said. "Get your ass up here. Now!"

Anthony's heavy feet hit the bottom of the stairs, and within moments he was at the top with us. For a big man, Anthony was *fast*.

"Hold her down or cuff her so she can't run off," Frank said.

I couldn't see the foyer since I was flattened on the ground and behind the railing, but the front door opened.

The wind howled, blasting into the home until the door closed. "Janie?" came Lina's voice from below.

"*Run!*" I screamed.

Frank clamped his hand over my nose and mouth, cutting off all air. Anthony drew his weapon and sidled his way to the edge of the balcony's railing, keeping the gun hidden.

"Anthony, was that Janie?" Lina asked. "What are you doing here? What the hell is going on?"

Frank held me down and kept low. Lina wouldn't be able to see me or Frank from the bottom floor. My lungs burned. I needed air.

"I came out to check on Janie," Anthony said. "She's up here but hallucinating from something she took. I radioed for an ambulance, but the storm has them tied up elsewhere, *if* they can even get out. Go back to your patrol. I've got this."

"I didn't hear anything over the radio," Lina said.

"Oh," Anthony said. "I used my cell."

"How? Towers are down."

Anthony's hand with the pistol twitched. I was a hot mess of mixed elation that Lina was there and dread that Lina was there. Anthony would shoot my sister.

I thrashed against Frank and got free enough to bite down on his fingers, clamping down until I tasted blood. He howled and jerked his hand away. Anthony ignored the commotion and raised his pistol. I clambered away from Frank and lunged for Anthony. He fired his weapon at his target downstairs right before I collided with him.

We flipped over the rail together, and I got my right hand on it. Anthony fell away from me, screaming. Granted, I had never heard what a body falling twenty-five feet to a marble floor sounded like, but I did not expect it to be so *loud*. The sickening thud of his body hitting the ground-level floor silenced his terror.

Anthony wasn't moving and blood pooled around his head. Lina was on her back and unmoving, her service weapon in her hand. Anthony had shot her anyway. I didn't see Goth anywhere, but I also didn't have a view of the kitchen to know if she was there.

I had to believe she'd gotten away.

Frank came toward me, snarling. I wasn't strong enough to pull myself up, and I didn't want to do that anyway. I would deliver myself to Frank with that move. If I let go, I'd fall to my death like Anthony.

I struggled to get my left arm up and another hand on the rail, but the knife wound hindered those efforts. The mushroom mix had my limbs feeling numb but not numb enough to make the stab wound stop hurting. My strength in my right hand was terrible, but I wouldn't fall yet. Pills and adrenaline kept me going.

I swung my legs a few times, hoping to get enough momentum to fling myself over the second-floor rail and to some measure of safety. The motion strained my arm, and I would lose my grip any second, causing me to fall.

Death by gravity or death by Frank?

When Frank reached for me, I let go.

Chapter Fifty-Seven

I had miscalculated several things. My body dropped much faster than I expected, but I *had* managed to twist and at least get my legs over the rail before the rest of me flipped upside down. The top of the rail caught me in the middle and I folded over it with a grunt. My body tipped more, threatening to pull me off the rail and down to join Anthony's corpse below.

I gripped the rail. It wobbled and pulled a few screws loose from the floor under my weight. I rolled off the rail, landing hard on my side on the second-floor balcony.

I lay frozen for a moment from the onslaught of pain brought on by my failed attempt to save Lina.

Frank unleashed a string of curses while going down the stairs. He'd kill me. No question. And that got my ass in gear.

I staggered away from the main set of stairs Frank was on. The secondary stairs at the far end of the second level seemed like they were miles away. I kept moving toward them. I could hide in one of the rooms on this level and lock the door. But Frank would beat it down and then beat me to death.

I was torn between wanting to go to Lina, finding Goth, and getting myself out of the house alive. Lina had a gun, but I didn't know how to shoot one even if I got my hands on it. Plus, Frank had used the kitchen knife against me. He'd take the gun and use it on me too. The gun was out, but I had made up my mind.

Frank reached the second floor and charged toward me. I arrived at the secondary stairs and froze when my feet sank into the flooring.

I closed my eyes, figuring I couldn't see hallucinations if my eyes were closed. I wasn't sure if it would work, but it didn't matter. I kept them pinched shut and had my hand on the rail, relying on my feet to carry me. I would've been more stable using both rails, but my left arm remained painful and useless.

I stumbled when I reached the first floor, and opened my eyes. Frank's form had morphed into nonhuman form again. The Shadow Man started down the stairs after me.

Lina remained flat on her back and unmoving. Instead of heading toward my sister and the front door, I passed by the kitchen and glanced in. Goth was gone. Good. I wanted her to stay hidden.

I moved along the wall toward the rear of the house.

The plan was to lead Frank down into the cellar. I could use the faux servants' tunnel to leave … to go where, I didn't know. The goal was to delay my death and lead Frank away from the house in case Goth was hiding somewhere inside it. Lina, I hoped, was alive and could find her way out too.

Simple (but not great) plan. It would have to do.

The walls bent inward toward me, and the floor liquefied with hundreds of writhing snakes on it. I recoiled from one of the walls threatening to fall on me.

I told myself it wasn't real.

"Janie!"

That voice was real, though, and I flinched when Frank called for me.

"You can't escape me."

As much as I didn't want Frank after me, I needed to keep

his wrath focused on me.

That part was a piece of cake.

"You're not my uncle, you piece of shit. Jack was my father, not Henry. Killing me doesn't get you any money. You don't get anything. I have a will in place that if I die, you get nothing."

"You're lying!"

I managed a hearty laugh. "Not this time, asshole."

"I'm going to make you suffer."

"Fuck you, Frank. You're going to prison for what you did to those kids. Hope you're ready to take it up the ass."

His feet landed on the first floor and he roared.

I had his wrath centered on me. I'd poked the bear, and the bear was coming to eviscerate me.

I faltered in my rush to turn back around and flee. The pounding inside my chest and head worsened. I assumed it was because of Goth's drugs since the walls moved a bit less. The snake floor was back to being a regular floor. The lights flickered again. A popping noise came from within the professional-chef-grade kitchen. A smoke detector screamed its warning and set off the rest of the detectors in the house. Lina, if she was alive, would be burned to death.

In my mind, I worked through how to lose Frank and reach Lina. My newest plan sucked with little chance for success, but I was spared from executing it. Goth crept out of the shadows from the opposite side of the house and went to Lina while Frank's attention was on me.

Seeing Goth made a little glimmer of hope inside me come alive, except Goth hadn't left the house. Lina stirred with Goth's arrival, and I decided it was worth being the prey to get Frank away from them.

"Hey, Frank, make sure you buy lubricant in bulk before they ship you off," I said. "You're gonna need it."

He no longer stomped toward me. He broke into a sprint.

I fled while trying to ignore the new hallucinations. I couldn't step on the child-sized skulls bubbling up from the floor. I even stutter-stepped around a few of them though I knew they weren't real.

I made a few turns, then headed for the cellar. I reached the heavy, old door with well-oiled hinges, except my hands were so slick with sweat that it took me a couple of tries to turn the knob.

Frank closed the gap in those few seconds.

I burst through the door and down the stairs. The cellar path would take me to the tunnel that led out of the underside of the house.

Frank was never too far behind me, and the ever-shrieking smoke detectors and strobe lights made it almost impossible for me to think.

Once at the bottom of the stairs, I raced past the covered furniture, grabbing what I could and flinging it behind me to obstruct Frank. I turned left through the double doors into the expansive wine storage room. I might have been able to use one of the older tools in the cobwebby workstation of the cellar, but I'd already had one of my weapons shoved through a part of my body. My throbbing and nonfunctioning left arm reminded me of that with each rapid thump of my pulse, so I chose the wine room.

I weaved around the first rack, and the cellar sank into total darkness when the power went out. Flipping a breaker wouldn't fix it this time. I could smell smoke.

Chapter Fifty-Eight

The battery backups in the smoke detectors kept them screaming like banshees but also turned on the sickly-yellow emergency lighting within them. The flickering strobes continued too.

I didn't know the cellar as well as I knew the other levels of the house. The strobe lights disoriented me. I made a few turns, and when I expected to be at the other end of the wine room, I instead faced another wine rack.

I'd lost Frank but had also gotten myself lost.

Janie.

I spun and Dead Hanna stood before me.

Come with me. Dead Hanna extended her tiny six-year-old hand.

My dead childhood friend was going to be my salvation or damnation. I wasn't sure which, but I had no choice but to trust the ghost, or hallucination, or subconscious something-or-other. My hand shook when I reached out to take Dead Hanna's. I expected her hand to be cold and deathly, but it was warm.

"Are you real?" I asked, squeezing her tiny hand, *feeling* the girl's skin against mine.

She smiled.

"Shit, Hanna. You're real. You're alive."

This way, Hanna said, tugging on me. I followed, and she brought me straight to the doors leading to the tunnel to take me out of the house.

Water and mud had flowed into the tunnel, and Hanna and I sloshed forward and through it. Frank was somewhere in the cellar and swearing.

I stayed with her until we emerged, reaching the storm and all its wrath. I released her hand to block the wind and rain from my face. Hanna remained at my side, the storm whipping her long hair, but my young friend smiled.

You know where to go next, Hanna said.

"What?"

Hanna pointed beyond me. I turned and there was nothing but blackness and violent weather between the house and the swamp.

"I don't know where you mean."

Hanna was gone, and I would have to figure that part out later. I didn't know where to go, but I allowed my feet to carry me farther from the house.

Frank was out of the tunnel, and his constant curses grew louder while he closed the distance between us. Wind lashed at the shrubs and trees in the garden. I clambered over a downed tree, then kept going.

I splashed through standing water, and rain stung with every wind-driven drop that met my skin.

A faint tinkling noise caught my attention, and I headed toward it, realizing it was the bottle tree. It made no sense that this storm would only make the bottles *clink* together instead of shattering them. But I'd also had a dead child lead me out of a cellar. The world made zero sense anymore.

What I would do once at the tree, I didn't know. Swamp water had risen and encroached on the periphery of the garden.

I neared the tree, gasping for air. Several bottles had already been broken from crashing into other bottles or the tree itself. Some bottles were gone with only their frayed strings left to be whipped by the wind.

I assumed the tinkling sound I'd heard was another hallucination, because there weren't enough intact bottles left to make the noise. Plus, Hanna stood at the base of the tree.

The swamp water had overflowed and surrounded the tree, causing me to go from ankle-deep water to almost knee-deep flooding. It slowed my progress too much, and I needed to keep running.

I glanced back to see where Frank was, and he slammed into me, taking me into the water and onto the broken glass under it. I landed on my left side, and shards dug into my shoulder and arm. My scream was muffled because Frank held me under water, pressing my head against the ground and more glass.

I thrashed against him, but he held me down. My flailing hand brushed against a sunken bottle, and I gripped it by the neck. I swung the bottle up and smashed it against the side of Frank's head.

He released me, and I slithered out from under him, using my hands and knees. I gasped for air as soon as my head cleared the water. I touched another sunken bottle, and picked it up. The tree bent with a violent gust of wind that also buffeted me.

The bottle in my hand was intact, full of water, and heavy. I struggled against the wind to stand. I would hit Frank again, and hit him again and again until he was dead.

I stalked *him* this time.

Hanna appeared behind Frank, and I paused.

My mind fogged over, and I wondered if Goth's pills had worn off and Frank's drugs had taken over. Everything around me went dark—more than it already was within the storm.

I wasn't sure what had happened, but when the space

around me cleared, Frank clutched his bleeding throat and dropped to his knees. Hanna was gone, and I no longer held the bottle.

Had Hanna sliced his throat? Had I cut him? Did flying debris tear his neck open?

Some broken glass was on the ground nearby, but it was somewhat submerged. There wasn't any blood on it, but the rain and flooding would've washed blood away.

Frank gurgled when he tried to speak. Not thinking clearly, I stepped toward him to hear what he tried to say, but I was forced back when a deafening *crack* erupted from the tree.

I lunged away from the half of the tree that fell. Its weight crushed Frank and slammed him down into the water. His arms flailed to escape the tree and its remaining bottles. Bubbles spurted up from his panicked, water-muffled shouts.

I could've helped him or tried to help him, but I didn't want to. Instead, I just watched.

The motion of his arms slowed, then stopped, lying limp in the water. I waited. He didn't move again and remained pinned by the bottle tree. I wondered if he had bled to death first or drowned first. It didn't matter. He was dead.

Maybe the bottles really did do something to protect against evil spirits.

"Hanna?" I turned, searching for my friend, but didn't see her.

My left arm had pieces of glass sticking out of it, and the kitchen towel was soaked with my blood and water. Blood streamed down my arm and dripped from my fingertips. Someone may have called my name, but the howling wind must have been what I had mistaken as a person's voice.

I was too weak to make it back to the house. I wasn't sure I could survive the storm. Either way, someone would find me once it had passed … unless my body floated into the swamp and I became dinner for gators.

None of it mattered. Goth and Lina were alive. Frank was dead.

I figured if I died too, I'd at least get to hang out with Hanna. I guess I fell, because I now lay in the water.

I closed my eyes.

Chapter Fifty-Nine

A hand touched my cheek. I figured Hanna was back to welcome me as one of the dead.

"Oh, no you don't."

I didn't recognize the voice, but someone shook my shoulder.

A different voice said, "Janie, wake up."

More shaking.

"Her arm's a mess. She's lost a lot of blood."

"We have to get her out of here."

More hands were on me, moving me. I was wet. My entire body ached.

My mind's gears ground together as some semblance of consciousness tried to return.

"Janie, wake up."

I thought I recognized that voice.

This time the voice was in my ear. "Wake up for me, Bougie."

I'd had that voice in my ear before, and I moved my head toward it, opening my eyes. "Goth," I said.

Goth kissed me. "I know you feel rotten, but you have to get up. Lina and I will help you."

I did my best to stand with their help, but I was a wobbling mess.

"What about him?" Goth asked Lina, nodding toward the downed tree.

I stared at the split tree and the body pinned beneath the half on the ground and in the water. I somewhat remembered what had happened with Frank except the part of how his neck had been cut open.

"Leave him," I said. "Wait. Are you okay?" I asked Goth. "You, too?" I asked Lina.

Both nodded.

"Anthony shot you," I said to Lina.

"Bullet hit the vest."

Lina's movements were limited. She was in pain even if the bullet from Anthony's gun had hit her bullet-proof vest. Goth seemed okay though. The rain had washed the blood off her face.

Guilt flooded me. "I'm so sorry, Lina. I didn't mean to kill Anthony. I swear, I didn't. I wanted to knock him off balance so he wouldn't shoot you, but I fucked up and took us both off the balcony. He fell, and—"

"Stop," Lina said. "You don't need to apologize. You saved my life." She shook her head. "He got mixed up in this shit somehow. I don't know why, but he was part of it and is dead. It wasn't your fault."

The buzzing inside my head returned, and Goth kept me upright. I couldn't stay focused anymore. I lost track of time. They could've led me into a pit of alligators, and I would've gone in without complaint. I moved my feet while my mind shuffled between reality and wherever else it went. I thought I saw Hanna again, but I wasn't certain.

When we neared the house, we slowed, and I blinked a few times. Part of the roof was missing. Flames burst through one of the windows on the first floor. The rain had eased up a little, but the wind stirred the fire.

"Oh, God," Lina said. "We need the fire department."

"No," I said. "Let that fucker burn."

"What?" Lina asked.

"Don't you or anyone else risk your life to save that goddamn house. Let it burn."

"They probably wouldn't get here in time anyway," Goth said.

We resumed walking, and I allowed them to lead me to Lina's deputy car. Goth and I climbed into the back seat. Goth pulled me close, and I leaned into her. Lina babbled into her radio, and the fiery glow inside the house expanded. Flames licked up the side of the house, and some erupted from the remaining roof. I laughed.

Lina shifted in her seat, radio mike in her hand. "Is she okay?"

Goth shrugged, and I laughed a bit harder.

"Let's go, Lina!" Goth said.

Lina drove the car on the long driveway, but we didn't get far. An oak tree was down across the road, and Lina hopped out of the car. I could not have gone with her even if I'd wanted to. My limbs had stopped working again. Frank's cocktail remained in my system.

"I feel like shit," I muttered.

Goth passed her fingers through my hair. "Well, Bougie, you have been stabbed, and you have enough drugs in you to throw a hell of a rave."

"You do too. Not the stabbing part. The drugs." I frowned. "I think I'm fucked up."

"You are definitely fucked up."

I chuckled.

"Frank gave me something like a paralytic," Goth said. "The pills had enough stimulants in them to override it. I'm jittery as hell, but I'm fine. Mostly. I should be fine," she said, nodding.

"I'm sorry you got entangled in this mess."

"Not much of a hurricane party. I've had better dates, ya know?"

I nodded. "Me too."

Smoke billowed up from the back seat, filling the car, and my smile vanished. I squirmed in the seat.

"What's wrong?" Goth asked.

"Are you seeing this? The smoke around us?"

"No. I don't know what Frank gave you, but it had hallucinogens in it for sure."

"I saw skulls. Kids' skulls."

"When? Where?"

"Hanna was with me."

"When?"

"She was real, Goth. Hanna was real. I felt her hand, and it was warm."

"Wow."

"You think I've lost my mind."

"Not at all. Hanna was real. I believe you."

"I didn't …" I glanced around inside the car. The smoke dissipated, and I forgot what I was talking about.

Lina jumped back into the car. "I can't drive around that thing without getting stuck." She got back on the radio.

I didn't follow everything Lina said; she talked too fast. Trees down. Needed an ambulance. Fire. Dead. Something-something. I stopped trying to listen.

"Fuck!" Lina pounded her fist on the steering wheel. "We have to wait till someone can get to us."

"How long?" Goth asked.

"I don't know. We can try walking to the main road, but there are trees everywhere. One of them or a limb might fall."

"We don't want to be like Frank," I said, and then giggled. I shouldn't be giggling over someone dying, but I did anyway.

Lina popped the trunk and hopped out of the car again. She slammed the trunk's lid down and was back in the car a moment later, this time crammed into the back seat with Goth and me. She opened a small, red duffel and pulled gauze and other first aid items out. "We've got to get this bleeding slowed. Untie the towel but continue to hold pressure on her arm."

Goth followed the instructions as Lina gave them.

"What happened to Frank?" I asked.

Both Lina and Goth paused, glanced at each other, then looked back at me.

"He died," Goth said.

"Did you see how he died?" I asked.

"Half a tree fell on him."

"Before that."

Goth tilted her head. "What do you mean?"

"I might have killed him." I shook my head. "I don't know what happened. I can't remember. His throat was gushing blood, but I don't know why. Hanna was there too."

"Hanna?" Lina asked.

"Um hmm."

"There was broken glass everywhere," Goth said.

"No. I mean, yes. There was, but …"

"But?"

"He was trying to drown me, and I hit him with a bottle. I was able to get out from under him. I picked up another bottle and planned to beat him to death. I was so angry … and out of it. I don't know what happened. Hanna was there. Then his neck was bleeding, Hanna was gone, I didn't have a bottle in my hand anymore, but there was glass all around. Did I cut his throat? Did you see that part?"

Lina and Goth shared another glance.

"What?" I asked.

"He's dead," Goth said.

"*How?* Was it me?"

Lina touched my shoulder. "We were too far away and didn't see what happened. Him bleeding from his neck might not have been by your hand. And if you killed him, it was self-defense. We saw the tree land on him while he was alive, and he was dead by the time we reached you. The tree ultimately ended him, not you."

I watched while they worked on my arm.

"Frank killed Henry and my mother," I said. "He said he rigged their plane to go down. I was supposed to be on the flight, too, but missed it because I was sick."

"I'm sorry that happened," Goth said.

I figured it would hurt more when they dumped whatever it was into the wound to clean it, but my body was numb. Goth picked a few pieces of glass from my arm and chin.

"Sorry if I'm hurting you," she said.

"Doesn't hurt," I said, noting my speech was slurred.

Lina frowned. "It should."

"No." My pain was gone. "I feel great." I closed my eyes, and Goth touched my face.

"Stay awake," she said.

I cracked my eyes open a little. "I'm going to sleep."

Hanna was in the front seat of Lina's car, turned so that she faced me. I smiled at Hanna.

"Janie," Goth said. "What's happening?"

"She's here," I said.

"Who?" Lina asked.

"Hanna."

"Our dead friend? *That* Hanna?" Lina asked.

"Yep."

Goth and Lina followed my gaze. Lina shook her head, but Goth turned back to me. "I can't see her, but I believe you."

Warmth surrounded me, and I closed my eyes again.

Goth shook my shoulder. "No, Janie, you can't sleep. Not yet."

My body relaxed as sleep began settling over me.

"Shit. Lina?"

"We have to get her to the main road to grab a ride to the hospital. Let's go. We're walking."

I wasn't sure why they were so worked up. I wanted to ask but instead allowed sleep to come.

They pulled me from the warm, welcoming arms of unconsciousness when they dragged me from the car.

Chapter Sixty

My left arm screamed its protest when I tried to roll to my side, causing me to stop. My sluggish mind worked a little better, and I recalled why I felt like shit. I eased my eyelids up. I was in a hospital, but I wasn't sure when I'd arrived or how long I'd been here.

My arm was in a sling, the hospital-issue oversized shirt was an ugly attempt at blue, and a small box with wires coming out of it lay on the bed next to me. The wires trailed out of the box and disappeared under the neckline of the shirt. Clear intravenous fluids flowed down a length of tubing into the back of my right hand.

The last thing I semi-remembered was impenetrable darkness and violent winds from the storm, and my insides twisted with fear.

Frank was dead. I had outlived him … barely.

Now there was no wind, no rain, no bodies.

Blinding fluorescent light was abundant, though. I used my working arm to shield my eyes.

"What's wrong?" a voice asked.

"Too bright," I said.

Light footsteps mixed with shuffling noises, and then the bright lights went away. The room dimmed more when someone adjusted the blinds over the window.

"Better?" the voice asked.

I opened my eyes more and lowered my hand. "Goth." I reached for her.

Goth smiled and I pulled her into a clumsy, one-armed embrace. I surprised myself when I wept—happy Goth was there, glad the nightmare with Frank was over, and sad for being the one who had killed Anthony. I wasn't sure how I'd been involved with Frank dying; that part was fuzzy. Sure, Frank's death meant the safety of numerous children and adults he would've killed had he remained alive, but I had had direct involvement with the end of two lives.

When I released her, Goth smiled, her eyes red. She placed her hands on the sides of my head. "You're going to be okay."

My gaze drifted downward to the sling and hospital bed. "I don't know."

"Look at me."

I did.

"You're safe, and you're alive. You will be okay."

I nodded, hoping Goth was right. She kissed me, and I believed she was right.

Someone knocked on the door. Goth left me to open it and allow Samuel and Clara, his mother, in.

My eyes burned, and I let the tears flow to see this precious, smiling child coming toward me while clutching something in his closed hand.

He wore pajamas with superheroes all over them and climbed onto my bed. "Hi, Janie," he said, slipping one little arm around the back of my neck.

I held on to him, wishing both of my arms worked so I could hold him tighter.

"I'm so happy to see you," I said.

Samuel released me and opened his fingers. The little

wooden giraffe rested on his palm. "I kept this with me."

"I'm glad. It's yours."

"It makes you safe if you keep it with you," he said.

I wasn't sure what he meant.

Clara spoke up. "Samuel had the giraffe with him when … during … you know."

Oh shit. The boy had the carved animal with him the entire time Frank had him.

"You need it back," he said.

"I … I'm safe now, too, Samuel," I said. "It's your giraffe."

He closed his little fingers around the animal and nodded. "When you feel better, will you come visit me?"

"Yes. Yes, of course."

He hugged me again, then slid off the bed. "Bye, Janie," he said, giving me a wave. He took his mother's hand and they left.

I wiped the tears off my face. Frank had stolen the lives of so many innocent children. I was sad for Letitia's family and them not getting her back. But I was happy for Samuel and his family.

Goth sat on the side of the bed and took my hand. "You good?"

"Yeah. He is the sweetest kid on the planet," I said.

"He is. Do you need anything? Hungry? Thirsty?"

"Can I get out of this bed?"

"Yes."

Goth helped me stand and held the wired box and pushed the pole with one hand. She kept her other one on my arm during my walk to the tiny en suite bathroom. Goth waited outside. I finished with the toilet, then stood at the sink. Using my functioning upper limb, I splashed water on my face, brushed my teeth with the flimsy hospital toothbrush, then ran my fingers through my hair. The dark circles under my eyes made me appear sickly and frail. Strips of tape were stuck to various spots on my face.

Glass. I'd fallen on glass. The strips kept the cuts closed.

"Slide that chair over," Goth said.

I didn't have a chair in the bathroom and feared I was hallucinating again. "What?"

"Sorry, I was talking to Lina. She's here."

I didn't want to do battle with my looks since it was a battle I would lose. When I emerged, Lina had a chair ready for me.

I sat while Goth tidied everything around me and managed the IV pole and wired box.

Lina, in civilian clothes, leaned against the foot of the hospital bed. "How are you feeling?"

"I'm not sure. What is that thing?" I asked, nodding at the box.

Goth perched on the side of the bed and crisscrossed her legs. "Portable heart monitor. You were a mess when you got here. Frank's drugs plus the pills and blood loss had your heart doing things it wasn't meant to do. Once you were out of surgery, they kept you on the monitor to keep a closer watch on things."

"You had Frank's shit and more pills than I did," I said. "Is your heart okay?"

"Yeah. They only kept me for one night, then released me. I moved into your room since you were rather baked."

"How long have I been here?"

"This is day three."

"*Three?*"

"Are you comfortable in the chair or do we need to swap?"

"The chair is fine. Why?"

Goth glanced at Lina. "We'll catch you up on everything, if you're up for it."

"Yeah. Go."

Lina relocated to sit next to Goth.

"What's the last thing you remember?" Goth asked.

"Uh." I scanned my memories. I had snippets of faces, some I knew, others I didn't. Being in Lina's deputy car was in the mix. A fire, maybe? More people. An ambulance. "Everything is jumbled. The last clear-ish memory is being by the bottle tree in the storm and Frank was dead. You were both there and helped me back."

"Yeah," Lina said.

"The tree fell on him," I said.

"Yeah." Goth grinned. "Karma in all its fucking glory, if you ask me. That's where your memories stop?"

"I think so. Maybe?"

"Okay," Goth said, nodding. "Speak up when you need a break."

I nodded.

"You were kinda delirious by the time we got back to the house, and we needed to get you to a hospital. Part of the roof of the house had been ripped off while we chased after you and Frank, and a fire broke out. The storm had knocked a tree down over the driveway. We sheltered in Lina's cop car while she reached out for help. You were busy laughing at the house as it burned."

"Is it destroyed?"

"Yeah. I'm sorry, Janie."

"Nothing but awful memories there. Karma in all its fucking glory."

"Oh," Goth said. "That explains why you thought it was hilarious seeing it burn. You weren't delusional."

"Well …" Lina said, a small smile playing at the edges of her lips.

"Sounds like I was delusional if I laughed at the house," I said.

"Yes, very much so," Lina said.

Goth continued. "We dragged you up that long-ass driveway to the main road. Stephen and his army of cousins, *your* cousins, arrived with chain saws and trucks while the storm raged on, and cleared the road as we went until we met the ambulance. All three of us got in."

"Anthony shot you," I said to Lina.

"Yep, bruised ribs from that," Lina said. "I'm off work for a bit, resting when I can, and coming by here every day. I'm happy to see you up and coherent this time."

"I am *so* sorry for all the horrible things I accused you of doing. I suck sometimes. Really suck. And that was one of those times."

Lina smiled. "Yeah, well, we all have our shit moments. I'm sorry I was sneaking around and did the protection spells without telling you."

"Maybe they worked. What happened after the ambulance?"

"You went to surgery," Goth said. "I got patched up and admitted. My nurse learned to come find me in your room until they let me go."

I'd almost gotten Goth killed, and she'd taken up residence in my hospital room to stay with me. My heart melted, and I knew I was screwed. I'd had to come to New Orleans for *one* funeral. Meeting someone I actually liked was never part of the plan, but it had happened. "That was kind of you to stay with me. Thank you."

"Anytime. The storm moved on, and Lina went back to the estate with a couple of feds and other po-po types." Goth glanced at Lina to take over.

Chapter Sixty-One

I observed Lina and Goth during the pause in my debriefing. They behaved like longtime friends. I figured that while I had been in my oblivious state in the hospital, they'd had plenty of time to talk. With them here, I felt safe.

Lina picked up the conversation, and I diverted my attention from my thoughts to her.

"I took them to Frank's body," Lina said. "We retrieved Anthony's body from the rubble. No," she said to me when I opened my mouth. "Don't apologize for what happened to him. When the feds and police raided Frank's home, they found more evidence. Frank had stolen Jacques's laptop. They also found Frank's stash of photographs. Creepy bastard had pictures of what they're guessing to be all his victims, kids and adults. His attacks on his adult victims were quite violent. He wasn't cruel to the kids, though he still killed them."

"Fuck," I muttered.

"Yeah," Lina said. "Forensics folks took his mushrooms and his various tinctures. The labs will do testing on the chemicals in them to see if he's tied to other dead children or adults in case there were some he killed but didn't photograph. They may be able to link him to other deaths through toxicology reports."

I shook my head, baffled by Frank's depravity.

Lina continued. "He kept meticulous notes on everything. People who were never found or never reported missing, well, we now know where we should start searching. He tracked everything. The money in the offshore account was in both Frank's and Henry's names and had been set up before Henry married Katherine. Feds are trying to figure out where the original funds came from. We're guessing that Henry was going to cut him off and that's what prompted Frank to kill him. Frank was able to use the account for bribes and other personal uses. The hush money Henry had shelled out had continued after his death because Frank took over the bribes. This scandal has exploded, and all sorts of warrants and arrests are active in several states."

"Good," I said. "Let those bastards rot for what they did."

"Remember that I told you about Frank's wife overdosing?"

"Yeah."

Lina shook her head. "According to his journal, his wife was his first adult victim. Several months later he killed his first child and dragged Henry into the mess. Some of his early kills of the kids were sloppy with fingerprints and DNA gathered on some of them. The feds took prints and DNA off Frank's body and have already linked him to those cases. But as Frank got better at cleaning the bodies before dumping them, the feds are using his journals and photos to ID other victims. Henry paid to keep things quiet the entire time."

"Why the kids?"

"From what we know thus far, they all had some sort of serious acute illness or something chronic. He had access to them through his prior paramedic work and volunteering in the communities and area hospitals."

I was both relieved and grateful that Jack was my father, and that I was not related to Frank *or* Henry.

"Anthony's involvement?" I asked.

"The family is rattled. We haven't released the details of his death. He had a history of bad debt and sometimes shady dealings with loan sharks, so no one has been too curious about *how* he died. They're more appalled, and so am I, that he was helping a serial killer."

I wanted to apologize again for knocking him off the balcony and killing him, but I didn't. Anthony was no better than Frank, and now he was as dead as Frank.

Lina sighed. "It sucks, but I can't change anything. The important thing is that you're in the clear. The police will want to chat with you later, but it isn't anything that will be a problem for you legally. Based on everything you dug up, they'll probably offer you a job."

I laughed. "No thanks. I'll have Mr. Landry present when I talk to them."

"That's a good idea," Lina said.

"What else?"

"Anthony killed our father. They found text messages between Anthony and Frank. Frank ordered Anthony to do it and make it look like a robbery. He lured Jacques out to New Orleans East, and Anthony killed him. They found Jacques's wallet and the probable knife used to kill him at Anthony's apartment."

"Fuck me. Killed by his own nephew."

"Yeah. I am not going to tell anyone else about Jacques being my biological father, but I told the family that he was yours. I also told them that you and I adopted each other as sisters because we'd known each other so long. That way we don't have to worry if we refer to each other as sisters. Only we'll know that we have the same biological father. Well, us and Eva. Mama Tess too, and I have told her to keep it quiet about Jacques's relation to me."

"I'm good with that."

Goth nodded. "I won't say anything."

"Thanks," Lina said. "Janie, you now have a massive number of aunts, uncles, and cousins itching to see you. A family reunion formed in the lobby. I tried chasing them off so you could rest, but they didn't leave till Mama told them to go." Lina chuckled. "They respect Mama's authority more than mine."

"Sounds about right," I said, smiling. "She's an old mother hen, but she's feisty."

"She is!" Goth said. "I adore her. She told me her secret for her sweet tea recipe."

"*What?*" Lina and I said in unison.

"She refuses to tell anyone her secret," I said.

Goth grinned. "She said we artists needed to stick together."

I shook my head. "Mama is full of surprises."

"She's planning a family gathering for when you're out of here and able to attend," Lina said.

"That should be interesting," I said, then stifled an unexpected yawn.

"Okay," Lina said, standing. "I'm going to let you rest. You're in good hands," she added, nodding at Goth.

I did my one-armed hug with Lina and she left.

"You have a smile stuck on your face," Goth said.

I hadn't realized it until Goth had said something. "A family reunion."

Goth grinned. "You're excited for this."

I paused, thinking, and then I nodded. "I guess I am after not having any family for so long."

"I'm happy for you. I imagine you'll be discharged from here by tomorrow. All the drugs have worn off. You woke up a few times yesterday to pee and such, but you crawled right back into bed and were out again. They were waiting for you to wake up more. You're doing much better today."

"I don't feel strung out like I did while dealing with Frank."

"I thought Lina might give us shit for taking the ecstasy, but she's fully aware that it is what saved us from Frank. You had weed and traces of cocaine in your system."

"I haven't had any cocaine. Weed, yes. Coke, no."

"No one's accusing you of anything. It'll be several days before all the results come back for what was in your system. We know he hit us with magic mushrooms. Some varieties can cause a feeling of paralysis like what we experienced. Given your hallucinations, I'm betting he gave you acid too."

"What a mind fuck."

"Yeah. The forensics folks are working on identifying what all he gave us … and the kids."

My gaze drifted to my lap. "Hanna. She was with me."

"You mentioned that when we were in Lina's car."

I met Goth's eyes. "She was *there*. She wasn't a hallucination."

"I believe you. There are things that happen in this world that we can't explain."

I shifted in my seat and grunted. "I'm *so* sore."

"You can have more pain meds if you need them."

"I'm not sure I want anything to do with drugs ever again, even if prescribed."

"They have other medications besides narcotics."

"Yes, true. I'll ride this out for now." I lifted the collar of my hospital shirt. My upper arm was wrapped in a ton of gauze.

"Frank and that knife did a number on you," Goth said. "Your arm is a mess, and your shoulder is even worse from all the glass you had in it. Nothing broken, but they had to put a lot of stitches in there. You'll need physical therapy to strengthen it."

"Ugh. I'm not doing physical therapy here." I noticed Goth's shoulders slumped after my remark.

"When, uh, do you think you'll head back to Boston?" she asked.

"I meant that I'm not doing it locally," I said. "I'll do the physical therapy in New Orleans. I'm done with this rural living horseshit."

Goth brightened and smiled. "If your bougie ass can handle not living in a swank hotel, you can crash at my place. I can move the futon from the studio into my apartment."

"You have too many plants to put a futon anywhere in your place."

Goth shrugged.

"Plus, I'd keel over on all those stairs trying to get to your apartment."

"Probably true."

"I appreciate the offer. It's very kind. Your place wasn't damaged by the storm?"

"Not really. Power is out in parts of the city. The building took some damage, but my apartment was fine. A neighbor is taking care of my plants until I get back."

"Did they say how long physical therapy would last?"

"The nurse mentioned several weeks' worth."

"Huh."

"Why?"

"Um, I think it's time I get into some therapy. I mean more than only physical therapy. I've been, well, not good for a while."

"You want to start that in New Orleans too?"

I nodded.

"Wait lists are terrible, but I know of someone and can give you their number."

"That would be great." Receiving counseling would be a good thing for me. Lying down would be good for me too. I levered myself out of the chair to stand.

"Whoa," Goth said. "Where do you think you're going?"

"Move over. I'm tired. No, don't get up," I said, gesturing with my good arm.

Goth scooted her rump, and I got into the hospital bed next to her. I rearranged my wired box and IV line, then leaned back. It was a bit cramped with Goth next to me, but I didn't mind. I rested my head on her shoulder.

"I had wanted to end things with you," I said. "I was going to fly back to Boston and get away from all the crazy shit here with hallucinations and missing kids. I almost did, but I chickened out and instead asked you to come to the estate to ride out the hurricane."

"Why didn't you leave?"

"Because I didn't want to. I know we only met … what? Not quite three weeks ago now. But …"

Goth remained silent.

My palms were sticky, and I resisted the instant urge to cough. "I like you, Goth. A lot."

"Is this the longest you've been with one person?"

My face burned. I didn't want to answer that question, but I nodded anyway.

"I'm happy when you're around," she said. "If it makes you feel any better, you're my longest-running fling too."

"That does make me feel better."

"Good."

"Wanna be my date at the reunion?"

"Of course."

I was content to have Goth next to me. "Ya know," I said. "This is the first time we've been in a bed together and haven't fooled around."

"There's still time."

I smiled, took Goth's hand, and fell asleep.

Chapter Sixty-Two

I stared at the television in my hotel room in New Orleans. National news outlets were losing their shit over breaking news in Boston about corruption and child abuse allegations perpetrated by two local caseworkers and a lawyer. I kept the volume muted and read the feed while images flashed of my former caseworkers being hounded by the press. The video of the lawyer showed him covering his face and darting back into a building. I chuckled.

I had started my physical therapy in New Orleans and finished it in Boston. While back in New England, I worked with someone Mr. Landry knew to hand off copies of my journals and the documents he'd gathered about Aunt Kim, the Boston lawyer, and the caseworkers involved in the fraud and abuses while I was in Kim's care. Several lawsuits were filed, and the shit was flying in a spectacular fashion. Two other people had also come forward with claims of similar problems with this lawyer and caseworkers.

It had exploded pretty much the way I had expected it to, except in reality it was only beginning. The next video cut was to a live broadcast of police at the house of the lawyer. I laughed for a moment, and then it morphed into tears. I let them fall.

A sliver of justice had been delivered, and I searched my

emotions … something I'd learned from therapy. I wasn't happy that these awful people were now the ones suffering. It was relief and some happiness that they couldn't hurt anyone else again. That's what I told myself. I think it was true.

I turned the TV off, left the hotel, and started walking. The heat hadn't relented much though the sun had set. New England temperatures already had a fall crispness to them by the time I'd flown out this morning. New Orleans remained hot and steamy.

I arrived at the entrance to Goth's building and smiled when I spotted her coming out. She looked amazing, as always. I pulled her close and kissed her.

"Mm. That was nice," she said. "It's almost like you missed me."

"Maybe a little." I took her hand. "I want to show you something before we find dinner."

We started down the street.

"Lina and I met with your architect today," she said. "Their redesign of the estate as a safe house is incredible. I know they emailed you the files, but Janie, you need to see the model in person. They've accounted for everything. People will be able to safely live and work there until they can get out on their own. The architect will have a list of potential contractors to you by the end of the week."

I enjoyed hearing the excitement in her voice. "That's great news. I appreciate everything you've done, Goth. I really do."

"I don't mind helping. It's been fun. Oh, Lina wants to meet for lunch on Monday here in the city."

I hadn't had any hallucinations (Hanna didn't fall into the hallucination category) or heard voices since my last night at the estate, but the nightmares of Frank and Anthony interfered with my sleep too much to be ignored. "I have therapy on Monday, but I'll arrange a time with Lina so I can keep the appointment and we can meet her after."

"I'm glad you're making yourself a priority."

"I am too," I said, smiling.

"Stephen and Mike love Jack's house—well, their house now. They insist we come out when all the painting and other work is finished."

"Yeah, we'll go out when they're ready."

"Where are we going?"

"We're almost there." My palms were slick with sweat. I hoped Goth assumed it was from the heat and not my nervousness.

We stopped at a building with a *For Sale* sign in one of the expansive but grimy windows. Revelers traversing the streets of downtown New Orleans maneuvered around us when we stopped on the sidewalk.

"I've looked into this building, and I want to buy it," I said. "The location is far enough away from other galleries to not oversaturate the block but close enough to the typical French Quarter activities to attract locals and tourists. What do you think?"

Goth released my hand and left me to walk back to the street corner. She turned and disappeared down the next street. A few moments later she rounded the corner, approached, and took my hand again. "I know this place. It's had a lot of different businesses come and go since I've lived here. It's an old building, but this corner lot is great. It'll be expensive to rehabilitate the structure and convert it."

"Yeah."

"I think that's what sank the other businesses ... the attempt to rehab it."

"It'll be worth it this time. I'm in this for the long game."

"The ground level will be perfect for a gallery. The windows are amazing. Well, they will be once they're washed. What's in the rest of it?"

"Old office spaces that need gutting and remodeling. I can convert them to studios for artists to lease."

Goth turned to me and grinned. "So you're interested in this building, or you've already bought it?"

I was grateful for the darkness of the evening, though I knew the streetlights had probably betrayed me and illuminated the hot flush flooding my face and neck.

"The purchase is in the works," I said.

"I thought you swore to never live in Louisiana."

"I'm going to be split between here and Boston. I'm keeping the two galleries there, but I'm going to unload the apartment there to move to one less expensive. I'll have some of the space in this building converted into a small, unofficial living area for when I'm staying here."

Goth nodded but remained silent. My gut twisted a little, and I was surprised I didn't feel the urge to cough. Goth's silence wasn't necessarily a bad thing. Her mind was always working, but it made me twitchy on the insides. I wanted her to love this idea as much as I did. She continued to have my hand in hers, so I hoped that was a good sign.

"When the renovations are done," she said, "do I get a bid on renting one of the studios?"

"Well, no."

Her eyebrows went up.

"I mean, yes," I said. "But no. Shit." I hated when I lost my bearings around her. "I wanted you to be one of the showcase artists, so a studio would go to you by default."

"There would be a contract?"

"Yes." I knew better than to offer a freebie to Goth. I'd learned from that prior fuck-up.

Goth nodded.

Seconds ticked by in relative silence. The flow of tourists

continued by us.

I tried to be patient, I really did. "Are you thinking about something in particular, or are you fucking with me to be cruel?" I regretted my outburst in an instant. Before I could apologize, Goth turned to face me. She didn't appear angry, but her eyes narrowed. At minimum, I'd annoyed the hell out of her, and she released my hand. Shit.

"I happened to be thinking about something," she said.

"I didn't mean … I did, but, it came out wrong. I'm sorry. When you go silent like that, it messes with my head. I can't always read you like you can other people. It's, um, I—"

"Jesus." Goth rolled her eyes. "Stop, Janie."

I snapped my mouth closed, but my shoulders remained tense.

"I was considering how this would work with the gallery owner in a relationship with one of the artists," she said.

My throat sealed shut with her mention of the *r*-word. I almost coughed but managed a tiny wheeze to keep oxygen coming in and going to my brain. We were a couple, no question. I had introduced her as my girlfriend at the reunion. But she was right. Our relationship could complicate things on the business side— or it could be amazing to work together in that capacity. It could be great or a total fucking disaster.

"Now *you're* the one who has gone silent," Goth said.

I nodded. I had hit her with a lot of information at once. Of course she needed time to think things through. I'd rushed her because of my own anxiety.

"I'm in," she said.

I blinked. "What?"

Goth waved her arm at the building. "What you're going to do here, I want to be part of it." She laughed. "You get the most bizarre look on your face when your brain hurts."

"It *does* hurt. I don't understand."

"The last time you were here and in the hotel, I mean before you left for Boston, I saw the papers you had on this place. I didn't say anything. I had a hunch you were up to something, so I contacted both your Boston galleries and spoke to the artists you represent today. They all confirmed what I'd already suspected."

"And?"

"There are some real sleazeball galleries out there that rob the artists, and you aren't one of them. You are very generous to the people who work for you and those you work with."

This was good news, except … "But you have concerns about our—" This time I did cough. Dammit. "Um, r-relationship being in the mix?"

"No."

Whatever expression I made when Goth said or did something to cook my brain, I had to be making it again, because I was beyond confused.

Goth smiled. "I think it will be amazing to work with you." She gave me a quick kiss. "I'm going to check out the other side view again." Goth disappeared around the corner. The glass windows were smudged and dusty, but I watched her form as she wandered the sidewalk with her eyes turned upward at the building.

A small, warm hand slid into mine. It used to startle me when Hanna did that, but now it was a welcome sensation. I squeezed her hand and gazed down. She smiled up at me.

I had known I would buy this building the day I walked the interior of it with the real estate agent … and Hanna. I didn't know what Hanna was to my life, but she always seemed to show up when I needed a boost of confidence. I had never trusted myself to make good decisions. I'd made plenty of good ones in the past. I'd also made loads of shitty ones. I was learning to trust my instincts and didn't mind Hanna's help.

"Goth likes it," I said.

Hanna nodded. *I knew she would.*

"Then why didn't you tell me she would? That would've saved me a ton of worrying."

You needed to ask her yourself.

"I guess so."

My incessant nagging thought resurfaced. "Please tell me who or what killed Frank."

Hanna did what she always did and gave me a sad smile and no words.

"Please?"

You're going to be fine now.

"What does that mean?"

You are.

"What do you mean?"

She squeezed my hand, then evaporated. I wheeled around, looking for her, but she was gone. My breaths quickened, and I rose up on my toes and shifted my stance to look around the other people.

Goth arrived. "What's wrong?" she asked.

"Um, Hanna. She's … She's gone. She was here but left, like vaporized left. She's never done that before. Is this permanent? Is she coming back?"

Goth took my hand. "I don't know."

Goth knew my dilemma. I needed to know if I had killed Frank or not. It didn't matter to her either way. I would like to know if I was sleeping with someone capable of killing another person, but she always shrugged it off.

"Did you ask her about Frank?" she asked.

My shoulders slumped. "She didn't give me an answer, as usual."

"You've trusted her before. Trust her now, too."

I took a deep breath. I'd been through some ridiculous

shit in my life, including surviving a murderous non-uncle. Trusting a ghost had become almost normal. I wanted to know why Hanna wouldn't give me the goddamn answer. What was behind that sad smile? Was I a killer? Anthony had been an accident. Frank remained a mystery.

Maybe I would never know.

Acknowledgments

First shout-out goes to Jen Thompson. We worked together at length discussing ideas and different ways to take this story. She allowed me to bounce ideas off her, and she provided ones for me to consider. Jen is more than a beta reader or a sensitivity reader. She is a wonderful person, and I'm so fortunate to have her as a dear friend.

Additional shout-outs to Bernadette and Tanya, who served as early test readers, then opted to read it again after I made significant revisions, including a complete POV switch from third person to first person. I had lots of great conversations with them about the story arcs and where a few things needed to be clarified or otherwise sorted out.

I had the pleasure of once again working with Ray Rhamey as my editor who, as always, provided plenty of helpful feedback. Each time I work with him, I learn more and improve my craft. Heaps of gratitude for Laurel Robinson and her copyediting skills. Working with her is always a delight.

Many thanks to Meredith who helped me as a final test reader and kept me sane during the final push to publication.

State police officer and long-time friend Jeff allowed me to pick his brain on police matters. Any mistakes in the novel regarding law enforcement procedures are my own.

Several other friends and family members remained supportive during my time working on this novel, whether it was to ask how things were going or asking when the hell it would be finished so they could read it. Those little check-ins meant the world to me.

I cannot claim that this novel was fun or a joy to write because of the dark subject matter. I will say that I enjoyed infusing elements of Southern culture into sometimes-clashing Northern mannerisms. As a South-to-North transplant, like Janie, I am often jolted by the contrasts when I make periodic visits South to see family and friends.

From the Author

The idea for *Bodies in the Bayou* began in 2019. I had a feeling that this novel, though fiction, about missing and murdered Black and Creole children was something that had to have happened before but had not been publicized. I couldn't recall any national news reports about missing children of color. The one widely broadcast missing child case that I remembered was JonBenét Ramsey, a six-year-old White girl who died in 1996. It was all over the news for months and later periodically resurfaced.

I continued writing my novel, and in 2021, a twenty-two-year-old White woman, Gabby Petito, disappeared. National news outlets erupted with widespread coverage of the search and later manhunt for her suspected killer. This brought a justified uproar over the lack of coverage for missing Black and Brown women. News outlets then covered a few stories of missing women of color, but it didn't last. Once Gabby's killer was found dead, the media went silent again. The murders of Ramsey and Petito were both tragic, but the deplorable racial bias with the media proved once again that anyone of color who went missing was not newsworthy.

While doing research for the novel, I stumbled upon the HBO documentary series called *Atlanta's Missing and Murdered:*

The Lost Children. That's when the memories returned. I was seven years old and living in Mississippi when the last of the Georgia victims was found. I remembered the reports of the missing and dead Black children being on television. I remembered the repeated lessons from my parents to never go anywhere with a stranger. I remembered the fear. Someone was taking and killing children, and it wasn't a fabricated story used to get kids to come home on time for dinner.

After watching the docuseries, I questioned continuing the novel. What right did I have as a White woman to create my fictional story about murdered Black and Creole children in Louisiana? My initial answer was none whatsoever.

If missing White children received the same poor media coverage as Black, Indigenous, and other children of color, our world would explode with outrage. Yet the world cannot know when another human is in danger because the media won't broadcast it unless the victim is White.

The National Crime Information Center's 2022 missing person and unidentified person statistics listed 339,469 entries for juveniles (seventeen years and younger). The number of reported missing Black children for 2022 was 133,628 (39.4 percent of the total) (https://www.fbi.gov/file-repository/2022-ncic-missing-person-and-unidentified-person-statistics.pdf/view).

According to the 2020 US Census and July 2022 population estimates (https://www.census.gov/quickfacts/), 13.6 percent of the population is Black. Yet, as mentioned above, over 39 percent of the reported missing children are Black.

AMBER Alerts are issued only if all criteria are met, and if they are not met, no alert is issued, and the missing child may be incorrectly categorized as a runaway. In 2022, 181 AMBER Alerts were issued. (https://www.missingkids.org/content/dam/missingkids/pdfs/amber/2022_Annual_AMBER_Alerts_

Report_Final.pdf). Almost 340,000 people seventeen years and younger were reported missing, and approximately 0.0005 percent of them were the subjects of an AMBER Alert.

I am desperate to see this imbalance and injustice corrected, but my desperation is nothing compared with the families' suffering when their children go missing while the media outlets remain mute. This must change.

Resources/Support for Impacted Families*

National Center for Missing and Exploited Children (https://www.missingkids.org/gethelpnow), including Native, Indigenous, and Tribal communities (https://www.missingkids.org/ourwork/nitc)

Black and Missing Foundation (https://www.blackandmissinginc.com)

Native Child Advocacy Resource Center (https://www.nativecac.org/)

When Your Child Is Missing (https://ojjdp.ojp.gov/library/publications/when-your-child-missing-family-survival-guide-fifth-edition)

*I am not affiliated with the above resources. I mention them as ones that I found and appeared to be good resources. There are many other organizations doing important work by providing information for those seeking to learn more and for those impacted by a missing family member.

About the Author

Cheryl Campbell has been creating stories since childhood. Her most recent writing adventures have been in psychological suspense and horror genres. She's won multiple awards for her YA fantasy and adult science fiction novels. Her varied background includes art, herpetology, emergency department and critical care nursing, and computer systems. She was born in Louisiana and lived there and in Mississippi before relocating to Maine for over twenty years. She currently lives in Massachusetts and calls New England home.

Photo Credit: Kelly Samia Photography

To see what she's been up to lately, visit cherylscreativesoup.com.